NO WAY OUT

David Kessler dropped out of school at the age of 15 and was self-educated from then on. He struggled for 25 years to become a published author before finally making his breakthrough with *A Fool for a Client*, a legal thriller set in New York. This was followed up by *The Other Victim, Tarnished Heroes, Reckless Justice* and *Mercy*. He also courted controversy by co-writing *Who Really Killed Rachel* (about the Wimbledon Common murder) with Colin Stagg, the man who was falsely accused of the crime. The book is now out of print, but since then, the real murderer – who was named in the book – has been convicted of the crime.

By the same author:

Mercy

DAVID KESSLER

No Way Out

AVON

AVON

A division of HarperCollins*Publishers*
77–85 Fulham Palace Road,
London W6 8JB

www.harpercollins.co.uk

A Paperback Original 2010
1

Copyright © David Kessler 2010

David Kessler asserts the moral right to
be identified as the author of this work

A catalogue record for this book is
available from the British Library

ISBN-13: 978-1-84756-183-1

Set in Minion by Palimpsest Book Production Limited,
Falkirk, Stirlingshire

Printed and bound in Great Britain by
Clays Ltd, St Ives plc

A very big thank you is due to Megory Anderson for her advice on San Francisco and also to Shelanda Adams for her advice on Oakland.

As is often the case with creative writers, I have nevertheless had to take literary license on some points. For example, the San Francisco Giants did *not* play at home to the LA Dodgers on the evening of 2 September 2009. Rather, on that date, the Giants were playing *away* to the Philadelphia Phillies. The Giants *did* play the Dodgers at home some three weeks earlier, but that was an afternoon meeting, at least the last day of the game was. None of this would have suited my intricate plotting and for that reason I had to rearrange the fixtures to suit the exigencies of the storyline.

To Eran, my brother in all but name

'He who fights with monsters should take care lest he thereby become a monster. And if you gaze for long into an abyss, the abyss gazes also into you.'

Friedrich Nietzsche, *Beyond Good And Evil*, Aphorism 146

Saturday, 4 July 2004 – 23.40

It was only a set of fingers flying across a keyboard, yet they could work so much malice.

She watched in awe as her words appeared before her, the letters on the screen keeping pace with her fingers. What was so amazing was how little she had to change to wreak so much damage. All she had to do to alter the behavior of an entire computer program was make minor alterations to just two of the lines of the program. Hackers and 'midnight programmers' would laugh at the absurd simplicity of it. Some of them might even have been mildly amused by the sheer audacity of it. But few of them would have condoned her objectives.

So what?

She wasn't doing it for fame or glory. She was doing it for justice – plain, old-fashioned justice.

As she continued her work, she glanced up and looked out through the window. In the distance she could see the flickering lights of the nocturnal city and they reminded her that there was a world out there beyond her private world of vengeance. But she forced herself to ignore the distraction. Her fingers continued to dance across the keyboard in the small pool of halogen light that fell upon the desk. The rest of the room was in darkness.

After a few more seconds she paused, satisfied with the

results of her labors. Then, with a couple of clicks on the left button of the mouse, it was done. She had created a *new* version of the program.

And what a new version!

She thought about it now, almost wistfully. Getting the original source code had been rather tricky. She'd had to use some of her old contacts to break down the bureaucratic barriers. But many States had public records or freedom of information laws. She wished that she could infiltrate the altered program *everywhere*. That would be something of a coup. But she had to be realistic.

When she first started out, she had no idea that she would even be able to do it. It was more idle curiosity than a firm agenda that had prompted her to explore the possibility. But when she studied the documentation and asked a few questions of a professor to understand how the software worked, it suddenly dawned on her just how easy it would be.

Of course, slipping it in *undetected* would be the hardest part. There were various ways she could do it. One was to hack into the server computers and upload the new program. But that was risky.

There was, however, another way to infiltrate the new version of the software that didn't involve hacking at all. That way was to get the systems administrator to install it themselves. The key to this method was to make it seem as if it were a modification of a current program that they were already using. By packaging the program complete with forged letterhead and then sending it out by special courier, she could trick their SysOps into installing the new version under the erroneous assumption that they were getting an upgrade from the software company. It would be the ultimate software hack followed by the ultimate in social engineering.

And now she was going to make the niggers pay.

Friday, 5 June 2009 – 7.30

Bethel was nineteen – too young to remember the Sixties and too bored to care about her grandparents' reminiscences – like how her mother was conceived at the Woodstock festival.

But the sound of Buffalo Springfield's 'For What It's Worth' was ringing through her head, via the earphones of her iPod, as she stood by the roadside, waiting for help. She knew little of the context of the song and nothing about the closing of the *Pandora's Box* nightclub or the Sunset Strip Curfew Riots. But the voice of Neil Young was haunting. It was easy to sleep through high school civics classes – even to sleepwalk through the assignments and exams. She knew a bit about the Vietnam War and the civil rights struggles of the Sixties. But it was all superficial academic know-ledge, of the kind she picked up almost by default while daydreaming about the football team quarterback.

It stayed in her mind not as a coherent picture, but as a collection of sound bites: 'We shall overcome,' 'I have a dream,' 'Power to the people,' 'Burn, baby, burn!' The voice of anger still echoed across the decades. But it echoed faintly. A time gulf separated Bethel from the turbulence that had almost ripped her country apart. And the time gulf was ever widening, so all that was left of the ringing timbre of history's voices were the fading reverberations of barely remembered heroes: Rosa Parks, Martin Luther King, Malcolm X, the Chicago Eight. Names and slogans to Bethel, but no substance.

But she liked the song. It had a pleasant hook that made it stick in her mind. What really sent shivers up her spine was that haunting phrase at the end of the chorus, urging the young listeners to pause and assess the situation. She had no more than the merest inkling of what it meant. Whatever it was had gone down already. *It doesn't really matter*, she told herself. It belonged to her grandparents' generation anyway. She belonged to another generation, the one that was more concerned with finding a job than changing the world.

Her full name was Bethel Georgia Newton and she was a mixed bag of human elements. In the looks department she was all bleached blonde and classic cheerleader figure, a carefully cultivated complexion and polished-tooth smile. Neither svelte nor buxom, a kind of perfect 'in-between' for her height of five foot six; athletic, but in that soft, not overdone sort of way, with well-toned leg muscles, but not rippling ones. She was middle class and far removed from the culture of the street, yet when it came to experience of life she wasn't entirely naïve. She might not exactly have been streetwise, but she had tasted the bitter side of life.

She stood by the roadside in her tight-fitting white t-shirt and denim shorts that showed every curve of her firm body, holding out her thumb every time a car went by. She thought it would be easy hitching a ride, with her breasts thrusting out in front, straining against her t-shirt, and the perfect ripe complexion of her thighs showing like white silk in the California sunshine. But people were paranoid about helping strangers by the roadside, she realized now.

A few yards away, her car had broken down and she

couldn't even call for help because the battery of her cell phone was flat. She had made a half-hearted effort to fix the car herself, but she didn't really have a clue when it came to car engines. So all she could do was flag down a Good Samaritan and ask them to take her to a garage where she could get proper help.

Secretly she was hoping that some good looking man with technical skills and a cool family fortune would stop and rescue her, not just from the roadside but from the aimless drifting boredom that seemed to have engulfed her life lately. But she would settle for an elderly couple taking her down the road to a pay phone if necessary. Only she wasn't even getting *that*. Life was unfair.

But then her luck changed.

An aquamarine Mercedes slowed down as it approached her. A recent model and from the up-market end of the European car industry, the owner was clearly affluent and probably young. By the time it had pulled over by the road-side she could see that the driver, in his late twenties, was a black man.

What would my parents think? she wondered with a smile at the fleeting fantasy of turning up on her liberal parents' doorstep with this young man in tow.

Think rather than *say*. She knew that they'd be warm and welcoming. But she wondered if they were capable of walking the walk as well as they could talk the talk. It occurred to her that she didn't really *know* her parents. And yet here she was away from home, trying to find herself.

As the young man leaned out, smiling, and asked if she needed help, she could tell from his confident voice that this was someone who was going places. She was drawn to his youthful good looks and quiet, cool self-confidence and she warmed to him instantly, even if his diction betrayed the lingering traces of a background that she half suspected he was trying to conceal – or maybe just forget.

He took a look under the hood and after about a minute shook his head and said, 'I'm not really all that good with engines. I'm better with people.' He won her over with that line and a disarming smile. Two minutes later she was in the Mercedes and they were rolling along down the road, getting to know each other better. Then, somewhere along the line, she noticed that he had turned off the main road.

She was about to ask where they were going when she caught a glimpse of his profile and saw his lips twist upwards into a smile. But she couldn't tell if the smile was friendly. And as the first traces of apprehension formed into a knot in the pit of her stomach, she realized that she was too afraid to inquire further.

Friday, 5 June 2009 – 8.50

'I've got butterflies in my stomach, Gene,' said Andi as the car snaked its way through the streets of Los Angeles.

'It's too late to go back now.'

They both laughed. This was becoming a bit of an in-joke between them. They had both been nervous about leaving the Big Apple and crossing the continent to a new life on the West Coast. But Andi's career had demanded it.

Andi Phoenix, sitting silently and brooding nervously, was in her late thirties. She had kept her looks through healthy eating, regular workouts and a bit of cosmetic surgery. Her breasts had been enhanced from 34B to 36D with silicone implants and she had taken a Botox injection to remove the first lines of age. But the rest was from hard work and healthy living. The blonde hair came from a bottle; the original had been a decent but boring mousy brown. Changing the color had been a form of therapy after the rough ride of her youth, but the enhancements as a whole carried with them the payload of attention from men that she could well do without. She was a few inches shorter than the black woman who sat next to her and in some ways felt in her shadow.

Gene touched Andi's forearm gently. 'Just remember this, honey: *they* don't know *you* either. But they were ready to take a chance on you.'

In the driver's seat, in more ways than one, was Eugenia Vance, the six foot, muscular black woman who had playfully wrestled with her in bed that morning, and won – as always.

They had met over twenty years ago, when Andi was still in her teens. Gene had helped Andi through her teenage crisis years, and they'd been together ever since. In all the time they had known each other, they never used the word 'lesbian' to describe their relationship. It wasn't denial. It was just that their every instinct railed against categorization. Neither Gene nor Andi loved 'women', they simply loved each other.

'I'm just wondering if this whole thing is a big mistake.'

Gene snorted her mockery at Andi's self-pity. 'You've picked a *hell* of a time to start wondering, girl!'

Here in California, Andi's specialty was much in demand. She had majored in psychology before going on to get her Juris Doctor degree from the Northeastern University School of Law where she thrived amidst its progressive atmosphere that encouraged social responsibility. But after graduation she had found the law to be an irritating environment in which to work. Most of her criminal work involved plea bargaining rather than trial work and usually that meant helping criminals plead guilty to lesser charges – hardly the service of justice and way off from the ideals that had driven her into the legal profession in the first place.

Matters had come to a head after she contracted pneumonia, forcing her to take a prolonged leave of absence from the law firm that had initially hired her. But when she went back to work, she found herself welcomed with less than open arms. She was protected by labor laws from outright dismissal, but found herself increasingly sidelined. She joined another firm but then spent the next eight months playing catch-up.

It was in this period that her interest in the subject changed. Although there were innocent people out there who needed to be helped, criminal law meant – for the most part – helping the guilty. And that was not something she particularly enjoyed doing. So she did the old poacher turned gamekeeper routine and got herself a job with the D.A.'s office, in the domestic violence unit, where she thrived for a while. Starting at the bottom of the ladder meant that she didn't get to do much courtroom work. Most of it involved working directly with victims, reading reports and collating evidence. But she was happy to do this. It gave her a sense of purpose.

Paradoxically, it was only when promotion gave her more courtroom work that disillusion set in for a second time. Because she found herself doing exactly the same thing as she was doing before, but from the opposite side of the table: plea bargaining with criminals. She found their lawyers to be vile, for the most part, and she realized how contemptible she must have seemed to the D.A. in her earlier days as a defense attorney.

At the same time, she had developed another interest: crime victim litigation. There was a growing industry involving the pursuit of civil remedies for crime victims and she very much wanted to be part of it. The only trouble was that she soon hit the glass ceiling and realized that this specialized field was more developed on the West Coast than on the East. She wasn't altogether comfortable about moving out West. But that was where the work opportunity took her.

'And what if I don't make the grade?' asked Andi, still seeking reassurance.

'Hey, listen,' said Gene firmly, 'I don't want to hear any of that. There's nothing to stop you except fear – and if you let that get to you, I'll be right behind you, ready to take a paddle to that cute little butt of yours.'

'My butt's not so little,' said Andi, but this time with humor rather than self-pity.

In truth, Andi's butt was fine, as any red-blooded male would have been only too happy to testify.

There was a hard edge to Gene. But it was precisely Gene's confidence in decision making that Andi loved most. On all the important matters, it was Gene who decided for both of them. It was Gene who had decided that they would come to live out here in California. Andi would never have demanded it for herself, much as she had wanted it. She still lacked the self-confidence to stand up to Gene – to the world yes, but not to Gene. And Gene herself knew that Andi needed to make the move for her career. It wasn't in Gene's personal interests to make the move, but she cared too much for Andi to let that stand in their way.

So when it came to the crunch, Gene was ready to uproot herself and start again on the other side of the country. *It's only a sacrifice if you give up the greater value for the lesser one*, she told herself, remembering the philosophy that had given her so much strength when she really needed it. *Andi's happiness means more to me than my two-bit career. So it isn't really a sacrifice.*

What Gene loved about Andi was that she was gentle and soft on the outside yet fiery and determined when her sense of injustice was aroused. It was a paradox that was expressed as eloquently in Andi's eyes as in her words. Her eyes had a kind of magic that was as frightening as it was fascinating: those eyes could look both menacing and vulnerable at the same time. It was Andi's eyes that Gene had originally fallen in love with. When Gene looked into Andi's eyes the first time they met, the beseeching, helpless look quickly dissolved into anger . . . no, not anger . . . tenacity.

As the car slowed down, Gene gave Andi an encouraging smile and then looked around at the office buildings of the town center. Andi smiled back, encouraged by Gene's contagious confidence.

'Looks like we're here,' said Gene, with an air of finality.

The car pulled up to a halt in front of a large office building.

'Wish me luck,' Andi said, taking a deep breath.

Gene looked at her firmly, 'I won't do that, honey, 'cause you don't need luck.'

Gene slid her left hand behind Andi's head, leaned over and kissed Andi on the lips. She had a way of making Andi feel good whenever the fear and self-doubt threatened to get the better of her.

That's why I love you, Gene, thought Andi, closing her eyes. But she didn't say it. She just held on a moment longer than Gene did, before letting go and getting out of the car. She wanted to say something, but the jitters were still with her and she knew that Gene could sense it.

'Get in there and knock 'em dead, honey!'

Andi closed the door and walked towards the building. Ignoring the names of the countless law and accountancy firms on the nameplates, she walked into the building and presented her ID to security.

Outside, Gene watched Andi enter the building like a mother watching her tearful five-year-old vanish into the crowd of other children on her first day at kindergarten. Then she brought the engine to life with a roar, made an aggressive U-turn and drove back the way she'd come. She knew it was going to be a tough day for Andi – first days always are.

Her thoughts were cut short by her cell phone. It was a call from the *Say No to Violence* rape crisis center.

'Hallo,' said Gene, pressing the button of the hands-free set.

'Gene, we've just had a call from Riley.'

Bridget Riley worked at the sex crimes unit in the local police department. And a call from Bridget Riley probably meant only one thing: another woman had been raped.

Friday, 5 June 2009 – 9.45

'You're kind of early, Alex.'

Alex Sedaka spun round to see a fifty-eight-year-old black man standing there with a beaming smile on his face. Elias Claymore was overdressed for SoCal at this time of year. But Alex knew that he was trying to avoid being recognized. Claymore didn't usually like to draw so much attention to himself because then he'd find himself surrounded by autograph seekers.

'I was at the front of the plane,' said Alex, reciprocating the smile. 'First one off.'

'How are you doing, old buddy?' asked Claymore, rejecting Alex's outstretched hand in favor of a warm, brotherly embrace.

Alex returned the greeting and then followed as Claymore led the way.

'What's happening with the show?' asked Alex as they walked towards one of the exits.

'The network renewed the syndication deal.'

Elias Claymore was the next big thing in talk show hosts, after his California-based show had gone national last year. He was tipped by some to become the next Montel Williams. But others criticized this appellation in view of Claymore's less than honorable past.

'How's the love life?' Typical Elias, filling the silence with his cheeky humor.

'You know I'm married to my work,' said Alex with a twinkle in his eye. 'That's why I haven't even got time to watch your show.'

'Oh really? That's not what I heard.'

'What *did* you hear?'

'Oh, a little bird told me something about you being in a relationship with a certain TV reporter.'

'You shouldn't believe everything you hear on the little bird grapevine.'

'Then how come we're meeting for breakfast not lunch?'

'I thought you were shooting the show after lunch.'

'You could come and watch that too.'

'I'll have to take a rain check. I'm seeing a . . .' Alex's smile was that of the proverbial angel caught out.

Elias smiled back, 'So the little bird was right after all.'

'It's early days yet. Anyway, these long-distance relationships don't usually work out. She's down here in SoCal and I'm up by the Bay.'

'And you ain't over Melody yet.'

Alex remained silent. They had been friends ever since Alex had represented Claymore, negotiating a plea bargain over 20 years ago. And they had learned to trust and respect one another. But they had also learned to *read* one another.

'Wait a minute,' said Alex. 'This isn't the way to the parking lot.' Alex was quite familiar with LAX and he had noticed that they were heading towards the curbside on the lower level.

'No parking lot today, bro. We're going by taxi.'

'Taxi? Isn't that carrying this incognito business a bit too far?'

'My car was stolen.'

16

'Stolen? When? How?'

'Two days ago.'

'Doesn't your insurance provide a rental one in the meantime?'

'They do when I have time to get onto them. So far I haven't even had time to report it to the cops.'

'When you say stolen, you mean like carjacked? At gunpoint?'

'Heck no! If they'd given me half a chance I'd've nailed the bastards. I got out to buy a paper.'

'I thought your Merc had digital ignition control? Isn't that supposed to be hotwire-proof?'

'Not if you leave the keys inside.'

Alex looked at him, wide eyed. 'You're kidding!'

Claymore held up his hands sheepishly. 'I plead guilty to stupidity, Your Honor.'

They both laughed and carried on their friendly banter oblivious to the storm that was brewing in the background.

Friday, 5 June 2009 – 10.15

The room was a cold, clinical white. It was supposed to be relaxing as well as hygienic but stepping into it felt like entering something out of science fiction.

'Okay, now just hold still,' said Doctor Weiner, holding the third swab between Bethel's legs.

Bethel held still and forced herself not to think about what was happening or what had happened. But the harder she fought to avoid it, the more painful the memories that flooded back.

'I don't understand,' said Bethel, fighting back the tears. 'How many swabs do you need?'

'We try to take several,' said Bridget, the twenty-something-year-old detective who was standing a few feet away.

'But why?'

Bridget could hear in Bethel's voice the inner strength that the girl was trying to draw on.

'Because sometimes the whole sample gets used up in the test and we may need to do back-up tests or give a sample to the defense in case they want to run their own independent tests.'

Bethel Newton had already been photographed from all angles, examined by a female doctor and had vaginal swabs and nail clippings taken. They had intended to take combings from her pubic hair, but she was shaven. They had also taken buccal swabs to use as reference samples. Bethel's body was now – in police investigative terminology – a crime scene. And the vaginal swabs and nail clippings constituted crime scene samples.

'I don't see what good this'll do,' said Bethel.

'We can distinguish between different contributors. That's what your reference sample is for. In fact, we now have powerful techniques for isolating DNA from sperm.'

'But he used a condom.' She remembered how deftly he had held her down with the weight of his body while putting it on, before he penetrated her. It was like he knew exactly what he was doing – like he had done it before. Some men are experts with bra straps. This man was an expert at rape – and an expert at minimizing the trail of evidence that he left behind.

'We don't expect to find any identifiable sperm in the vaginal swab,' explained Bridget. 'But we have to check anyway.'

Bethel shuddered, but kept her mouth shut. She hadn't expected it to be like this.

'You scratched him too, don't forget,' Bridget added. 'That could give us a skin sample or even a blood sample and that in turn will give us his DNA. Also we might find traces of the condom itself. He might have thrown it away nearby.'

'So what?' said Bethel, bitterly. 'How does that help you catch him in the first place?'

Bridget took a deep breath and spoke gently. 'Okay, well let's say we find an empty condom packet by the road near where it happened, if it has fingerprints on it, and if he has a criminal record, we'll be able to identify him and issue a warrant. And let's say we find some exchangeable traces from the condom in the swabs we took from you – that means substances like lubricants and spermicides and anti-stick powders – we can compare them for chemical similarities to any condoms we find in the suspect's possession or for that matter any chemical traces in any condom that he discarded nearby. Or if he discarded the whole packet, we can analyze the exchangeable traces in them and compare them to your evidence sample.'

'So what'll that prove?' Bethel spat out contemptuously. 'That he has the same type of condoms?'

Bridget put a comforting hand on Bethel's shoulder. 'Evidence is like a jigsaw puzzle, Bethel. If we can put enough pieces together we can nail him. And if we can match his DNA to the DNA from any other crimes then before you know it he's going down on multiple counts of rape. And *you'd* be the one who can claim the credit for stopping him.'

Bethel knew that the flattery was part of a well-meaning game. Still, she warmed to the compliment and nodded, pretending to accept Bridget's logic.

In fact, a bond was beginning to form between them. But this was only natural. From the moment Bethel had staggered into the police station, Detective Bridget Riley had accompanied her.

Bethel had been reluctant to go through the whole rape examination procedure. Several times she had almost backed out of it. But Bridget had convinced her to continue, pointing out that the bruises and internal injuries showed that the rapist had used considerable force.

'There's virtually no danger he'll be able to argue consent,' Bridget assured her. 'They sometimes get away with that in date rape cases, but this wasn't a date. Unless we goof up badly, there's no way he can use it here. And once we ID the man, if we've got a good sample from any of the swabs or nail clippings, the DNA'll get him.'

'But first you've got to catch him,' said Beth tentatively.

'We'll check his DNA against the National DNA Index

System as well as the California DNA Index which may have some more detail.'

Bethel smiled nervously. But then she said something that struck Bridget as rather strange. 'What if his lawyers dig up stuff that they can throw at me?'

Friday, 5 June 2009 – 11.05

'So how big is this department, then?' Andi asked the lean, bespectacled man in a light gray suit as they walked past the desks in the open-plan office.

A mix-up about her starting date had meant that she had spent half the morning sitting in a room reading brochures and web-based material about Levine and Webster instead of beginning her induction and being introduced to the staff. The human resources manager wouldn't be back till Monday, so it was left to Paul Sherman, one of the partners in the firm, to lead Andi along through the maze of desks, as some of the younger (male) members of the staff leaned out from their shoulder height partitions to get a glimpse of the new girl. The women, for the most part, kept their attention to their photocopying or papers on their desks, only glancing round briefly to size up the competition.

'It's not really a department,' Sherman replied nervously. 'It's more of a section in *my* department.'

Andi experienced a hint of unease as these words wafted over her. 'I don't understand. I thought I was going to head up a department over here.'

Sherman squirmed with embarrassment. He was only slightly shorter than Andi yet she seemed to tower over him. 'Well, my department covers all forms of negligence and, for our purposes, tortious liability of criminals is a sub-section of that.'

'I'd've thought there's a difference between malicious acts and negligent ones.'

'It's all part of torts.'

'Well so is trespass,' she replied, as if addressing a child. 'So is nuisance, so is defamation.'

'Yes, but slander and libel are intentional.'

'Just like crime.'

Sherman seemed embarrassed, as if perturbed by Andi's confrontational approach, but reluctant to follow suit. 'Well, anyway, I won't try to second guess you. When we've got a victim case to litigate, you'll be the one whose desk it lands on. You're the expert in that field. I'm just a humble negligence lawyer.'

The uneasy feeling was growing in Andi. This wasn't what they'd promised her when they offered her the job. They had given her the job without an interview, based on nothing more than her résumé and the recommendation of her head of department back in New York. But what Sherman was describing now wasn't anything like what they had described when they made the job offer. If anything it was a step backwards.

She had made this move because it had become clear to her that in New York she could only move sideways. But now it looked like she had been suckered into this and was going nowhere just as fast. She felt betrayed. *No*, she told herself. *Don't prejudge. Maybe it's not what it seems. Maybe they just have a less formal structure in this firm.*

'So let me get this straight, Mr Sherman. Any crime victim wanting to sue the perp is mine?'

She was watching his face carefully now.

'As long as it falls exclusively within your remit. There

might be some areas of overlap, in which case we'll have to discuss it. But nobody's going to go behind your back, let alone over your head. Everything'll be done on a consensus basis.'

It was obvious that he was trying to sound encouraging, to make her feel at home. It was clear that they respected her or they wouldn't have hired someone from the other side of the country and made such a generous pay offer, not to mention paying her relocation costs.

'I guess it makes sense. It's just not what I had in mind.'

'Well, let's see how it goes,' he said encouragingly. 'You'll have a lot of autonomy. And in most cases no one will try to second guess you. The other partners will probably defer to your judgment too. You're the specialist after all.'

'Okay,' said Andi brightening up. 'Let's get to work.'

'That's the spirit.'

'So, where's my office?'

Sherman looked embarrassed. 'Well, it's not really an office,' he said nervously. 'As you can see we're open plan here.'

'You mean only the partners have private offices?'

'Well, no, some of the others do too. But we didn't have a spare room, apart from the conference rooms. You'll get one when we've got things sorted out. It's just a matter of rearranging things. In the meantime, you'll have a booth in the corner – away from most of the noise.'

He had noticed the expression on her face. 'What?'

'Look, maybe I shouldn't say this, but I'll spell it out to you. This isn't what I signed on for. I signed on to have an office, even head a department. Not to be an orphan or a stepchild.'

Friday, 5 June 2009 – 14.40

'Well, check out the ass on *that!*'

Alex shot an angry look at the leering redneck in torn jeans who was nursing a near-empty can of Bud. The man looked back as if to say, 'Wanna make an issue of it, buddy?'

The truth of the matter was that Alex didn't want to. But he was ready to. He was more afraid of the legal and professional consequences to himself as a lawyer than the possibility of getting beaten up. The guy was bigger than Alex. But Alex had trained in *Krav Maga* – an Israeli martial art – and reckoned the odds at about 50-50.

Not wanting to feed the redneck's desire for attention, Alex returned his attention to the snooker table that the lithe, thirty-four-year-old, dark-haired, Chinese-American woman was bending over.

They were in the Embassy billiards club in San Gabriel. The place had been packed for the men's event – the fourth in the six-venue US tour. But the hall seemed half empty as the woman in black pants and matching vest lined up her most crucial shot of the frame – if not the entire semi-final match.

After a few seconds, the chattering settled down to a respectful silence as the crowd held its breath with eager anticipation, wondering if Martine Yin could pull it off.

She took the shot with cool ease, not tentatively but with the firm confidence of someone who knew that there were no prizes for second best. And when the red ball dropped into the right corner pocket and the cue ball rolled slowly to a halt a foot away from the left cushion, the small crowd of appreciative aficionados who were there to watch the game and Martine, let out a whooping cheer. And Alex was amongst those applauding wildly – although he had to admit that he was one of those who was there to see Martine more than the game.

They had been going out together, on and off, for over a year now – if you could call it going out together. It had started after the Clayton Burrow case, when Martine had spent several months pursuing Alex for an interview. She was a TV reporter and she had covered what had become Alex's most famous case. She had been one of the reporters in the observation room adjacent to the death chamber when they got the fateful call to abort the execution.

And she had witnessed, albeit from a distance, Alex's intense conversation with his legal intern followed by the intern's arrest. This whole surreal episode had culminated in a high-speed car chase in the dead of night, ending in a fatal crash that unfortunately evaded the cameras of the news helicopters.

After the case, Alex had offered some considerable resistance to Martine's interview request, and when they did finally talk about it, she got the impression that he was holding something back. At first, she had been determined to break his resolve and get in under his guard. But somewhere along the line, she sensed that what Alex was holding back had more to do with his personal feelings than any hard facts about the case itself. She realized that Alex was all too human – nothwithstanding the predatory reputation of his profession – and thus realized also that there were limits to how predatory she could be in her own chosen vocation.

It was only after that, and because of this softening in Martine's character, that the relationship between them really started to develop. And even then it was a relationship at a distance, which tended to stunt its growth. She was based in Los Angeles; he in San Francisco.

'I'd like to put one in *your* pot, babe,' the redneck called out, as he swaggered to the bar for a refill.

'Why don't you can it?' said Alex turning round again.

'Wanna step outside and settle it like a man?' the redneck challenged.

'Why don't you *both* can it!' Martine snapped. 'I'm trying to concentrate.'

By this stage, the referee could no longer hope that the situation would play itself out without his intervention. He called a couple of bouncers to escort the redneck off the premises.

Martine turned back to the table and, taking a deep breath to regain her composure, potted the black and then another red. She had come to the table with four points and eight frames on the board against her opponent's sixty-one points and eight frames, after a nail-biting battle of safety shots. Her opponent, a petite blonde, had missed a two-cushion escape from a tricky snooker and this gave Martine a final chance to save the match on this final frame.

But only if she made every shot.

Keeping her cool, she made another black and then a red. But this time, the cue ball drifted towards the baulk end of the table and she had to settle for a pink instead of a black. She knew that there were no more chances. After the pink she had to pot the last red and get on the black. She sank the pink and came a little too far on the final red. Not that she couldn't pot the red. It was an easy shot in itself. But if she just rolled it in she would be on the wrong side of the black. She had to play it with pace and come off three cushions in order to get back down the table to the black. But if she played it with pace, she also had to play it with deadly accuracy.

She took the shot with pace . . . a lot of pace.

Alex held his breath and prayed.

The ball dropped into the pocket to shrieks of delight from the crowd. And to top it all off, the ball came to rest with perfect position to pot the black one final time.

From there Martine cleared up: yellow, green, brown, blue pink and black. But when the frame ended, there was thunderous applause. She had made a break of fifty-eight and a frame-winning score of sixty-two.

The crowd loved it when a match came down to the wire, however nerve-racking it might be for the players, and Martine found herself having to sign many autographs before she finally got to talk to Alex.

'You were great,' he said.

'Do me a favor,' she replied. 'Don't ever do that again.'

'What'd I d—'

'You *know* what I'm talking about. I don't need you to get into fights for me. You don't have to prove anything.'

'But he was—'

She held up her hand.

'Let's go grab a bite,' she said, taking his hand.

Friday, 5 June 2009 – 15.15

'The reason we got a drug problem is 'cause the *man* flooded the ghetto with cheap cocaine!' the black militant shouted into the microphone. 'And the reason things haven't changed, brother Elias, is because we've still got Uncle Toms like *you* blaming the *brothers* for what the *white man* did to us!'

The audience broke into loud spontaneous applause, especially the large group of the black militant's own supporters. The white supremacist on the other side of the studio struggled above the roar of approval to make his answer heard.

Elias Claymore was enjoying himself. It was fiery guests like these who made Claymore's ratings. The militants might get the anger off their chest, but it was Claymore who'd make more money thanks to the syndication deal.

Claymore was just as black as this militant guest of his. Now in his late fifties, tall and broad-shouldered, his colorful life had run the gamut from left-wing radical to Islamic fundamentalist to neo-conservative and born-again Christian.

This was meant to be a three-way debate between secular black militants, Black Muslims and the Ku Klux Klan. But the black militant had turned the debate on conservative blacks, including Claymore himself, and made the white supremacists in the studio – who had raised the drug issue in the first place – largely irrelevant.

'What *they* did to *us* is no excuse for what we're doing to *ourselves,* brothers!' Claymore replied. 'We have to stop blaming others. We used to be slaves to the white *man*. Now we're slaves to the white *powder*. I say it's time for us to break the chains and set ourselves free once and for all!'

Again the audience burst into thunderous applause, except the small cadre of militants. Claymore looked around and saw the approval on the faces of most of the audience, black and white. The black militant had almost won them over, but Claymore knew that with a few well-chosen words he had won them back.

Then a man wearing a suit and a bow tie with a crescent on it spoke up. 'If you think that joining the white establishment is a solution,' said the besuited man, 'then you're as big a fool as he is.'

'What are you talking about?' asked Claymore.

'I mean you've jumped out of the frying pan into the fire. You've betrayed your people twice over.'

He was a tall, slim, dapper figure and he was known to be Claymore's arch enemy. The man was a leading member of the Nation of Islam. Claymore had once belonged to his sect, but had later become disillusioned with it.

'Would you care to elaborate?' Claymore challenged.

'I'm talking about Islam, the religion of the black man, the religion you turned your back on when you became an apostate.'

'An apostate to Islam or an apostate to the Nation of Islam? The two are not the same. Malcolm X left the Nation of Islam but never turned his back on Islam. Yet that didn't save him from getting murdered.'

This was one of his favorite challenges to his former sect.

Malcolm X had left the Nation of Islam in disillusion both at its policy of separatism and at the practices of its leader.

But the well-dressed man in the audience was not going to be drawn into a debate about who killed Malcolm X. The Nation of Islam had subsequently re-adopted their former enemy and tried to distance themselves from his assassination.

'You're not like Brother Malcolm, Claymore, and you never will be! Brother Malcolm never did what *you* did.'

There was wild applause at that one. Everyone knew that Elias Claymore was not quite as respectable as he had now become. But Claymore was prepared for this.

'It's precisely because of my own guilt that I must speak out,' said Claymore, casting a professional eye at the studio clock. 'As a sinner, I have a duty *not* to remain silent. In the meantime, let's all say a loud "Thank God" that we're living in a country where no one has to be a slave unless he chooses to be. Thank you all, good afternoon and God Bless America.'

There was thunderous applause. The show was over.

As one of the cameras pulled back to let him pass, Claymore walked away, talking to various eager members of the audience and shaking hands with some of them.

He left the set to be confronted by two uniformed policemen and a female detective who couldn't have been more than thirty, if that. But what frightened him most was the implacable look on their faces. He didn't know what was going on, but sensed that it was something serious. The faces of the TV staff hovering around them looked tense. The detective stepped forwards and flashed her shield at Claymore.

'Elias Claymore?'

'Yes?' replied Claymore, slightly nervously.

'Detective Riley. I have a warrant for your arrest.'

'What for?'

'Rape.'

Claymore shot a look of panic at the producer and swallowed. 'Call Alex Sedaka. Now!'

Friday, 5 June 2009 – 15.30

'This is the best Chinese food I've ever tasted,' said Alex, expertly picking up a mouthful of chicken chow mein with a pair of wooden chopsticks.

'Best *at this price*,' said Martine, her voice still tense from the incident back at the snooker tournament. 'Let's not exaggerate.'

They were eating at the Embassy Kitchen, just across the parking lot from the billiards club. The area itself seemed like a bit of a dump. But Alex was used to slumming it, in his line of work. And he suspected that the same was true of Martine.

'Look, about what happened earlier . . .' He was nervous, sensing that Martine was still angry.

'You don't have to apologize. Just don't do it again.'

Alex felt deflated. He hadn't been going to apologize. But he wanted to clear the air. 'You shouldn't have to put up with that kind of crap.'

'And you shouldn't have to get into fights to prove your masculinity. Okay! You fathered two children. You paid your dues in life. You win battles in court – which is the battle-ground where *thinking men* fight and win battles. I don't need you to beat up some redneck to prove yourself.'

He was flattered that she said 'beat up' not 'get beaten up by.'

'I wasn't trying to prove anything. But the way he was going, I figured it was distracting to—'

'Oh gimme a break! You think arguing with him made it *less* distracting? Come off it, Alex. You wanted to play the hero. You wanted to show me that you're not the wimp lawyer in a suit but the tough guy who can take care of his lady – like I'm the sort who's gonna be impressed by that macho bullshit. Like I haven't seen it, done it and bought the t-shirt.'

'All right, maybe I overreacted. And maybe I'm old-fashioned.' He was leaning close to her now. 'But then again, I think that it *is* a man's duty to protect his lady.'

'And maybe you've also got some unfinished issues.'

'What's that supposed to mean?'

'It means you're still thinking about another lady you felt you should have been able to protect.'

She saw the hurt in his eyes.

'I'm sorry,' she said softly. 'I was out of line with that.'

'No it's true. You're right. I wasn't there for Melody.'

'You *couldn't* have been there for Melody. How were you to know that some loony-tunes with a Saturday night special was going to bushwhack her on the way home? Don't beat yourself up about it.'

Alex's wife Melody had been killed by a gangbanger in the parking structure of the hospital where she worked. Melody was a doctor who had been working in A & E when two gangbangers from opposite sides of town were brought in the same night. What she didn't know was that the one she was treating had shot the other one. She saved the one on her operating table, but the other doctor lost his. And the dead man's homeys couldn't get at the guy who killed their brother, 'cause he was in jail – in solitary. So they held a council of war and decided that Melody had to pay.

By that stage, she probably knew she was in danger, but

she refused to take it seriously. She even rejected an escort to her car, saying she was too old for a nanny.

Call it arrogance, call it self-confidence – either way, she paid with her life.

And Alex still blamed himself in some way.

'I just wish I could . . .' He trailed off. But Martine knew what he was going to say. He wished he could turn the clock back. Just like everybody does. But as his son David, a physicist, had once told him: time doesn't run backwards.

He tried to take his mind off it. 'Tell me how you made that trick shot?'

'You should get David to explain it. You see it's all about Newtonian mechanics. If you hit the object ball at quarter ball with pace, the cue ball moves off at an oblique angle, while—'

Martine's cell phone went off. She whipped it out and answered it with polished, professional speed. 'Martine Yin.' For the next half minute, she appeared to be listening intently. 'Okay, I'll be there in ten.'

She turned to Alex, looking acutely embarrassed.

'I know,' he said. 'Duty calls.'

She thanked him for his understanding and left briskly. Seconds later, the roar of a car engine outside brought a wry smile to his lips as he realized that the predator in her might lie dormant but was far from extinct. She was still a newswoman, poised to pursue a good story at a moment's notice, just as he was a lawyer 24/7, even if he didn't quite resort to ambulance chasing.

He managed one more mouthful of food before his own cell phone blared out the familiar musical phrase from the Allegro of Dvorak's *New World Symphony*.

'Mr Sedaka?' said an almost desperate-sounding male voice at the other end of the line.

'Yes.'

'I'm the producer of the Elias Claymore show. We've got a situation here and I was wondering if there's any possibility of you coming to LA—'

'I'm in San Gabriel.'

'Oh, thank God for that! Mr Claymore asked me to call you. He's been arrested.'

'Arrested? What's the charge?'

'It's some kind of phony rape charge.'

Alex knew at that moment why Martine had left in such a hurry.

Friday, 5 June 2009 – 16.50

'Okay, there we are,' said the evidence technician, as she took the third buccal swab.

Like Bethel a few hours earlier, Claymore was giving a DNA sample from the lining of his mouth. They hadn't told him that the rapist had worn a condom or that the victim had scratched the rapist's arm. The less they told him, the better their chances of getting him to incriminate himself by revealing first-hand knowledge of the crime. But they did subject him to a full examination in which they looked for signs of scratches and found several.

Nevertheless, this was far from conclusive. The real test would be the DNA. They had several good samples from Bethel and now all they needed was a good match.

After the reference samples had been taken, Alex sat with Claymore for twenty minutes, going through where Claymore had been at the time of the alleged rape. Claymore had been very clear that he had nothing to hide and wanted to answer police questions. But Alex was wary of this; he knew that even guilty people sometimes think they can get away with the crime by talking to the police. And he also knew all about the naivety of the genuinely innocent man who thinks he has nothing to hide. Alex had known Elias for a few years now – ever since he had represented him at the plea bargain for unlawful escape, after he came back to the United States to face the music – and he had been impressed at the time by Claymore's sincerity and genuine sense of shame at his past. But that meant little now. If a man could change once, he could change again. The only thing it *did* mean was that Alex had a certain amount of influence with Claymore.

But lawyers take their instructions from clients, not the other way round. So when Claymore made it clear that he was determined to answer police questions, all Alex could do was say his piece and then step aside while the interview took place. He would be present during the questioning and he'd step in if he had to.

Alex sat in silence while Lieutenant Kropf, the tall, thin man who headed up the investigation, used his aggressive rapid-fire technique to try and trip Claymore up.

'Okay, so you admit that no one saw you at home at that time?' barked Kropf.

Alex wanted to tell the lieutenant to stop wasting time; he'd had his answer and was just repeating himself ad nauseam. But Claymore held out a restraining hand to silence his lawyer.

'It's not a question of *admitting*,' Claymore replied, trying to keep his voice level. 'I was alone. That's a fact. It's not a crime to be alone.'

'No, but it helps to have an alibi.'

'You think I don't know that?' asked Claymore wryly.

In the tense silence that followed, Claymore looked around. The room was stark and bare. The furniture was limited to a table and three chairs, one for the lieutenant and one each for Claymore and Alex. Light entered the room from a high window located very close to the ceiling.

Another police officer, a detective, stood by the door but said nothing. He was there in case the suspect decided to get 'physical.' He was also there to be a witness to protect the lieutenant from false accusations. Although the interrogation was being videotaped, with Claymore's consent, and there was a technician on the other side of the one-way glass, there were times – on the way in and the way out – when the people were out of the watchful eye of the camera.

'Can you think of anything else that might prove you were at home?'

'Like what?'

'Like a phone call. Did anyone call you? Did you call anyone?'

Claymore shook his head. The monotonous drone of the air conditioning was beginning to take its toll. It was more irritating than the monotonous drone of Lieutenant Kropf's voice as he kept up a steady stream of questions that carried with them more than a hint of quiet menace.

'I don't remember.'

'If you called out from your phone then there'll be a record on your phone bill. It's all digital now so you should get an itemized bill.'

Alex sensed that the lieutenant was actually trying to be helpful, almost like he didn't believe that Claymore was guilty.

'Okay,' Kropf continued, 'if you're confident on this one, we can get it now.'

The lieutenant was looking at Alex when he said this.

'At *this* time?' asked Alex skeptically, looking at his watch.

'I know a friendly judge we can ask.'

'And you think the phone company's going to haul ass tonight just 'cause we wave a subpoena in their faces? Get real!'

Alex knew well enough what the lieutenant was up to. He was testing to see how confident they were. It wasn't a legally binding test of innocence. But it was a good way to know whether or not he was wasting his time on a sure-fire loser.

'Okay,' said Kropf, finally. 'We're not going to charge your client.'

Claymore breathed a sigh of relief.

'At least not right now. We'll wait for the DNA results to come in and we'll take it from there.'

Alex smiled. It was beginning to look like the storm had blown itself out before it hit dry land. But he noticed that Kropf looked far from deflated – like he still had one more card up his sleeve.

'Just one more question, Mr Claymore. What car do you drive?'

'Well I've been using taxis for the past couple of days.'

'Any particular reason?'

'My car was stolen.'

'Did you report it?'

'Not yet. I haven't had the time.'

'What make of vehicle was it?'

'A Mercedes.'

'What color?'

'Blue.'

'A blue Mercedes?'

'Aquamarine, if you want to get technical.'

Friday, 5 June 2009 – 19.30

'I'm beginning to think that nothing's changed,' said Andi, bitterly.

They were sitting on the porch of their house, dining alfresco in the California evening sun.

'How d'you mean?' asked Gene, with measured sympathy. She wasn't one to encourage self-pity, having seen in the course of her work what a self-destructive force it can be. Self-destructive and thoroughly seductive.

Andi attacked her food with such ferocity that Gene was forced to smile. It meant that Andi wasn't succumbing to the demon of surrender. She was in fighting spirits and that was surely a good sign. She'd snap out of it completely in no time at all!

'We uprooted ourselves from New York and relocated for *what*? It's not a *department*. It's just a meaningless title.'

'Give 'em a chance, honey. I mean it's only your first day. Let's see what they let you do.'

Gene was calmly reassuring. She knew that Andi expected no less of her. It was a game they played: Andi bitched about life and Gene pulled her back down to earth.

'I can just feel the vibes from the start,' Andi continued.

'I'm supposed to be on the fast track for a partnership and yet I haven't even got an office. They've stuck me in a glorified broom closet.'

Gene touched Andi's forearm gently. 'I'm sure that's only temporary.'

They ate on in silence for a few seconds. Andi was still sulking. But Gene was content to leave her to it. If Andi preferred to sulk for a while longer, that was her business. *I can't be her mother all the time.*

In the end, it was Andi who broke the silence, changing the subject.

'So how was *your* first day?'

She couldn't understand why Gene looked so upset.

'*My* first day? What? At the Center? Pretty hectic. I guess I should be used to it.'

'Are you understaffed?' asked Andi.

She knew perfectly well that they were understaffed. Rape crisis centers always suffered from a chronic shortage of employees, exacerbated by the low pay.

'Understaffed and underappreciated,' Gene replied. 'Everyone rails and rages against crime, but they're more concerned with punishing the perpetrator than helping the victim recover from the trauma. Who needs to help the victim when you can get revenge? That's the American way.'

This was unfair, and they both knew it. They both understood the desire for revenge all too well. But it was strange how guns always counted for more than bandages on the human balance sheet.

'You've got something on your mind, haven't you?' The voice was gentle, sympathetic. It was one of those spontaneous mid-conversation role reversals that characterized their relationship.

'I had a case this morning . . .'

44

She trailed off, but Andi could read the rest of the sentence in the silence.

'They threw you in at the deep end?' This was something that Andi had been hoping for in her own job. But it wasn't to be. Instead it was Gene who had the dubious privilege.

'Wha'd'you expect? Like I said, we're understaffed.'

Andi put a gentle hand on her lover's bare arm. 'What's bugging you? You've seen it all before. You know the score by now.'

A pained expression flipped briefly across Gene's face. 'I've seen *this* before all right,' Gene muttered bitterly. 'It's the kind of case that sets off the talking heads on TV. Feminism versus race politics. A white girl raped by a black man.'

Andi, who had been taking a sip of her orange juice, gulped and put the glass down. 'The press'll have a field day. It'll probably turn into another black rights versus women's rights circus.'

'And don't I know it! The defense will raise the specter of the Scottsboro Boys and the prosecution will use everything they can throw at the defendant from Mike Tyson to O.J. Simpson.'

Andi nodded sympathetically.

'And caught in the middle of it is one frightened little girl, not yet out of her teens.'

'You think you can handle it?'

'Oh, *I* can handle it all right. I've been there before, remember. The question is, can the victim?'

'And *can* she?'

Gene shook her head, sadly. 'She doesn't know what she's letting herself in for.'

'Have they got a suspect?'

'Yes.'

'Has she ID-ed him?'

'Yes. Only they released him pending DNA results.'

Andi sat forward, part eager, part concerned. She had known Gene long enough to pick up the nuances in her words as well as her tone.

'Well if she ID-ed him then maybe she's tougher than you think.'

'She's not tough. She's just naïve. She doesn't realize that she's going to carry the can for two centuries of racial persecution.'

Saturday 6 June 2009 – 11.00

Albert Carter was an old man. Not a wise old man, not a crusty old man, not even really a frail old man, just an old man who had lived a full life and been around the block a few times. He wasn't in the best of health, having done his share of smoking and drinking, before he gave it up when he noticed it slowing him down a bit. But he was a lonely old man, having lost his first wife to divorce and his second to the Grim Reaper.

Oh yes, the Reaper.

There were many weapons in the Reaper's arsenal, and Albert Carter couldn't even *pronounce* the name of the disease that had claimed Hildegard.

His children were still around, but he had lost them to professional migration. He saw them at Christmas and on his birthday, but that was pretty much it. One lived in Utah and one in Boston. The one in Utah was a store manager and the one in Boston some kind of academic. He understood the work of the former more than the latter, but, both had families and neither came out west very often.

So he spent his days watching TV, reading the newspaper and – with diminishing frequency – bowling with his old friends. It was a dull, repetitive chapter towards the latter part of his book of life, but he had his basic needs and he didn't want more. All he yearned for was a bit less arthritic pain. Oh, and he wished that the cops would do more to round up those gangs who were turning the neighborhood into such an unpleasant place. He *knew* who *they* were . . . in a generic sort of way, at least.

It was while he was watching the TV alone one night, he saw a news report about the Bethel Newton rape case, saying how a famous local talk show host had been arrested and then released. They didn't have any footage from the police station, but they showed a still photograph of the girl and stock footage from the man's talk show. Apparently he'd been arrested after shooting the latest show, yet to be broadcast.

And that was when Carter got the feeling.

He didn't remember the details too clearly – the whole thing had happened just too fast. But there was one thing that he remembered.

For a moment he hesitated, realizing that criminals could sometimes be vengeful towards people who snitched. But then he remembered his own, all-too-frequent words about the cowards who don't speak out when criminals destroy their communities. He didn't want to be like one of those people whom he routinely criticized. He knew now that it was his civic duty to speak out and he didn't want to be like all the shirkers.

So he dragged his weary bones out of the comfort of his tattered, dust-ridden armchair and trudged over to the phone.

Friday 12 June – 9.40

Detective Bridget Riley was a victim chaperone, not a counselor. She was the principal point of contact between the investigating officers and the rape victim. The detectives investigating the case put most of their questions through Bridget. When they had to put questions directly or when others had to have contact with the victim, such as during the medical examination, the victim chaperone had to be there.

She had a sporty, athletic look about her, the tough look of a kick boxer. Male colleagues found her attractive and her face, highlighted against her raven-colored hair, was potential photographic model material. But what would be a blessing in the world of show biz, could be something of a curse in the locker room culture of the police.

Because of her looks, Bridget had been the target of sexual harassment by her colleagues. And it had made her tough. She could take the compliments with a smile and a shrug and when they became vulgar she hit back with a glib 'in your dreams, buster.'

When one of the rookies was bold enough to try to pin her against a locker, showing off in front of three of his friends, she deterred him from further action with a well-placed fist to the groin. Then she added insult to injury by

49

asking him if he wanted her to kiss it better. The rookies never bothered her again; nor had anyone else in the department during the four years since.

Bridget was sitting at her desk typing up a report on a domestic violence case for Sarah Jensen at the D.A.'s office, when a female officer dropped a fax on her desk. But Bridget did not look up.

Sarah Jensen, the Assistant District Attorney in charge of the domestic violence division at the Ventura County D.A.'s office, was no less determined than Bridget to nail these bastards who beat their wives or girlfriends. But Sarah Jensen was a realist. She was also very ambitious. She knew that unsuccessful prosecutions damaged the reputation of the department, and gave her a poor track record, personally. So Bridget knew that she had to word every sentence carefully to give Sarah the impression that this was a winnable case.

When she looked at the fax, her eyes lit up. She scooped it up and rushed out of the room.

Friday, 12 June 2009 – 10.30

Sitting on a lounging chair on the deck of his Mediterranean-style villa, looking out onto the ocean, Elias Claymore realized that crime and repentance had served him well. His present surroundings were a far cry from the ramshackle hut where he had been born and the rat-infested 'hood where he had grown up.

The villa stood in landscaped grounds on the sands of Montecito's most prestigious beach and had breathtaking views of the ocean from nearly every room. There was a huge living room with fireplace, bar and ocean view, a beachside kitchen, two beachside bedrooms each with a fireplace, and a third at the back. Even the office had an ocean view. There was also a separate guest apartment, a large beachfront deck, a sunset view seaside spa, majestic trees and flowering gardens and seventy-five feet of private beachfront.

But how far had he really come?

'You can take the man out of the ghetto,' the racists had taunted, 'but you can't take the ghetto out of the man.' And much as it pained his troubled conscience, the racists were right on this one, albeit in the most literal sense. A ghetto is a place of retreat where one is surrounded by one's own kind yet is constantly under threat from those outside. And right now Elias felt besieged.

His mind drifted back to what his life had once been like. He used to think that the pain was all over. He had never forgotten what he had done. But after all these years he thought it would no longer come back to haunt him. Yet the events of the past week had proved him wrong – and it was like a slow, drawn-out torture.

He tried to soften the pain by reminding himself what had driven him to do the things he had done and become the man he became, thinking back to the time he was nine when two white policemen raped his mother before his eyes. He had tried to stop them, but one of them had grabbed him and twisted his arm behind his back, forcing him to watch while the other had pinned his mother to the ground, ripped her clothes and forced himself into her as she screamed and begged for mercy.

She had brought up Elias alone, without the help of a man, and she had always been a strong figure in his early years, dishing out the punishment while protecting him from the bigger kids in the 'hood. But she couldn't protect herself from *this*. And Elias Claymore learned in those few minutes that his mother, who had been like a pillar of support for the entire world as he knew it, was powerless in the face of this invading force in their own home.

And through his childish eyes, little Elias knew why. She was a woman – and women were weaker than men. He couldn't expect a woman to protect him. It was for men to be strong and to protect women . . . or violate them. That was how it was in other households. He had seen the local pimps slapping their girls around and he quickly learned that this was the natural order in the world. It was normal for men to dominate women.

But these men who had invaded his house and raped his mother were not *their* men. They were an alien presence.

These were the pigs who beat up blacks just because they were black. These were the people who called him 'Nigger' and made him afraid whenever they walked by, knowing that he daren't respond to their racist taunts. And now they were here in his home, doing . . . this thing . . . to his mother.

He couldn't blame her for being weak. But it *was* her fault that they didn't have a man to protect them. She had driven him away. That's what one of his brothers had told him. She had called Elias's father a no-good, drunken deadbeat and thrown him out of the house. But now he realized how much they needed a man in this household . . . and they didn't have one because of her.

He realized in that moment that one day *he* would be a man. *He* would be big and strong and then there'd be hell to pay! Because *then* he'd be able to fight back . . . and he'd hit them where it hurt. He'd hit *their* weakness – *their* women.

He was shaken out of his unhappy daydream by a loud, aggressive knocking on the front door.

'Who is it?' he called out.

'This is the police! We have a warrant for your arrest.'

Friday, 12 June 2009 – 13.00

'This time we've got a witness,' said Lieutenant Kropf.

'Who?' asked Alex.

'You'll find out soon enough.'

Alex had flown down to Los Angeles from San Francisco as soon as he heard of Claymore's second arrest, having told his client not to say a word until he got there. He knew that the cops would try their usual tricks – telling the suspect that they were more likely to believe him if he spoke freely on the record, without getting all 'lawyered up.' But Alex had been firm.

'Don't fall for it,' he had warned. 'The issue is not whether they believe you, but whether they've got a case. They're capable of talking themselves into anything. You just stay cool and hang on till I get there. If they've got no case, they can't act. If they think they've already got one, then nothing you can say will make any difference.'

'What exactly did this witness see?' Alex assumed that someone hadn't just stood there watching a rape and doing nothing about it.

'He saw your client running away from the crime scene,' said Kropf, regretting it a moment later.

He.

Alex picked up on it. So the witness was a man . . . or

a boy. And he had only seen Claymore allegedly running away from the crime scene, not the rape. That was a very different thing.

And Kropf had also let slip that an ID had already been made.

'Wait a minute, you put my client in a line-up when I wasn't there?'

'We didn't need to,' said the lieutenant. 'He recognized him from the news reports.'

They hadn't said anything about a witness at the time of Claymore's first arrest. And even if he was right about the identity of the man running away, how did he know that it was from the scene of a rape? If he had known at the time, would he not have stayed to help the victim? Or given his name to the police? And would they not have said something about a witness at the time of the first arrest? And put Claymore in a line-up? But now they were saying that this man had recognized Claymore from the news reports. That meant that he didn't stick around at the time.

Why not? Had he been afraid? Why would he be afraid if the rapist had run away? Was he afraid to get involved? Was he afraid of the police? Was he a criminal himself? Had he really seen something? Had he even been there? Or was he one of the legion of freeloaders who come out of the woodwork in high profile cases, looking to make a quick buck?

'Can I see his statement?' asked Alex.

At a certain point, if they decided to proceed against Claymore, they'd have no alternative but to show him the statement. However at this stage, they owed him nothing, not even the name of the witness.

'You'll get it from the D.A. with the rest of the discovery material.'

That sounded ominous, like they had already made up their minds to charge Claymore.

'I don't suppose you'd like to give my client an opportunity to explain what he was doing there?'

'What, you mean why he was at a crime scene at the time of the crime when he had previously claimed to be at home? No, as a matter of fact, we wouldn't.'

Alex realized that he was in a tight spot. The police were under no obligation to give Claymore a chance to explain himself, now that they had a witness to put him at the crime scene. They *could* do so, if they wanted to. But they didn't *have* to. If they decided to go to trial, Claymore would have to take his chances with a jury.

The door opened and Bridget entered. She signaled the lieutenant over and whispered in his ear while showing him a piece of paper. The lieutenant was nodding seriously and the expression on his face looked grave. Alex suspected that this scene was being staged. He had seen this sort of thing dozens of times before.

The lieutenant came back to the table. 'Do you want the good news or the bad news?' he asked Alex.

'Just cut the crap and spit it out,' said Alex.

'We just got back the results of the DNA test.'

Alex suspected that they already had the results before re-arresting Claymore. They wouldn't have arrested him on the strength of the witness's ID alone, when the test results were still pending.

'And?' asked the lawyer tensely.

'We didn't have any DNA in the vaginal swab because the rapist used a condom. But the victim scratched the rapist's face and so we were able to get a good DNA sample from under her fingernails. Want to know what the results were?'

'Spill it,' said Alex, realizing where this was going.

The lieutenant handed the fax over to Alex, watching his face for a reaction with a growing sense of excitement. But when Alex perused it, the emotion he felt was anger – not towards Kropf, but towards his own client. And when he showed it to his client, the look on Claymore's face was one of confusion . . . and fear.

Friday, 12 June 2009 – 14.30

'Your Honor,' Alex Sedaka's voice rang out confidently, 'although my client has a criminal record, his last criminal conviction was over twenty years ago.'

They were in Court 13 of the Ventura Courthouse, in the same building where Claymore was being detained. It was a crowded courtroom with backless spectators' benches and a large cage for holding prisoners. Being based up north in the Bay area, Alex had never had to practice here before, but he knew that this was one of the busiest courts in the country, essentially a meat factory for arraignments, scheduling motions and defendants' pleas. With 200 cases a day to process, user-comfort was a luxury that they couldn't afford.

'Mr Claymore has strong roots in the community,' Alex continued. 'And for the last ten years has been a model citizen.'

In truth, Alex was rather less confident than he sounded. The warrant for the second arrest had been a no-bail warrant, because of Claymore's past, a powerful indicator of which way the judge's thinking was heading. Alex would have liked to file for an interim appeal. But he knew that his grounds were weak to nonexistent. Denying bail to a man who had previously escaped from prison and stayed at liberty for several years was hardly unreasonable.

But his training and experience as a trial lawyer, permitted him to conceal the doubt – indeed *required* him to conceal it.

So it was with this turbulent mixture of emotions that Alex was addressing the judge. Except that he was all too aware that he wasn't addressing *only* the judge. This was Claymore's first appearance in court since his arrest and predictably enough it had attracted a lot of public attention. The courtroom was packed with reporters and Alex knew how important it was to get the message out there into the stream of news as quickly as possible, to counteract the negative effect of Claymore's well-known past.

It was inevitable that the media would dredge up Claymore's history; there would be no restrictions on public discussion of the facts of the case. Gag orders could be imposed at the judge's discretion, but there was no automatic sub-judice rule.

As Alex sat down, a woman of about forty, of average height with neat, jet-black hair, rose from her chair to dispute the point. She was Sarah Jensen, the Assistant District Attorney who headed the domestic violence division of the D.A.'s office. Alex had never crossed swords with her before but he was well aware of her reputation. Some prosecutors are tough but not good. Others are good but not tough. Sarah Jensen was both tough and good.

'Your Honor,' there was an angry, almost contemptuous edge to the voice, 'Elias Claymore's record is well known and the defense counsel conveniently failed to mention that he not only raped six women in the past, but he also escaped from prison last time he was convicted and remained at liberty for several years. For this reason alone, he is a very serious flight risk.'

Alex was back on his feet. 'Your Honor, the Assistant

District Attorney seems to have *conveniently* forgotten that my client returned to America *voluntarily* to serve out his sentence.'

It was Alex who, as a young law graduate, still learning his craft, had negotiated the plea bargain.

'And why should that outweigh the fact that he fled in the first place?' asked the judge, raising a skeptical eyebrow.

The judge was an old man, close to retirement from the bench. He had seen and heard just about every piece of bullshit that lawyers were capable of throwing at him, and if there were any new tricks to be learned – even from a veteran like Alex – he would have been most surprised.

'Because it's a more *recent* event, Your Honor. And in judging a man's character, the court should give more weight to his *recent* past than his *distant* past.' He placed the emphasis on his key words, in the hope of neuro-linguistically programming the judge to respond as he wanted.

'You mean the fact that he returned to the United States to serve out his sentence *after* he escaped?'

'Precisely, Your Honor.'

The judge squirmed with mock embarrassment and scratched his head. 'Forgive me for pointing out the obvious, Mr Sedaka, but he could hardly have done it *before* he escaped.'

The courtroom erupted with mirth at the judge's wisecrack and Alex felt the frustration that goes with knowing that one faces an uphill struggle against a hostile judge – especially when the hostile judge has the law on his side.

The gallery, packed with journalists who had got wind of Claymore's arrest, sensed that this was the beginning of another media event, like the O.J. Simpson trial.

Sarah Jensen shook her head. 'Your Honor, if I might just add something at this juncture. There is nothing particularly confidence-inspiring in Mr Claymore's return to the United States, after he'd spent several years on the run as a fugitive from justice. He stayed away as long as he could hold out, until he decided that he preferred the comforts of an American prison to the hardships of a Third World dictatorship.'

Alex bristled with anger. 'Your Honor, anyone who thinks a prison is a comfortable place to be, should spend a couple of nights there.'

'I believe,' the judge replied solemnly, 'that prison is *supposed* to be an unpleasant place . . . so that the inmates don't get too attached to it.'

Again, laughter erupted from the spectators.

'My point, Your Honor,' Alex replied, with growing irritation, 'is that the court should be guided in its judgment by considering the *new* Elias Claymore, not the *old* Elias Claymore. His absconding, like his criminal record, belongs to his *past.*'

'That's something that the prosecution will no doubt dispute, and something that the jury will have to decide,' said the judge in his world-weary tone. 'However, I'm inclined to accept that the defense has a valid point regarding the flight risk. The fact that Mr Claymore returned to the United States to serve his sentence is a strong point in his favor. Also he does now have roots in the community. On the other hand I must also bear in mind the severity of the alleged crime and the fact that Mr Claymore has a record for this sort of crime and the fact that he did once escape lawful custody.'

Alex and the A.D.A. waited in silence while the judge considered his options.

'I feel that in this case, the accused's record of escape outweighs any other factors. Bail is denied.'

Alex was angry. 'In that case my client stands by his right to a speedy trial.'

'That *is* his right, Mr Sedaka. I'll set the prelim fourteen days hence in Court 12.'

In general lawyers are more amenable to a delay when their client is out on bail. Alex's motive for refusing to waive the right was twofold. Firstly to put pressure on the D.A. – and thus indirectly on the judge – to reconsider the bail question. Secondly, if bail *was* to be denied, then he didn't want his client sitting in jail for long. Jail is an unsafe environment at the best of times, and for a black man who was thought of as an 'Uncle Tom' it was particularly dangerous. He would be in danger from both sides.

Whether either of them would go as far as to try and kill him was another matter, but prison beatings were almost impossible to prevent. The only way Claymore would be safe was if he asked for isolation from the general prison population. But that would involve being put in a special section with all the sex offenders, including child molesters. Alex wasn't sure if Claymore would be ready to seek this. Knowing Claymore, he'd probably try to tough it out – until it was too late. And this wasn't an area in which Alex could advise his client. It was something Claymore would have to decide for himself.

After a brief whispered exchange, Claymore was led away to the county jail that was located in the same building.

As Alex was walking away, he was approached by a dignified, sixty-something gray-haired man, who stiffly proffered his business card to Alex, by way of introduction.

'I'm Arthur Webster of Levine and Webster.'

'How do you do, Mr Webster,' said Alex, tensely. 'What can I do for you?'

'Let's walk,' said Webster, indicating with his hand to the side exit from the court building. Alex was happy to comply, but felt alienated by the man's manner, that appeared to straddle the fence between embarrassment and conde-scending arrogance.

'I should explain that we're a local law firm, based in Los Angeles. We're retained by the network that broadcasts Mr Claymore's show and we work extensively with SoCal Insurance where Mr Claymore carries his liability insurance.'

'I've heard of you,' said Alex.

Webster seemed pleased by this.

'The reason I wanted to talk to you is because I under-stand that you're actually based in San Francisco.'

'What of it?'

'Well Claymore's insurance policy with SoCal Insurance includes *legal* liability and it occurred to us that it might be rather hard for you to represent Claymore down here in Ventura when you're based up in the Bay area.'

'And you want . . .'

'We'd like you to step aside as attorney of record and let us represent Mr Claymore.'

Friday, 12 June 2009 – 15.40

'But as I'm sure you know,' said Alex, 'the policy only covers *civil* liability.'

Alex was seated with the partners of Levine and Webster, including Paul Sherman, around the long oval rosewood table in the main conference room. The atmosphere was tense.

'Well obviously it can't cover criminal *liability*,' said Webster with a puerile grin, 'because an insurance company can hardly serve a custodial sentence. But the policy includes payment of legal *fees* as well as liability payouts, and the insurance company has specifically asked us to take the case.'

Alex had kept his cool when Webster had first approached him and had agreed to this meeting without prejudice. But he was getting irritated now.

'That means, presumably, representation and legal fees in a *civil* suit, when there's an issue of liability.'

'It covers all legal *representation*,' Webster insisted, 'including criminal.'

'You seem to be assuming that you can do a better job of defending him on criminal charges than I can.'

'Oh, come on Mr Sedaka, you're a one-man band. We're a large law firm. We've got dozens of lawyers and a network of experts and other contacts that you can only dream about.'

'I'm not disputing your size, but that's not necessarily an

65

advantage. If the accused marches into court with an army of lawyers, that can actually count *against* him.'

'There's also the logistical aspect. You're up there in the Bay, we're down here in the Basin. Ventura's in our backyard. What are you going to do? Commute down from San Fran every day?'

'You seem to be assuming that the trial is going to stay in Ventura.'

'Are you going for a change of venue?' asked Sherman.

'I might. It certainly wouldn't hurt if we could get it transferred to a county with better demographics.'

'I thought you wanted a speedy trial,' said Webster. 'A change of venue motion will give them a pretext for a delay.'

'Also we're in a better position than you when it comes to a change of venue,' added Sherman.

Alex's ears pricked up at this. 'How so?'

'We've got a whole department for demographic analysis.'

Alex thought about this for a moment. 'You may have a point. But it's not for me to decide. It's Claymore's call. I'm his lawyer and I'm here for him as long as he wants me.'

'But you could talk to him,' said Webster, 'convince him.'

'I'm not even going to try. I'm not convinced that you can do a better job, so why should I try and convince *him*?'

Arthur Webster leaned forward to speak again. But a frail-looking man, who must have been pushing eighty, held up his hand to silence him. This was Aaron Levine, the senior partner in the firm. Webster slumped back into his seat and left it to his lifelong friend to address Alex.

'Could I ask you a question, Mr Sedaka? Please don't take this the wrong way, but is it a matter of professional pride? Because, if so, you needn't worry. Your reputation precedes you. We all remember your remarkable achievement in the Sanchez case.'

Alex was no longer angry. But neither was he assuaged by the flattery. In truth he was simply relieved that their real concerns were finally coming out into the open. He noted that this man was tactful enough not to mention the Clayton Burrow case.

'It has nothing to do with professional pride. But I'm not just Elias Claymore's lawyer, I'm also his friend. I'm not going to abandon him or do anything to give him the impression that I want to unload the case onto someone else.'

'We're not asking you to do that, all we're ask—'

'I *know* what you're asking. But the fact of the matter is I'm *not* convinced that anyone in your criminal law department is in a better position to help him than me.'

Webster leaned forward again, unable to contain himself any longer.

'But *we* have the resources to—'

'Then let's *pool* our resources,' said Alex.

This silenced them for a few seconds.

'What do you mean?' asked Levine, the only man in the room with the gravitas to break the silence, or the moral courage to meet Alex's eyes.

'I'm offering you second seat.'

Webster's intensity flared up again.

'We're not *asking* for second seat. We want you to—'

Again, Levine's hand silenced his partner.

'Could you elaborate?'

'Yes. Let's work on this case together, with me as point man and your formidable resources to back me up. You pick your best man – or woman – to take second seat to report back to you.'

'But you lead?' said Levine, half-question, half-statement.

'I take first seat,' Alex confirmed in a tone of finality that made it clear that this position was not open to debate.

A cheerful smile graced Aaron Levine's face, changing the mood for almost everyone.

'I think we can live with that,' he said, looking at Webster in a way that demanded his agreement. Webster nodded, his face taut to maintain its neutrality.

'Good. Then I guess we can roll up our sleeves and get on with it.'

The tension was collectively released from the lungs of those present and the awkward smiles spread like a contagion round the table.

'I think it stinks,' said Joanne Gale, a woman in her late thirties, sitting forward to meet Webster's eyes. She was the only women partner in the firm.

'Why?' asked Webster.

'You *know* why. The man is a rapist.'

'A rape *suspect*!' Webster corrected. 'And it's never bothered you before.'

This was true. The firm had defended rape suspects before. Indeed Jo herself had taken first seat in several rape defenses – and in some of those cases there was little room to doubt the guilt of the accused.

'This is different. He's done it before.'

'And he's served his sentence,' said Alex. 'But that doesn't make him guilty this time. He's not the same man now that he was then.'

'He got off lightly last time.'

'That's not for us to judge.'

This was Webster again. Everyone else remained silent, including Alex. It was tempting to speak up in defense of Claymore, or even to lecture this woman on the finer points of legal ethics. But it wasn't his job. If she had a problem

68

with Levine and Webster being involved in Claymore's defense, that was between her and her colleagues.

Again, it was left to Aaron Levine to break the silence. 'Do we have a hope in hell of winning? There's not much kudos in *losing* a high profile case.'

The other partners looked down or away, anything to withdraw from this pragmatic way of looking at the issue. Alex realized that the question was directed at him. He met the old man's eyes.

'It's going to be an uphill struggle.'

'How steep is the hill?'

Alex thought about this for a moment.

'There's a lot of evidence for us to refute – not to mention that we still have to overcome the effect of Claymore's past. It won't be easy. The problem is I can't desanctify the victim without seeming like a bully.'

'Desanctify the victim?' Levine echoed softly.

Jo Gale spoke into the silence that followed, 'A euphemism for character assassination used by sleazy shysters who like helping rapists and wife-killers beat the rap.'

Alex smiled, not in mockery, but out of respect for Jo Gale's feisty attitude.

'I prefer to think of it as leveling the playing field after the D.A.'s finished milking the sympathy of the jury for all it's worth.'

'Well if you can't "*desanctify* the victim",' asked Jo Gale, 'how do you propose to level the playing field?'

'By making Claymore seem harmless.'

'And how do you propose to do that?'

Alex looked around the table to gauge the mood. It was obvious that no one else had anything more to say. This was turning into a grudge match between himself and Jo Gale.

'That's very simple. A picture paints a thousand words.'

She rested her elbows on the oval table, and leaned forward, meeting Alex's eyes implacably.

'And how do you propose to paint a picture for the jury?'

'By putting an attractive woman next to Claymore. She doesn't have to say a word on his behalf, just sit there looking comfortable and relaxed. That's all it takes.'

Jo recoiled. It was an actual, *physical* retreat.

'You can forget it, Mr Sedaka,' said Jo. ''Cause it *ain't gonna happen.*'

Alex had to fight hard to resist the urge to smile.

Sherman, who until now had been leaning back in a desperate effort to make himself invisible, now sat forward, sensing an opportunity to earn some brownie points with the senior partners.

'There's Andi Phoenix.'

All the other heads in the room looked round at him. But it was Jo who spoke – and her tone was audibly defensive.

'Who's Andi Phoenix?'

'She's from our New York office. We needed someone to fill our victim litigation slot and she took the bait. She knew she wasn't going anywhere in the Big Apple so she came out here.'

'Will she do it?' asked Webster.

'She's hot and she's ambitious. I know she'd just *love* a piece of the action. If you want a cute piece of ass to sit next to Claymore looking comfortable and keeping *shtum*, you won't have any trouble convincing Andi Phoenix to take the seat.'

Friday, 12 June 2009 – 16.30

'I *won't* do it!' said Andi, flatly.

They were in one of the smaller conference rooms: Andi, Paul Sherman and Alex Sedaka.

'Why not?' asked Alex. 'It'll be great experience for you – and a challenge.'

'Don't patronize me, Mr Sedaka. I'm past the stage when I need that sort of a challenge. And I've had plenty of experience back east—'

'Oh, my mistake, I thought you came out here because you hit the glass ceiling in the Big Apple.'

Andi felt like punching him in the face for his sarcasm. She felt like punching Sherman too for exposing her to it. But she contained her anger.

'That doesn't mean I have to scramble for the dregs.'

'No one's asking you to scramble. I'm coming to *you*, remember. All I'm asking of you is your help for our client.'

'He's *your* client not *mine*.'

'He's Levine and Webster's client,' Sherman stepped in. 'That makes him *your* client too.'

'That doesn't mean I have to prostitute myself defending him.'

'We're not asking you to prostitute yourself,' said Alex.

71

'We're just asking you to stand up for the principle that a man is innocent until proven guilty.'

'Oh, come off it, Mr Sedaka. What do you need me for? I'm a *civil* litigator.'

'You've had criminal experience,' Sherman cut in. 'Working both sides of the fence.'

'There are plenty of criminal lawyers here with a lot more experience. Why do you need me?'

'Okay, I'll be honest with you,' said Alex. 'I don't want you to play an active role. I just want you to sit next to him, make him look harmless. Look, you know the kind of pre-trial publicity this case is going to arouse – the sort of publicity it's *already* aroused. They'll drag in every incident from Claymore's past. They've already compared him to O.J. Simpson. They're going to savage his reputation before the case ever gets to trial. That's what we're up against.'

'And how do you think me sitting there next to him is going to refute the negative pre-trial publicity?'

Alex met her eyes, trying to read her.

'When the jury sees a beautiful young woman sitting next to him, it'll dissolve their prejudice. It'll make him look like a normal, everyday human being. It'll show them that he's safe, harmless, inoffensive . . . not the monster that the prosecution is to going to try and make him out to be.'

'And you say you're not asking me to prostitute myself?'

She was looking at him hard; she wasn't going to make it easy for him.

'Look,' he said after a long pause and a deep breath. 'Claymore has an image problem with Middle America. Everyone knows about his past, how he raped white women and said it was political. How he broke out of prison and fled to Libya. But he has the right to be judged by the evidence

72

in *this* case – not his past when he was an angry and embittered young man.'

'I don't deny that Claymore's got a problem,' she conceded, shifting uncomfortably. 'But asking me to sit next to him and make him *look* harmless is like . . . like trying to use my body to sell a product.'

'What *product*? We're talking about a man's reputation.'

'Then *sell it* like a reputation, with *reasoned argument* – not with a head of bottle-blonde hair and a pair of silicone-enhanced tits.'

Alex was about to argue, but he fell silent as his face melted into a smile. He realized that there was an element of satire in Andi's description of herself.

'Okay, you've nailed me. We've got to use Madison Avenue techniques. But you know what? We're doing it in a worthy cause.'

'What you're proposing goes way beyond Madison Avenue . . . more like Sunset Boulevard or Old Moulin Rouge.'

'All right, Ms Phoenix,' said Sherman. 'Let me lay it on the line for you. You're an employee of Levine and Webster and I'm pulling rank.'

'Pulling rank?'

'Yes,' he said stiffly.

Alex said nothing. They were playing the old good cop, bad cop routine, and now it was Sherman's turn.

'You seem to think you've got something to back it up with.'

'How about your future at this law firm?'

'My future?' she echoed, more amazed than afraid, more puzzled than angry. 'I have a contract.'

'That cuts both ways. You're refusing to work for one of our biggest clients.'

'Elias Claymore?' she asked incredulously.

'His insurance company.'

'Well if it comes down to it, I have a valid reason for not representing Claymore.'

'What reason?' asked Sherman.

'My . . . partner . . . she works at the *Say No to Violence* rape crisis center. She might even be assigned to this case.'

'She could agree to hand over to another member of staff.'

'She may have had some contact with the victim already.'

'We can cite the defendant's right to his counsel of choice. And you can agree not to talk to your partner about the case.'

'It'll . . . put us under . . . strain.'

Alex noticed that she had mellowed in her objections: the tone of her refusal was no longer outright. But he also knew that if he waited any longer, they'd lose her completely.

'Okay,' Alex cut in. 'Try this.'

He turned and grabbed a couple of newspapers from a nearby wooden trolley and threw them on the table.

'What are you doing?' asked Andi, her tone betraying her confusion.

'Wait!' he said, thumbing through the papers. 'Just listen. "Elias Claymore is the kind of man who expects people to believe he's right whatever side he takes and whatever he says or does. When he was raping white women and calling it a revolutionary, political act, he expected us to think of him as a freedom fighter, not a criminal. When he fled to Libya and started preaching Islam, he expected to be thought of as a religious scholar. Then he 'saw the light' and found Jesus – as well as capitalism – and expected us to welcome him with open arms. And like fools, we did. Now he's accused of rape once again and, having come full circle, he asks us to believe that he's an innocent man who is being victimized because of his outspoken political comments in the recent past."'

74

'So what? Of course he's going to get some hostile press.'

Alex wasn't finished yet. 'Okay, that's the mainstream press. And it's typical of the rest. Trust me, I've read through them all.'

He pointed to a stack of newspapers on the cherrywood trolley beside the table. 'Now let's see what black radical journals are saying.'

He grabbed another paper. This one was already open on the right page.

'"The chickens are coming home to roost for a Judas who betrayed his people for thirty pieces of silver. Elias Claymore, who once stood for the rights of his oppressed brothers, now stands exposed as a hypocrite who places self-indulgence above any cause. This perennial campaigner, who keeps reinventing himself whenever it suits him, has now run out of ideas and has finally reverted to type as a narcissist and egomaniac. Having turned against his own kind and sold his soul to the devil, he has now compounded his crime by bringing his brothers into disrepute.

'"When Claymore was a respectable figure of the middle-class establishment, he was held up by conservatives as an exception to the rule, the black man who worked within the system and succeeded. The rest of us only had ourselves to blame for our miserable plight because we were lazy and refused to abide by the rules and make use of the system. But now that he has been exposed for what he really is, he will be held up as a *typical* example of the black everyman and the old stereotype of the black male as sex-driven monster will be resurrected yet again."'

'Okay. *That's* what we're up against!'

'And you think . . .' She stopped. There was no easy way to brush off an appeal to the fighting spirit within her. Bullying hadn't worked, but this was quiet persuasion.

'Well, what do you say?'

'I say . . .' She hesitated again, wondering if Alex could see the civil war raging within her.

Alex and Sherman looked at Andi, inviting her final answer. Ignoring Sherman, she stared back at Alex for a few seconds, breathing heavily. Then, not trusting her voice, she nodded her head in reluctant truce rather than surrender. He smiled gently as if accepting it with good grace.

'Okay,' said Sherman. 'I'll go now and leave you to start working.'

And with that, Sherman packed his papers into his attaché case and left.

Friday, 12 June 2009 – 18.10

'The case took a dramatic turn today when it was revealed that Andromeda Phoenix – a civil litigator with Los Angeles law firm Levine and Webster, is to serve as co-counsel with Alex Sedaka.'

Martine Yin's voice was coming from the television window in the web browser on a computer.

'Ms Phoenix is in a relationship with Eugenia Vance, a counselor at the *Say No to Violence* rape crisis center. In order to protect Elias Claymore's right to the counsel of his choice, the judge issued an injunction against Ms Vance having any contact with the alleged victim.'

Standing outside the courthouse, Martine was wearing her snooker vest, speaking to the camera in a dry, clipped tone. She wasn't sure if it was a good idea to depart from her trademark blue jacket, but she had worn the snooker vest a couple of times before and had got a positive response in her mailbag. And she had a particular reason for wanting to emphasize her figure today; the network had been talking about putting her behind a desk in the studio and were evidently getting some funny ideas about parachuting in some ambitious spring chicken to fill her slot.

'Ms Phoenix's participation was opposed by the prosecution. But after a long sidebar, the prosecution's motion was denied. The D.A.'s office declined to say afterwards whether they would file an interim appeal.'

A woman's hand reached out and paused the news report. Then she returned her attention to the computer in front of her. With a click of a button she launched an e-mail package and started preparing a message to aphoenix@levineandwebster.com.

This would put the fear of God into the bitch.

Friday, 12 June 2009 – 19.45

'So how did you manage to overcome her objections?' asked Martine over her hors d'oeuvre of torchon of duck foie gras with poached Adriatic fig in Muscat wine.

Ten minutes earlier, Martine and Alex had entered the Little Door, one of Martine's favorite haunts. As they'd stepped through the wooden doors to the patio, it had been like passing through a gateway into another dimension. In an instant, they had left the city behind them and entered a rustic world of bougainvilleas, ferns, a tiled fountain and a Koi pond. A succession of light waves from the wrought-iron candelabra rippled across the lace tablecloth. They could even see the moon through the open skylight.

'I don't want this to end up on the evening news,' said Alex.

'Strictly off the record,' Martine assured him.

'We used a bit of gentle persuasion.'

He didn't really feel comfortable telling her about the incident. It would probably make him sound like a bully. But the practice of law was a dirty business. They both knew that.

'We?' Martine raised her eyebrows with a delicate smile.

'Paul Sherman and I.'

'You mean you blackmailed her?'

'I prefer to call it bribery,' he said with a guilty smile, after a short pause.

He attacked his own hors d'oeuvre of farmer's market butter lettuce and steamed spring vegetables, a light starter to allow room for his main course of filet mignon and roasted fingerling potatoes.

'So what was the carrot?' she smiled, alluding to the piece of carrot poised at the end of his fork with a smile.

'I sold it as a fight for a man's right to a second chance.'

His facial expression was nervous, as if he was expecting a torrent of skeptical laughter or a cutting response. But Martine's smile was both piercing and bewitching.

'And what did Sherman use as the stick?'

'What do you mean?'

'Come off it, Alex. You were playing good cop, bad cop.'

He held up his hands in a gesture of helplessness, caught in the glare of Martine's headlamps.

'Okay,' he acknowledged reluctantly. 'You've got me. We did a little arm twisting.'

'That doesn't surprise me. It must be pretty hard for her, with her lover working at a rape crisis center.'

'That's a personal matter. They'll just have to work it out for themselves.'

'You make it sound so easy. Imagine what it must be like for Eugenia Vance: one minute she's doing her job, next minute she gets handed an injunction telling her she's not allowed to have any contact with the victim.'

'I'm sorry. I may have sounded a bit callous. But the judge didn't exactly have a choice. He had to do it to avoid a conflict of interest.'

Martine's face turned suddenly serious. 'Actually, that's what I wanted to talk to *you* about.'

Alex had an uneasy feeling when he heard the words . . . and the tone. 'What do you mean?'

'I *also* have a conflict of interest. I can't cover the case and carry on going out with you.'

Friday, 12 June 2009 – 21.15

It was quite late when Andi arrived home. She had spent the day going over the case file with Alex and then stayed on for a few hours after he left. It had been exhausting. They were racking their brains trying to figure out how they could refute the DNA evidence. All the other evidence could be challenged and the seeds of reasonable doubt sown.

But the DNA was a problem, a *real* problem. It couldn't just be swept under the rug. In the past, they might have been able to attack the science itself or throw up smoke screens to confuse the jury. But post-O.J. Simpson that was no longer an option. Defense ploys are like magicians' tricks – they can never be repeated in the same form. The most Alex and Andi could do was point out that the particular form of the DNA technology used in this case was less discriminating than other methods.

But all of this was still way down the line. First they had to resolve the issue of trial venue. That was the big question that was going to come up at the pre-trial in two weeks' time. And that was what Andi had to focus on now.

Gene was lying on the bed in her underwear in the dimly lit room, watching the wall-mounted TV when Andi entered. Andi took off her street clothes in the walk-in closet by the door and then shuffled back into the bedroom barefoot and in her underwear, expecting Gene's usual warm welcome. But Gene didn't even turn to look at her. Andi was hurt and confused; Gene was never cold like this, even if she was in a bad mood.

'Where have you been?' asked Gene, her eyes glued to the TV.

Andi sensed that Gene had had a bad day as she climbed onto the bed behind her lover, gently massaging Gene's raised shoulder.

'At the office. I had a lot of paperwork to clear up. I've just started on a major case.'

'I know. Some flunky from the court came round to the center to serve an injunction on me.'

Andi stopped massaging, but left her hands in place. She *knew* now what this was about. 'Are you angry?'

Gene turned round, brushing off Andi's hands in the process. There were tears of anger in Gene's eyes. This surprised Andi. It was very rare for Gene to cry.

'What do you think? I quit my job in New York and crossed the continent with you 'cause you couldn't make it over there and now you stab me in the back by getting me thrown off the case, so I can't even help the victim. And why? To defend a rapist!'

Andi understood Gene's anger, and she could hardly blame her for it. In a way she knew that Gene was right. The anger that Gene was feeling towards Andi was every bit as intense as the anger that Andi had felt towards Alex. But the fact was, she had signed on for the defense and all she could do was fall back on that last standby of litigants and lovers: anger of her own.

'It's my job,' she snapped, rolling off the bed. 'And it's *alleged* rapist!'

With these words, Andi stormed out of the room.

Tears now streaming down her own cheeks, Andi went downstairs to the living room. She crossed over to the alcove that housed a desk and bookshelves, which they had set aside as a study and office. On the desk was a laptop PC, a docking station and a large monitor. Andi switched on the computer to download her mail. There were five messages. Four were from old friends wishing her luck in her new job. But it was the fifth message that startled her. It read:

That rapist scumbag Elias Claymore is unworthy of your assistance and deserves everything he gets. Make sure that you are not around when justice is finally delivered or you will only have yourself to blame.

Lannosea

An alarm bell went off inside her head. Who had sent the message? And where from? She scrolled up to the 'From' field, and saw that it had come from a webmail address. It could have been sent from a public library or an Internet café. There would be no way to trace it to a person.

A range of emotions swept over her like a quick succession of waves: confusion followed by fear followed by anger. But if the first was a ripple and the second a surfer's tube ride, the third was a tsunami.

Who the fuck was Lannosea?

Monday, 15 June 2009 – 10.25

'What's *she* doing here?'

Elias Claymore's reaction appeared to border on paranoia when Alex first brought Andi into the room at the Ventura pre-trial detention facility that had been allocated for their conference.

'Allow me to introduce my co-counsel on this case,' said Alex. 'Andi Phoenix.'

Claymore's eyes darted away to Alex for a moment before returning to Andi, the suspicion lingering in his eyes.

'You didn't say anything about co-counsel. Nothing personal, Ms Phoenix.'

'Oh, please, call me Andi,' she said, in a reassuring tone calculated to put him at ease.

She held out her hand warmly. Claymore hesitated before reaching out to shake it. Then he sat down, not taking his eyes off Andi. Andi followed suit, leaving Alex last to take his seat round the table.

'The first thing we need to talk about,' Alex began, 'is a change of venue.'

'Why?'

'Perhaps I can explain,' said Andi.

She looked at Alex. He nodded.

'According to the latest stats, Ventura County has just

under 700,000 Caucasians and 17,000 African-Americans. That makes the State 2.1 per cent black and 87.5 per cent white.'

'That's not necessarily a bad thing. I'm probably more unpopular with my own people at the moment.'

'I doubt that,' said Andi. 'We're talking about *ultra-conservative* whites.'

Claymore tried to sound jovial. 'Well, hey . . . I'm a conservative!'

'I know, Mr Claymore, and that might have worked if it was a minor charge. But this is rape and a lot of your natural supporters have already turned against you.'

'You've done an opinion poll?' He grinned, desperately, trying to make light of the situation.

Andi maintained her neutral face. 'We're keeping an ear to the ground and those are the vibes we're getting.'

Claymore looked over at Alex, who nodded imperceptibly, content to let Andi earn her keep.

'In any case,' Andi continued, 'we know from the stats that Ventura juries tend to be convicting juries.'

'What about Hispanics?' asked Claymore.

'Hispanics can be either race and they're included in the black and white stats. But we have a separate figure of 287,000 Hispanic and Latino citizens. Of those, 272,000 are classified as white Hispanic. There are also some 50,000 Asian citizens who are likely to be hostile to *working class* blacks, but might admire *you* and a further 17,000 of mixed race who may be a bit more friendly. But those two groups combined are less than 10 per cent of the population.'

Claymore looked crestfallen. 'And what do we need? If we had the ideal choice.'

Andi was about to speak when Alex finally entered the discussion.

'Ideally, we'd have a jury of liberal whites.' He was going to elaborate on his reasons, but held back, realizing that it would sound just a little too cynical.

'Or Hispanics,' Andi added. 'Even white Hispanics won't be tainted by the prejudice of the more conservative non-Hispanic whites. Even if we can't use collective guilt on them in quite the same way.'

'So what *can* we do?'

Alex and Andi exchanged glances. In the end it was Andi who spoke.

'In the real world, the outcome of one controversial case can often have a knock-on effect on the next. In the O.J. Simpson case, the acquittal of the cops who viciously beat Rodney King was still fresh in the minds of the jurors. The truth of the matter is that a case that may be cast iron and watertight in the courtroom can fall apart in the jury room.'

'So are there any recent cases we can take advantage of?' asked Claymore. The cynical words fell uneasily from his lips.

'Unfortunately not. In this case, the key to winning is getting the right jury,' said Andi. 'And that means holding the trial in the right district and then using challenges to prune and cherry pick the jury. Sometimes that might be as simple as getting a jury of the right ethnic group. In the O.J. Simpson case, the defense was able to get a predominantly African-American jury. In the Rodney King case it was an all white one in Simi Valley where a lot of cops lived.'

'And can we do that?'

Again Andi looked at Alex. Again he nodded to let her know that he was content to let her speak.

'In this case it's a little more complicated. Even if we can get an all black jury, it's by no means certain that such a jury would favor you. Like you said, a lot of blacks have been alienated by your outspoken views.'

'Could I ask a personal question, Ms Phoenix? Did you volunteer for this job?'

Alex felt a stab of fear, wondering if Andi's answer was going to be tactful or brutally honest. But he knew that he couldn't interfere now.

'That's *not* a personal question,' she replied with a reassuring smile. Claymore was watching her closely. 'I . . .'

She looked at Alex. But his face offered her no hint of assistance. 'I was asked by Mr Sedaka to help, and I agreed. Alex was . . . most convincing.'

Alex coughed nervously.

'Okay, I think we'd better get a move on. We're working on some research for the change of venue motion, but in the meantime we need to review the evidence.'

He handed copies of the evidence report to Andi and Claymore.

'The case against you appears to be made up of the following. One: a statement of the alleged victim including the second of two photo line-ups. Two: a medical report about the victim's physical condition right after she reported the incident. Three: police photographic evidence of same. Four, a DNA comparison between crime scene DNA and reference samples taken from you and the alleged victim. Five: eyewitness evidence after the alleged rape that you were seen running from the crime scene. Six: your arrest record – six counts of rape.'

'I don't know where they got this stuff,' said Claymore shaking his head. 'I mean the record I admit. But the rest is just a load of garbage.'

'Some of it is easy enough to demolish,' said Alex. 'The witness who saw you running away is weak, I need to get a PI to look into the girl's background for anything we can use to impeach her. The real problem is the DNA and the

90

medical and photographic evidence. The DNA points to you and makes it hard for us to deny that a sexual encounter took place between you and Miss Newton.'

'I don't understand how they could've got DNA evidence.'

'How do you mean?' asked Andi.

'I never touched her. I've never even *met* her.'

'All right,' said Alex. 'We'll go into that in a moment. But first let me make one thing clear: we can't argue that it's both a case of mistaken identity *and* that she consented. We have to nail our colors to the mast early. In effect you've already committed us to saying that it's mistaken identity because of what you told the police. Technically we can still change your story, but it won't look good.'

'But why *should* I change it? I never even met the bit—'

For a few seconds they all avoided each other's eyes as they realized what Claymore had been about to say.

Monday, 15 June 2009 – 13.00

'There goes Uncle Tom.'

There was mocking laughter and jeering as Elias Claymore shuffled his way to the end of the table.

'Watch where you're sitting!' snarled the man next to him, as Claymore barely brushed against him when he sat.

Claymore tried to ignore the taunts. But when he raised the food to his mouth, he felt a sharp elbow in the rib cage, making him drop it. He knew that this was the first and final test. If he showed weakness now, they would make his life a living hell. He had to stand up to the bullies before they saw him as easy prey.

'Look, cut it out!' he shouted, leaping to his feet and turning to face his attacker.

The man rose to face Claymore. They were evenly matched for size, but the man was a lot younger and probably a lot fitter.

'You talkin' to me, Tom?' The words were backed up by an open-handed shove.

'Yeah, you!' Claymore shot back, shoving the man equally hard.

The man took a swing at Claymore. Claymore ducked and dove in under his guard, clamping on a side headlock and hooking his right leg around the younger man's left leg in a grapevine. The other man took a swing at Claymore with his left fist, which Claymore deflected with his open right. But he couldn't avoid the younger man's rabbit punch to the back of his head, a second before he swung the man round and grappled him to the ground.

The whole place erupted into pure chaos as a nervous guard hit the panic button.

Monday, 15 June 2009 – 16.35

'So when are you going back to LA?'

Alex was sitting with his secretary Juanita in the reception of their San Francisco office on the 15th floor of the Embarcadero Center. He had flown back that afternoon, after the consultation with Claymore, and was now briefing his paralegal on the background to the case.

'We've got the prelim in twelve days and I'm planning on pushing hard for a change of venue.'

'What are the chances?'

'Well the D.A. will fight us all the way. It's Sarah Jensen. I don't know if you've heard of her?'

'I've heard of her,' said Juanita. 'Ventura County domestic violence section. The rumor mill says she's got her sights set on her boss's job.'

'And her boss has his sights set on Sacramento.'

'I know.' She nodded.

'Anyway,' continued Alex, 'we already had a fight on our hands about Andromeda Phoenix taking second seat and we won that. But that's because she didn't really have a leg to stand on. That means she'll be even *more* determined on this one. And she's got time to do her homework so it's going to turn ugly.'

'Maybe you should step aside and let it turn into a catfight. Assuming she's good enough.'

'Oh, Andi's good. But I don't know if she's fully—'

The phone rang. Juanita picked it up.

'Alex Sedaka's office . . . oh hallo, Ms Phoenix . . . I'll put you through right away.'

She put the call on hold.

'I could have taken it here,' said Alex.

'I need this line free for other calls,' said Juanita in her sharpest tone. 'This is an office.'

'Okay boss,' he said, with a smile, as he rose from his chair.

Juanita put the call through to his office before he got there, making sure that his phone was ringing by the time he went through the door.

'Hi, Andi,' he said into the handset.

'Hi, Mr Seda—Alex. Listen, I've been working here with the demographic department at my firm and we've been trying to figure out which are the best counties to try the case. We've come up with a list of counties based on demographic analysis and some public prejudice questionnaires.'

'And which counties are they?'

'Well the best is Alameda. I emailed a file over to you. Take a look at the demography. It has about 300,000 Hispanics to 200,000 African-Americans and half a million white non-Hispanics. It's also got 350,000 Asians, who may or may not be friendly to Claymore. We'll have to run some surveys to check that out.'

'Okay. But the 200,000 African-Americans won't necessarily be too friendly to Claymore.'

'No, but I was thinking about this white liberal issue.'

'What about it?'

'Well, you can cherry pick the liberals at the voir dire.'

'Yes, but whatever cherry picking we try and do, the

prosecution will do the opposite. And they've got ten peremptories too.'

'I know that. But it's a question of how many liberals there are on the panel.'

'Yes, but like you said, Andi, there's no such thing as a white liberal county.'

'By and large there isn't. But I was thinking: Berkeley's in Alameda and at Berkeley you've got the liberal academic contingent. And they tend to live around that area. So with that and the Hispanics and the Asians as well as the blacks, you might just be able to cherry pick a sympathetic jury.'

'You could be onto something,' Alex conceded. 'The trouble is, the prosecution will fight us every inch of the way.'

'Only if you let them know what you want. If you make it look like you're afraid of a black jury and wary of Asians, they might just go for it themselves. The trick is to let the judge suggest it as a compromise.'

'Andi, if you were here right now, I think I'd kiss you.'

Friday, 26 June 2009 – 11.20

'In addition to the unfavorable comments on the talk radio stations, an opinion poll has shown that ninety-six percent of the women and seventy-eight percent of the men in the county believe my client to be guilty.'

The judge in Court 12 at the Ventura County Superior Court appeared to be listening attentively to Alex.

'Clearly,' Alex continued, 'it would be impossible for my client to receive a fair trial in Ventura County under these circumstances. On the other hand there have been no such signs of prejudice in Sacramento.'

Andi was watching Alex as he spoke. Sacramento was eleven per cent black and eighteen per cent Hispanic.

'Any addition to your earlier response, Ms Jensen?' asked the judge, looking over at the prosecutor. Sarah Jensen rose, sweeping a strand of her black hair out of her eyes. She paused for a moment, as if trying to assess the judge's current state of mind. This was a tricky matter, and one so sensitive that the entire outcome of the trial could hinge upon it. What happened here today could render everything that followed largely irrelevant. So the A.D.A. had to pitch it *just* right.

'My only argument is what I said in response to the defense counsel's earlier argument, namely that the voir dire should be sufficient to weed out any prejudiced jurors, as long as the panel is large enough. However, I would also point out that defense counsel appears to be trying to relocate the trial to a venue with more favorable demographics.'

'Are you suggesting that the demographics of Sacramento are likely to be pro defense?' the judge prompted.

'Not necessarily. But it does have a higher percentage of bla— of Mr Claymore's own ethnic group.'

Alex knew that the A.D.A. had to choose her words carefully. She wanted to accuse the defense of trying to get more blacks onto the jury, but by opposing it, she was effectively saying that prosecution wanted the opposite.

'But there's nothing constitutionally improper about the demography of Sacramento is there?'

The judge was smiling as he said this. Sarah Jensen's embarrassment was palpable.

'I . . . we . . . that is, the prosecution accepts that there is a case for a change of venue. And obviously it should be away from the south and possibly in the Bay area. But Sacramento would not be the best choice.'

Alex saw his opportunity and pounced. 'If the A.D.A. is concerned about the demographics of Sacramento, the defense is quite amenable to a county where the demography is more to their liking, like Santa Clara.'

Sarah Jensen blushed. They both had the stats in front of them and Sarah knew that while Santa Clara County – Silicon Valley – was 2.7 per cent black and 62 per cent white, many of those white people were working in the computer industry, where there was a high proportion of liberals and libertarians, unlike the traditional conservatives of Simi Valley in Ventura. But Sarah Jensen could hardly use this in her argument.

'We would prefer San Mateo or Marin County – or even Napa.'

'What do you say, Mr Sedaka?' asked the judge.

Alex knew that he had succeeded in the first part of his objective: getting the A.D.A. and the judge to accept relocation to the Bay area. Now he had to get the judge to choose the county he wanted. That meant making it look as if he wanted somewhere else.

'Your Honor, we believe that many of the people who are most prejudiced against my client are actually those who the prosecution seems to think are biased in his favor.'

'Does that mean you agree to Ms Jensen's suggestions?'

'Well we'd prefer San Joaquin or Solano. Maybe Contra Costa.'

'What about Alameda?' asked the judge. Sarah Jensen looked as if she was about to say something, when Alex spoke up quickly.

'Sidebar, Your Honor?'

The judge nodded. Alex and Sarah approached the bench.

'Your Honor,' Alex said putting on his most embarrassed tone of voice. 'Alameda County is 20 per cent Asian. It's a well-known fact that a lot of Asians are prejudiced against blacks and this would deny my client a fair trial.'

'Oh, do me a favor!' said Sarah. 'There may be some limited residual prejudice against working class blacks. But Claymore is hardly working class. Besides, Mr Sedaka can use the voir dire to weed out any biased jurors.'

The judge turned back to Alex. 'That makes sense doesn't it?'

Alex fought hard to maintain a neutral face and shrugged his shoulders. 'That depends on how reasonable the judge is when it comes to accepting challenges for cause.'

'Well I have to assume that another judge will be reasonable,' said the judge. 'And if you think he abused his discretion you can always appeal.'

101

Alex used the full range of his acting skills to look like a man who was trapped.

'There's also the problem of transportation. My office is in San Francisco and that means I'll have to cross the Bay Bridge during commuter times.'

'Yet you were ready for San Joaquin or Contra Costa,' said the judge, sarcastically.

'Those were second choices,' said Alex feebly. 'I still think a Sacramento or Santa Clara jury would be more likely to approach this case with open minds.'

'Well you can file an exception for the record. In the meantime it's decided. The trial will be transferred to Alameda County.'

As they returned to their places, Alex continued his struggle to suppress a smile that was just itching to appear on his face.

Friday, 26 June 2009 – 12.05

'So what's this weakness you've found in their case?' asked Claymore.

They were in a meeting room at the Ventura County pretrial detention facility, where Elias Claymore was being held. Alex was taking the lead this time, while Andi sat in almost total silence.

'She changed her story . . . about the attacker's age.'

'How do you mean?'

'Well, initially she told the police that her attacker was in his *twenties*. They did a photo line-up – they even had a suspect tucked in there with the pictures – but she didn't choose him.'

'I don't understand. When they said she picked me from a photograph, I thought that meant she picked me from a book of mug shots.'

'No, they don't do that anymore. They discovered a long time ago that after looking at hundreds of pictures, the witness's vision becomes so blurred, they can't tell a stranger from their own mother. It actually led to erroneous arrests in the past and also let guilty people slip through the net. They sometimes use an artist's impression or e-fit picture when they're planning on asking the public to help find an unknown suspect.

'But in this case they used mug shots as a cheap alternative to a line-up as they already had a suspect. It's called a "photo line-up." Instead of hauling a suspect in and risking a civil rights suit, they use photographs of suspects mixed in with pictures of law-abiding citizens that match the description. In fact they can even use out of date pictures. As long as the picture of the suspect is up-to-date and as long as the faces in all the pictures matched the description of the suspect given by the witness, then the identification is valid.'

'But can they do that without my knowledge? Without an attorney present?'

'Sure can. US versus Ash, 1973. But we can challenge it before the jury.'

'But if she told them I was in my twenties, then what picture of me did they put in there? As I am now or when I was in my twenties?'

'When you were in your twenties.'

Claymore looked confused.

'Doesn't that invalidate the whole thing?'

'No, you don't understand, Elias. She didn't pick *anyone*.'

'So what was all that bullshit about her picking me from a photograph?'

'That was later. After lunch she went back and told them that she'd had second thoughts and that the man who attacked her was *older* than his twenties.'

'But I'm fifty-eight. How'd she get from twenties to fifty-eight?'

'Good question. I think they were probably skeptical too, although their reports don't make it obvious what they were thinking. You have to read between the lines.'

'But what did she say? I mean did she just come out with something like, "He was twice as old as I said at first"?'

Alex handed Claymore a copy of the statements. Claymore picked it up and started reading through it as Alex spoke.

'She said she *now* thought that he was in his *fifties*. But she explained that the reason for the change of heart was because she had actually seen him again.'

'What do you mean seen him again?'

'I mean saw *you*. Not in the flesh, but on the TV. She said she was passing an electronics store and she saw you on a TV screen in the display window. It was your show. And that was when she realized – so she said – that it was you.'

'But didn't they notice the age difference? Didn't they ask her to explain the discrepancy?'

'They did, but she just said she was mistaken. She claimed that she was under stress. Which is reasonable.'

'But how can stress make her mistake fifties for twenties?'

'That's the question they don't seem to have asked. Or if they did, they didn't receive any answer, as far as I can determine. And that's the question that we're going to ask if this case goes to trial.'

Wednesday 15 July 2009 – 12.40

'The defendant, Elias Claymore is charged with Rape under section 261, Part a, Paragraph 2 of the California Penal Code. How do you plead, Elias Claymore: guilty or not guilty?'

'Not guilty.'

Claymore sat down, looking around the courtroom nervously. They were in Court 11 of the Rene C. Davidson Courthouse on Fallon Street in Oakland, before Justice Roberts.

Alex remained standing. 'Your Honor, at this stage I would like to renew my request for bail in accordance with my written submissions.'

Sarah Jensen, who had hung on to the case for the time being, rose to reply. But the judge stayed her with a raised hand.

'I've considered your submissions carefully, Mr Sedaka, but I see no reason to reopen the original decision to deny bail. This is truly an exceptional case, but I am bound to consider the defendant's past as an escapee and for this reason I cannot grant bail.'

Alex gritted his teeth. It was particularly hard on Claymore, because he was still being held at the pre-trial detention facility in Ventura. To get to this ten-minute hearing, he had been driven for 6 hours across 375 miles.

'In that case, Your Honor, I move that the defendant be transferred to the Santa Ritter jail in Alameda County.'

'So ordered. Now, regarding the trial date. I see that the Information was filed in Ventura County on June twenty-sixth. That means the trial must commence by August twenty-fifth. I also see that there's a vacant slot on Justice Ellen Wagner's docket in Court Seven between August seventeenth and September fourth. Does that allow enough time for the trial?'

'Yes, Your Honor,' said Alex, nodding.

'Yes, Your Honor,' Sarah Jensen confirmed.

'So I'll assign the case to that slot. Voir dire to commence on August seventeenth.'

Wednesday 15 July 2009 – 15.15

Elias Claymore looked around uneasily as he was escorted to his assigned block. He had survived at the Ventura pre-trial facility, but this was somewhere new. He wondered if it was going to be the same here.

As he shuffled along, he was torn between whether to keep his head low and avoid antagonizing anyone, or to hold his head up to show that he wasn't a natural victim.

He opted for the latter and was surprised to hear some of his fellow inmates actually cheering him. That was an encouraging sign. But it didn't alter the fact that prison was prison. He was familiar with it, but that didn't make it any more pleasant. He had never become institutionalized and lately he had become used to living in the lap of luxury.

But the last month had reacquainted him with prison and all its horrors. And in many ways, this time it was worse. Last time around he had been a hero – at least in the eyes of his brothers. He was the freedom fighter who had stood up to the enemy. But this time he could feel the hostility all around him, and he could count on no one.

So when he walked now, it was with caution.

He was not looking forward to the trial. Alex was a good lawyer, but the evidence was strong. And he feared that Alex didn't believe him when he said he was innocent. It was hard to take his mind off the case but if he didn't think about the future then all he had left to dwell on was the past. And that was even more painful. For it was not just his childhood that he had to contend with, but also his young adulthood – when he had turned from victim into victimizer.

He remembered the time he had followed a white woman home at the start of his campaign of vengeance and then forced his way into her house, smashing open the French windows from the garden to get at her. As he approached her and clamped his hand over her mouth, she had screamed. He threw her onto the sofa and ripped her clothes off her. Then, as she begged and pleaded, he raped her.

But he didn't hear her cries. He heard only those of his mother – those of his memory. But even those cries were drowned out by something else. In his mind he heard the smug voices of the callers to the talk radio station who had phoned in when they were discussing the rape of his mother. They came on the air one after another to say that the 'black woman' was 'lying' and that she was 'probably just a hooker who didn't get paid.' He was seeing the skeptical looks on the faces of the people on the TV show as some long-winded liberal lawyer tried, but failed, to defend his mother's reputation. And he remembered that the slanderous comments about his mother came from white *women* as well as men, speaking in their smug, sanctimonious middle-class accents about how they 'felt sorry' for this woman, but she 'only had herself to blame.'

His mother had been raped before his very eyes, but whenever people discussed the case, those who claimed to speak for his mother were on the defensive, while the viciousness of the fascist pigs was never even talked about. His mother had complained to the police. But after his uncle had been beaten up and arrested on trumped-up drugs charges she withdrew the complaint.

That was white man's justice – and white woman's.

So when he raped white women as a revolutionary act, the pangs of guilt were numbed by the anger.

His thoughts were cut short by a large shadow in front of him and a sharp pain in his abdomen. He looked up to see a man appear in front of him, and then disappear within seconds. Then he felt something wet against his flesh and he looked down to see black blood accumulating on his torso. He had been stabbed in the liver. And he knew this meant that he had maybe twenty minutes to live.

Wednesday, 15 July 2009 – 16.30

While Andi sat in the lounge at San Francisco International airport waiting for her flight, she checked her e-mail on her BlackBerry. Most of the messages were routine and work-related, but one of them gave her pause even before she read it; it leapt out at her because of the sender's name: *Lannosea.*

> You are playing with fire by helping that rapist
> nigger and that blackmailing sleaze-ball lawyer of
> his. If you had any guts – which you obviously don't
> – you'd have told that slimy Sherman and that
> hypocrite Sedaka to fuck off when they badgered
> you into helping him. Instead you just lay down and
> spread your legs. I guess that makes you a rape
> victim too – or maybe just a whore!
>
> Lannosea

A mixture of fear and revulsion broke out inside Andi as she stared at the message. Who was sending these messages?

She logged on to the Internet and quickly looked up Lannosea on Wikipedia.

Nothing.

She did a general search for the name but only found

113

three listings. Two were flagged by warnings that they were dangerous websites that might contain spyware. The third was one of those question-and-answer websites and all it said was that Lannosea was one of the daughters of the ancient English queen Boudicca.

What on earth did it mean?

But there was another question nagging away at Andi. How did this Lannosea know that Sherman and Alex had badgered her into working on the Claymore case? She hadn't told anyone.

Wednesday, 15 July 2009 – 18.05

Alex was reading through the report about the case, trying to find other weaknesses. So far, Bethel's change of mind was the only one. But it looked like the most promising. The only thing that Alex was worried about was that it seemed like such an unlikely change of mind that he was wondering if the prosecution had a trick up their sleeve.

Aside from that, he knew that this case did not depend on the testimony of the victim. They also had DNA evidence. If Claymore had said that he had consensual sex with Bethel then it would have been a whole different ball game. Although the medical evidence and pictures of Bethel's injuries made it difficult, the defense would have at least had breathing room.

But Claymore had closed the door on a consent defense by claiming that there had been no sexual contact between himself and Bethel Newton – and even that he had never met her.

That left Alex and Andi with the problem of explaining why she had accused him. Of course the obvious answer was that she had been attacked by someone who looked like him. Alex had even played a long shot by asking Claymore if he had an identical twin. But Claymore responded with such a withering look that Alex knew perfectly well what the answer was.

The phone rang. Juanita told him that it was a call from the Santa Ritter jail.

'Hallo, Elias.'

'Pardon?' said an unfamiliar voice.

'Oh, I'm sorry,' said Alex, 'I thought you were someone else.'

'This is the deputy governor of the Santa Ritter jail. I'm afraid I have to tell you that your client, Elias Claymore, has been stabbed.'

'Stabbed?'

'Yes, but not fatally. He's in the jail hospital.'

'How did it happen?'

'Usual story . . . a fellow inmate with a shank.'

Alex was surprised to hear this described as usual. 'How serious is it?'

'Pretty serious. He was stabbed in the liver. They're still operating, but it looks like he's gonna make it.'

Alex breathed a sigh of relief. 'Did you catch whoever did it?'

'Not yet, but we've got CCTV so we'll look at the tapes.'

'Okay. What about security for my client?'

'We've got guards posted outside the recovery room and we'll keep him in protective solitary until the trial.'

Until the trial.

Alex sensed the full import of these words. If he was found guilty, he wouldn't be kept in solitary any longer. He might be transferred to another prison, but he'd have to join the general population. Alex realized in that moment that this wasn't just about his client's freedom. If he didn't secure an acquittal, Elias Claymore's life wouldn't be worth two bits.

Thursday, 16 July 2009 – 16.20

When he opened his eyes, he didn't know where he was. All he could see was the white walls. He tried to gather his wits. The last thing he remembered, he had been thinking about his early life and the crimes he had committed. Was that where he was now? In prison? Had it all been a dream? Had he never really been released? Or had he escaped?

He struggled to remember.

He had joined several black power groups as they struggled to liberate themselves. After serving a one-year stint in prison for firearms offences, he came out angrier than ever and over the next two and a half years he raped five white women, after practicing his technique first on three black ones.

By this time, the brothers regarded him as more of an embarrassment than an ally and it was widely rumored that it was one of his own who betrayed his hiding place to the FBI. He still remembered the day the feds came for him. It was anger, not fear, that he felt as he saw the flickering lights in the distance and knew that he had nowhere to run from the vast convoy of lawmen that it had taken to bring him down.

He considered fighting to the death and taking down as many of the pigs with him as he could. He fully expected to be killed in prison – while the guards looked the other way – and saw no reason not to make his last stand here and now. But he realized that if he could at least have his day in court, he would have the one thing that the white man's 'free press' had denied him until now: a platform from which to speak and from which his message would surely be heard.

He was arrested and charged with six counts of rape. Sentenced to nine years, he escaped after one, under the cover of a prison riot, with the aid of another group – this one basing its ideas on a racially separatist version of Islam rather than secular revolution.

But three years in Libya and Sudan had shattered the illusion. He had seen corruption and double standards in Libya. Then when rumors of a US government plot to kidnap him started floating around, he moved on to Sudan. It was there that he saw how the blacks in the south of that country were treated as second-class citizens. No amount of excuse-making and weasel words could change that.

Yes, many of those blacks were Christians and their persecution was partially religious rather than racial. But so what? If that was their belief system, were they not entitled to it? Did it make any difference if their oppressors claimed that it was religion rather than race that reduced the blacks of Sudan to the status of second-class citizens? Oppression was oppression and if he wasn't prepared to make excuses for oppression in America then why should he make excuses for it here in the Third World?

And the more he spoke to the Christian blacks in the south of Sudan, the more he learned about their culture and ideas and the more he realized that he had fallen for someone else's illusion. He had been led to believe that Christianity was the religion of the oppressors and that Islam was the natural religion of the black man. But it was here that he saw the other side of the coin. And America too was changing. Whatever its faults, America was growing and learning from its past mistakes. At least the American way had a future.

He had once said that indifference was impossible: if you're not part of the cure, you're part of the disease. But as he looked toward his homeland – his real homeland, America – he saw that many people were becoming part of the cure. He had seen the first glimpse of it back in the Sixties, in the freedom riders of all races. He saw it now in the newly enfranchised young who were asserting themselves politically as well as in more trivial ways. The same wind of change that had once swept colonialism out of Africa had blown 'Jim Crow' out of America.

Yes, there was still injustice in America. But there was also resistance to that injustice. Yes, there was still suffering. But there was also hope. Yes, there were the lingering aftereffects of past injustice. But those lingering aftereffects would be swept away too, as long as people kept trying and never gave up working together.

And it came to this: after seeking the truth in a foreign desert – a truth that almost eluded him – Elias Claymore saw the light of day and found happiness where he had started out, in his own backyard.

So at the end of three lonely years in exile, the prophet of bitter conflict finally returned home.

Monday, 17 August 2009 – 10.00

'Hear ye! Hear ye! Hear ye! The Superior Court of the State of California, Alameda County, is now in session, the Honorable Justice Wagner presiding. All persons having business before the court come forward and give your attendance and you shall be heard. God save this Honorable Court and the United States of America.'

Justice Ellen Wagner – a senior judge of the California Superior Court – took her seat in Court 7 of the Rene C. Davidson Courthouse in Oakland and the others followed suit. In her sixties, she was a striking, bespectacled African-American woman who projected dignity and gravitas from every pore. A veteran of the civil rights struggle, she had, in her youth, endured threats and even beatings as a freedom rider in the Sixties. Along with a quarter of a million others, she had stood on the National Mall when Martin Luther King made his immortal 'I have a dream' speech.

She had always claimed that her education began with the 1954 Brown decision in which the Supreme Court ruled that racial segregation in publicly funded education was unconstitutional. As a precocious eleven-year-old she had followed the case closely, encouraged by her aunt, who taught her to read. She had sat on her aunt's porch, enthralled, as her aunt explained the more difficult words of the eloquent arguments used by civil rights lawyer Thurgood Marshall.

Thirteen years later, Marshall was appointed by President Lyndon Johnson to serve as the first African-American justice in the highest court in the land. One year after that, Ellen Wagner fulfilled her own childhood dream by winning a coveted place to clerk for Marshall at the Supreme Court.

A venire panel of 150 was assembled in about twelve rows, sitting looking nervous. This was quite a large panel, even for a felony case. But the judge was mindful of the fact that this was a high-profile case involving a popular and controversial public figure and it was necessary to ensure that there was a large enough panel to allow for the many challenges for cause that were expected.

The venire panel had been shown a video explaining all about their duties as jurors and now, after a day and a half of waiting around, they had finally been brought into the courtroom. The question they had all been wondering about was whether they would be selected for the Claymore case. Not all of them wanted to be. They knew that it was going to be a long case and they had jobs to do and lives to lead.

But some of them did want to be on the jury, for various reasons. Serving on a jury in a high-profile case could be a passport to easy money. It was not unusual these days for jurors to sell their stories to the press. Some of them 'knew' that Claymore was guilty and wanted to 'nail that bastard.' Others 'knew' that he was the victim of a white man's witch-hunt and wanted to save him from the clutches of a racist legal system. Yet others just wanted to tell their friends that they were on the Claymore trial jury.

Sarah Jensen was still on the case, in the prosecutor's first seat. But now, she was assisted by Nick Sinclair, a short-bearded African-American lawyer in his mid-thirties, assigned to the case by the Alameda D.A. The choice was not accidental. The D.A. wanted to show that this was a crime against women, but also to reassure society that it was not a race issue.

At the defense table, Claymore sat uncomfortably. Alex – a quintessential trial lawyer – was very much in his element. He leaned over and whispered a quiet last-minute word to Andi.

'I don't know this judge, but she looks kind of tough so I think we should set the program to assume that she won't allow any of our challenges for cause.'

They were using a piece of software called *JuryWizard*. It allowed them to grade jurors according to how good or bad they were for their case. They could challenge jurors 'for cause' such as a conflict of interest, but it was up to the judge to decide if their reasons were valid. However they could also challenge up to ten jurors without giving a reason – *peremptory challenge* it was called.

The plan was that Alex would ask the voir dire questions and Andi would input the data.

'Something's bothering me about this panel,' said Andi, her eyes glued to the prospective jurors.

'What?'

'There are hardly any blacks on it.'

'I know,' said Alex. 'But we've agreed that that's not necessarily a disadvantage.'

'Yes, but it doesn't make sense.'

'I guess it's because they're under-represented on the voting register. A lot of blacks still don't register to vote.'

'You're living in the past, Alex. This is the Obama age. Besides, the jury's also drawn from driver's license registration.'

Alex waved his hand dismissively. 'It could just be a statistical blip. Let's not make a mountain out of a hill of beans.

There's nothing we can do about it now. We've got bigger things to think about.'

'Is the prosecution ready?' asked the judge.

'Yes, Your Honor,' said Sarah Jensen. 'I appear on behalf of the people. Mr Nicholas Sinclair of the Alameda County D.A.'s office is my co-counsel.'

Alex rose. 'Your Honor, I appear on behalf of the defense. My co-counsel is Ms Andromeda Phoenix.'

He sat down.

'The people may proceed.'

'Thank you, Your Honor.'

Suddenly, Andi rose, leaving Alex looking surprised if not downright terrified.

'Your Honor, may it please the court, before we begin voir dire, I wish to lodge an objection to the panel.'

They all looked at her in confusion, including Alex.

'The *entire* panel?' asked Justice Wagner, with measured composure.

'Yes, Your Honor.'

'Your grounds, Ms Phoenix?' asked the judge, her curiosity aroused.

'Fourteenth Amendment, Your Honor: systematic exclusion of jurors on grounds of race in clear violation of the principles of *Batson* v *Kentucky*, 476 U.S. 79, 1986.'

Justice Wagner peered down her varifocals at Andi, somewhat bemused. Alex, by contrast, was struggling not to show his irritation.

'I'm not quite sure I'm following you, Ms Phoenix. The jury hasn't been empanelled yet. The voir dire hasn't even started.'

'I'm referring to the under-representation of African-Americans on the panel of veniremen. Alameda County is nearly 14 per cent black. On that basis there should be about twenty-one or twenty-two African-Americans on this panel.

I can only see seven – sorry, eight. This under-representation is clearly contra to *Strauder* v *West Virginia*, 1880, upon which the previously cited *Batson* ruling was founded.'

'Ah yes, *Strauder*,' said Justice Wagner, with a wry smile. 'The case that held that States have the right to exclude women from juries.'

Andi looked flustered.

'I believe that at the time, the Nineteenth Amendment had not yet been passed, whereas the Fifteenth had. So the ruling merely reflected the state of play with regard to the constitutional position on voting rights for blacks and women respectively. In any event, the ruling remains in force and has been cited in other rulings.'

'Yes, Ms Phoenix, one of those rulings being *Hoyt* v *Florida* in 1961, in which the court ruled that making jury service compulsory for men and voluntary for women did not violate the Fourteenth Amendment.'

Andi gritted her teeth. 'With *respect*, Your Honor, the Fourteenth Amendment has always been interpreted as referring to racial rather than gender discrimination. The fact is—'

'The fact is, Ms Phoenix, that the *Washington* v *Davis* case of 1976 held that the legal test to be applied is *intention*-based not *effects*-based. The issue that the court must consider is therefore *not* whether the *result* of a practice is racial disproportionality in the jury per se, but rather whether there was a *deliberate intent* to wholly or partially exclude a particular ethnic group from the jury.'

An astute observer would have noticed a pained expression on Ellen Wagner's face as she said these words. But they might not have realized that the reason for this was because her own, highly respected Thurgood Marshall had dissented in *Washington* v *Davis*.

125

Andi tried again. 'Your Honor, that precedent was set in a *federal* case under the Fifth Amendment, citing the due process clause. My citation is of the Fourteenth Amendment at the State level, referring not to its *own* due process clause but rather to its *equal protection* clause. It was the wording of the equal protection clause that was explicitly cited by the court in *Strauder*.'

'Be that as it may, Ms Phoenix, the ratio decidendis for holding that disproportionality per se is not a constitutional violation is as applicable to the Fourteenth Amendment's "equal protection" clause as to its "due process" clause.'

'In that case, Your Honor, I would also cite my client's *Sixth* Amendment right to trial by an impartial jury.'

'Are you saying that failure to ensure racial proportionality in the venire panel would negate the impartiality of the final jury?'

Andi paused. She knew she would have to be careful here because this was in the presence of the venire panel. She didn't want to alienate them by accusing them of bias.

'Sidebar, Your Honor?'

'Approach.'

She approached the bench with Alex, who didn't trouble to hide the anger on his face. Sarah Jensen and Nick Sinclair also approached, but took their time in doing so. The judge switched off her microphone and Andi leaned forward as she spoke in a low voice, forcing herself to sound less strident and more appealing.

'Your Honor, my point here is that with blacks so severely under-represented on the venire panel we have no *chance* of getting a truly representative jury. In a case such as this, with all its ramifications, it is *vital* that the jury be a true cross-section of the community. It is *inevitable* that there will be strong feelings all round in a case like this. All I'm asking is that we get at least a fair shot at an ethnically diverse jury to represent a true cross-section of the community.'

The judge looked over at the prospective jurors. It was obvious that there were indeed only eight blacks there. And based on what Andi had said, this was indeed a statistical aberration to say the least.

'I can understand your concerns, Ms Phoenix. But there's no constitutional requirement that juries be ethnically balanced or diverse. Even venire panels can sometimes be imbalanced. It means nothing in the broader scheme of things.'

'But there *is* a constitutional requirement that there be no *systematic* exclusion on grounds of race, Your Honor. The fact that blacks are so *grossly* under-represented in the panel – and I can give you the statistics to back that up – means that they are effectively being excluded from the final jury. If they're not on the venire panel in the first place then they can't possibly get onto the jury.'

Justice Wagner looked over at the panel again, as if for reassurance.

'But jurors are summoned at *random*, Ms Phoenix. Do you have any evidence that blacks have been deliberately excluded from this panel?'

'No, Your Honor. But it is statistically unlikely – *extremely* unlikely – that in so large a sample, blacks would be so *grossly* under-represented. For this reason there must be a prima facie assumption that something has gone wrong in the selection procedure.'

Sarah Jensen – who had been content to leave it to the judge to shoot Andi down in flames – decided that it was time to enter the fray.

'Your Honor, this is ridiculous. Statistical aberrations happen all the time. With such a large number of trials, it's only natural that in some cases there should be a disproportionate number of one race or another. Has Ms Phoenix ever heard of mean standard deviation? Does she actually know anything about statistics? Or is the defense merely trying to cherry pick the jury?'

The judge looked at Andi.

'Ms Phoenix, do you have any statistical evidence that a deviation of this size is statistically dubious, given the large number of jury cases that take place altogether?' Her tone was firm but not aggressive.

'No, Your Honor,' replied Andi sheepishly.

'Do you have any *causal* evidence that blacks were intentionally excluded from *this* venire panel?'

'No, Your Honor.'

'Then your objection is overruled.' Ellen Wagner leaned back and looked at all of them. 'You may return to your places.'

Monday, 17 August 2009 – 13.00

'What the fuck were you trying to do?'

It was the lunchtime adjournment, after they'd spent the morning on the voir dire. Alex had barely waited to put some distance between himself and the reporters who had followed them out of the courtroom before letting rip at Andi. The press pack was out of earshot but only just.

'I found a discrepancy in the jury panel and I had a duty to act on it.'

'You don't have a duty to do anything without *my* permission!'

'If I hadn't put our objection on the record before the voir dire, we might have lost the chance to invoke it on appeal!'

'"*Our* objection"? "*We* might have lost"? Let me tell you something, Andi. There's no *we* and no *our* in this case. You're not here to fight the case. That's *my* job. Your job is to provide the softening, humanizing touch.'

'You're evading the issue. If I hadn't spoken up, we'd've been fucked.'

'That's bullshit! We could have said we didn't notice at the time.'

'Didn't notice? It was practically reaching out and hitting you in the face. And if you didn't notice until I pointed it out to you, *then you must have been blind!*'

'Look, I don't think you're hearing me too well. You don't do anything in there without my say so.'

'I told you the problem, but you just ignored me.'

By now Alex was on the verge of shouting, a rare occurrence for him. 'And you think it's good tactics to stand up in front of the people who are going to make up the jury and say to the judge, "I don't want any of this lot, I think they're biased!" Look, let's get this straight once and for all. *I'm* running this show. You're just here for the ride. *Got it*?'

'I thought you wanted my help on this case.' Her voice was weak, the self-confidence all gone.

'Look, I know you want to help,' he said more quietly. 'But if you're going to work with me, you have to play it according to my game plan. I picked you for my team because you look good and having Claymore sitting next to you makes him look non-threatening.'

'I told you back then, I'm not a prostitute.'

Alex lost his patience. 'We've already been through all that!'

Andi stormed away, angry and frustrated.

Monday, 17 August 2009 – 17.30

They had finally concluded the voir dire at around 16.45 p.m., with neither prosecution nor defense using up all of their peremptories. Justice Wagner had made it clear that she would extend the session past the normal time and, faced with that prospect, a kind of fatigue had set in amongst the lawyers, making them less acrimonious and more amenable to compromise. Ellen Wagner prided herself on having a stronger constitution than most of these 'spring chicken lawyers' and today proved to be no exception.

Consequently, they managed to select twelve jurors who they were more or less able to agree upon, even if the defense wasn't completely happy. Andi had been wary of leaving some of their peremptory challenges unused, as precedent suggested that this might block their prospect of appeal based on her objection to the panel. But she had been equally wary of incurring Alex's anger any further and besides, she felt confident that the specific grounds for her objection to the entire panel fell outside the scope of existing precedent.

After the last juror was selected, the judge decided to adjourn the session and postpone the swearing in till tomorrow. So Alex and Andi returned to the office to get some paperwork done. The tension between them had mellowed somewhat, but had not disappeared in its entirety.

Back in the office in the Embarcadero Center, Andi took the opportunity to spend the rest of the day looking at demographic statistics for other juries. Alex had given her use of the conference room as her temporary office for the duration of the case. She felt rather guilty about this, considering that Alex's own office was considerably smaller and had no natural light, let alone a stunning view of the Bay. Juanita, whose reception desk was in the large open area of the office, had told her in confidence that the conference room had once been used by a legal intern and that it had some painful memories for Alex.

Clicking on one link after another as she pursued the chain of data, she didn't really expect to find anything. She knew that blacks were under-represented in juries for a variety of reasons. But she suspected that the results of her labors would be to find a high degree of variation from case to case – proving the common opinion of the judge, the prosecutor and even Alex, that it was just a statistical blip in this case with no significance whatsoever.

And yet part of her was still hoping.

'Would you like a cup of coffee?' asked Juanita.

'Thanks,' said Andi, barely looking up. Juanita had seemed hostile when Andi first started working here, and Andi couldn't escape the feeling that it might have something to do with their differing sexuality. But after less than a day, Juanita seemed to be much nicer – almost suspiciously kind – and Andi even began to have doubts whether her initial assessment of Juanita's sexuality had been correct. At any rate, Juanita was a gentler soul than Alex . . . and certainly a gentler soul than Gene.

While she waited for the coffee, Andi returned her attention to the computer screen and thought about the issue that had been bugging her in court. Yes it was true that many blacks didn't register to vote. But that was precisely why the State didn't rely solely on the voting register, but used driver registration too. The one type of ownership that was impervious to socio-economic discrimination was car ownership. The widespread availability of cheap used cars meant that all but the most poverty-stricken members of society could afford one. And even if they didn't own a car, most adult Americans could drive. And all of those drivers were included in the jury pool.

That was why it was so troubling to Andi. In a small panel, one might sometimes get uneven or disproportionate results. But this was a panel of 150. An imbalance of this size was quite an anomaly. Could it have been just a random accident? Contrary to what Sarah Jensen had assumed, she did understand statistics – having taken a course in the subject as part of her psychology studies – and was fully conversant with such concepts as standard deviation and mean standard deviation. But she wasn't satisfied that the small number of blacks on the panel was the result of such random deviation.

And she was determined to find out for sure.

The door opened and Juanita came in with the coffee and a smile. Andi returned the smile, but quickly turned her attention back to the computer monitor, making it clear that she had no time for small talk.

The first thing she had to do was log on to the census bureau and pull up the jury records for the various voting districts. Then she started looking at the statistics for jury composition. It was a slow and tedious procedure but it had to be done. Finally, after several hours of painstaking work, she had enough data to build some graphic display charts, showing the demography of the populations and the corresponding average jury pools.

When she looked at the results it was frightening. There *was* a statistical imbalance. But it wasn't just this one county. It was quite a few others too.

And it went back five years.

Monday, 17 August 2009 – 18.10

'Once again, even before the trial has started, the case of Elias Claymore for the rape of Bethel Newton has managed to produce a surprise,' said Martine Yin.

The television flickered as the young man sat with his eyes practically glued to the screen.

'This morning in court, Alex Sedaka's co-counsel, Andi Phoenix, stood up to challenge the entire panel of prospective jurors in a surprise move for the defense. In a challenge that hasn't been seen since Sam Leibowitz's celebrated defense of the Scottsboro Boys, Ms Phoenix told the court that blacks were under-represented on the jury panel and moved that the panel be dismissed.'

The young man smiled with amusement as he pondered the irony of what was happening. He had been surprised when he heard about Andi Phoenix and her relationship with the woman who worked at the rape crisis center. It was a complete and utter coincidence. But an amusing coincidence nevertheless.

'However, the judge threw out the motion after some heated debate which culminated in a brief sidebar.'

He considered going to the trial to sit in the spectators' section. But he realized that might be pushing his luck. There was however one aspect of the case that intrigued him: he had read a rumor on the web that this reporter and Alex Sedaka were in a relationship.

Monday, 17 August 2009 – 18.20

Alex was reading through the jury selection notes when he heard a knock on the door.

'Come in,' he said, not looking up.

The door swung open and Andi burst into the room holding a computer printout, unable to conceal the excitement on her face.

'I've got something that'll knock your socks off!'

Alex looked up, responding to her mood as much as her words. 'Surprise me.'

'It's about the representation of blacks on the jury.'

'You're not still going on about that are you?'

'There's been a new development.'

She was gushing now. Alex's face remained skeptical, but he put his pen down to show that he was giving her his undivided attention.

'What about it?'

'I've checked the figures for jury selection in California for the last five years and guess what? The pattern holds. Blacks are under-represented on venire panels in *many* counties, not just Alameda.'

Alex thought to himself for a moment. 'What does that mean?'

'It means that jury panels in many counties have consistently under-represented blacks by a statistically significant amount. I can show you some charts to prove it.'

'Okay now, let's slow down here. First of all there are certain somewhat mundane factors that might have the effect of reducing the number of blacks on jury panels.'

'Such as what?' Andi challenged.

'For example, rightly or wrongly, a disproportionate number of blacks are incarcerated in penitentiaries and corrections institutes and jails. Prisoners are ineligible to vote.'

Andi shook her head. 'I got the stats for that and used the statistical analysis software to hold constant for it.'

'Hold constant?'

'Factor it in. The imbalance is still there when you take it into account. Don't forget, I have the figures from the voting register as well as census data.'

'Wait a minute, you have to be careful how you handle the data. The voting register excludes people incarcerated for *felony* convictions, but those serving time for *misdemeanors* can still vote. However, they can't serve on juries.'

Andi folded her arms and pursed her lips.

'Please give me credit for a modicum of common sense. I held constant for *all* incarcerations, including pre-trial detention. The pattern still holds.'

'Pattern?'

'I don't mean the size of the imbalance stayed constant. Obviously it was reduced when I held constant for those variables. But a statistically significant discrepancy remained.'

'Meaning, in plain English, that it was too big to be a—'

'Random deviation? Exactly.'

'Okay, but you base that on the assumption that the use of driver's license records would be sufficient to plug the gap left by under-representation of blacks on the voting register. But not everybody drives. Some people use the bus.'

'The DMV also issues non-driver IDs.'

'But only to those who request them.'

'Come off it! There isn't an eighteen-year-old in the State who doesn't want to buy smokes or booze. And once they've got the ID, they're registered at the DMV. And that makes them eligible for jury service.'

Alex shook his head, as he struggled to take it all in. 'Okay, hold on a minute, let's rewind. First of all, how are juries chosen?'

'We've been through that over and over: from voting registers and car license records. I think they use property tax records too.'

'No, what I mean is, once they've got the records how do they make the actual selection?'

'Well nowadays it's done by computer.'

'And how does the computer actually do it?'

'What do you mean?'

'I mean, according to what criteria does the computer make its decision?'

'It's random! That's the whole idea!'

'Yes,' Alex persisted, 'but *how* does something as deterministic as a computer make a random decision?'

'Okay let's say the court needs 200 prospective jurors for that week,' Andi began. 'And there are 50,000 eligible people in the district or county. The computer first divides 50,000 by 200 and gets 250. That means they need to summon one person for every 250 in the district. So the computer chooses every 250th name on the list.'

'That's it?'

'Well no, not quite. If the computer just did that, then it wouldn't be random. So instead, what the computer does is it creates what's called a "random offset."'

'Random offset?' Alex repeated.

'Yes. What that means is that it picks a random number between 1 and 249. Then it counts that number in and picks that as the *first* name on the list. So let's say it picks the random number 187. What it does then is pick the 187th person on the list as its first selection and then pick every 250th person thereafter, until it gets to the end of the list.'

'And that makes it random?'

'It's supposed to.'

'Okay,' said Alex. 'But how does it choose a random number in the first place?'

'It uses something called keyboard latency.'

Alex was looking at her blankly.

'It means the speed at which the person at the keyboard types. What the software does is get the computer operator to type on the keyboard at random. It ignores what keys they press, because that might not be random, but it measures the time between keystrokes – or rather the differences in *microseconds* between one keystroke and another.'

'Okay.'

'But it doesn't take the whole figure, it takes what it calls the least significant bit. That means like the last digit on the list of microseconds – that's *millionths* of a second. It takes the least significant bit from several keystrokes. Then the program uses this random input as the seed or initialization vector for the randomization algorithm that calculates a number between – in this case – one and two hundred and fifty.'

Andi paused to catch her breath.

'But none of this explains *why* blacks are under-represented,' said Alex.

'That's exactly my point. If the software does its job properly, then they shouldn't be. But all the stats I've looked at show that they are. *That* means that something's going wrong.'

'But what?'

'I don't know. But the judge did say causal evidence *or statistical* evidence. This is clear statistical evidence!'

'I don't think it's enough.'

'Why not?'

'Because she rejected it once and she'll reject it again.'

'But then it was just one panel. Now it's across the State for the last five years.'

'That's going to make it even harder.'

Andi was surprised at this. 'Why?'

'Because if you tell her this, then any decision she makes will have implications for thousands of other cases, not just this one. And I don't think she's going to want that sort of responsibility. She'd rather leave it to the Court of Appeal instead of taking it on her own head.'

'So what are we going to do? Just drop it and walk away like we haven't discovered anything?'

'No but we're going to need to bolster our arguments.'

'How?'

'By finding some causal explanation for these stats.'

'And how are we going to do that?'

'That's what I was hoping you could tell me.'

Andi thought about this for a moment. 'Maybe if we could find some glitch in the software.'

'Do you have the skill for that?'

'Probably not. I mean I tried to learn programming in C++ once, but I kind of . . . dropped out of the course.'

Alex pursed his lips.

'If it *is* a software glitch, I think I may know someone who can help.'

'Who?'

141

'My son. He's a physicist at Berkeley. Get his number from Juanita and call him. Tell him you're working for me.'

'*For* you?'

'*With* me.'

She rose, resignedly, but didn't leave the room. She just stood there saying nothing.

'Was there anything else?' he asked.

Now was the time to tell him about Lannosea, to ask him if he had told anyone about their private conversation when he had pressured her into sitting at the defense table. It should be simple enough to tell him about the messages and ask him if he had any idea who could be sending them. But something made her hold back and she wasn't sure what.

'No, nothing,' she said, realizing that now was not the time. When she opened the door, Juanita was standing there with a sheet of paper in her hand, poised to knock. Alex looked up as Juanita and Andi slipped past one another.

'We just had an e-mail from Leary,' said Juanita. She approached the desk and put it down in front of Alex. 'He's found some dirt on the Newton girl. This isn't the first time she's made a rape accusation.'

Tuesday, 18 August 2009 – 12.40

'I need hardly tell you about Elias Claymore's background,' Sarah Jensen was saying.

The sea of faces in the spectators' section of the courtroom on Tuesday reflected the interest in this case that had lingered beneath the surface for the last two months.

They had been told all about Elias Claymore's background by the newspapers and broadcast media when the case first broke back in June. Some of them were old enough to remember Claymore from his revolutionary days. But much of what they had been told by the media had faded from their memories. A spate of political crises, tornadoes in the Midwest, violence in the Middle East and stories about wife beating among the Hollywood glitterati had driven the tales of Elias Claymore from their minds. So now the prosecutor had to remind the four Caucasians, six Hispanics and two Asians of what sort of man Claymore was.

'The most militant member of the Black Leopards, he raped white women for – in his own words – "*political* reasons." Convicted and imprisoned for his heinous crimes, he escaped and fled to Libya where he became a Muslim—'

'Objection!' snapped Alex leaping to his feet. 'My client's religious views – past or present – are irrelevant.'

'Sustained,' said the judge firmly. 'The jury will disregard that remark. Counsel will refrain from making any further references to the accused's alleged former religion.'

'While he was there,' Sarah Jensen continued, 'he saw the oppression of the people and the corruption of the government and he became disillusioned. He realized that for all its faults, America was not as bad as he had thought. So he came back to the United States to serve out his sentence. This took a lot of courage, and I would be the first to give him credit for it. But a single act of courage doesn't make a man a hero, just as a single act of virtue doesn't make a man a saint.

'After his return, he served out the remainder of his sentence before being released on parole. But the prosecution will show that the leopard didn't change its spots. On the fifth of June of this year, he picked up a girl called Bethel Newton, whose car had broken down. He then took her to a deserted spot where he brutally raped her.

'You will hear testimony to this effect from the victim herself – the girl whom he raped.

'You will hear medical evidence of her internal and external injuries proving that this was rape and not consensual sex.

'You will see photographs showing the girl's external injuries, so that you will be able to judge with your own eyes whether the girl was a willing participant or an innocent victim.

'You will hear eyewitness testimony of a man who saw the accused running from the scene of the crime towards his car in which he made a quick getaway.

'Finally, most irrefutable of all, you will hear scientific DNA evidence showing that the man who raped Bethel Newton was none other than the accused, Elias Claymore.'

Sarah Jensen sat down, keeping her face completely neutral. Alex knew that she had ended her opening statement at almost precisely one o'clock, to make sure that her summary of the case stuck firmly in the minds of the jurors over lunch. It was the oldest trick in the book, and Alex had expected it. But there was very little he could do about it. He just had to pace himself right too, making sure that his own bombshells coincided with the appropriate adjournments.

Four hundred miles away, Eugenia Vance sat before a television set watching the proceedings on Court TV.

Tuesday, 18 August 2009 – 15.40

After lunch, Sarah Jensen began presenting her case, calling Bethel Newton first. Her approach was gentle, putting Bethel at ease by leading her through the noncontentious events leading up to her encounter with the rapist: her car breaking down, the Mercedes stopping and the man giving her a ride. At all times, Bethel testified in a voice that was quiet but not weak.

'Then he dragged me out of the car, behind the bushes, and clamped his hand over my mouth. I managed to bite him but then he slapped me across the face. I felt a sharp blow and then I could feel blood in my mouth and I realized it was futile to struggle.'

'And then what happened?'

While she paused to compose herself before answering, Andi quickly scribbled a note to Alex saying: 'We need to ask her if she knows my e-mail address.' Alex looked at her blankly. Andi still hadn't told him about Lannosea. But she knew that she could hardly expect him to probe this area, and risk the judge's disapproval, without offering him at least *some* explanation. So she added to the note, the words: 'I've been getting abusive anon e-mails.' He seemed to take it in very quickly and did not look altogether surprised. He nodded his head gently, as if understanding.

'He started tearing away at my clothes, not so much ripping them off me, more pulling them out of the way. Then he unzipped his pants and pushed them down slightly and then . . .'

She started to cry. Everyone in the courtroom sat in absolute silence while she pulled out her handkerchief and sobbed into it.

'Take your time, Miss Newton.'

'And then he raped me.'

'How did he penetrate you?'

'Vaginally,' she said weakly, the words barely audible. 'From the front.'

'And do you see the man who did this in this courtroom?'

The words seemed to have a toughening effect on her, as if she sensed the opportunity to regain control. She put her handkerchief away, no longer crying. Then she leaned forward and looked over at Claymore.

'Yes I do,' she said pointing at Claymore. 'That man over there.'

'May the record show that the witness identified the accused, Elias Claymore,' said Sarah Jensen.

'So ordered,' the judge responded.

Sarah Jensen then went through a series of questions to put on record the events that happened afterwards: Claymore running away and driving off, a member of the public calling the police, the medical examination, the DNA sample, the photographs.

When she had finished, Sarah Jensen looked over at the judge and said, 'No further questions.'

Then she sat down, trying to look sad or at least solemn, rather than triumphant. Andi noticed that Justice Wagner was looking over at the clock. It was just after five pm. *She had done it again!* She had timed it perfectly to coincide with the afternoon adjournment. That meant that once again the jury would leave the court with the girl's tearful testimony locked firmly in their minds, and they would have the whole night to think about it.

'Your Honor,' Alex interrupted leaping to his feet. 'I know that we only have half an hour left tonight. But I would like to at least *start* my cross-examination now—'

'Is that really necessary, Mr Sedaka?'

'There are one or two points I'd like to clear up right away.'

'Do you think you can finish your cross in a short time?' asked the judge with a disarming smile. 'Because if so I might be ready to allow you some latitude and extend the proceedings. As long as you feel confident you can wrap it up tonight.'

Alex frowned for a second and then almost smiled.

'In order to know that, Your Honor, I would have to ask one question of the witness first. Depending on the answer to that question I will know whether I can wrap it up tonight.'

'Go ahead.'

'Miss Newton, have you at any time, since first making your complaint, contacted anyone involved with the defense?'

Oh that's good, thought Andi. *Plant the idea in the jury's mind. Even if it all fizzles out, it'll keep them preoccupied with it now, so they won't think so much about her testimony.*

Sarah Jensen was on her feet. 'Your Honor, is counsel making any specific allegations? Or is he just trying to cloud the issue with unsubstantiated allegations?'

'Approach the bench!' snapped the judge.

Alex and Sarah approached. Andi hesitated for a moment and then approached, ignoring the forbidding stare of the judge. Only Nick Sinclair stayed in his seat.

'Are you going anywhere with this, Mr Sedaka?'

149

'Your Honor, my co-counsel has been receiving anonymous e-mail messages of an abusive and harassing nature. We wouldn't for one minute suspect the prosecution of involvement, but this witness is another matter altogether.'

'How do you know it isn't one of the thousands of whack jobs looking for his fifteen minutes?'

Alex turned to Andi, to let her answer.

'Your Honor, the content of the messages suggests that it's someone with intimate knowledge of the case.'

'Knowledge that only this witness or someone on the prosecution team would have?'

Andi hesitated for a moment, embarrassed by the truthful answer. 'Well, some of the knowledge . . . appears to be . . . things that not even this witness would know.'

'What do you mean?'

'Private conversations that I've had.'

Sarah was shaking her head, smiling with utter contempt. Justice Wagner ignored her.

'So what are you saying? That your office is bugged?'

'I don't know what I'm saying. It just doesn't make sense.'

The judge was silent for a few seconds, as if weighing up what she had just heard.

'Well, when you *do* know what you're saying, I may revisit the issue and allow the defense to resume this line of questioning. Until then, such questions are out of order.'

Andi was looking at the floor, unable to meet the eyes of either the judge or Alex.

'I think we'll adjourn for now.'

When they had returned to their places, Justice Wagner addressed the jury. 'Members of the jury. You will ignore that last question and refrain from any speculation about it. We will now adjourn until ten o'clock tomorrow morning. The jury are admonished not to form an opinion on this case until they have heard all the evidence and the case has been put to them, nor to discuss this case among themselves or with others or to permit it to be discussed in their presence. Court is adjourned.'

They all stood up as the judge left. But one thing stuck in Andi's mind: when Alex had asked the question about contacting anyone on the defense, Bethel Newton had looked absolutely terrified.

Tuesday, 18 August 2009 – 17.15

Outside, Alex walked over to Andi's side to speak to her. 'I want to know about these anonymous e-mails – including why you didn't tell me about them before.'

'I've had a couple. The first one right after I agreed to sit at the defense table. The second one came just after I challenged the venire panel.'

'What did they say, the e-mails?'

'Like I said, they were full of abusive language. I can't remember verbatim, but I've saved them. I can show them to you back at the office.'

'You said something about the writer knowing intimate details that not even the victim would know.'

She noticed that he had said 'victim' rather than 'alleged victim.' He would never have been that careless in court.

'Whoever sent them seemed to know about things that happened during our private conversations.'

She was watching him carefully as she said this.

'What do you mean "our" private conversations?'

'Yours and mine. Things that occurred when you and I were alone together.'

'Such as what?'

'Such as you practically blackmailing me into working with you on the case.'

'I didn't blackmail you—'

'That's the way *they* described it.'

'What else did they say?'

'They said I should have resisted your pressure and that I'm a "whore" and Claymore is a "nigger scumbag."'

'And this was anonymous?'

'More or less. It was signed "Lannosea."'

'Does that mean anything to you?'

'Nothing.'

'Did you look it up?'

'Wikipedia, Yahoo *and* Google. Apparently she was one of the daughters of the old English queen, Boudicca.'

'I assume you did an Internet search for other people with the same name?'

'There were only four results altogether: two foreign, one meaningless, one that gave the answer.'

'Alternative spellings?'

'Loads of results, but mostly foreign.'

'What about tracing the source of the e-mails?'

'They were sent via a webmail account.'

'From what my son told me, I understand they can still trace it through the message header.'

'Yes, but anyone sending this kind of message would probably use a public computer, like in a library or an Internet café.'

'They might have security cameras at places like that.'

'We'd have to convince them that it's important enough. That means getting law agencies involved. And at this stage we don't even know which *country* they're sending it from.'

'Okay, let's hold off on that, Andi.'

'The thing I don't get is how they knew about private conversations.'

Alex was looking at her with a skeptical smile. 'You think they really *did* bug the office?'

'It may sound crazy, Alex, but there has to be *some* explanation.'

Alex smiled, mockingly. 'Well in that case, I'd better tell you what I've decided before we get back to the office.'

'What?' Andi felt apprehensive at Alex's tone.

'*You're* going to conduct the cross-examination tomorrow.'

Wednesday, 19 August 2009 – 9.10

Jerry Cole had never really amounted to much. At forty years of age, he was a lean, nondescript figure of average height and receding hairline. Such hair as he had was greased back, not in a stylish fifties style, but more in the manner of a lazy man who doesn't want the bother of unruly hair and who uses grease as the easiest option for keeping it in place.

He had been working at the forensic science laboratory in Ventura County for half his life and all he had to show for it was a rented roof over his head. He didn't own a car and didn't even know how to drive. He was, according to everyone who knew him, feckless and barely capable of doing anything other than by rote. His job title was 'Lab Technician' but this could just as easily have been translated as 'Gopher.' Unlike other, younger, technicians at the lab, he was never sent on courses that could improve his job skills because it was widely assumed that he lacked the aptitude for them.

Most of the time he worked in the Forensic Alcohol section, but occasionally he had to run errands for the Toxicology or Controlled Substance sections. Never for the DNA section. But he knew how they worked and he knew that at times it could get chaotic. That was why he didn't always remember to do things he was supposed to, you see, not because he was lazy or incompetent.

But his bosses didn't always see things that way. That was why today he had been summoned by the Forensic Alcohol supervisor, the head of his administrative section.

'You remember a month ago you received an official caution about using a stale batch of testing solution?'

Cole remembered the incident very well. He had been acting under intense pressure in a busy lab and had grabbed the nearest batch of made-up testing solution. What he hadn't realized was that it was an old solution that another technician had been using and was about to throw away. It could have been disastrous if he had used it because he was running tests on real crime samples. Fortunately the other technician had spotted it just in time and intervened.

'Yes, sir, but I'm more careful now. I always make sure it's a fresh batch.'

'Well, that isn't exactly true now is it, Mr Cole?'

Jerry Cole's face flushed. 'I don't know what you mean, sir.'

'You know that every three months, the Department of Health Services sends blood samples spiked with alcohol to verify that facilities such as the crime lab are getting accurate results?'

'Yes, sir.'

In fact he didn't know anything of the kind. But he was afraid to admit it.

'Well, they did such a test last week and we have the results back. I'm sorry to have to inform you that you failed the test.'

'What . . . me personally?'

'Yes, Mr Cole. The samples were coded and the other technicians passed. You were the only one who failed.'

'I must have been under pressure sir, otherwise—'

'It's the same pressure for everyone, Mr Cole. You were

the only one who failed and this was on top of your mistake a month ago. You were given an official written warning then, so I'm afraid there can be no further warnings. We're going to have to let you go.'

'But this isn't fair, sir.'

'It complies with the labor laws and I'm afraid the decision is final. We're giving you one month's pay in lieu of notice, plus lay-off pay for twenty years' service which should see you through until you find a new job, also you're entitled to three weeks' holiday and again we've given you pay in lieu of that. I'll send a member of security to help you clean out your locker.'

Fifteen minutes later, Jerry Cole was on the streets and unemployed.

Wednesday, 19 August 2009 – 10.15

On the third day of the trial, the tension in court was even greater than before as the judge took her place. This was to be the first time the defense had a crack at the accuser. Claymore was sitting at the defense table uncomfortably, the fear visible in his eyes.

Andi realized that Bethel had had to go to sleep last night knowing that the following day she would be subjected to a thorough and rigorous cross-examination. Indeed Andi herself had had an almost sleepless night at the hotel last night. And to make it worse, she didn't even have the comfort of Gene to hold her and reassure her. When she finally woke up – late – she felt as if she hadn't slept at all.

After the court was called into session, the judge looked up at the defense table and told Alex that he could begin his cross-examination.

Andi rose. 'Your Honor, I will be cross-examining Miss Newton.'

Claymore tensed up when he heard this. Andi realized that Alex hadn't warned him about the change of plan.

Sarah Jensen rose from her seat. 'Your Honor, I object. Lead counsel began the cross-examination yesterday. Absent a compelling reason, it would be quite improper for co-counsel to take over in the middle.'

Andi well knew why Sarah Jensen was objecting. A cross-examination of an alleged rape victim by a *man* would inevitably elicit sympathy for the victim, no matter how gently it was conducted. Whereas a cross-examination by another woman – especially an attractive one – allowed scope for some probing questions, and even a modicum of aggression.

Justice Wagner hesitated for a moment.

'No, I'm going to allow it. Cross-examination barely started yesterday. And the defendant has the right to have his defense handled according to the best judgment of his counsel.'

Sarah Jensen sat down reluctantly. Andi gave her a knowing look and then returned her attention to Bethel Newton.

'Miss Newton, would it be correct to say that when you got into the car, you didn't know the man whose car you were getting into?'

'Yes.'

'In other words, you were getting into a stranger's car?'

'Yes.'

'And were you not aware of the danger to which you were exposing yourself?'

'I know that it isn't all that smart to hitch a ride, but I didn't have a choice.'

'Are you saying that he forced you into his car?'

'No. But my car had broken down and I couldn't use my cell phone. It had a flat battery – the phone, I mean.'

Andi kept a neutral look on her face. She was forcing Bethel to elaborate on her answers, taking her into unfamiliar territory.

'But you were aware that there was an element of danger in getting into a stranger's car?'

'Yes.'

'Assuming of course that you didn't *want* what ultimately happened?'

'Objection,' Sarah Jensen interrupted.

'Sustained. Counsel will refrain from embellishing her questions. The jury will ignore defense counsel's last remark.' Justice Wagner turned back to Andi. 'Ms Phoenix, if you wish, you may repeat or rephrase the first part of the question.'

'Miss Newton, if you didn't want to have sexual relations with the driver of the car then would not the wisest course of action have been *not* to get into his car in the *first* place?'

'I suppose so.'

'Yet you *did* get into the car?'

'I didn't think about it.'

'Nevertheless would you not concede that by getting into a stranger's car you advertised that you had less concern for the consequences than the average female?'

'Objection!'

Again Sarah Jensen was on her feet. Andi tried to sound calm as she replied. 'Your Honor, if I may quote a ruling of Justice Compton in the California Court of Appeal: "Under such circumstances it would *not* be unreasonable for a man in the position of the defendant here to believe that the female would consent to sexual relations."'

'Your Honor, counsel for the defense forgets that Justice Compton specified that it only applied to situations in which there was no emergency. In this case, the victim's car had broken down in the middle of nowhere. Furthermore, the official grounds for the reversal was that the trial judge allowed the jury to consider the defendant's previous conviction for a sex offense – for which he was still on a suspended sentence.'

Ellen Wagner nodded, 'I believe that it was also pointed

out that if it were applied consistently it would also allow homosexual rape as well as heterosexual rape – of both drivers *and* hitchhikers.'

Andi was feeling flustered. She had overplayed her hand and Alex was now looking at her with unconcealed anger.

The judge continued, 'I am directing the jury as a matter of law that the act of getting into a stranger's car does not in itself entail an absolute forfeiture of the protection of the law against rape.'

Sarah Jensen sat down, casting a smug sideways glance at Alex, who looked somewhat frustrated.

'Miss Newton,' Andi continued, 'is it possible that the reason you felt you had no choice but to hitch a ride is because you were *tired* of trying to get your car started and anxious to get back into town?'

'Yes,' said Bethel, grateful for the chance to revert to one-word answers. She had said in direct examination that she had been *unable* to restart the car on her own. She hadn't noticed the subtle shift in wording that Andi had introduced into the questioning.

'And is it not also possible that, being *tired*, you may have been mistaken about at least *some* of the details of the event – not the major details perhaps, but at least the minor ones.'

'Yes, maybe,' said Bethel nervously.

'For example,' Andi continued, 'if you say you were raped, then there is certainly no reason to doubt you. If you say you didn't give your consent to sex then *you* ought to know what you wanted and no one should question *that*. But is it not *possible* that you might be mistaken in what is, at the end of the day, just one of the details? Like the *identification* of the rapist?'

'The man who raped me is your client, Elias Claymore,' she said with grit in her voice.

'But did you not initially tell the police that the man who raped you was in his *twenties*?'

'I did, at first.'

The voice was weak. But more significantly, Alex noticed that she was no longer relying on one-word answers, even when she could get away with them.

'Would you say that the *accused* is in his twenties?'

She looked round at Claymore.

'No. But when I came back after lunch, I told them he was older.'

'Ah yes, when you *came back*. And that was when you also told them that you'd seen the rapist on a TV talk show.'

'Yes.'

'And how old does the accused look to you now?'

'About fifty.'

'Fifty-eight actually. So how could you confuse him with a man in his twenties?'

'I don't know,' she replied weakly, wiping a tear from her eye.

'And what made you realize that he was older?'

'Like I said, I saw him on a TV in a store window. He was presenting the talk show. But I didn't know who it was. Only I realized that it was him when I saw his face in close-up.'

'But you saw the rapist in close-up, didn't you?'

'Yes.'

'And you thought he was in his twenties.'

'I was frightened.'

'Frightened would hardly make fifty-eight seem like twenties, would it?'

'I was confused.'

'Are you *sure* you're not confused now?'

'No.'

165

'You're *not* sure if you're confused?'

'No. I mean I'm not confused now.'

'Is it possible that you saw an older man on TV who *looked* a bit like an *older version* of the man who raped you and so you decided that this man *was* the rapist?'

'No. Look, I know what I'm saying! The man who raped me is that man sitting over there!'

Andi paused, put on the look of one who was hurt but still defiant, and spoke in a slow but impassioned voice.

'Is this the first time that you've accused a man of rape?'

Bethel looked over to Sarah Jensen who nodded discreetly. Andi could have made an issue of such non-verbal communication, but she chose to ignore it, putting pressure on Bethel to answer.

'No.' The voice was weak and accompanied by a girlish sniffle.

'Is it not a fact that two years ago you made a similar accusation against a fellow high school student called Luke Orlando?'

'Yes.'

'And then you retracted it and admitted that you were lying?'

'I *wasn't* lying.'

'Then why did you admit that you were lying at the time?'

'Because after I withdrew the accusation my family and friends were all pestering me to reinstate the accusation and that was the only way I could get them off my back.'

'Oh, so you admitted you were lying *after* you withdrew the accusation?'

'Yes. But it wasn't a lie! He *did* rape me!'

'So *why* did you withdraw the accusation if it was true?'

She opened her mouth to speak, but no sound came out.

'Take your time, Miss Newton,' said the judge, gently.

166

'It's complicated.'

'Would you like another glass of water?' asked the judge.

Without waiting for an answer, the judge signaled one of the bailiffs to refill the water cup that Bethel had emptied slowly while testifying under direct examination. When Bethel had taken a few sips and calmed down, the judge nodded for her to continue.

'I knew that if I followed through with the accusation I'd be subjected to this sort of thing . . . and . . .'

'What sort of thing?'

'Like . . . *this* . . .'

The tears were flowing again.

'Oh, you mean cross-examination.'

'*Yes*,' said Bethel in a little-girl voice, her eyes squinting to dam up the tears.

'But isn't that my *job*?'

'Yes.'

'So you were afraid because you knew the prosecutor would do his or her job?'

'I was afraid of how he'd make me seem.'

'And how was that, Miss Newton?'

'Like a slut.'

'Why do you think he'd make you seem like a slut?'

'Because that's what they do.'

'They?' asked Andi, raising her eyebrows.

'Lawyers. Defense lawyers.'

'Is it only defense lawyers who do that sort of thing, Miss Newton?'

At the prosecution table, Sarah Jensen tensed up. She knew that Andi was leading Bethel into dangerous territory. She could object, but she couldn't afford to let it seem to the jury as if she was protecting the witness from being tested.

167

So she held back. With any luck Andi would just create sympathy for Bethel by attacking her in this way.

'I don't know what you mean.'

'Oh, I think you do. Didn't the boys in your high school vote you "slut of the year" in their student magazine poll?'

'Yes,' she cried, sobbing bitterly into her handkerchief. 'But I wasn't like that at all. I wasn't a slut. It was just the boys being silly.'

'But *they* evidently thought it was true, Miss Newton.'

Sarah Jensen finally rose to her feet like an avenging angel, realizing that she had let it go on too long. 'Your Honor, this is hardly relevant to the proceedings. The witness objected to the way the boys had characterized her even at the time.'

'That may be, Your Honor,' Andi responded, 'but the witness's past behavior pertains to her veracity.'

Sarah Jensen tried again. 'That may be the case with the previous rape accusation, Your Honor. But how she was characterized *by others* is another matter. This poll was done in a high school by a group of *adolescent boys*. It merely reflects the adolescent boys' *mentality*. It hardly represents reliable evidence of the witness's past behavior.'

Justice Wagner hesitated. After a few seconds, she spoke slowly. 'It may not be the most reliable evidence, Ms Jensen, but it is evidence.'

'But it is not evidence of a form that permits cross-examination. If defense counsel wants to introduce this evidence, she should call the author of the student magazine article and the rules of hearsay evidence should be strictly applied.'

'That would surely restrict the content of his testimony to the point of rendering it worthless,' said the judge.

'In that case, let defense counsel call the boys who *answered* the opinion poll.'

'That would be extremely impractical, Ms Jensen.'

'In that case I reiterate my objection to the evidence. If this evidence is deemed to be relevant, then at least it should be admitted in a form that lends itself to the test of cross-examination of its sources.'

'No, I don't agree, Ms Jensen. I think it's important to protect the accused's right to a fair trial, and that includes testing this witness's testimony, by allowing defense counsel to put these points to her.'

Sarah Jensen sat down, frustrated. Emboldened by the judge's decision, Andi pressed her advantage home, determined to make up for the earlier debacle about the Justice Compton decision.

'Miss Newton,' Andi continued. 'Can you think of any reason why fifteen boys should unanimously vote you "slut of the year"?'

'Because they're a bunch of fuckin' creeps!' she cried, sobbing profusely.

'And is it not true, Miss Newton, that you took part in a student charity event dressed as a slave girl?'

'Yes,' she said, continuing to cry. She had been dressed more modestly than a girl – or man – on the beach. But in court it sounded so different from the reality.

'And on another occasion did you not appear as a strip-ogram?'

'It was a *kiss*ogram!'

The court erupted into laughter, crushing her with the weight of total humiliation.

At the defense table, Claymore lowered his head and stared at the table in front of him, unable to watch what was unfolding before his eyes. But no one noticed Claymore. The last thing everyone remembered of that session was Bethel Newton's face with the tears of humiliation streaming down her cheeks. And amidst all the politics and legal shenanigans, it was all too easy to forget that this was a human being.

No one looked at Andi, either. If they had, they would have noticed that she too was crying.

Wednesday, 19 August 2009 – 12.30

'You know that according to Bethel's statement about Orlando, he assaulted her with one end of a baseball bat?'

Andi and Alex were in the car driving back to the office across the Bay Bridge to finish some paperwork. The atmosphere was tense. They had been sitting there in stony silence until Andi spoke.

'I know,' said Alex, uncomfortably.

'And you also know that Orlando forced her to perform several sexual acts while threatening to bust her head open.'

'I know she *said* he did,' Alex replied, not giving anything away by his tone.

'And you think she made all that up?' asked Andi, contemptuously.

Alex shrugged.

Andi spoke again. 'You know that another girl came forward at the time of the Orlando case and confirmed that Orlando had done the same thing to her?'

'Yes.'

'She said he pulled her hair and treated her like a rag doll, just like Bethel Newton said.'

'So?'

'And he boasted to her about having assaulted other girls

and threatened to "rearrange her face" if she told anyone. Do you think they *both* made it up?'

'How do you know all this?' asked Alex glancing sideways briefly to assess what she was thinking.

'It's in the report. Pity you didn't bother to read it.'

Alex's face was neutral.

'I *did* read it,' he said coolly.

Alex kept his eyes on the road, but when he turned to check his blind spot she saw that his expression had given way to a faint trace of an embarrassed smile.

'You bastard,' she said coldly.

It was too quiet for anger; too lacking in intensity for passion. It was revulsion; the sort of revulsion one might feel towards an old piece of decomposing food. She turned her face to the road, unable to bear the sight of him any longer.

'We're up against a century-old stereotype,' said Alex. 'The black man as sex-driven predator who goes hunting for white women to violate. We have to counter that stereotype any way we can – even if it means fighting dirty.'

'You're still living in the past, Alex. That stereotype died with *To Kill a Mockingbird*. It's been replaced by another stereotype, and one that's no less pernicious: the lying woman who consents the night before and then screams rape the morning after.'

172

Wednesday, 19 August 2009 – 13.05

'The trial of Elias Claymore crossed an important milestone today as alleged rape victim Bethel Newton was subjected to a grueling cross-examination by defense co-counsel Andromeda Phoenix on the third day of the trial.'

Martine Yin was standing in front of a news camera giving her report, while a group of women behind her demonstrated outside the court building, shouting slogans demanding justice for rape victims.

'Cross-examination had been expected to last several days, but appears to have been cut short to avoid creating any more sympathy for the alleged victim.'

Andi was watching the report via the Internet at her desk in Alex Sedaka's conference room office when she heard a knock on her door.

'Come in,' she said, not looking up.

The door opened and Juanita walked in with two ice-cold cans of diet Coke.

'Oh, hi, Juanita.'

'How are things going?' asked Juanita, pulling up a chair and practically yanking the ring out of her diet Coke can.

'Okay. Still slogging away trying to make sense of these demography and jury stats.'

'I thought you'd put that on the side.'

'Alex wants me to. He thinks we can break the prosecution case with old-fashioned courtroom methods. But I'm not so sure. And in any case there's something not quite right going on. And I want to know why.'

Part of the cause of Andi's obsession was the feeling that someone was operating against her in the background. All her efforts at demographic analysis seemed to have come to nothing when she walked into that courtroom and looked at the jury panel. To add to that, the obscene messages she had received had both angered and frightened her. She sensed that there was an enemy out there trying to stop her – and she was determined to stand up to that enemy.

'What exactly are you hoping to find?' asked Juanita.

'Well, firstly I guess I want to rule out any other explanation. But the more I look, the more obvious it seems that the other explanations don't work.'

'Maybe you just haven't considered the right one.'

'Like what?'

Juanita shrugged and her eyes squinted as she gave Andi an awkward, embarrassed smile. 'Like whatever you haven't thought of. If I knew, then one of us would have thought of it and we wouldn't be having this conversation.'

'Great,' said Andi at the wry humor.

'What did David say, when you phoned him?'

'David? Oh, Alex's son. He told me about some case in Kent County, Michigan a few years when they found a glitch in the software that had been running for eighteen months. It excluded the higher number zip codes – which just happened to be the ones with the black population.'

'And what was the outcome?'

'Well, I looked up the case and it turned out that the Michigan Jury Commission determined that the error was accidental so it didn't result in any successful challenges to

174

convictions. But I did a broader Internet search and found that the Grand Rapids area has been plagued by other problems concerning minority representation in jury pools. They found things like greater laxity of standards in requesting jury exemption from black applicants than whites and also problems with locations they were summoned to appear at.'

'And is it possible that that's what's happening in Alameda?'

'Well first of all it isn't just Alameda. It's . . . not exactly every county in the State, but certainly quite a few of them. I haven't yet been able to check all the counties, but I'd say around a third of the ones I've looked at seem to have the same problem. The stats vary but it's all to within one standard deviation.'

'It's strange that it should be only a third.'

'Well, no, that's the other thing. You see not every county uses the same jury selection software. I've checked up online and there are at least four companies that supply jury selection software for the courts.'

'And?'

'Well, I was wondering if maybe the ones who are having the problem are all using software from just one of these companies. In other words, maybe one of the companies is selling defective software.'

'Have you checked it out?'

'I've tried to. But it seems that nobody in the court administration knows what software they're using and nobody knows who *does* know – at least nobody I can get on the phone.'

'Well, *somebody* must know! And they can't just refuse to tell you.'

'Well, they'd have to go back through the court admin financial records to when the software was purchased and no one wants to be bothered with that. Also the courts are exempt from the California Public Records Act, except for statements of itemized expenditure. So I requested statements from every county in the State from five years ago. Hopefully we'll find it listed. But they have up to ten days to comply. And some of them have even written back to invoke the statutory fourteen day extension. And that's time we can't afford. So far only one of the counties has got back to me.'

Juanita smiled. 'And is it one that has the low minority stats or one of those that doesn't?'

'One that doesn't.'

'So why don't you presume that the problem is with software from one of the other three companies?'

'That's exactly what I *do* think. But until I've got responses from the others, I don't know *which* and that means I can't prove anything.'

'No, but can't you in the meantime, analyze the software from those three other companies? Or get David to?'

'I got the impression that David didn't really have the time. He only agreed to help because his father wanted him to. Besides, there's still the problem of *getting* the software. We still don't know which of the other three companies it's from.'

Juanita thought about this for a moment.

'Maybe it would quicker to buy copies of the software from the various companies?'

'Probably would. The trouble is then all we'd have is the executable – or at best the object code.'

Juanita was shaking her head. 'Now you've lost me.'

'We need the source code to figure out what's going wrong, if anything.'

'Oh, I see.' Juanita was actually more knowledgeable about computers than she liked to let on. 'But isn't it possible to – what's that word? – decompile it or something like that?'

'It is. And I can probably get a freeware decompiler online. But the output from a decompiler is so cryptic that it takes an experienced computer programmer to understand it.'

'And you're not an experienced programmer?'

'Unfortunately not,' said Andi. 'Barely more than a beginner.'

'I'm sure David can help.'

'Until we've got the software, that's a moot point. Also it's not like off-the-shelf software. It's very expensive and you pay for the number of seats.'

'Seats?'

'The number of parallel users. That means they'll want to know where and in what manner we'll be using it. And what are we going to tell them? "We want to analyze your software to see if it has a defect that causes African-Americans to be under-represented on juries"?'

Juanita smiled. 'I see what you mean. The thing I don't understand, Andi, is how come you got the demographic jury data so quickly, if they're so slow under the Public Records Act.'

'That's easy. A lot of counties have already compiled their own demographic reports to monitor these things for internal admin purposes. The data was already out there. It was just a case of tracking it down on the Internet.'

Juanita leaned forward conspiratorially. 'You see, I was just wondering if we could somehow get a copy of the software and present David with a *fait accompli* . . . get him to haul ass.'

Andi realized that Juanita was trying to be helpful. And maybe she was right. 'Do you think Alex would be ready to fork out for a copy of the software?'

Juanita smiled. 'Maybe as a last resort. But let's try something else first.'

'What?'

'Are you in court this afternoon, Andi?'

'No. The judge has some other business to clear up so we've got the afternoon free.'

'Private business or court business?'

There was an eager smile on Juanita's face. It left Andi feeling awkward.

'Court business, I assume.'

'So she's still in the court building?'

'I assume so. Why? What do you have in mind?'

'Give me a moment.'

She picked up the phone and called a number.

'Hallo, is that the clerk to Justice Wagner? Yes, I wonder if you can help me. My name is Juanita Cortez and I am the secretary to Alex Sedaka in the Elias Claymore case. I was wondering if you could find out from Justice Wagner if she would consider an ex parte motion from the defense for a court order to obtain the software used by the court for jury selection?'

There was a long pause, and Andi could hear indistinct voices in the distance.

'Yes we can obtain the executable program from the court itself, but the source code would have to come from the supplier I assume . . . Yes we can be there in person in half an hour. Thank you.'

Juanita put the phone down, here eyes gleaming. 'She'll grant us an order for the executable from the court and schedule a hearing for the source code from the company that supplied the software. It's called LegalSoft. But she'll have to give them forty-eight hours' notice of the hearing.'

Andi's face lit up. 'Yes!'

'We'd better get going.'

Andi stood up and grabbed her purse. 'And on the way, I'll tell you my theory about what's really going on – assuming I can trust you.'

Wednesday, 19 August 2009 – 13.20

Martine Yin had wrapped up her reporting from the Claymore trial for the day. The court wouldn't be reconvening in the afternoon and the TV station would simply run her earlier report again in the evening and on the late night news, filling in any additional details from the studio.

Feeling somewhat down and dejected, she made her way to her car, which was parked in the parking structure a couple of blocks down from the courtroom between Jackson and Madison. She was missing Alex's company and was frustrated at having to stay away from him. Perhaps if she had felt in a better mood, she would have been more alert. But as it was, she was barely aware of what was in front of her, let alone what was behind.

Consequently, she didn't notice that she was being followed by a young man. A young man whose excitement was growing at the prospect of what he was planning to do.

Wednesday, 19 August 2009 – 13.30

'So let me get this straight,' said Juanita. 'You're saying that you think it's not a glitch but deliberate tampering?'

'That's right. And it goes back for the last five years.'

They were crossing the Bay Bridge into Oakland, on their way to the court administration building in Oakland. Juanita was at the wheel.

'But what does that mean? That it's an inside job? Someone in the software company?'

Andi leant her head back, considering this. 'Possibly.'

'Well, I mean, like, what else could it be?'

'Maybe someone created a different version and switched it for the original.'

'What, like someone who worked at the court?'

'At this stage we need to keep our minds open.'

'Yes, but . . . hold on a minute, Andi. Anyone working in the court would only be working in *one* county. They'd have an opportunity to install it in one county but not a third of the counties in the State.'

'No, that's why I said we should keep an open mind. But you're right, that's not a likely explanation. But maybe somebody hacked into the computers at the courts?'

Juanita pondered this in the dim light of the lower section of the bridge as heavy traffic thundered overhead.

'Wouldn't that be kind of hard? I mean don't they have . . . what are they called? *Firewalls*?'

'Of course. If it was easy, everyone would be doing it. But some people have that kind of skill. But they wouldn't just have to modify the software. They'd also have to find some way to slip it past the firewalls – and that's probably a lot harder. Firewalls these days are quite sophisticated. A good server would only allow local super user privileges.'

'So a remote installation would be blocked automatically.'

'Exactly.'

'There's something else I don't get,' said Juanita. 'If someone had tampered with it – or even if it was just plain defective – how come no one discovered it until now?'

'Don't forget, the only reason *I* discovered it now was because I noticed that there weren't enough blacks on what was quite a large panel. Usually the venire panel is smaller to begin with, so this sort of imbalance wouldn't stand out so visibly.'

'A smart lawyer like Alex would notice it, Andi.'

'From case to case, yes. But he'd probably just think of it as bad luck or look for other more mundane explanations. I mean that's exactly what he did think.'

'But you didn't agree.'

'No, and I'll tell you why not. You see, we went to a lot of trouble to get a change of venue and I did a lot of prior research about the demography of the various counties. That meant that I approached the trial with some *very specific expectations* about the venire. When those expectations weren't met it stuck out like a sore thumb. And it was particularly surprising because it was such a big venire pool. That meant we couldn't explain it away as a random deviation.'

'But you haven't told Alex your theory that the software's been *deliberately* tampered with?'

'It's not a theory. Just an idle speculation at this stage.'

'You mean you're afraid he'll laugh at you.'

Andi didn't reply. It occurred to her that Alex would confide in Juanita. And Alex was one of the few people who knew that they had put pressure on her to take second seat in the Claymore defense.

Wednesday, 19 August 2009 – 13.35

Alex had been surprised to get back to the office from a deli downstairs to find it empty and a note on his desk saying: 'Taken a long lunch break to have a chat with Andi.' But he knew better than to make a big deal of it. Juanita was too useful an asset to reprimand. And if she thought it was more important to have a heart-to-heart with Andi than to answer the switchboard then he wasn't going to argue.

He realized that Juanita was better attuned to women's issues than he, and he assumed it was something important. He was well aware that Andi still felt uncomfortable about working for the defense in this case.

And today's events had been particularly traumatic. It was obvious why Juanita might have felt the need to take her to lunch and encourage her to get it off her chest. The important thing was that the case was going surprisingly well, and that was due – in no small measure – to Andi. She had seriously undermined Bethel Newton's testimony without seeming like a bully. Yes, she had reduced the girl to tears. But the tears came only when it was revealed that Bethel had made a rape accusation in the past and then withdrawn it. That was not something that would sit well with the jury. And they would have serious doubts about her claims now.

He noticed that the switchboard message light was flashing – there was one message waiting. He pressed the button to retrieve it.

'Hallo, this is a message for Alex Sedaka. My name is Jerry Cole. I'm calling from Ventura County. I worked in the lab where the samples from the Claymore case were processed. I have some very interesting information about the lab and how those guys operate. Please call me on . . .'

Alex scrambled to grab a pen and write down the number.

Wednesday, 19 August 2009 – 13.45

'Andi? Earth to Andi.'

'Oh. I'm sorry.'

Her embarrassment was palpable.

'Where were you?'

'I'm sorry.' Even now, back in the real world, Andi seemed confused, reluctant to talk. 'Sometimes when I'm thinking about a problem I immerse myself in it so completely, the world could end and I wouldn't notice.'

Juanita brushed it off.

'The thing that puzzles me is how could anyone fiddle the jury software in such a way as to exclude blacks? I mean, the data on the voting register and driver's license records wouldn't include any reference to race – at least not the data that's fed to the court administration for jury selection purposes.'

'I don't understand either. But if I'm right then they must have found *some* way. Maybe they rigged it to screen out certain selected names?'

'Like what?' asked Juanita, almost laughing. 'Jackson? Washington?'

'Or maybe first names.'

Juanita's smile widened. 'LaToyah? Denzel?'

'Okay! Okay! I get the point.'

'Look, I'm sorry. I'm not trying to make fun of you. But that's one explanation that's not going to fly.'

'Well, maybe they rigged the software to screen out names from street addresses with large numbers of people with the same surname. In other words, big families.'

'That would screen out a lot of Roman Catholics. Oh yes, and a lot of Mormons!'

They both burst out into girlish giggles at the absurdity of it. As they fell about laughing, Juanita put a gentle hand on the back of Andi's hand – a brief moment of intimacy, camouflaged as friendship.

'There's something I've been wanting to ask you, Andi. Are you still uncomfortable working on this case?'

Juanita realized that she had allowed a note of seriousness to intrude into her tone. But she sensed that Andi would be grateful for the chance to get her worries off her chest. She knew about Andi's dilemma over Gene and the rape crisis center. But she wanted to know how Andi felt about it now. Was she comfortable about what she was doing herself – regardless of what her lover thought about it?

Andi hesitated for a few seconds before answering. 'I don't know why defending a person has to be based on attacking the victim. I mean, sometimes you've got no alternative, but why can't it be done gently?'

'How do you assassinate a witness's character gently?'

Andi thought about this, realizing that she was thinking with her heart and not her head. 'Well, I tried to with Bethel Newton. I tried to focus on the possibility that she made a mistake. But I was also obliged to use the dirt we dug about her previous rape accusation. If I hadn't, Claymore might have been convicted, but then he'd've got it overturned on the grounds of inadequate legal representation. That would have hurt Alex too – and Levine and Webster.'

'That's the way it works, Andi. That's the adversarial system. They put up *their* strongest case and we put up *ours*.'

'And for that we have to put the victim on trial.'

'That's the way of the world, Andi – the legal world at any rate.'

'And what if you don't find any dirt?'

'We can usually find something using the hundred to ten approach.'

'Hundred to ten?' Andi echoed.

'Well, you know, even a living saint has *some* enemies. And enemies means people who are ready to speak ill of that person. The idea is that if you talk to *enough* people who knew the victim, sooner or later you'll find someone who's ready to give you some dirt to throw at them. In fact you can usually find several people. Then you call as many of them to the witness stand as you can and turn the jury against the victim.'

'But why is it called the hundred to ten approach?'

'It's based on the theory that for every hundred people who knew the victim, about ten are ready to say something mildly negative about the victim, four or five are ready to say something very negative and two or three are ready to say something *extremely* negative. Then you use as many of these as the judge lets you get away with.'

Andi thought about this. 'I suspect that if the victim was Alex you'd probably only have to speak to a handful of people to get the dirt you needed.'

They broke into giggles again.

'We're here,' said Juanita, still laughing, as the car pulled up at the white stone building.

189

Wednesday, 19 August 2009 – 15.15

'It's going to be quite tricky without the source code.'

They were in David Sedaka's office at the Berkeley Center for Theoretical Physics in the renovated LeConte Hall. The room was surprisingly large and flooded with light from an enormous window at one end. David was sitting on a high-backed blue chair inside a huge wraparound cherrywood desk while Juanita and Andi – on similar chairs – sat facing him. It was the only part of the desk that wasn't cluttered with papers, and that was only because David had stacked them all up and moved them to the other side of the table to give them space.

'But you can decompile it at least,' said Andi.

'Oh, sure. But without the original source code, I have nothing to compare it to for errors. And no explanatory documentation. All I can do is try to figure out how it works. I hope I can finish before I fly out to Switzerland.'

David was due to visit the Large Hadron Collider, where his theory that anti-matter could decay into photons without colliding with matter, was going to be tested.

'I guess the first thing to look out for is lack of randomness,' said Andi. 'Anything that interferes with the randomness of the selection, whether it has anything to do with African-Americans or not. I mean the glitch in Grand Rapids wasn't about race per se, it was about zip codes.'

'I'll look for that and for anything that might interfere with referencing the database. Ideally we'd have a copy of the database itself. Maybe that's where the problem lies.'

Computer programming, as such, wasn't his field. But like many physicists, he had some programming skills, along with his mathematical background and training. Also, he had a network of contacts on whom to call for assistance.

'We've got a hearing to get the source code on Friday. The software company'll fight it vigorously and if they lose, they'll appeal. So anything you can get from the executable will help. We might get the source code, but *when* is anyone's guess.'

Andi noted – for all it mattered to her – that he was quite good-looking, even at only five feet six and with boxy, TV-screen glasses and his unruly black hair.

'I'll decompile it right away, but I don't expect to have time to look at it before the weekend.'

'Whatever help you can give us,' said Andi, 'I'll appreciate.'

Thursday, 20 August 2009 – 10.10

The prosecution's first witness on Thursday was Dr Elaine Weiner, the doctor at the sex crimes and domestic violence unit who had examined Bethel. She was in her late twenties, but she exuded an air of confidence, like someone who had testified in court before and wasn't intimidated by it. Of course, the real test would come when she faced cross-examination. But she showed no sign of nervousness. Quite the contrary, she gave Alex a brief, challenging eye contact that almost seemed to suggest that she was looking forward to crossing swords with him.

The first questions that Sarah Jensen put to Dr Weiner, established her qualifications, occupation and the fact that she was on duty on the sex crimes and domestic violence unit that night. Then the questioning turned to the facts of the case.

'And could you describe the events that occurred at ten-fifteen of that morning?'

'Well, at about that time, a girl whom I now know to be Bethel Newton was brought in by Detective Bridget Riley.'

'Can you describe her appearance?'

'She was bruised and shaken and visibly distressed. Her clothes were in disarray.'

'And what did you do?'

They were using a digital evidence system, in which the judge, jury and lawyers looked at the images on computer monitors in front of them.

'I took her to the rape suite for a physical checkup and to collect evidence samples. Once at the suite, I had pictures taken showing external bruising to the alleged victim and conducted a forensic medical examination with a view to establishing the cause of her condition and to gather any potential evidence. Specifically, I took clippings from her fingernails and vaginal swabs for future DNA analysis. I placed these in the appropriate containers, sealed them and marked them for chain of custody. I then handed them over to Detective Riley.'

Sarah Jensen pressed the button that showed the pictures on the court screens.

'And can you confirm that these are pictures of Miss Newton on the day in question?'

'Yes, I can.'

The pictures showed bruising around her wrists consistent with restraint by a strong hand.

Sarah Jensen pressed the button to move on to the next image, which showed the evidence bags bearing Dr Weiner's signature. The doctor was asked to confirm the authenticity of the signature, which she duly did. Later Sarah Jensen would ask the lab staff who had conducted the DNA tests to identify those same markings against the lab's record log to confirm that this was the same evidence.

At the end of this direct examination, Sarah Jensen said, 'Your witness,' to Alex and sat down.

The prosecutor expected some pyrotechnics on cross-examination, but Alex surprised her and the doctor by rising just long enough to say, 'No questions.'

The judge announced a twenty-minute recess.

'How come you didn't challenge her over the editorializing about Bethel's state of mind?'

'The jury already heard it. And it wouldn't make sense. Our defense is mistaken identity. Why shouldn't she be visibly distressed?'

Andi shrugged.

In the press section, Martine left to do her report. She didn't notice that a young black man in the spectators' section was following her – just as he had yesterday.

Thursday, 20 August 2009 – 11.05

'So, do you think it'll help?' asked Alex. 'Or is it a complete waste of time?'

Alex had decided to phone David during the recess to find out how he was doing with the jury selection software.

'Like I told Andi, it might. But it'll be a lot easier if we can get the original source code.'

David Sedaka was in his office poring over a huge printout.

'But I thought you said you could convert the finished program back into its original source code.'

'Yes, but the idea is to compare one to the other – what it is to what it *should* be, if you see what I mean.'

'We have a hearing on Friday to try and get it. But I can't be sure we'll succeed. Can't you just break it down into sections or something and work it out that way?'

'Not from the machine code alone, no. That's why I need the source code.'

'Okay, well, we'll do our best. Gotta go now. They're going back into court now.'

Thursday, 20 August 2009 – 11.10

'The morning session of the trial got off to an uneventful start today, with police doctor Elaine Weiner testifying about her initial examination of Bethel Newton.'

While Alex was talking to his son, Martine Yin was delivering her report facing Lake Merritt on the grass triangle between 12th and 14th Street in front of the main entrance to the Alameda County Courthouse. To her left and right were other news vans, and journalists from other stations doing their reports.

'Though some observers expected experienced criminal attorney Alex Sedaka to conduct a probing cross-examination, testing Dr Weiner on her recollections of the events, especially after the withering questioning faced by alleged victim Bethel Newton yesterday, Sedaka chose instead to waive cross-examination altogether.'

The white stone façade of the majestic court building provided the backdrop as she continued to outline the events that had occurred in the courtroom minutes before. Her report would be accompanied by pictures by the press artist that had been scanned in the broadcast truck and transmitted to the TV station.

'It is not clear if this marks a change in his courtroom

strategy or simply a recognition that some evidence stands on too solid ground to be worth challenging.'

The young man who had followed her yesterday was watching nonchalantly, from the corner of Fallon and 12th Street.

'It should be stressed that at no stage did Dr Weiner's testimony directly implicate the defendant, Elias Claymore. But it was used by the prosecution to establish chain of custody over the DNA evidence which is to be presented later today.

'Martine Yin, *Eyewitness News*, Alameda County Court-house.'

She smiled at the lanky cameraman, but noticed that he was looking unhappy.

'We had some cloud cover bang in the middle there. It may have screwed up the lighting. Do you think we can do the bit about waiving cross-examination again?'

'We haven't got time. They're going to start again, any minute.'

'Okay, in that case we'll get a bite to eat and get back here for the lunchtime adjournment.'

And with that the cameraman and soundman got into the van and drove off. Martine decided to walk across the grass to get back to the court building. However, even though she was wearing practical shoes, all it took was one misstep and she lost her balance. She fell rather awkwardly on her side, taking a hit on her left arm. To their credit, the other news crews didn't laugh or even smile. They just looked away with embarrassed smirks on their faces. Martine sensed their reactions and felt a stab of anger, or at least irritation. But she took a deep breath and rose above it.

She looked at her left sleeve. There was no mistaking it: the mud was visible on the blue, and wiping it would make no difference. She could do the report in her blouse and

200

snooker waistcoat. But then she looked at her matching blue skirt and saw that it too had traces of mud.

She looked at her watch again. She still had seven or eight minutes – and they never returned from the recess bang on the dot. She knew that if she walked briskly, she could get to her car, freshen up, change clothes and still be back in the court before they got to the substantive questions. They always started off with preliminary questions to establish the expert's credentials and she knew that this time would be no different.

So she set off down 12th Street for the parking structure, two blocks away, unaware of the man who was walking a few yards ahead of her.

Thursday, 20 August 2009 – 11.20

'All rise!' said a bailiff as the judge returned. When the judge was seated, the others followed suit.

Alex was tense when the court reconvened after the short recess. He knew that they were now about to hear the crucial make-or-break portion of the prosecution's evidence.

'Are you ready to proceed, Ms Jensen?' asked the judge.

'Yes, Your Honor,' said the prosecutor. 'My next witness is Dr Victor Alvarez.'

A bailiff opened the doors to the witness anteroom and said: 'Call Victor Alvarez!'

Victor Alvarez, a man in his sixties with an air of the academic about him, entered the courtroom. He was in fact the technical leader of the DNA section of the Ventura crime lab and had done the DNA analysis himself because this was such a high-profile case. He was sworn in and then asked a few preliminary questions to establish his qualifications and the fact that he worked at the lab where the DNA profiling was done. This was followed up by a detailed explanation of what DNA is, using the court's DOAR Digital Evidence Presentation System to illustrate his testimony with a series of diagrams and pictures.

He explained that DNA is made up of four so-called

'bases,' referred to by the letters A, C, G and T, and that these bases formed pairs, but only in very specific ways.

'A always pairs with T,' he explained, 'and C can only pair with G.'

When he fell silent from this preliminary explanation, Sarah Jensen was ready to move on. 'Now could you explain how you use this to identify the source of the DNA?'

'There are certain sequences of DNA that vary a lot from one person to another. It is these sequences that we use for DNA analysis in criminal detection.'

'And how do you do this?'

'We look for something called Short Tandem Repeats, or STR for short. These are short sequences of DNA, normally of length two to five bases, that are repeated several times in a row at particular locations or loci. For example a sequence like—'

He clicked to show the next chart. It showed a sequence of letters:

G-A-T-A- G-A-T-A- G-A-T-A- G-A-T-A- G-A-T-A-G-A-T-A

'That's a sequence at a location known as D7S280. It shows six *repeats* of the sequence G-A-T-A. Such a sequence is called an allele. At each location you have a pair of alleles which might be either the same or different. So a person might have the sequence six times in one allele and eight times in the other. Or they might have identical sequences in both alleles.'

'And how does this help identify the person?'

'Well, different people have different numbers of repetitions. In this particular case it can vary between six and fifteen repetitions.'

'But between six and fifteen means only ten possibilities?'

'Yes indeed.'

'So there must be lots of people who match that particular sequence?'

'Yes indeed. But we don't look at just that one sequence. We look at thirteen *different* sequences. For any *one* sequence, many people may have the same number of repetitions. But once you start looking at all thirteen different sequences at different locations, then the likelihood of two people having the same number of repetitions as each other in each of the various sequences is extremely small.'

'So, to make that clear, you're saying that you can narrow the DNA down to one person?' Sarah summed up.

'Exactly,' Alvaraz nodded.

Thursday, 20 August 2009 – 11.30

Martine took the elevator to the fourth level of the parking structure feeling tense and flustered at the amount of time it had taken her to get there. She knew that the trial would have already started, but there was nothing she could do. She just hoped that she could get one of the stringers from the print press to fill her in on anything that she had missed.

There was nothing unusual as the elevator doors opened and she walked over towards her car. She pressed her combination on the remote key to unlock her car, ignoring the man moving things about on the passenger seat of his aquamarine Mercedes in the adjacent parking spot. At the back of her mind was the recollection that Elias Claymore's missing car – like the one used in the rape of Bethel Newton – was the same make and color. And this man was . . .

She dismissed the thought, opened the driver's door and slid into her car. She was just about to close the driver's door when the young man standing on the passenger side of the adjacent car lurched at her, shoving her hard into the passenger seat and slamming the door behind him. Before she could scream, he clamped an iron right hand over her mouth, his thumb under her jaw holding it shut. With his free left hand, he operated the mechanism to incline the chair back until it was almost horizontal. Then he started ripping at her clothes.

It was only at this stage that terror truly engulfed Martine. They were high up on the fourth level of the parking structure, so people were less likely to come here than to the lower levels and there was no chance anyone would hear her outside on the street. It was not the beginning or the end of lunchtime so this would not be a key time for people to arrive or leave. And this man was holding her down so that she couldn't be seen even if anybody did come. The man was strong and easily able to withstand her attempts at resistance.

Her skirt had been hitched up and her panties and pantyhose ripped off completely. Her attacker was now struggling with his own clothes and Martine could feel from the contact between them that he was already aroused physically as well as psychologically. The only thing she didn't know as she struggled was whether he intended to let her live when he was finished with her.

Thursday, 20 August 2009 – 11.40

'So Polymerase Chain Reaction is a method of increasing the amount of DNA available for testing?'

Sarah Jensen was continuing her direct examination of Victor Alvarez.

'That's right.'

'And how does it work?'

Alvarez pressed a button to show an animation to illustrate the process graphically.

'It involves heating and cooling the DNA in a special chamber called a thermal cycler, together with certain enzymes. This causes the DNA to split into separate strands and then each strand forms a new pair of strands in the same way as it does in the body, with the bases forming pairs like I said before.'

'And how many times do you do this?'

'It can be anything from twenty-eight cycles to thirty-four. Each cycle doubles the amount of DNA.'

'But once you've got enough DNA for testing, how do you distinguish between DNA from the victim and DNA from the perpetrator of the crime?'

'We start off by defining a threshold quantity. Anything that shows up in the test in a smaller quantity is simply ignored. Then we look at the relative quantities of what's left to identify what we call the "major contributor" and the "minor contributor." Next we compare the evidence sample to the victim's reference sample to determine if the victim is the major or the minor contributor. We do the same with the suspect's reference sample to see if the suspect matches the other contributor. If we find a sequence in the evidence sample that matches one found in the suspect's reference sample, then we call that an *inclusion*. The more inclusions we find, the more likely it is that the suspect is the source of that DNA. On the other hand, if we find even one sequence that can't be matched to the suspect and also doesn't come from the victim's part of the sample, then we would call that an *exclusion* and that would eliminate the suspect from the investigation.'

'Now you spoke about the major and the minor contributor. Does that mean that the DNA in the evidence sample is always a mixture?'

'Not always. We can isolate the DNA from sperm. We tried that in this case with DNA from a vaginal swab, but established that there *was no sperm* in the sample. We then compared the *non-sperm* DNA from another vaginal swab to the reference samples of both Bethel Newton and Elias Claymore but found that it contained only DNA from Bethel Newton and none from Mr Claymore *or anyone else*. This is consistent with the rapist using a condom.'

'So what did you do then?'

'We had to turn our attention to the nail clipping samples from when Miss Newton scratched the attacker.'

210

Thursday, 20 August 2009 – 11.45

Martine was gasping for breath now, struggling against the man's weight upon her. He had now unfastened his belt and pants and for a brief, fleeting moment he lifted his weight off her so that he could pull them down. It gave her the chance she needed. Quick as a flash, she twisted her body and pulled out the small pepper spray canister she always kept in her pocket. She knew, from her limited training, not to waste any time or effort trying to carefully position the canister. That would merely telegraph her intentions. She swung it close to his face, closed her eyes, held her breath, and let out a large burst of spray.

The man cried out in agony and anger, twisting away from her onto the driver's seat and rubbing his eyes. Martine herself was gasping and coughing from the back spray. She sat up to make it harder for him to resume his assault and at the same time grabbed his throat, digging her thumb hard into the soft tissue. He let out another cry of pain, but this time managed to deliver a vicious punch to the side of her face.

Dazed by the force of the punch, she recoiled, grabbing the handle of the front passenger door, tugging at it. But it wouldn't open. Then she remembered – it had a security lock. Fortunately, she knew where everything in the car was. She pressed a button under the dashboard and the passenger door was unlocked. On her second attempt she managed to open the door, but before she could push it wide enough to escape, the man grabbed her arm again. She let out a scream of 'Fire!' remembering the old rule that people were more likely to respond to the word 'fire' than 'help.'

He silenced her by placing his hand firmly over her mouth. But it was the same hand that he had used to grab her arm – his other hand was still rubbing his burning eyes. With her arms and hands free, she pushed the passenger door open wider with one hand while using her other – reinforced by a powerful biting action of her teeth – to remove his hand from her mouth. Again he cried out in pain and retracted his hand to suck on the wound.

Without waiting for him to make another move, she twisted away through the open door and ran out of the car continuing to scream, 'Fire!'

The man knew that there was nothing more he could do to her. He heard the sound of other people coming and realized that he was now in danger. He didn't know how many people were responding to Martine's cry, and whether they were security guards or just members of the public. But whoever they were, even if they couldn't stop him, they would still be witnesses who could identify him.

So he knew he had to flee as quickly as possible. He couldn't start her car as it was one of those modern high-tech ignition systems and he didn't have the key. She must have put it in her pocket when she reached for the pepper spray. So he leapt out and dived back into his own car via the passenger door, slamming it shut, sliding across the seat and starting the engine as quickly as possible. By the time he had got the engine started there were two security guards charging towards the vehicle, apparently more concerned with stopping him than with helping Martine.

But he knew that even if they were armed, they wouldn't shoot. They might have grounds to detain him, but they sure as hell didn't have grounds to shoot him. Not in this State. They didn't know it was an attempted rape. For all they knew it could have been a falling out between a pair of lovers or an argument over a parking space. And the word she had shouted that had brought them running was not 'rape' but 'fire' – hardly grounds to shoot a man.

They tried to run into his path, but he just kept going, sending them spinning out of the way as they dived for cover.

He permitted himself a brief chuckle as he thought about their pathetic and futile effort to stop him. And now he was screeching his way down a series of ramps to get to the exit of the parking structure. A couple of times other cars came perilously close to crossing his path. But the ferocity with which he was driving forced them to hold back or swerve out of the way. So it took him only a minute to get to the exit on 13th Street.

But when he got there, in his desperation to escape, he forgot the most basic rule of driving: to look. And a second later, a speeding police car that was answering the call from the security guards, slammed into the left side of the aqua-marine Mercedes, sending him reeling.

Thursday, 20 August 2009 – 11.50

'The problem with nail clipping samples in cases where the victim scratches the attacker,' said Alvarez, 'is that you normally find a large amount of DNA from the victim and only a small amount from the assailant.'

'And can this be resolved by the method you described earlier? Identifying the major and the minor contributor?'

At the defense table, Alex had noticed that Martine wasn't sitting in the press section. He was idly curious about why but continued to concentrate on the Alvarez testimony.

'Unfortunately that is often impossible, because the sheer volume of DNA from the victim dwarfs the amount of DNA from the perpetrator. And if you try to get round this by setting the detection equipment at a highly sensitive level, you end up with a lot of background "noise" as we call it.'

'So how do you solve the problem?'

'We look at something called Y-STR. That means the DNA from the Y chromosome. You see in the human genome we have twenty-three pairs of genes. One of these is either an XX pair or an XY pair, the double X if it's a woman and the XY if it's a man. The Y chromosome is unique to the man. We look at a set of seventeen carefully selected markers on the Y chromosome looking for tandem repeats of between two and five sequences.'

He clicked the button and showed an illustration of a strand of Y chromosomal DNA with arrows pointing to various marked sections.

'And how do you determine how many STRs there are at these various loci?'

'We start by cutting the DNA using a similar technique to that used for ordinary autosomal DNA.'

'When you say cut, you mean like with a pair of scissors?'

'In a way, yes. It's sort of like chemical scissors.' This was the cue to go on to the next animation on the screen. 'The DNA is placed in solution with certain enzymes that cut the DNA at particular points just before and after the sequences we're looking for. We then wash away the rest of the DNA with chemical solutions.'

The animation showed this in time with Alvarez's words. He noted the smiles on the jurors' faces as they took in this explanation.

'Ok,' said Sarah, 'that shows how you cut the DNA into the right fragments. But how do you actually find out *which* sequences are there in the mixture?'

'First of all bear in mind that the more repetitions in the sequence, the *heavier* the fragment. And the heavier the fragment, the *slower* it moves.'

'And how does this help?'

Alvarez pressed a button to show the next animation.

'We add a mixture of various different colored dyes to the DNA mixture. The different colored dyes attach themselves to different fragments. This enables us to distinguish between the fragments later. Then we put the fragments into one end of a thin metal tube, and pass an electric current through it. This makes the DNA fragments move through the tube. But the thing is, the *lighter* fragments move quickly and the heavier ones move slowly. As these fragments arrive at the other end of the tube, we use a laser to determine both the *order* in which they come out and the *quantities* of those different fragments.

'Now let's review what this means. The *time* when the fragments emerge tells us the *length* of the fragment, with the lighter or shorter, fragments coming out first and the heavier, i.e. longer, fragments coming out last. The *color* of the light tells us which fragment it is, that is what *location on the DNA sequence* it comes from. Finally, the *brightness* or *intensity* of the light tells us *how much* of that fragment is present; in other words, it tells us the *quantity*. We then get the computer to print out a report showing the length of the sequences at each of the marker locations. It doesn't tell us the quantity, but ignores anything below the pre-set quantity threshold.'

Sarah now assumed control of the presentation system and pressed a button. A report appeared on the screen.

'And is this your report in this case?'

'Yes.'

It was the first page of the report, stating that the suspect, Elias Claymore, could not be eliminated as a suspect. Sarah pressed another button.

'And this is the second page?'

'Yes.'

The second page showed the breakdown of the different fragment lengths at the different locations on the crime scene samples and the equivalent for the suspect.

	DYS 19	DYS 385a	DYS 385b	DYS 389 I	DYS 389 II	DYS 390	DYS 391	DYS 392	DYS 393	DYS 438	DYS 439	DYS 437	DYS 448	DYS 456	DYS 458	DYS 635	Y-GATA -H4
Newton Finger nail (Index finger)	4	5	2	4	5	3	2	5	2	2	2	5	5	4	3	5	2
Ref, Elias Claymore	4	5	2	4	5	3	2	5	2	2	2	5	5	4	3	5	2

'I see from this table that the quantities for the suspect and crime scene sample are identical. What does this tell us?'

'It tells us that there were no exclusions. This means that the suspect could not be eliminated as a possible source of the DNA in this sample from the victim's fingernails.'

An eerie silence hung over the courtroom before the prosecutor spoke again.

'And were you able to establish the probability of a randomly selected male matching this particular DNA profile?'

'Yes. In the general population as a whole, this profile or "haplotype" as we call it, is likely to occur in one in every four thousand males.'

'Your witness,' said Sarah Jensen, turning to the defense table.

But as Alex was about to rise, the judge spoke. 'We'll take a fifteen-minute recess.'

Thursday, 20 August 2009 – 11.55

'Will he live?' asked the driver of the police car as the gurney was raised into the ambulance outside the parking structure.

'Oh yeah,' said the ambulance attendant. 'It's not life threatening.'

'Pity.'

There was a certain amount of macho posturing in this interjection. The cop was not, in fact, as hard as he was trying to sound. He was a rookie and had never killed a man before. Even the sight of Martine couldn't make him wish that the man was dead.

'It'll be okay,' said his partner.

The rookie backed off as the ambulance crew closed the doors and drove off.

Martine was being treated in situ by a second ambulance crew. Another squad car had been summoned and a victim chaperone was taking her preliminary statement.

'So, what do we know?' asked the rookie.

'Name's Manning, Louis Manning. Has a string of priors for possession and dealing.'

'Anything for rape or indecent assault?'

'No. Just dope.'

'I guess that's gonna change now.'

'Uh huh. He cornered her as she was getting into her car. She's a reporter on the Claymore case, you know.'

'No shit.'

'That her car?'

'No, his. Hers is up on level four. She was getting into her car when he jumped her.'

'Didn't she see him approaching?'

'His car was right next to hers.'

'Sounds like a setup.'

'Probably was.'

'She okay?'

'Think so. She maced him in the face so she must be pretty tough.'

The rookie looked at the Mercedes.

'You say he was a dealer?'

'That's what his rap sheet says.'

'He must've been making some serious dough.'

'Oh yeah, that's another thing. She said that one thing that caught her attention just before he jumped her was his car, because it matched the description of the one in the case she's covering.'

'What, the Claymore rape case?'

'Yeah.'

'Well, maybe we should check it out.'

'I was planning to.'

The older cop put in a call on his radio. About twenty seconds later the dispatcher replied.

'Those license plates come from a 1993 Pontiac Firebird licensed to one Louis Manning in New Mexico.'

'Okay, thanks,' said the older cop. He looked over at his partner to make sure that had heard it.

'So he used his old plates,' said the rookie.

'Looks like it.'

'But he didn't transfer the registration.'

'He must've stolen the Merc to replace his aging Pontiac.'

'We'd better check the VIN to see who it belongs to.'

They walked over to the car as it was being hitched to the tow truck.

'We need to check it out,' said the rookie.

The tow truck team stood back while the rookie and his partner opened the driver's door and looked for the plate on the dashboard with the serial number. The rookie spoke into his radio.

'We need a name check on Vehicle Identification Number 4DB-NG-7-zero-JX-9K-234-299.'

The dispatcher came back even more quickly on this one.

'That vehicle is registered with the California DMV as a Mercedes belonging to Elias Claymore.'

'Okay, thank you,' said the rookie, letting out a whoop of delight.

Thursday, 20 August 2009 – 12.10

Martine was in the rape suite at the police station in the Frank H. Ogawa Plaza. Unlike Bethel Newton, they hadn't taken any vaginal or oral swabs or even nail clippings. But they had taken photographs of her injuries and tapings from her clothes to show fiber matches with Louis Manning's clothes.

The victim chaperone dealing with her had told her not to be surprised if Manning tried to use a consent defense, but pointed out that her injuries would be corroborative of her version of events. There seemed to be a sense of gloom however, as if to make her aware of the fact that she could expect her reputation to be attacked by the defense lawyers as a matter of course.

That reminded her about one very particular defense lawyer whom she wanted to call. She checked if it was okay and whipped out her cell phone to put in a call to Alex. She was expecting to get his message box, because he was in court, but was surprised when he answered in person.

'Martine. Where are you?'

'I'm at the police station up at the Ogawa Plaza.'

'Why, what's happening there?'

'I was attacked.'

'What?'

'Someone tried to rape me.'

'Holy shit! Who?'

'I don't know his name. I got him with pepper spray and the cops busted him.'

'Are you all right?'

'A bit shaken, but everything intact.'

'Thank God.'

'Anyway, I just wanted to let you know. I'm okay. Don't worry.'

'I'm coming round there.'

'No need. I'll probably be through here in half an hour or so.'

'I'll ask for an adjournment.'

'There's no *need*.'

'But I *want* to.'

She gritted her teeth, but felt a tinge of amusement at Alex's reaction.

'Did anyone ever tell you, you're very stubborn?'

'Only my mother.'

Martine couldn't help but smile.

'Okay, you do whatever you must. Like I said, I'll be here for at least the next half hour.'

Thursday, 20 August 2009 – 12.15

'Let me see if I've understood this, Mr Sedaka. You want me to grant your request for an adjournment, so you can visit your girlfriend a few blocks away?'

Justice Wagner's tone was condescending rather than indignant. But Alex was left in no doubt as to how she felt about what he realized might seem like a frivolous request.

'She's not my girlfriend, Your Honor, just a professional friend. And she's pretty badly shaken up.'

'But you said yourself that this was only an attempted rape and she hasn't even been hospitalized.'

'Yes, but she must be in shock. It'll probably hit her later.'

'And when it does, you can comfort her – this *evening*. But right now, we have a case to try.'

'Your Honor, if I'm forced to conduct my cross-examination while I'm thinking about this, it might affect my performance.'

'I hope you're not going to try and make your client pay for your concern about your girlfriend – sorry, your "professional" friend.'

'I'm not saying I'll do anything less than my best. But my concern for Miss Yin is genuine and may affect my performance. And even if it doesn't, my client might claim that it did.

He might claim incompetent representation by counsel and use it as grounds for appeal.'

'Which would hurt your reputation.'

'And threaten to undermine the verdict.'

Sarah Jensen stepped in. 'Why can't Ms Phoenix conduct the cross-examination?'

All eyes turned back to Alex.

'This is a very complex area of law and science, Your Honor, and my co-counsel may not be sufficiently well-versed in this area to—'

'Come off it, Mr Sedaka. Ms Phoenix is an experienced trial attorney. She has been a prosecutor in New York City as well as defense counsel. Unlike you she's worked the criminal courts from both sides and she's more than capable of conducting a rigorous and thorough cross-examination of the witness.'

Alex found himself almost stuttering. 'Well . . . I don't know. I mean my client might not agree to it.'

'Oh really?' sneered the judge. 'A minute ago you were saying that your client wouldn't want *you* to cross-examine because you were in emotional turmoil over what's happened to your— to Miss Yin. Now you're saying he desperately wants you.'

For once, Alex was lost for words.

'May I confer with my client, Your Honor?'

'Please do.'

Alex went over to Claymore and told him what had happened, prefixing his remarks by telling Claymore not to show any reaction on his face – an instruction with which Elias Claymore proved singularly incapable of complying.

'I don't want her doing it,' he replied vociferously. 'I want *you* to cross-examine.'

'But why? She's a very good lawyer – and in some ways it'll look better in the eyes of the jury if she does it.'

'She doesn't understand the DNA science as well as you do. She's too wrapped up in this computer business.'

'She can use my notes. It's all there.'

'I don't want it. Look, you pushed me into accepting her as second seat. And she did a good job on the Newton girl. But for this job, I don't think she's up to it. I'm the client and I ain't taking any chances. I want *you* to cross-examine Alvarez.'

Alex could see from the look in Claymore's eyes that he wasn't going to give way. But he also noticed something else. Claymore was afraid – it was the DNA that frightened him more than anything else.

Seconds later, Alex was back at the judge's bench.

'My client doesn't agree, Your Honor. I'll do the cross. But may I at least be excused after that?'

'Okay, we'll adjourn for lunch when you've finished and cancel the afternoon session.'

'Thank you, Your Honor.'

On the way back to the defense table, Alex said, 'I don't want Elias to hear this, but don't be surprised if I race through the cross.'

'I understand,' Andi replied.

Seconds later, Andi and Sarah Jensen were seated at their respective tables. Alex remained standing.

'Proceed, Mr Sedaka.'

'Thank you, Your Honor.' He looked down at his notes, flicking through several pages, and then looked up to meet the eyes of Victor Alvarez.

'Dr Alvarez, you told us in direct examination that the test you carried out looked at seventeen markers on the Y chromosome. Is that correct?'

'Yes.'

'But is it not a fact that the generally accepted profile for Y-STR uses only the first eleven of those markers?'

'There are four commercial Y-STR kits available for anything from ten to seventeen markers. But the seventeen-marker test has attained the status of general acceptance.'

'Is it not a fact, however, that many of those persons actually in the reference database are profiled with only ten or eleven markers, so that six or seven markers of the seventeen are in fact extraneous and cannot be compared either negatively or positively?'

Alvarez nodded.

'Yes, that's true. But in such cases, the markers are simply ignored. So it doesn't affect the final result one way or the other.'

'But it does mean, does it not, that the result is based on less data than the seventeen markers would seem to imply.'

'Yes, but you have to remember that the markers are not independent anyway, so the result isn't really dependent on the number of markers as such.'

Alex had to suppress a smile as Alvarez walked into this. Although it would have come out eventually, regardless, the way in which it was coming out would make it look all the more strongly in favor of the defense.

'What do you mean, "the markers are not independent"?'

'I mean that the Y-STR markers, unlike regular DNA, are not independent of one another. That is they're not randomly inherited from one or another parent, like regular DNA. Instead the Y chromosome's DNA is inherited entirely from one's father. That's why the probability of a chance match isn't as low as with regular DNA. That's also why we can't estimate the probabilities by multiplying the probabilities of the individual sequences. Instead we use a counting method, looking at how many times the profile occurs in a database used for reference.'

'So if Y-STR DNA is passed on intact from fathers to all

their sons, who in turn pass it on to theirs, you're bound to have *many cases of the same haplotype in the general population*?'

'Yes,' Alvarez replied, squirming a little.

'And is it not *also* a fact that Y-STR haplotypes are more common in some ethnic groups than in others?'

'Yes.'

'So in other words, even if the probability of this particular haplotype in the population as a whole is 1 in 4,000, it's somewhat more common in the African-American population.'

'Yes.'

'What is that probability?'

'About 0.2 of one per cent.'

He put it this way to make it still seem rare. But Alex had other ideas.

'So you're saying that *one African-American man in five hundred* has this *same* haplotype profile?'

'Yes, if you care to put it that way.'

Alex most certainly *did* care to put it that way. Alvarez was desperately trying to take the sting out of this point. But Alex was not going to let up.

'Well let's try it another way then. *How many* African-American males in the United States would you expect to match this profile?'

Alvarez looked uncomfortable and appeared to be thinking about how to phrase his answer.

'About 37,000.'

The spectators gasped. The jury, to their credit, held their breath silently, although some did lean forward keenly. Alex knew that he had them.

'Let me be clear that I've understood this correctly. You are telling this jury that from a *scientific* point of view any one of those *37,000 African-Americans could have been the source of the DNA found in these nail clippings?'*

Alex had phrased the question cleverly. Of course, Alvarez could say that the real question should be what was the likelihood that a man who was identified by the victim, who had a prior record of interracial rape – a rape committed by someone driving a car that matched *his* car that he claimed had been stolen two days before the rape but hadn't bothered to report – was innocent. But it was not for him to say that. That was an argument for the prosecutor to make out in her closing. He was here not to present arguments but to answer questions. And he could only answer within the scope of his field, DNA science.

But Alex had asked *from a scientific point of view* and it was from a scientific point of view that Alvarez had to answer. He could try to embellish it or emphasize that his portion of the evidence was indeed only one small portion of the evidence. But the more he quibbled, the weaker and less significant and convincing his evidence would sound.

And his duty was to answer truthfully without taking sides.

'Yes,' said Alvarez finally, swallowing awkwardly.

Thursday, 20 August 2009 – 12.50

'I'm okay, I'm okay,' Martine squealed as Alex practically crushed the life out her.

'I was so worried about you.'

'I'm okay,' she said, looking at him with amusement, tinged with embarrassment.

He well knew why. He was making a fool of himself in front of other people. But he had lost a woman he loved, also in a surprise attack. And at the back of his mind was the thought that the same had so very nearly happened again. He didn't know how to handle this kind of trauma other than with an over-the-top show of affection.

The man had tried to rape her. But he might just as easily have killed her to silence her. That was why being here, holding Martine in his arms right now was more important than defending a thousand Elias Claymores, however innocent they might be and however worthy their cause.

'Alex . . .'

'Yes?'

'My . . . ribs.'

He released her apologetically.

They looked at each other in silence. Martine was the first to speak.

'Look . . . I just want to say I'm sorry about . . . that day in the restaurant . . . after the snooker tournament.'

'What do you mean?'

'I laid into you over you trying to be my knight in shining armor.' He was about to speak, but she held up her hand. 'No, let me say it. I still think it's a bit old-fashioned, you know. I mean, we're not living in the age of Errol Flynn – and not John Wayne either. But that's your nature. You're always going to want to be the Great Protector, because that's what you are. Even your work is that of the protector – the protector of the innocent and the falsely accused. And I can't fault you for that. That's what makes you the man I . . .'

She trailed off.

'This isn't going to work,' he said, almost regretfully.

A pained expression appeared in Martine's eyes. 'Our relationship?'

'Putting it on hold. It's not gonna work. We can't fight it.'

She looked at him for a few seconds, fighting back the tears. 'You can't pull out of Claymore's defense. He's counting on you. I'll ask the network to take me off the case.'

Thursday, 20 August 2009 – 13.05

'So we got the call about the 261A at the parking structure on the Jackson–13th Street intersection,' said the eager young rookie at the other end of the line. 'And we race there with the siren clearing the way. But as we get close, we see the road is clear, so we cut the siren and keep cruising. Then the perp just shoots out of the parking structure exit without looking and *wham* . . . we t-bone him.'

Detective Bridget Riley had been reluctant to hand over the case to one of her counterparts in Alameda County, but there was no way she could have gone up there to be with Bethel. She had too many other duties down in Ventura. So she was surprised when she got the message from the Oakland police after leaving her desk for ten minutes to get a hot pastrami on rye sandwich.

They said it was about the Bethel Newton rape and that it was urgent. Bridget thought at the time that they might need her after all – or maybe that there was some problem with the written reports. Whatever it was, she called back as soon as she got the message.

'How hard d'you hit him?'

'Hard enough to deploy our airbags.'

'What about his?'

'His front airbags opened but it didn't really save him 'cause it was a side impact. He wasn't even wearing a belt.'

'Well, he wouldn't if he was fleeing from an interrupted 261.'

'No, and he paid the price for it.'

The patrolman sounded almost happy.

'What happened to him?'

She was half expecting the patrolman to say he'd died.

'Broken collarbone, broken leg, concussion and whiplash.'

'You got him in custody?'

'They took him to ER and his leg's in traction. But we've got him under arrest and there's a pair of officers stationed there – one at his bedside and the other in the corridor.'

'I'm crying for him already,' said Bridget, taking a bite out of her sandwich. They'd put too much mustard on it again. 'Have you been able to question him?'

'Not yet. He's still heavily sedated. But get this: who do you think the victim was?'

'Of the 261A?'

'Uh huh.'

'Britney Spears?'

'Nah, come on . . . be serious.'

'I *am* serious. Who do you think I am, Uri Geller? How the fuck am I supposed to guess!'

'Okay. It was Martine Yin.'

'The news reporter?'

'Right.'

'Well, that's very interesting, but you're surely not suggesting that he picked her 'cause she was covering the Claymore trial?'

'Not in itself, no. Although that's a possibility to consider after what else we found out.'

Bridget was getting irritated with this young patrolman and his puerile games. 'And what *did* you find out?'

'Well, here's where it starts getting really interesting. We noticed that his car was a Merc.'

A chill went up Bridget's spine. 'What color?'

She already knew the answer before it came back over the phone line.

'A sort of dark blue. I think it's called aquamarine.'

'Please tell me you impounded it.'

'Well, obviously! And we've got a CSI team going over it even as we speak.'

'Thanks. Now the next thing you need to do is check the ownership.'

'That's actually what I'm calling you about.'

Something in the way the patrolman said this made Bridget realize that he was way ahead of her. It also made her realize that the bombshell was yet to come.

'Spill it.'

'We already checked the ownership. First, we checked the license plates and they belong to one Louis Manning.'

'Have you traced him?'

'No need. That was the name of the perp. We checked his driver's license and it's him all right.'

'Okay, so he also owns an aquamarine Merc and he tried to rape a reporter who's covering the Claymore trial.'

Bridget was no longer as excited as she had been a few seconds ago.

'Now, hold on a minute. I said the *plates* belonged to the perp. But they didn't belong to the car. They were New Mexico plates and they belonged to his old car – a Pontiac Firebird.'

'You should've checked the VIN.'

'What kind of a jerk do you take me for? Of *course* we checked the VIN.'

'And?' prompted Bridget, not daring to get her hopes up.

'It's registered to Elias Claymore.'

'Holy shit!'

Several other people in the open-plan office turned to look in the direction of Bridget's booth when she uttered this exclamation. Profanity wasn't exactly taboo in a police station, but it was rare for Bridget.

'Wait, it gets better! You see, I thought it was kind of a big coincidence, this guy having possession of Claymore's car and trying to rape a woman who just happens to be covering the Claymore trial. So I pulled the records on the Newton rape and guess what?'

'I already told you, I'm not into guessing. Just tell me what you got.'

'This perp, Louis Manning . . . he's the spittin' eye of the artist's impression of the man the Newton girl described.'

Bridget practically choked on her sandwich.

'But we've already got the man who raped Bethel Newton.'

'You mean you *think* you've got the man.'

'Do you know something I don't?'

'All I know is we're holding a man on an attempted rape charge who was driving Claymore's stolen car and who looks just like the original description of the rapist.'

'So did *Claymore* when he was younger,' said Bridget, realizing that she was rationalizing.

'So what should we do?' asked the rookie. 'I mean we can't just *ignore* what we've got. We have to check it out.'

'Have you taken a DNA sample from him?'

'Not yet. We're waiting for a warrant.'

'Why?'

'We weren't sure if we had probable cause.'

'Are you kidding? On a 261?'

'261A – it was only *attempted* rape.'

'That should still be enough to pass a Hayes test.'

'My captain didn't want to take any chances.'

'Okay, well as soon as you get it, take the sample and have the lab upload it to the California DNA database. Tell them to do a Y-STR comparison with the Bethel Newton rape evidence sample. In the meantime, I'll tell Sarah Jensen, the A.D.A on the case, what you've told me.'

'Okay. Just one thing?'

'Shoot.'

'What if you find something you don't like?'

The patrolman sounded genuinely concerned.

'I don't think we will. But we've got to cover all the bases 'cause if we don't, the defense certainly will.'

Thursday, 20 August 2009 – 13.30

Alex had lunch with Martine at the Slanted Door, the classy Vietnamese restaurant in the Ferry Building overlooking the Bay: a generous plate of Niman Ranch shaking beef with broken jasmine rice for him and grilled five-spice chicken with Massa Organics brown rice for her.

She had made it clear that she wasn't the delicate little flower that he seemed to think she was. She reminded him that she had fought off the attacker with pepper spray and it was Louis Manning who had fled in agony and was now in a hospital bed with a broken leg and collarbone.

But she had agreed to tell the network to take her off the Claymore case because of a conflict of interest. That meant that she and Alex were now free to start dating again. Alex even hinted that he wanted her to move in with him, but Martine made it clear that she valued her freedom too much for that. Alex understood. He also remembered her reaction the first time she visited the house in Elizabeth Street, when she saw Melody's strategically placed picture in several places. They had never discussed it, but he had made it clear that his late wife was still too important in his memory to remove the pictures and she had made it equally clear that she wasn't sure if she could compete with a ghost.

So they had let it stand, dating but not living together,

taking it one day at a time, faithful but not committed to each other. And now they were ready to resume where they had left off.

It was mid-afternoon when Alex returned to the office. Juanita was at her desk, reading a law book as part of her night-school course. She reacted, almost imperceptibly, to his entry, but didn't greet him. Alex sensed that something was up – it was almost as if she was deliberately ignoring him.

'Everything all right?' he asked.

'Yes. Andi has someone in there. Jerry Cole. You remember, you invited him over?'

'Jerry Cole? *Oh yes.* From the forensic lab in Ventura. I thought he was coming this evening, after work.'

'His flight arrived at two-thirty and he didn't have anything else to do. So he phoned in and I put him through to Andi. She got him to come by taxi and she's been talking to him for the last twenty minutes.'

They heard a door opening. It was the office that had recently been assigned to Andi.

'Alex, is that you?'

'Yes.'

'I've got Mr Cole with me.'

He noted the use of the respectful title and surname and sensed that their guest had a fragile ego.

'I'm just coming.'

Juanita signaled Alex over to her desk with a flip of her index finger. He leaned forward when she touched her lips conspiratorially.

'He takes his coffee weak, with plenty of milk.'

Juanita smiled and leaned back smugly, as if this was supposed to be telling Alex something. He had no doubt that it was, but couldn't for the life of him figure out what.

Seconds later he entered the room where Jerry Cole and Andi were standing. Andi ushered him in, while Cole hovered nervously by the chair opposite the desk from which he had just risen. Andi closed the door behind Alex who found himself facing a thin man of about forty with a stooped posture who kept rubbing his hands together in an almost obsequious manner.

'Alex, this is Jerry Cole. As you know, he works in the same lab as Victor Alvarez.'

'Please, sit down,' said Alex, pointing to the chair. Cole sat down, awkwardly, looking around as if another chair for Alex might materialize from nowhere if he just waited long enough.

To put him at ease about the fact that he was standing, Alex went and stood by the window, while Andi took her seat.

'Did you have a good flight?'

'Oh, er, yes.'

They had paid for his two-way flight and even for him to stay overnight and return the next day, so it wouldn't be so stressful, making the round trip in one day.

'Mr Cole,' said Andi, 'why don't you tell Mr Sedaka what you told me.'

Cole took a nervous breath and started speaking. 'First of all, I can tell you something about the conditions in the lab. We were hopelessly understaffed. That's why we have a huge backlog of cases and that means there are loads of samples waiting to be tested and scanned into the system.'

'And is that relevant to the Claymore case?' asked Alex. 'I mean are there samples sitting there that you think could clear my client?'

'I didn't personally see the tests being done on the Claymore or Newton samples but it's relevant in the sense that we work under so much pressure that it's very easy for mistakes to be made. Sometimes we had lab assistants with no college qualifications working virtually unsupervised.'

'And what sort of things can go wrong in practice? With DNA I mean?'

'Well the most obvious danger is cross-sample contamination.'

'How can that happen?'

'Well you know about Polymerase Chain Reaction to increase the evidence sample?'

'Yes.'

'And you know that if there's even the slightest contamination that gets into the sample *before* they put it into the thermal cycler then the contamination gets multiplied along with the evidence sample.'

Alex nodded. 'I believe it's called allele drop-in.'

Cole looked surprised. 'Oh you *know* about it.'

'Of course.'

Alex was getting irritated. He thought that this man would have some specific information that would help them. But all he had were the vague generalizations about DNA labs in general that they already knew.

'Well, the thing is, I remember they were very busy on the day the Claymore sample was tested. I know because the lab assistant who tested it seemed very nervous.'

Alex picked up on this. 'What was his name?'

'Steven, I think. Yes . . . Steven Johnson.'

'And do you have any idea what he was nervous about?'

'No, not really. I just noticed he was nervous. You have to remember it was busy for me too.'

'Do you also do DNA analysis?'

Cole appeared not to have heard the question, almost like he was in a trance.

'Mr Cole?'

'Oh sorry . . . no . . . no I didn't. I worked in the Forensic Alcohol Section. Sometimes I had to cover for someone in the Toxicology or Controlled Substance sections. But not DNA.'

Alex noticed the flicker in Andi's eyes. She had picked up on the past tense. Alex, of course, had already known this. Cole had told him. But he hadn't been so willing to say why and Alex wasn't ready to close in on that yet.

'Any particular reason for that?'

'No, it's just the way it was. We all had our jobs to do and different lab assistants worked in the different departments.'

Alex decided to plump for a wild guess, based on Jerry Cole's age.

'But weren't you the most senior of the lab assistants working there?'

Jerry smiled proudly. 'Yes, I was.'

'Then surely they should have let you work in the DNA section. I mean, let's face it, that must be the most important section there – certainly the most prestigious.'

'Yes but the head of the lab was against me because . . .'

He trailed off into embarrassed silence.

'Anyway, I didn't work in the DNA section.'

Alex realized that the time had come to probe the issue of the past tense.

'But you don't work there anymore? At the lab, I mean.'

There were two possibilities and both involved Cole being pushed rather than taking a walk of his own free will. The better scenario was that Cole knew too much and was sacked to silence and discredit him. The less attractive alternative was that he was sacked for some legitimate reason and was now looking for revenge. In fact it was more complicated than that because even if it was the former, the lab would probably claim the latter and if it was the latter, Jerry Cole would no doubt hide his shame behind the former.

'No, they fired me.'

'What for?'

'They said I made some mistake on a test batch. Normally, if you make a mistake like that, they send you for retraining. But in my case they decided to sack me.'

'But you *did* make a mistake, though,' Alex pressed on. 'I mean it's not like they made it up, surely?'

He left it to Andi to monitor Cole's face. Alex just wanted to *hear* Cole's reply.

'I don't know. I mean they say I did, but I have no way of knowing. It's not like they showed me the results in writing. They just told me I'd messed up, pointed out that I'd had one warning already and then gave me fifteen minutes to clear out my locker. They didn't even let me work out the day or the week or let me say goodbye to my friend.'

Alex picked up on the singular, but ignored it.

'Did you say you already had a warning?'

'Yes, I mean I did make a mistake before that with a live batch. It was just an accident, using a stale solution that I thought was fresh. But that just goes to prove what I said about working under pressure.'

'Did you say anything to anyone about Steven Johnson looking nervous?'

'Oh . . . er . . . no. I didn't even really think about . . .'

Alex realized that this precluded any possibility that they might have sacked him because he knew too much. Realizing this, Alex also realized that there was nothing more that they could get out of Jerry Cole – at any rate, nothing useful. Feeling only mildly sorry for the man and not wanting to waste any more of his valuable time, Alex looked at his watch.

246

'Yes, well, thank you very much, Mr Cole. You've been a great help.'

Cole got up awkwardly as Alex walked to the door and opened it.

'So when are you calling me?'

'We'll let you know,' said Alex, hustling Cole towards the door. Cole became slightly agitated at being forced to make such a rapid departure.

'Because I really want to testify,' said Cole, anxiously. 'I think I can make a difference.'

Alex was nodding towards the open doorway for him.

'Well, thank you again. And don't worry. We *will* let you know.'

Cole looked like he wanted to say more, but the implacable look on Alex's face warned him that he could only expect anger if he persisted. Alex gently but firmly hustled Cole out across the reception area and closed the door behind him. Then he turned back to Andi who was looking at him expectantly. He straightened his tie and took a deep breath, looking first at Andi and then Juanita.

'Are you gonna tell us what you're thinking, boss?' said Juanita with that taunting smile across her face.

'We can't use him.'

'You think he's a psycho?' Andi asked.

'Oh, no, he's legit. It's just that the prosecution will tear him to pieces. Trust me, Cole won't thank you for putting him through it and it wouldn't help Claymore in the least.'

Andi nodded at Alex's logic. 'I agree with you but I can't help thinking that what he said was actually true.'

'I'm *sure* it's true. Look, we know what it's like in forensic labs these days. Everything he said made perfect sense. But it's all just a collection of cheap generalizations. It'll take more

247

than sweeping statements to save our client – especially against a lioness like Sarah Jensen.'

'No, I don't mean that, Alex,' said Andi.

'Mean what?'

'About the generalizations. About the high-pressure atmosphere at the lab. I think he may have been onto something when he said that the technician who handled the crime sample looked nervous. I think he may have been telling the truth. I think he may well have seen something specific.'

'Oh come off it, Andi. You don't think they sacked him 'cause he saw too much? I made sure to cover that one – he said he never told anyone.'

'No, I'm not saying they sacked him for it. I'm sure they sacked him for a legitimate reason. I'm sure he was careless and they gave him a warning and he screwed up again and they decided that enough was enough. I accept all of that. It's just . . .'

'What?'

'It's just that I still think he may be right about the lab technician. Just because they sacked him for a legitimate reason doesn't mean he's lying when he says the technician was nervous. Cole may have seen it at the time and thought nothing of it – or at least not cared enough to do anything about it. But that doesn't mean he's lying . . . or even imagining it. I think he may have really seen it. And he's been thinking about it ever since they sacked him.'

'But what if he is right?' Juanita stepped in. 'How are we going to prove it when we haven't got a reliable witness to put up there on the stand?'

Andi thought about this for a few seconds. 'I think maybe we need to subpoena the worksheets from the lab's log book.'

Friday, 21 August 2009 – 10.20

The Friday morning session was taken up with legal arguments in the judge's chambers. It started off pretty well for the defense, when they filed a discovery motion for the log book worksheets from the Ventura forensic lab. Sarah Jensen responded that the prosecution didn't oppose the motion and even had a copy of relevant pages in her file already. The copy was handed to the clerk who made copies for the defense and judge and it was marked as an exhibit for future reference.

The truth of the matter was that it would have been hard to impossible for Sarah Jensen to oppose the motion. But in any case, she was grateful to the defense for stipulating to the chain of custody on the DNA, which spared the jury having to hear several boring witnesses and shortened the trial by maybe a day or two. So she flagged them through on this point, confident that there was nothing in the worksheets that they could use against the prosecution. She had been through the worksheets very carefully and it all looked routine. Everything was signed in and out. There were no gaps in the timing and no excessive handling of the evidence as far as she could see. The fact that the defense had waived the right to question the chain of custody witnesses, meant that they didn't expect to find anything in that regard. Still, she was curious as to their sudden interest in the worksheets.

However, after the agreement of the parties on the work-sheets, matters became somewhat acrimonious when a third party entered the picture.

That third party was LegalSoft, the software company that had created the jury selection software used by the Alameda County courts, as well as time-management software, also used by the courts.

'Your Honor, the source code to this software is clearly proprietary information and a trade secret,' argued Melvin Kenney, the lawyer for the company, a six foot five former Notre Dame fullback. 'Furthermore it is not covered by the California Public Records Act as it's private. And as to the fact that it is being used by the court, I would point out that the courts are also exempt from the CPRA. Accordingly my clients should *not* be forced to hand it over.'

Andi – who had been given the green light to argue the matter herself, because of her superior knowledge about such matters – pressed on with her arguments.

'Your Honor, counsel is attacking a straw man. Our motion has nothing to do with the CPRA. It's a subpoena motion for evidence relevant to the defense, pertaining to our client's Sixth Amendment rights. The court has already conceded that if the defense can establish that there has been intention-based interference with the ethnic composition of the jury then it would amount to a Sixth Amendment violation. We have been able to establish some fairly severe statistical discrepancies but the only way we can establish their *cause* is to analyze the software. As to the secrecy element, we will of course be bound to refrain from disclosing what we discover outside the confines of the courts and we accept that. So LegalSoft has nothing to fear in that regard.'

'Your Honor,' Kenney continued. 'This information could be prejudicial, as it could lead to law suits against LegalSoft

– and could have other severe consequences to the smooth operation of justice.'

He smiled smugly at this, prompting a look of anger from Justice Wagner. But she contained her anger. Kenney was hinting that if the defense found anything wrong with the software that could open the floodgates to appeals in criminal cases, leading to large numbers of convicted criminals – most of whom were probably guilty – being released onto the streets. In theory such people could be re-tried, but with the passage of time and fading witness memory – not to mention logistical problems – that would be unlikely in practice.

However, no judge could allow herself to be swayed by this argument. Ellen Wagner's decision had to be based on law and let the chips lie where they fall.

'Your Honor, if the software is defective, then it is right and proper that there *should* be lawsuits—' Andi began.

'But not right and proper that our client should be forced to incriminate itself,' Kenney interrupted

'It isn't incrimination if it's a civil matter.'

'But there *is* no automatic right to access to trade secrets to help in a lawsuit against a private company.'

'But we're not *trying* to start a lawsuit against anyone, Your Honor. Our aim is purely to protect our client's Sixth and Fourteenth Amendment rights.'

'But it could have that effect, Your Honor,' Kenney shot back, 'as a by-product of the defense's actions.'

'Your Honor, the rights of a company against the vague – at this stage, phantom – threat of a lawsuit must take second place to the rights of a defendant in a major felony case to a fair trial.'

Justice Wagner homed in on this. 'But you must admit that the same potential findings that could trigger concerns

251

about the fairness of the trial could also trigger likely lawsuits against the company.'

Andi thought about this for a moment. 'Actually the opposite is probably the case, Your Honor.'

'Would you care to elaborate on that, Ms Phoenix?' Ellen Wagner prompted.

'We don't think there actually *is* a problem with the source code. Our belief is that it is *not* the source code that is flawed but rather the executable program.'

'Then I don't understand why you need the source code at all. Why would it help?'

'Because, Your Honor, it can help to show discrepancies between what the executable program is doing and what it is *supposed* to be doing.'

'In what respect?'

'We think that the original software was problem free but that it has been tampered with so as to produce these anomalous results. In other words, the problem is in the *executable program*. But in order to prove that, we need to compare it to the original source code.'

'*If* there is any tampering, Your Honor, which counsel has yet to prove.'

'We've already established the statistical discrepancy that cries out for an explanation, not only in this case and not only in this county, but in quite a number. The defense submits that this is sufficient probable cause to give us a court order to obtain a copy of the source code.'

The judge looked over at Kenney to see if he had anything to add. He shook his head, having already made his position clear.

'I think I'm going to grant this order.'

Kenney's frustration was palpable. It was inevitable that he would file an appeal before the day was out. But in the meantime, Ellen Wagner was satisfied that she had done the right thing.

She turned to Andi. 'Do you want it in printed form or electronic?'

'Electronic is quite sufficient.'

'Okay, LegalSoft is ordered to provide the defense with a copy of the source code in electronic form by ten o'clock Tuesday morning.'

Friday, 21 August 2009 – 12.30

'The arguments took place not only outside the presence of the jury, but also away from the press.'

Martine Yin's replacement – a twenty-something blonde – was reporting on the latest events from the court. She had been pulled at short notice from her duties as the weather girl and she thought this was her golden opportunity. But she didn't really have a firm grasp of what she was reporting on, because although she had followed the case on TV, she didn't really understand the finer points of criminal law. Most of what she was reporting now was on the advice of Martine, who had kindly agreed to advise her, to help make sure that her reports were accurate and clear.

'We do not know what was decided in these discussions, but we can confirm that in addition to the lawyers for Elias Claymore and the prosecution, there was a third party present in the judge's chambers. This third party was believed to be a lawyer representing LegalSoft, the software company that supplied Alameda County Court – and many other courts in the State – with software used by the court service, including jury selection software.

'Earlier on in the trial – on the first day, in fact – co-counsel Andromeda Phoenix objected to the entire panel from which the jury was to be chosen on the grounds that

African-Americans were under-represented on that panel. Ms Phoenix's objections were overruled, but the matter could be raised again on appeal.'

Gene Vance used the remote in her left hand to turn the sound down on the TV, while picking up the phone handset in her right hand.

'Hallo, I'd like to book a flight to San Francisco International . . . yes, this afternoon.'

Friday, 21 August 2009 – 14.50

In court, on Friday, the prosecution was rounding off its case. They had presented Bethel's heartrending testimony, albeit dented by Andi's surgical cross-examination. They had called the medical expert who had examined Bethel to confirm that she had internal injuries consistent with rape. This would go a long way to corroborating Bethel's claim that she had been raped. But to bolster her identification of the rapist, they had relied on Victor Alvarez, who had been forced to concede that because of the quality and type of DNA, the statistical probability that Claymore was the rapist was not as strong as they would have liked it to be.

So now Sarah's 'second seat' – Alameda A.D.A. Nick Sinclair – was questioning Albert Carter, an independent eyewitness, unconnected to any of the other parties, in an effort to put Elias Claymore at the scene of the crime. The idea was that even if the defense could attack any and all of the elements of the people's case, the prosecution could counter that it was the combination of several different *types* of evidence that made their case so strong: victim, eyewitness, medical, DNA *plus* the defendant's criminal record.

'Then I started walking over in the direction of the screaming,' the elderly Carter was saying. 'But I didn't want to get too close . . . I guess, I was afraid.'

'And then what happened?' asked Sinclair.

Carter hesitated, looking around the court nervously.

'Well, I hid behind a tree, just in case I was seen. I mean I didn't want to be seen.'

'And what happened then?'

It was clear that Carter needed prompting, or at least encouragement. But the A.D.A. knew that he couldn't lead the witness. This was direct examination and leading questions were not allowed. Sinclair knew that he was getting there, but slowly. But he was growing increasingly worried about how he would stand up to cross-examination. With a little bit of gentle coaxing he was telling the jury what he saw. But how coherent would he sound when subjected to one of Alex's withering cross-examinations?

Of course Alex would have to tread carefully: he wouldn't want to create sympathy for Carter. But even with a few quiet, polite questions Alex could completely disarm a witness and throw him into confusion. And Carter was a timid old man to begin with.

'Mr Carter?'

'Then?' echoed the witness nervously. 'Well that was when he ran past me.'

'*Who* ran past you?'

'Well . . . the man.'

He was getting nervous.

'Could you tell us if you see the man in the courtroom?'

Carter pointed to Claymore with an unsteady hand. *At least it brings out the jury's sympathies, thought Nick Sinclair.*

'That man over there.'

'Let the record show that the witness indicated the accused, Elias Claymore.'

'So ordered,' said the judge.

'And from which direction did he run?'

'Well . . . from the direction of the woman screaming.'

'And where did he run?'

'To a car. He got in the car and drove off.'

'And what sort of car was it?'

'One of those European cars. I think it was blue . . . I didn't get the number.'

'Thank you,' said Sinclair smiling with relief. 'No further questions.'

The A.D.A. sat down. Carter was about to leave the witness stand.

'Oh, just a minute,' said Justice Wagner. 'The counsel for the defense wants to ask you a few questions too.'

Carter turned back and reentered the stand, looking somewhat disoriented. Nick Sinclair resisted the temptation to smile at this. When Carter wilted under Alex's bullying, it would create sympathy for him, and thus for Bethel too.

But after a brief conference at the defense table, it was Andi who rose to cross-examine. She flashed a reassuring smile at the witness. He knew that she was supposed to be the enemy. But she seemed so inoffensive that he was forced to smile back nervously.

'Mr Carter,' Andi began gently, 'you say that you were hiding behind a tree, is that right?'

'That's right.'

'And were you hiding your face as well?'

'I don't understand.'

'Well if you stuck your head out from behind the tree, then wasn't there a danger that someone might see you – the very thing you were trying to avoid?'

'But I didn't stick my head out. I kept it hidden.'

'So how did you see the man when he ran past you?'

'Well, he ran past the tree. I saw him when he ran past the tree.'

'Are you saying that he turned to look at you as he ran past the tree? Like he knew you were there?'

'No. He just ran straight past like a bat out of hell.'

'Like a bat out of hell?'

'Yes.'

'So he didn't turn to look at you?'

'I just said he didn't,' snapped Carter, irritated.

'Then how did you see his face?'

'Well I saw . . . I mean he . . . well, I mean he didn't look at me but I could see part of his face. I mean . . .'

Carter looked over at Nick Sinclair. He lowered his head, avoiding his eyes.

'Okay, let's review what we've got,' said Andi. 'You heard screams, you were scared, you hid behind a tree and a man ran past you very fast without turning to look at you.'

'I didn't say he was running fast.'

'You said like a bat out of hell.'

'Did I?' asked Carter, confused.

Andi paused to let Carter's response sink in.

'No further questions.'

Andi sat down, letting her head drop. Nick Sinclair rose with as much dignity as he could muster.

'I have no redirect, Your Honor.'

'The witness is excused,' said the judge.

Carter was escorted gently from the witness stand by a bailiff, as Andi looked on with what appeared to be a trace of sympathy. Sinclair sat down and Sarah Jensen rose. She regretted rounding off on a low note. It would have been better if Carter had been bullied on cross-examination, instead of simply being made to seem like the absent-minded old man that he was. But Carter's testimony was intended as the icing on the cake. It wasn't really essential. Even Bethel's evidence, with its uncertainty over the attacker's age and her past accusations of rape wasn't really essential.

The scientific evidence was what counted in this case. In cases where the eyewitness or victim testimony is weak, scientific evidence was crucial. And in this case it was conclusive. The danger was that the jury would hold this debacle with Carter closest to the forefront of their memories. Therefore Sarah Jensen would have to remind them of the formidable scientific evidence in her closing.

She would take advantage of the O.J. Simpson trial, in which the DNA evidence was classified by one ignorant juror as 'a whole lot of nothing.' This jury was educated enough to understand DNA evidence and would react differently. But there was something else she had to do first.

'Your Honor, the prosecution rests.'

Justice Wagner looked up at the clock on the courtroom wall opposite her and then at Alex Sedaka. 'Will the defense be ready to proceed on Monday morning?'

'Yes, Your Honor.'

'Then this court is adjourned until ten o'clock Monday morning.'

'All rise!' the bailiff intoned.

The lawyers, Claymore, jurors and spectators all stood. The judge rose with her customary dignity and left the courtroom. Andi and Alex started gathering up the papers in front of them. Claymore was standing with them, looking embarrassed. He wanted to ask them what his chances were, now that the prosecution's case was nearly over.

Throughout the case against him, Claymore had sat there in silence, not even leaning over to Alex when he wanted to tell him something. Alex had warned him against any behavior that might make him seem anxious or concerned. Instead, if he had anything important to say, he was to write

261

it down on a note in front of him. Alex would see him writing and read it without turning his head.

But now before he was led away back to jail, he wanted to know where things stood.

'What do you think?' asked Claymore, quietly.

'How do you mean?' replied Alex, not really anxious to answer the question that he understood only too well.

'What are my chances?'

Alex didn't look at his client as he put the last of his papers into his attaché case. He still believed in his client, but he had a duty to be candid and honest.

'I won't bullshit you, Elias. We've got an uphill struggle ahead of us.'

Friday, 21 August 2009 – 22.15

'Mmm, that feels good,' said Andi as Gene's hands moved up and down, her thumbs squeezing her shoulders and upper back.

The room was dimly lit. Andi was lying on the bed in her underwear, while Gene gave her an intense yet soothing and relaxing massage. When Gene had turned up unannounced at Andi's hotel room, a beaming smile had lit up Andi's face. But now as she recalled the week's events, the stress and strain of the trial began to take its toll.

'And the judge isn't going to do anything about it unless we can *prove* that there was deliberate tampering,' Andi continued. 'But the thing I'm worried about is that we just find some accidental glitch in the software that's reducing the number of African-Americans on jury panels.'

By tacit agreement, Andi and Gene had suspended their rule against talking about the case together even though Gene was still prevented by an injunction from any contact with Bethel.

'But at least that'll help in the future,' Gene comforted.

'Yes, but it won't help in this case.'

'You shouldn't lose any sleep over it. Claymore isn't exactly the most deserving client.'

'But he *is* the client and I've got a duty to do my best for him.'

'Then *do* your best. But don't beat yourself up over it if the judge doesn't accept your arguments. You've done your best by *presenting* the arguments. The rest is out of your hands.'

'It's just that I can't help feeling that this is some sort of a test of my integrity.'

Gene's hands stopped working Andi's shoulder muscles.

'*You're* not on trial, Andi. Elias Claymore is. The only duty that you and Alex Sedaka have to Claymore is to give him the best of professional services.'

'But how can I be sure that I *am* giving my best?'

'Judging by the TV coverage of the trial, I'd say you're going *above and beyond* the call of duty.'

'Then how come I feel this case slipping away from us?'

'Maybe that's because the outcome of the case isn't in your hands.'

Andi turned her head slightly.

'How do you mean?'

Gene's voice became surprisingly gentle.

'Has it occurred to you he might be guilty?'

'It occurred to me. But I think – and I know as a lawyer I should be thinking with my head, not my heart – but I *think* that he's innocent.'

'Are you sure that isn't just what you *want* to think?'

Andi swung round into a sitting position, her feet touching the carpet. She looked lost in thought.

'Are you coming to bed now?' asked Gene.

'Not yet. I forgot to check my e-mail today.'

Andi stood up and went over to the desk. She switched on her laptop and logged on to the office network at Levine and Webster to download her e-mail. There was only one message, but when she saw it, she felt that claw of fear and anger ripping at her insides. The screen contained the following message.

You are still helping that slimy nigger rapist. By helping him you are stabbing your sisters in the back and your blood will be upon your own hands!
                                                          Lannosea

The first thing Andi felt was a jolt of anger. But as she thought about the message, she realized that she had never really made any effort to find out who this Lannosea was. She knew that Lannosea was the name of one of the daughters of the ancient English queen Boudicca. But why would anyone choose such a name?

Andi was determined to find out more. She typed in Boudicca and looked up the Wikipedia entry. It didn't give the names of Boudicca's daughters but it stated that when their father Prasutagus – a vassal of Rome – died, the Romans seized his kingdom, flogged Boudicca and raped her daughters.

Raped her daughters?

So that was it! Lannosea was a rape victim – maybe even one of Claymore's former victims.

All of a sudden, things were different. Andi realized that she was not being taunted by some evil creature motivated by hatred, but rather by a victim who was motivated by *anger*.

And she couldn't hate a victim.

She tried to tell herself that she was only doing her duty. Once she took on the case, she had to give it all her professional skill. But that sounded like the pathetic excuse of every other pragmatist who ever sold his conscience down the river for a quick buck or an easy life. She knew now that she had been rationalizing when she justified taking the case. She had become like one of those people whom she despised – a mercenary, devoid of conscience.

As this ugly realization swept over her, she broke down in tears, her face resting her on her arms on the desk, her whole body shaking from the violent sobbing.

Saturday, 22 August 2009 – 09.00

It was Saturday morning and David Sedaka was in his apartment in Berkeley, studying the decompiled jury selection program. He didn't yet have the original source code – LegalSoft had until Tuesday to produce it and even then they would probably appeal. So all he had to work with in the meantime was the decompiled source code, without any programmer comments and with hopelessly counterintuitive names for the variables and arrays.

Still, now that his working week was over, and he was relaxed and in his own home, he was able to give it his undivided attention. The trouble with most modern computer programming is that it doesn't really have a beginning, a middle and an end. It jumps around and branches off in all directions. But it does have a so-called 'main object' which is the control center of all this branching. So if he wanted to debug the program, it made sense to start off by looking at its main object and see where these branches led.

It was at the main object that David was staring now, as he tried to figure out how it held the other parts together. To make it clearer he started drawing a flow chart, showing how the parts connected and branched. In effect he was reverse engineering the way in which the program was created in the first place.

It was then he noticed a small discrepancy. He chased it up by looking at how the program handled duplicates – names that were on both the voting register list and the Department of Motor Vehicles list.

And that was when he realized!

Saturday, 22 August 2009 – 09.20

'Just ignore it,' said Martine.

Alex had been about to reach for the phone when Martine spoke. He had invited her for Friday evening dinner and she had stayed the night, entranced by his homemade gefilte fish, chicken soup with kneidelech and chicken schnitzel with potato kugel. His mother had taught him to cook, but it was from Melody that he had learned that sometimes the way to a *woman's* heart was through her stomach. He hoped that the ghost of Melody had been smiling down on him last night, as he availed himself of this knowledge to take the first delicate steps towards moving on from the pain of the past.

'It could be important.'

'Isn't it supposed to be the Sabbath?' she asked with a girlish grin, as he reached over her for the phone.

'Don't be cheeky,' he said, picking up the phone with one hand and smacking her bottom playfully but firmly with the other.

'Hallo,' said Alex, his greeting almost masked by Martine's squeal of pain, or delight.

'What was that?' asked David.

'Oh, er, hi, David. Nothing. I was watching the TV.'

'That's not like you. You're usually all work and no play.'

'I guess the case is taking its toll. Anyway, it's not like *you* to phone this early on a Saturday.'

'I know, it's just that I've had some results from looking at the jury selection program.'

Alex sat bolt upright and signaled Martine to be quiet. David's tone had been so calm and measured that anyone else hearing it would not have known how tinged with excitement it was. But Alex Sedaka had known his son for twenty-six years and he could tell when he was gripped by excitement.

'What did you find?'

'The solution! To the jury selection software problem. I've found out how the software was rigged. I mean I've discovered what the tampering actually *does*.'

'So tell me!'

David's tone took on the aura of embarrassment. 'I'm not sure if I can explain it to you.'

Alex wasn't in the least bit offended. He was, at worst, mildly irritated. 'Oh, don't do the old "ignorant father" routine. I *need* to know.'

'Okay, but look, it's hard to explain it in words alone. I may need to show you some things. I can drive round there.'

Alex didn't want David coming round there now. Obviously he would have to tell him at some point about how the relationship with Martine had progressed. But now was not the time.

'Can't you e-mail them over? Besides, Andi needs to hear it too.'

'Maybe you can get her to come round as well. That way I can show you the printouts and diagrams and everything.'

Alex had to think quickly.

'I've got a better idea. Let's do one of those three-way video conferences that you're always on about.'

'Okay. Phone Andi and tell her to log in, then you log in and I'll log in and I'll invite both of you. You just have to accept the conference and we're up and running.'

Saturday, 22 August 2009 – 09.30

It was Saturday morning and Bethel was miserable. Last night she would normally have been out on the town with her friends. As a double rape survivor she kept trying to tell herself that she had almost recovered. Almost, but not quite. The experience of testifying at the trial and listening to the other witnesses brought it all flooding back. And now when she should have been out having a good time, she was sitting at her friend Linda's home feeling miserable and depressed. She was staying with Linda for the duration of the trial. At the end of the trial she would go back to her parents' house and try and get on with her life. Not that she was sure what 'getting on with her life' meant anymore.

She had planned to go back to college. But not now. She couldn't face people after the rape – the second rape. She couldn't face men. She had gone out on a few dates since the rape, but they always made her feel cheap and dirty. Not that they were aggressive. Most of them went out of their way to be respectful, almost to the point of timidity. But the kid gloves treatment reminded her that she was damaged goods. It was as if they were saying to her that they didn't want to touch her. Or if a few of them became bold enough to touch her, she flinched away from them.

And this rape had in some way affected her more than the first.

The first was date rape. It had hurt her deeply at the time. But somewhere along the line, she had seen it coming. Orlando had been building up to it the whole evening. Although she didn't want to have sex with him, she had been mentally prepared for the rape as she saw Orlando's frustration steadily degenerate into anger and then violence when he didn't get his way, like a frustrated child throwing a tantrum. And because he was such a big child and she was alone with him, it was obvious long before it happened that she wouldn't be able to hold him off.

Also, she knew that Luke Orlando had suffered for it too in some ways. He had lost friends as a result of it: his friends knew full well that he had raped her – just as they knew he had raped the other girl who came forward at the time, but whose case was never heard.

But this time it was different. When she got into the Mercedes with that smooth-talking man, she hadn't expected it all. She had heard all the racist generalizations, but it was precisely for that reason that she was determined not to be intimidated by them.

This last time she was raped, some of the men she knew had even offered to 'beat up that bastard.' But that did nothing to ease her pain. They were seeing it in terms of revenge. But they were missing the point. What she wanted was not revenge but *empowerment*. Perhaps, in a way, that was really what men wanted too. Perhaps revenge *made* men feel empowered.

But in any case, the feelings of empowerment eluded her. When she had testified in court she didn't feel empowered, in spite of all the pep talks they had given her at the rape crisis center.

The opening bars of 'For What It's Worth' rang out from her cell phone. It startled her out of her thoughts abruptly. She looked at the display but she didn't recognize the number. She didn't like answering the phone when she was alone. Since the rape she had been afraid of strangers. Even strangers at the other end of the phone frightened her. And so now, listening to the phone ring, the apprehension grew inside her. Eventually, her curiosity overcame her fear. She picked up the receiver.

'Hello?' she said abruptly, putting on a Mexican accent that she could hide behind, in case it was someone she wanted to avoid, by pretending to be someone else.

'Is that Bethel?'

It was a woman's voice . . . a familiar voice . . . but it sounded distorted.

'Who is this?'

'You don't know me. My name is . . . You can call me "Lannosea."'

Hearing such a strange name made Bethel nervous. Anyone using a name like that had to be a weirdo. And she didn't need a weirdo in her personal space on top of all her other problems. But the fact that it was a woman was reassuring.

'What do you want?'

'I want you to know that Claymore isn't going to get away with it.'

'What . . .?'

'I want you to know that there's someone out there fighting for justice . . . fighting to give *you* justice.'

'What are you going to do?'

'I intend to make sure that all those who have harmed you are punished. I intend to give you the justice that the system has denied you.'

Bethel was apprehensive, but no longer fearful. This woman was not her enemy. But she knew that she had to be careful what she said. It was one thing to wish for revenge, it was another to be associated with it. And yet the voice gave her a note of hope. This woman was in some way her kindred spirit – a woman who could read her thoughts, feel her pain, almost with the same heart beating inside both of them.

'Thank you,' said Bethel quietly. 'Thank you,' she said again her eyes squinting against the tears that were now flowing freely.

'Be strong,' said the woman's voice at the other end of the line, gentle yet hard. 'Be strong and courageous. Justice will soon be with you.'

Saturday, 22 August 2009 – 10.20

'Okay, let's hear it,' said Alex.

They had set up the three-way video conference, with Alex sitting at his desktop computer in his home office on the main level of the house, while Andi was sitting with her laptop at the desk in her hotel room.

'It's *supposed* to work like this. First of all, the original jury selection program was written in such a way that it didn't have to use its own database. It logs on to the databases for voting and drivers' registration in the relevant district of the State and take the names of all prospective jurors in that district from both databases. That way it's assured of the most up-to-date voter and driver records.'

'Okay,' said Alex, nodding.

'The next thing it's supposed to do is screen out any duplicates – that is any names that appear on both the voting register and the driver's license records. There are usually quite a lot. So far so good?'

'I'm still with you.'

'All right, the next stage is to screen out persons known to be *ineligible*. That means people in prison, people with felony convictions or recent misdemeanors. All clear?'

'Absolutely.'

David was being brisk about it; Alex gave him credit for

that. He was also being careful not to go *too* fast, summarizing each stage quickly and then stopping to make sure that Alex had understood.

'Okay, finally when all that's done, the algorithm picks the jurors using a randomization procedure.'

'Okay, I understand all that,' said Alex impatiently. 'But how has it been tampered with?'

'Well, remember I said that *first* it draws up the list of *potential* panelists living within the relevant district. *Then* it cuts out the duplicates from the list *before* going on to make the actual final selection.'

'Yes?' said Alex hesitantly.

'Well, I don't know if this is the result of tampering or just bad programming, but what actually happens in the program is that it doesn't cut out the duplicate names from the overall list *before* it draws up the panel. Instead it draws up the panel *first* and only then cuts out the duplicates from the actual list of panelists *if there are any.*'

'Holy shit!' said Andi.

'Does that make a difference?' asked Alex, confused.

'Do you want *me* to explain it, David?' asked Andi.

'If you want to.'

'It's all a matter of statistics. It means that people who are on *both* the voting registration and the driver's registration are more likely to be chosen. And because blacks are under-represented on the voting register – or at least were – it significantly reduces the likelihood of them being chosen for jury service.'

Alex was struggling to take it all in. 'And you think this could explain the discrepancy on the panel we had at the start of the trial?'

'That was probably a pretty severe case,' said Andi. 'The discrepancies that I discovered in my research are somewhat

278

less extreme than that. But when combined with other factors like African-Americans being excused more easily from jury service upon request, I think we have a credible explanation of the extent of the problem.'

Alex was still confused.

'I don't understand. Are you saying that lots of factors caused the problem?'

David stepped in. 'I think that what Andi is saying – and I would agree – is that this defect with the software has made a *significant contribution* to the problem. There are other factors that have aggravated the problem – factors that are quite well known in certain jurisdictions. But the problem wouldn't be nearly so big if it wasn't for the peculiar way that this software deals with duplicate names.'

Alex could finally permit himself to smile. 'We're going to have to take this to the judge. We've finally got the proof.'

And with that, they ended the three-way conference.

'Good news?' asked Martine, as she slinked into the room in a t-shirt and black lace panties, carrying a tray with some sheets of paper and two cups of coffee.

'You should know,' said Alex with a smile. 'You were eavesdropping.'

'I was *not!*' she said with mock indignation.

'Honey, I know you. You're a reporter – as well as being a woman. That means you can't help yourself.'

'Well for *your* information what I was *actually* doing was looking through these worksheets from the lab's log book.'

'*What?*' he blurted out as he snatched the papers from the tray, practically spilling the coffee in the process. 'That's a *privileged* document. It's not supposed to be looked at by *anyone* outside the defense team – least of all a reporter.'

'I already told you. I'm not on duty.'

'You're on duty 24/7. Like I said, I know you.'

'Then you should know that my word is my bond.' And just to twist the knife she added, 'Like a lawyer.'

'Like a gangster, more like,' said Alex, his tone still gruff. But he couldn't conceal the smile on his face.

'Well in this case, I'm acting more like a paralegal for the defense, because I've actually discovered something that might be useful.'

'What do you mean?'

'Take a look Steven Johnson's last entry before he did the amplification on the nail clipping sample.'

Alex flipped through the pages and scanned the relevant lines. 'He checked out reference samples for both Bethel Newton and Elias Claymore.'

Martine smiled and nodded. 'But hadn't those samples been amplified, separated and detected already?'

Alex thought about this for a moment. 'Er, yes,' he said, sensing where this was going.

'So why did he need to check out the back-up samples? Especially as he signed them right back in a few minutes later.'

Monday, 24 August 2009 – 10.15

'And how does that amount to racial discrimination?' asked Justice Wagner.

She was sitting at her desk in her chambers, on Monday morning, with Andi, Alex, Sarah Jensen and Nick Sinclair. A court stenographer also sat in the room. Although this hearing was being heard in camera, it still formed part of the record and therefore the proceedings had to be transcribed, in case the judge's decision became the subject of an appeal by one of the parties.

Alex had filed the dismissal motion as soon as the morning session opened, but left Andi to do the talking, as she had a better understanding of the technical aspects of the issue.

'Your Honor,' Andi continued, 'it is a well-known fact that African-Americans are less likely to register to vote than European-Americans. That's why the State tries to even the odds by using driver's license records. This problem with the jury selection software effectively undermines that equalization measure and causes African-Americans to be under-represented on jury *panels* and thus on *juries*. This is clearly in breach of the Sixth and Fourteenth Amendments.'

Justice Wagner raised a skeptical eyebrow and turned to the prosecutors. 'Do you have any response to that?'

Sarah looked over at Sinclair, to give him the first chance

to respond. He nodded and took his cue. 'I understand the essentials of the defense argument. However, I would remind them that the *Fifteenth* Amendment right to register to vote has been enshrined in the Voting Rights Act of 1965. If some African-Americans have chosen not to *avail* themselves of this right, then it is entirely by their own choice. Personally, I would encourage all citizens to avail themselves of all their rights. And I think it's safe to say that recent political events have encouraged many more to do so. However, this is a free country and people cannot be forced. Voting is a *right* not a *duty*. I therefore cannot see that the exercise of this choice in a particular way by certain people is in any way a violation of the accused's Fourteenth Amendment rights to the equal protection of the law.'

Alex stepped in, knowing that however much Andi might know about computers and statistics, when it came to matters of constitutional law, she was out of her depth. That was *his* specialty and it was for him to explain it to the judge.

'Your Honor, I have no wish to dispute the argument that the failure of *some* African-Americans to avail themselves of their voting rights is a matter of personal choice. However, I would argue that the issue that the court must concern itself with here is not the choice *itself*, but rather the *consequence* of that choice as it affects a *third party* who has no control over their behavior, namely the defendant. Voting may be a civil *right*, but jury *service* is a civic *duty*. The failure to be available for jury service – in conjunction with this software flaw – effectively infringes the constitutional rights of defendants.'

Alex realized that by putting his argument in the plural, he was jeopardizing his chances – as he was alerting the judge to the fact that the ruling would have monumental implications for other cases. So he quickly reverted to the singular.

'The defendant is entitled to a fair trial by a jury *that truly represents the community at large*. The defense would further point out that the need to ensure at least the *possibility*, not of racial *proportionality* in the jury, but rather of racial *diversity* is the reason *why* jurors should not be excluded on grounds of race. Indeed, *this was the basis* for the decision to use driver's registration records in addition to voter registration. As this need has already been recognized and enshrined in the law by the decision to use driver's license records, it would be wrong to retreat from it now.'

When Alex fell silent, Sarah Jensen jumped in, quick to cash in on the psychological weakness in Alex's arguments.

'Your Honor, I would point out that a ruling in favor of these arguments would have dangerous implications not only for other cases pending but also for past convictions by juries selected by this—'

'I am well aware of that!' Ellen Wagner snapped back angrily. 'And it is not something that I can take into consideration in reaching my decision.'

Nick Sinclair leaned forward hesitantly. 'Your Honor, there is one other aspect of this matter to consider.'

'Yes?' the judge prompted.

'The defense has not yet had a chance to view the source code from the original jury selection software. Their entire argument has been based on their analysis of the executable program that they have decompiled.'

'But that's the one that the court service is actually using,' said Andi.

'Yes, but we don't know whether the original was like that too.'

'What are you saying?' asked the judge, looking squarely at Sinclair.

'I'm saying that if the original source code is *different* to

283

the current version, then the defense can argue that the software has been tampered with deliberately and then the people would have to concede that this shows that any discrimination arising out of the tampering is indeed *intention-based*. But if on the other hand the original source code is substantially the *same*, then it would imply that the problem is simply a *flaw* in the program design, and any adverse consequences to ethnic minorities would thus simply be a *by-product* of this flaw. As the court is applying an intention-based test of discrimination, in accordance with the earlier precedents, and not merely an effects-based test, the court does not *yet* have any basis for granting this motion. Only if and when the defense is able to prove that the software has been modified by some unauthorized party outside the company that designed it, can they argue that there is evidence of intention-based discrimination.'

The judge turned to the defense lawyers. Andi looked crestfallen. Alex's face and body language showed no emotion.

'Assuming that LegalSoft's appeal is blocked and you get the source code tomorrow, how soon after that do you think you can have a definitive answer to this question?'

Alex turned to Andi. This was her territory – and David's.

'I'd say that if we get the software by ten o'clock tomorrow, as per the ruling, then we can have a definitive answer within a few hours. We can rename the variables and arrays in the decompiled version to match their counterparts in the original source code and then just run a straight text comparison to look for any changes.'

'So you think you can come up with a definitive answer by, say, Wednesday morning at the latest?'

'I'm sure of it,' said Andi.

The judge turned to the prosecutors. 'Will the prosecution want a copy and a chance to call its own expert?'

Nick Sinclair looked at Sarah. She was leading the case and it was her call.

'No, Your Honor. But could I ask if, in the event of the defense establishing that there was such tampering, is the court minded to grant the defense's motion for a mistrial, bearing in mind the people's *other* arguments – and if so will this be with or without prejudice?'

Sarah Jensen wanted the reassurance, that if a mistrial was declared, they would at least have the chance to bring a new trial with a fresh jury.

Ellen Wagner thought about it for a moment. 'I will take this matter under advisement. There's no point jumping the gun until we know whether or not this was deliberate tampering.'

The judge was about to adjourn the hearing, when Alex remembered something. 'There was one other small matter, Your Honor.'

'*Yes*, Mr Sedaka,' said the judge, sighing irritably.

'The defense would like to call Steven Johnson, the lab technician who processed the scene sample from the nail clippings.'

Sarah Jensen became highly animated at this.

'Your Honor, we have had no notice of this – and Mr Johnson is not on the defense witness list. If the defense wanted to call him, they had *ample* time to notify us.'

'Your Honor, something has come up that makes it vital to the defense case that we call this witness – if the trial goes ahead. In any case, the prosecution has forty-eight hours before the trial continues to look into this witness. Furthermore it's not as if this witness is *unknown* to the prosecution. He works at the very lab that they have relied upon in this case. And he was the lab technician who processed the evidence sample upon which the prosecution has placed such heavy reliance.'

'Yes, I can't see any valid reason to deny this request, Ms Jensen. You may call Steven Johnson, Mr Sedaka. Will that require an adjournment for the five-day notice period, Ms Jensen?

'Mr Johnson is an employee of the State and I'm sure the Ventura lab would be ready to release him at short notice.'

'In that case, this court is adjourned until ten o'clock Wednesday morning.'

Monday, 24 August 2009 – 11.50

The forensic laboratory in Ventura was as busy as it had been the day they had processed the nail clipping sample from the Bethel Newton rape case. The initial evidence samples from the vaginal swabs had already been processed with the intention of uploading the profile into the National DNA Information System database and crosschecking against other crimes. But the failure to find any sperm DNA had thwarted that. They would have pressed ahead if they had felt confident of finding any autosomal DNA from the perpe-trator in the crime scene sample. But they realized that the nail clippings were probably only good for Y-STR DNA, and this could not be uploaded to the NDIS.

So it was only when they had a suspect and after they had processed the reference samples that they got round to the amplification, separation and detection of the nail clipping evidence sample.

It was like any other day at the lab today. Evidence was checked in, registered, filed, in some cases processed and reports written up. It was like a factory. The staff had no emotional attachment to any of the cases, whether it was about blood alcohol, illegal substances or DNA. They simply did their bit, according to the work roster assigned to them.

Consequently, Steven Johnson was thoroughly engrossed

in his work when the process server appeared. Ordinarily, unauthorized personnel would not have been allowed into the lab. But the server was a bailiff attached to the court and as such was able to flash her credentials at security and get waved through without even putting in a call to the DNA section where Steven Johnson worked.

'Steven Johnson?' said the bailiff.

'Yes?'

She noticed that he was smiling. Young men often smiled when they saw her. She took advantage of his disarmed state to hand him the envelope. He took it without question but with a look of curiosity in his eyes.

'You've been served.'

The bailiff was such a battle-hardy and seasoned veteran of this kind of mundane legwork that she didn't usually pay attention to the recipient's reaction to being served with a subpoena or court order. The only thing she was on guard against was the possibility of the recipient becoming violent. In this case, Johnson's slight frame and meek manner precluded that danger. But still, she noticed that even before Johnson opened the envelope, he already looked afraid.

Monday, 24 August 2009 – 21.30

The hotel room was in semi-darkness, the light coming from a floor lamp. Andi was sitting on the couch working on her laptop computer. It had been a frustrating day, culminating in the judge postponing her decision on the dismissal motion. Now they had to wait till tomorrow to get the source code.

And there was no guarantee that they would get it. LegalSoft would almost certainly file an appeal. Whether the appeal court would agree to hear it was another matter. But if they did then they would grant a stay and set a date for a hearing with all parties present. That could drag the matter out for another week. The best thing they could hope for was that the appeal court would refuse to hear the appeal or grant a stay and the company would have to hand it over by tomorrow morning at ten. The trouble was that *hope* was all they could do. They certainly couldn't count on it.

Of course, the defense could also go on the offensive and file an interim appeal against the court's decision not to grant their dismissal motion based on what they had already found out. But there was no guarantee that such an appeal would be upheld – the judge's reasoning regarding the intent-based test was legally sound. Besides, it was premature. It was just that even waiting till ten o'clock tomorrow was maddeningly frustrating for Andi.

In the meantime, tonight, she just wanted to unwind and forget about it. So she logged on to her Internet account and downloaded her e-mail. There were several messages from her friends from Europe and the Far East. But there was also one that struck fear into her heart yet again when she saw the name: Lannosea:

So your dirty little plan to get that rapist shitbag off on a technicality didn't work? And that leaves you back at square one, you cheap little cunt. That's what your sisters think of you, you know. That's really all you are! You didn't really think you'd get away with it, did you? By the way, I was the one who changed the software to keep the niggers off juries. And if you try and fuck with me, bitch, you'll be fucking with the wrong woman. You understand?

Lannosea

The language was getting more vitriolic. This person was angry. But who was it? The name Lannosea and her reasoning about it being another of Claymore's victims suggested that it was a woman. But the language was what one would expect of an ultra-misogynistic man.

And how did Lannosea know about her attempt to get Claymore off 'on a technicality?' How many people knew about that? And which of them could be doing this? Which of them might have said something indiscreet and let other people know?

She couldn't think. Her head just wasn't clear enough. She needed help; she knew that now. She reached for the phone and called David Sedaka. *He* knew about computers and the Internet. He could help her. And she could trust him, she knew that.

'Hi, David, it's Andi here, Andi Phoenix . . . Listen, I need your help, that is, I'd *like* your help . . . if you think it's something you can do. But you must keep this completely secret from everyone, at least for the time being.'

Over the next few minutes, they set up a plan to try and trace the person sending the messages. It started with her copying the messages she had already received to him, including the full Internet header. This showed the path that the messages had taken over the Internet. It couldn't trace the message all the way to its source. But it might just lead them back to the service provider for the place where the messages were sent from. This would probably be somewhere like an Internet café. But at least it was a start.

The next thing she had to do was give David direct access to her Internet account. This entailed a loss of privacy. But he made it clear that this was something she would have to do if she wanted the person caught.

There was a knock on the door, shaking Andi out of her concentration. She looked up. 'Who is it?'

'Your lover.'

Andi tossed the laptop aside, raced to the door and opened it.

'You were supposed to be going back to LA,' said Andi as Gene stepped forward.

'You sound disappointed,' Gene replied, encircling Andi's waist with her arms.

'I'm sorry. I didn't mean to,' Andi replied, sliding her hands up Gene's arms and interlocking her fingers behind her lover's neck.

'I couldn't stay away from you, babe.'

Gene was about to kiss her when Andi turned away. 'But don't they need you back at the rape crisis center?'

Gene looked long and hard into Andi's eyes and tightened her grip around her, emphasizing that Andi was a prisoner in her arms.

'They need me all right. But right now I need you more . . . and I think you need me too.'

There was a questioning tone in Gene's words, and Andi felt a slight, barely perceptible, slackening of Gene's grip – as if Gene too needed reassurance.

'Of course I need you.'

There was a few seconds of hesitation and then their lips met in a tender but hesitant kiss.

Tuesday, 25 August 2009 – 10.30

David Sedaka was at his desk in his office when he got a phone call from his father.

'Hi, Dad.'

'Busy?'

'I'm always busy,' said David, looking around his cluttered office.

'We've got the source code.'

'Great! Send it over.'

'Can you look at it right away?'

'Like I promised.'

Barely a minute later, David had downloaded and opened the source code. As soon as he scrolled through the code, he could see that he was right. The original version correctly removed the duplicates from the combined temporary database *before* selecting the panel just as it was supposed to. For that reason it had a large area for the temporary database, but a small area for the array that held the names and details of the venire panel. But on the decompiled version this was reversed. The array had been enlarged to allow for the theoretical possibility that *all* the names would be duplicated. And the removal of duplicates took place after the panel selection was made, with the address pointer for the program redirected to the jury panel array instead of the temporary database.

And *that* could only mean one thing: this program had been deliberately tampered with. Someone had evidently modified the source code and then recompiled the program and distributed the modified version.

But how could they do that? How could they get the court service in many counties to accept the modified version of the program? Could it have been an inside job? Someone within the company?

That would explain how they obtained access to the software – and also might explain how they had managed to get the court services to accept it.

But was it likely that someone inside the company would have the motive to do that and the means to avoid detection? Or had it been some very clever and devious outsider?

David had no way of knowing. All he knew was that he had discovered enough to be able to testify under affirmation that this software had been *deliberately sabotaged*.

He knew that he would have to give a statement or affidavit. And they might even need him to testify in court.

He reached for the phone to call his father.

Wednesday, 26 August 2009 – 11.40

'However, I am not convinced by the arguments of counsel for the defense that the facts when taken as a whole amount to a violation of the defendant's constitutional rights.'

They were in the judge's chambers on Wednesday morning. Justice Ellen Wagner had heard the defense's factual submissions about the software, which the prosecution did not challenge and had then retired for an hour to consider her judgment. Neither side wanted to present any more legal arguments, because they both felt they had covered that ground already.

When the lawyers trooped back into her chambers at the end of that hour, Justice Wagner looked solemn. But neither side had any inkling of which way her judgment would go. Now she was delivering her devastating judgment, with the court stenographer present to record the decision.

'I accept in the light of the defense's uncontested claims of fact that the jury selection software has indeed been tampered with and that it is a strong possibility that this tampering was done with the express intention of reducing the likelihood of African-Americans and possibly other ethnic minorities from being selected for jury service.

'However, a strong possibility falls short of a probability, let alone a certainty. It is quite possible that the person or persons who tampered with the software did so for reasons entirely unrelated to racial discrimination. They may, for example, have thought that they were *improving* the software in some way. In this regard I would note that the defense has failed to offer any evidence of fact that the modification of the software was done by someone *outside* of the company that developed the software. It is still within the bounds of possibility that the modification was done by someone within LegalSoft and that there is another more recent version of the source code within the company archives, that has been inadvertently overlooked.

'Furthermore, even if the modification was done by someone outside the company, and even if it was done for the explicit purpose of causing racial discrimination in the composition of jury panels, that would only be the motive of the malicious party who *modified* the software. That does not mean, however, that such was the intention of the court service or the government in *using* the maliciously modified software. Inasmuch as the test to be applied is intention-based and inasmuch as the court service appears to have used the software in good faith, I cannot see that this constitutes a Sixth or Fourteenth Amendment violation.

'I should also point out that in the case in Kent County, Michigan, cited by the defense – where there was an entirely *different* but *accidental* glitch in the software that had a deleterious effect on the ethnic diversity of juries – they did *not* at the time select their juries from anything other than the voting register. Indeed they did not start using driver's registration and State income tax records for jury selection in parallel with voter registration until the year 2007. Thus, it can be seen, there was and is no constitutional requirement that any source of data other than voter registration be used for jury selection. As Mr Sinclair has noted, the right to vote exists for all, even if some fail to avail themselves of it. And whilst I am persuaded by Mr Sedaka that the effect of that choice upon third parties such as the accused, is of *some* relevance, I am *not* convinced that the magnitude of such effect is sufficient to find in favor of the defense in the present case.

'I would note, in this regard, that under-representation of African-Americans in the voting register is probably less prevalent now than it used to be at any time in the past, and also probably less prevalent in this state than in many other states.

'Finally, I would note that my reasons for this decision are cumulative and that it is for all of these reasons, taken *as a whole*, that I am minded to come to this decision.'

Oh, very clever, thought Alex. *Make it a mixture of law and fact to avoid giving the defense an opening to apply for an interim appeal.*

'Accordingly,' the judge continued, 'the defense motion for dismissal of the charges is denied.'

For a few seconds, nobody said a word. However, there was a subtle difference in how the parties took the ruling. While Sarah Jensen looked smug, Nick Sinclair looked decidedly uncomfortable. And while Alex remained calm, Andi gritted her teeth angrily.

Wednesday, 26 August 2009 – 11.55

'There's no doubt that some other lawyer in some other case will raise this issue at some point in the future,' said Alex. 'And my guess is that it'll be up to the Court of Appeal to deal with this whole can of worms – maybe even the Federal Supreme Court. But there's nothing more we can do about it now.'

They were in a meeting room on the same floor as the courtroom. Alex and Andi were trying to explain the judge's ruling to Claymore. But it was rather hard, if only because the judge's ruling had been so unexpected.

'Why is she so hostile?' asked Claymore.

'She wants to prove that she's not taking race into account,' said Alex.

'Oh, that's bullshit!' Andi cut in. 'She's been around the block more times than the two of us put together. She doesn't have to prove jack shit!'

'That doesn't mean she doesn't *think* she has to. But anyway there's another thing: what we've uncovered has the most awesome implications for countless cases throughout the State over the last five years – and possibly other States too. That's probably why she's so reluctant to find in our favor – even though she's probably as concerned as we are. She doesn't want the responsibility. It's too big for her. It's too big for any one single judge.'

He caught the skeptical look on Andi's face and hoped that Claymore didn't see it. He moved swiftly to win her back onside.

'Look, let's face it, this is a insidious piece of sabotage that we've uncovered.'

'Has it occurred to you that maybe she's *right*?' asked Andi. 'At least technically.'

Claymore looked at her accusingly.

She plowed on. 'Look, I don't *like* her decision any more than you do. But as far as the law goes, it reads like the Sermon on the Mount. She's got all the bases covered and everything she says makes perfect sense.'

'Does that mean we can't appeal?' asked Claymore, nervously.

'Not at this stage. We can only do a fact-based appeal after the trial . . . *if* they find you guilty.'

'But I thought you can sometimes do an interim appeal – I mean in cases like this where there's a major constitutional issue.'

Alex smiled and remembered a line by Alexander Pope: *A little learning is a dangerous thing.*

'If it was a purely legal issue we might be able to do that. But this isn't a purely legal issue; it also has a factual dimension. The judge pointed out that we don't know who did the tampering or what their motive was. And there were also a few other things that we needn't get into. But the bottom line is we have no grounds to get the Supreme Court involved.'

'Well what about the Court of Appeal? I mean if the judge is wrong on factual grounds, why can't we appeal on factual grounds. I thought you could *always* appeal to them on factual grounds.'

Again Alex smiled tolerantly.

'Yes, but that's only after the trial. We have to wait until then – and let's hope it doesn't get to that stage.'

'Do you think we will?' There was no disguising the fear in Claymore's eyes.

'It's up to the jury.'

'And what are my chances?'

Alex shook his head. 'I gave up trying to second-guess juries a long time ago.'

He looked at Andi.

'I don't know what the jury will say. But you sometimes get a gut feeling about what a jury *wants* to find. It's no guarantee of the final verdict because sometimes juries are responsible enough to follow the law even if they feel uncomfortable about doing it.

'And what's your gut feeling telling you in this case?'

'My gut feeling is telling me that they feel sorry for Bethel Newton. In other words they *want* to believe her.'

'So what do you want me to do?' asked Claymore nervously. 'Change my plea?'

'No, of course not,' Alex cut in, determined to head off any more of Andi's negativity. 'We've still got grounds for appeal based on the refusal to grant a dismissal with prejudice. But there are no guarantees.'

'The thing I'm getting at,' Andi explained, 'is that the *reason* they want to believe her is because they've heard her. That's *why* they feel sorry for her. Because they've seen that she's human . . . and vulnerable. And they want to protect her. The way they see it, she could be *their* daughter. So far, they haven't seen you. They haven't seen your human side. As far as they know, you're the man they fear. Yeah, I know you've sat next to me and that softens you and makes you less threatening in their eyes. But they still don't know you.'

'But they must have seen me on TV.'

'Yes, but on TV you're powerful and forceful. Yes, you're one of the good guys – into law and order and all that. But now they wonder, is this the real you? Or is the real you that angry man from thirty years ago? The evil predator who preyed on their daughter?'

'Then the only way to show them I'm human is to testify.'

'That's not without its *own* problems,' said Alex. 'The thing that bothers me is that Sarah Jensen is quite a wily prosecutor.'

'But if I just tell the truth—'

'It's not as simple as that, Elias. Let's say she gets to cross-examine you and you *do* manage to get the better of her. To the jury that'll look like a strong man getting the better of a weak woman. Which is exactly what rape is.'

He didn't see the bitter look on Andi's face when he said this.

'And if she gets the better of me, then I look like a liar getting trapped by someone smarter than me.'

'Exactly.'

'That's if she cross-examines you herself,' said Andi. 'She might leave it to Nick Sinclair. That way, it won't look quite so much like a race issue to the blacks on the jury.'

'No, she won't do that,' said Claymore. 'He'll come over as an "Uncle Tom." She'll question me herself. I *know* she will.'

'Well, if she does,' said Alex, 'go carefully. 'Cause *whatever* you do, you'll look bad.'

'So it's heads she wins, tails I lose.'

'That's what I'm saying,' said Alex.

'And if I don't take the stand?'

'Then the judge will direct the jury that they're not allowed to infer guilt from your silence and they'll ignore her as soon as they get into the jury room – if not before that.'

'Jesus!' Claymore sounded frustrated as he raised his head and looked up to the ceiling, as if praying for help from the God that he still believed in. 'The thing is, I *want* to tell my side of the story.'

'I accept that. But we have to be realistic and decide which is the lesser of two evils.'

Andi spoke up. 'For what it's worth, my opinion is that you *must* testify. They have to see your human side. Otherwise they won't *want* to believe you.'

Alex didn't like the way Andi was pushing Claymore. It had to be *his* choice, not hers. 'Wait, let's not get carried away here, Andi. Whether they want to believe or not, the prosecution still has to have a convincing case. Let's take a step back a minute and consider where the prosecution's case stands as it is, in the eyes of the jury. Bethel Newton sounded sympathetic but implausible. They believe she was raped, but the fact that she said a *young* man first and then changed her story to an *older* man means they know she might have got it wrong – hell, she *must* have got *something* wrong.'

'On the other hand,' said Andi, 'she sounded emphatic when she ID-ed you in court and they can't see any reason why she should lie about that.'

'But she *is* lying!' snapped Claymore.

'Okay, but we have to come up with a *reason*. Can you think of any reason why she should pick on *you* to accuse?'

Claymore looked at Alex helplessly. But Alex remained silent.

'Maybe she knows about my background – about what I did in the past. Maybe she thinks I'm some kind of a symbol of everything she hates – everything she has a *right* to hate.'

'That's ridiculous,' snapped Andi. 'She didn't even know who you were when she picked you. She's new in this State and she's too young to remember the Seventies or Eighties.'

'Well, maybe she isn't lying. Maybe she's just mistaken.'

'But she *was* very emphatic.'

'It just doesn't make sense,' said Claymore looking up at the ceiling, desperate.

'Okay, let's move on,' said Andi. 'The *medical* evidence says she *was* raped and the *DNA* evidence suggests it may have been you, but statistically it's far from conclusive. I mean the statistical evidence that the jury selection software was tampered with was stronger than the statistical evidence against you.'

'Good point,' said Alex making a note to be used in his closing.

'But the fact is that we've now established that the software *was* tampered with. The jury might decide to trust the DNA statistics and believe that you're guilty too.'

Claymore looked at her with an intensity that she hadn't seen before. 'Do *you* think I'm guilty?'

She squirmed with embarrassment. Alex looked like he wanted to intervene on her behalf, but held back. It was obvious that Claymore wanted an answer and wouldn't accept any evasion.

'Look, Mr Claymore, you've got to understand, lawyers don't act on their personal feelings. They act on their professional skills. You were accused of a serious crime and it's my duty to help Alex give you the best defense. I can't say if you're innocent or guilty. But sometimes the greatest test of courage is standing up to the enemy within. My duty is to put aside any doubts I might have and fight this case to the best of my ability.'

'Then let me ask you another question, Ms Phoenix. You said she's too young to remember the Seventies or Eighties. Do *you* remember me from then?'

There was a hesitant silence. 'Why do you ask?'

'I want to know how much prejudice there is against me in that jury of thirty-somethings that Alex empaneled – with your help.'

'I was only fourteen when you were arrested for the rapes in 1984. I remember reading about the case. But I was more into parties and dating at that age. I wasn't exactly civic-minded or politically precocious. But even if they didn't read about it then, they would almost certainly have read about it now, when this case broke.'

'I'm *not* proud of what I did,' said Claymore tensely. 'But remember that I came back to the United States to serve out my sentence when I saw that all those Middle Eastern countries weren't exactly heaven on earth for the black man.'

'That may be. But there are some people who think that you should have been sentenced to life for what you did. Raping six women isn't something that middle America forgives easily – even if you did become a born-again Christian afterwards.'

'Eight,' Claymore's choked-off voice came back at him.

When Alex met Claymore's eyes he noticed a couple of tears forming in the corners. 'What?'

Claymore took a deep breath and the tears start to roll down his cheeks as he spoke. 'I raped a total of eight women. Only six of them came forward and testified against me.'

Alex stared at his client in stony silence for a few seconds and said, 'I stand corrected.'

The tears were flowing more freely from Claymore now.

'Look . . .' Claymore began, in a tone that seemed to be almost pleading. 'I can't expect forgiveness for my past. I know that I caused pain to other people – and the pain and suffering that my brothers and sisters went through was no excuse for what I did to others. But I've paid the price for it in more ways than one. Since I came back to America to serve out my sentence I haven't been able to touch a woman. In a way I'm still in prison.'

A cynical smile graced Alex's face as he watched Claymore dry his eyes with the back of his hand. 'If you can do that again in court, we're home and dry.'

Wednesday, 26 August 2009 – 12.05

'Why don't you just come clean and tell us the truth. You know we're going to get you when the DNA results come through.'

Detective Bridget Riley had already had quite a tiring morning. Starting early, she had driven to LAX from Ventura then flown to San Francisco International and finally driven to Oakland in a rented car, getting caught up in the morning logjam on the Bay Bridge.

Now she and Detective Nadis of the Special Victims Unit at the police station in the Frank H. Ogawa Plaza were questioning Louis Manning in his hospital bed at the Alta Bates Medical Center. They would have preferred to haul him in, but his leg was still in traction and would be for several weeks. He was, however, under arrest and able to talk. So they read him his rights and started questioning him. The only trouble was, he wasn't talking. He had waived his right to an attorney, but that was just about all he waived.

'If you're so sure of that, why do you *need* me to confess? Besides, I could be lying if I *do* confess.'

Manning smiled smugly. Nadis leaned over him and spoke quietly. 'Maybe, but DNA doesn't lie.'

'You haven't got the DNA results yet.'

'But we will,' said Nadis, leaning over Manning aggressively. Bridget put a hand on the detective's shoulder and eased him back. She didn't want him doing anything that might undermine their case, if the DNA *did* prove positive.

A part of her felt sorry for Manning. He'd never had a chance. He didn't even know who his parents were. To him a parent was an indifferent social worker who changed every few months. But other people get over that sort of thing. Not everyone who goes through the social services system comes out a criminal at the other end.

'What if I confess and then the DNA shows I'm innocent. Then folks'll go round sayin' you beat a confession outta me.'

'I somehow don't think that's going to happen,' said Bridget.

'Then I don't see why you want me to confess.'

'The judge might go easier on you if you confess.'

Manning smiled again, taunting them with his good spirits. 'Do you *want* the judge to go easy on me?'

Nadis leaned over the table practically shoving his face into Manning's. 'You know what *I* want, you piece of shit? I want the judge to throw the book at you!'

'Then maybe it's better if I *don't* confess.'

Detective Nadis was about to grab Manning by the throat, when Bridget stepped forward and stopped his hand. 'You think it's clever, terrorizing innocent women?'

'Not all women are as innocent as they'd have you believe.'

Wednesday, 26 August 2009 – 12.10

Andi was standing before the judge in the fully assembled courtroom, looking somewhat nervous. 'Your Honor, the defense calls Elias Claymore.'

A gasp of surprise went through the courtroom. Alex had decided that once again, she should do the honors. Claymore was accused of raping a woman. So a woman must guide him through the minefield of his direct examination, before she abandoned him on the even deadlier minefield of Sarah Jensen's cross-examination. Claymore stood up and walked to the witness stand. The clerk held out a Bible for him.

'Place your left hand on the book and raise your right hand,' said the clerk.

He complied.

'Do you swear, so help you God, that the evidence you give shall be the truth, the whole truth and nothing but the truth?'

'I do.'

The clerk took back the Bible and withdrew and Andi Pheonix began her direct examination. 'You are Elias Joshua Claymore?'

'Yes.'

'Could you tell the court where you were on June fifth of this year between seven-thirty and nine in the morning?'

'I was at home, reading through background material for my afternoon show.'

'How can you be so sure?'

'It was a weekday. I always read the background material in the morning. The show goes out live in the afternoon and I read the material in the morning to prepare for it.'

'Did anyone see you there?'

'No.'

'Mr Claymore, did you rape Bethel Newton?'

'No,' Claymore replied, it was only a moment's hesitation. But it was enough to damage his case.

Damn! thought Alex, as he looked on helplessly.

No matter that there were a dozen legitimate reasons for his hesitation. No matter that he was a man carrying the burden and baggage of his guilty past. That momentary hesitation was enough to inflict a mortal wound upon his defense. Andi didn't seem to notice this. She just plowed on with her questioning.

'Have you had any form of sexual contact with a woman since you came back to America of your own free will to serve out your sentence?'

'I've been haunted by what I did for many years. Since I came back to America I haven't been able to touch a woman.'

'No further questions.'

Andi sat down. Sarah Jensen rose slowly and waited a few seconds before commencing.

'Mr Claymore, you say that no one saw you at home during the hours in question. Did anyone telephone at that time?'

'No.'

'So no one can actually confirm your alibi?'

'That's right.'

'Tell me something. You say you haven't been able to touch a woman since you came back to America, is that correct?'

'Yes.'

'Have you ever *fantasized* about touching a woman, since you came back?'

Andi was about to stand up to object. Alex put a subtle, restraining hand on her forearm.

'I . . . I guess so.' He was hesitant again. 'Sometimes I've thought about it.'

'Have you ever fantasized about *raping* a woman since you came back?'

Andi looked round at Alex, the look on her face bordering on desperation. He shook his head gently. Claymore who had seen this, remained silent, a glazed stare in his eyes, as if he were remembering something.

'The witness will answer the question,' said Justice Wagner firmly.

'I could never do a thing like that. Not now. When I look at women, I see people I've hurt.'

Andi glanced at the jurors with her peripheral vision.

'I didn't ask whether you *did* anything like that now. I asked whether or not you fantasized about it.'

'No, of course not. I've been a different man since I came back. I put my past behind me. I've never thought about that sort of thing. Not since I came back.'

'So does that mean you don't remember raping those girls?'

'I . . . I remember it. I'll never forget it.'

'But you don't remember their faces?'

'Oh yes . . . I remember their faces. I see them every night, in the darkness . . . when I'm alone in my bedroom.'

'You relive the ordeal?'

'Yes.'

'So you *do* think about raping women?'

'I . . . I . . .'

He didn't know what to say. What to him was reliving a

nightmare from which he couldn't escape, was to her the savoring of sadistic memories from his past – and he could see by the looks on the jurors' faces that they accepted the prosecutor's version, not his.

'According to the records from the TV station, a call to your number from your producer was logged out at nine-twenty. How do you account for that?'

'I must have been in the bathroom. The toilet must have been flushing when the phone rang. Sometimes you can't hear the phone when the toilet's flushing.'

Sarah waited in silence, to allow the jurors' skepticism to kick in.

'Was your car in the driveway on the day in question?'

'No, it was stolen two days before.'

'You mean you *reported* it stolen?'

'I mean it *was* stolen.'

'Did it ever show up again?'

'You know what happens when a car gets stolen. They strip it down and you never see it again.'

'Just answer the question, please.'

'It hasn't been found. I rented one.'

'And what make and color was the car that was stolen?'

'An aquamarine Mercedes.'

'Just like the victim described. No further questions.'

Sarah Jensen sat. Andi stood up to salvage as much as she could on redirect.

'Just a couple of questions to clear up some things. Mr Claymore, your car was stolen on the *third* of June?'

'That's correct.'

'And at that time, Bethel Newton wasn't even in the State of California.'

'So I understand.'

Andi sat down smiling. Claymore looked at her tensely, then at Andi.

'Recross?'

Sarah Jensen stood up again. 'When did you *report* your car stolen, Mr Claymore?'

'I . . .' he trailed off. 'I told the cops about it when I was arrested in connection with this case. I intended to report it before that but—'

'I'm not interested in what you intended, Mr Claymore, only what you *did*. No further questions.'

The judge looked over at the clock above the main entrance. 'In view of the hour, I think we'll adjourn for lunch. The court will reconvene at two-thirty.'

'All rise!'

Everyone stood. The judge left through the door beside her bench. Alex and Andi started gathering up their papers as Claymore walked up to them from the witness stand, a member of the sheriff's department standing nearby just in case he got any funny ideas. He was looking at Andi, and the look was gentle, almost embarrassed.

'I just want to thank both of you for what you've done for me.'

He was looking, not at Alex Sedaka, but at Andi. She nodded, embarrassed.

'I have to go,' she said uncomfortably. 'I'll meet you back here at two-thirty.'

Wednesday, 26 August 2009 – 14.45

'So, Mr Johnson,' said Alex, 'you amplified the sample in twenty-eight cycles in the thermal cycler?'

'Yes,' said the nervous eighteen-year-old boy on the witness stand. He was thin, but not tall and could easily have been mistaken for two or three years younger than his age.

Alex had called Elias Claymore first in accordance with the general rule that the defendant should be called first, if he was to testify at all. Alex realized that Andi was right about the jury having to hear from Claymore to make them more sympathetic to his cause. She had done a creditable job, despite Claymore's early slip-up and Sarah Jensen's skillful cross-examination.

But now Alex was planning to unleash both barrels and expose a vulnerability that he thought he had discovered in the people's case.

He had obtained the judge's permission to treat Steven Johnson as a hostile witness. This meant that he could ask the witness leading questions directly. Thus many of his questions sounded like statements.

'Twenty-eight used to be the standard number of cycles for evidence samples, wasn't it?'

'Er, yes.'

'But since then it has become routine to do as many as thirty-four cycles, hasn't it?'

Alex's tone was quiet. He didn't want to alert the witness to how much he had already figured out. Nor did he want the jury to sympathize with the witness and resent the defense.

'It can be,' Steven Johnson replied, 'but it doesn't have to be.'

'But in this case you were dealing with a nail clipping sample, where there was likely to be only a small amount of offender DNA present.'

'Yes.'

'And yet you chose to run only the minimum of cycles.'

Johnson thought for a moment. 'Well there's also a risk of overproducing the victim sample.'

'But why would that matter when it was the offender DNA that you're interested in?'

'Well, if we amplify the evidence sample too much, we might make it impossible to distinguish between a major and minor contributor. And that would make it hard to identify a distinct offender component.'

'With Y-chromosomal DNA?' asked Alex sarcastically.

Johnson blushed. 'I didn't know they were going to do a Y-STR test. I thought it was going to be a standard autosomal DNA test.'

'No one told you what sort of a test it was going to be?'

'No, I merely assumed . . .' He trailed off, uncomfortably. 'I know I shouldn't have assumed. But I did.'

'And that's why you only ran the evidence sample through twenty-eight cycles?'

'Yes.'

'So no one actually told you how many cycles to run?'

'No.'

'You decided on your own initiative?'

'Yes.'

'Is that normal?'

'Sometimes.'

Alex paused for a moment and appeared to be thinking. He had actually thought about this line of questioning very carefully and knew exactly where he was going. But he wanted to give the impression that he was a bit hesitant himself, partly in order to avoid creating sympathy for Johnson but largely in order not to alert the witness himself as to what was coming.

'Does Dr Alvarez keep a close eye on you when you work?'

'What do you mean?' asked Johnson nervously.

'Well, you're only eighteen. And you're not a scientist, just a lab technician. Doesn't he have to keep a close eye on you to make sure you don't make mistakes?'

'Not at all. As a matter of fact, he lets me work unsupervised.'

'Isn't that a bit risky? I mean, wouldn't it lead to a certain amount of jealousy and conflict and interfere with good working practices?'

'Why should it lead to jealousy?' asked Johnson, sounding confused.

'Well if he lets you work unsupervised, while he keeps such a close eye on the others . . .'

'He doesn't keep a close eye on the others.'

'Oh, you mean *all* the lab assistants work unsupervised.'

Johnson suddenly realized that he had said too much, 'No. I mean . . . not all the time.'

'Oh, I see, you mean some days he says, "Today I'm going let you all work unsupervised," and other days he says, "Today I'm going keep a close eye on you." Is that right?'

'No, it's not like that.'

317

'Then what is it like?'

'It depends on . . . the circumstances.'

'You mean on the workload?'

'Yes.'

'So when the lab's not busy he keeps a close eye on you?'

'Yes.'

'And when it's busy he doesn't?'

'Yes – I mean, no!' He had already realized that he had gone too far, and he knew that there was no way of covering his tracks completely. But with every answer he gave, he seemed to be digging himself in deeper. 'I mean he always keeps an eye on us, but not as close when it's busy.'

'But not on you.'

'I don't understand.'

'He doesn't keep a close eye on you at all. Is that right?'

'No. He keeps a close eye on me too.'

'But you said he lets you work unsupervised.'

'Yes, but not completely unsupervised.'

'What do you mean not completely unsupervised? Isn't that like being a little bit pregnant?'

'I mean, he doesn't stand looking over my shoulder but he'd notice if I made a mis—'

'Yes, Mr Johnson?'

'If I made a mistake.'

Alex asked his next question, quietly but firmly. 'And did you make a mistake?'

'No.'

But he was squirming when he said it. The mere fact that the lawyer asked the question, and looked at him with those piercing eyes, was enough to make him squirm. He could have been innocent and had nothing to hide, but those piercing eyes would still have made him squirm.

'Were you busy that day?'

Johnson looked over at Sarah Jensen. Alex half turned and looked back and forth between the two, emphasizing Johnson's helplessness and making clear to the jury that Johnson was seeking help from the prosecutor.

'The witness will answer the question,' the judge said firmly.

'We were fairly busy.'

The word 'fairly' was a desperate attempt to straddle the fence – and Alex knew it. He could see right through Johnson's attempts to stick to the safe middle ground. With 'fairly busy' the witness knew that he could go either way, depending on the thrust of the next question.

'So busy that Dr Alvarez had to let you work unsupervised?'

Johnson could evade no longer. 'I guess.'

'Why were you busy?'

'I don't understand.'

He was genuinely confused, and thought he had made another blunder.

'It's a simple enough question. Why were you busy?'

'Because . . . I guess . . . because we had a lot of work to do.'

'And not enough people to do it.'

'I guess.'

'In other words, the reason you were busy is because there wasn't a big enough staff to handle the workload?'

'Yes,' replied Johnson.

'And so, if you had a lot of work to do at the lab and not enough people to do it, you would have been under pressure to get a lot of work done in a short amount of time?'

'Yes,' Johnson admitted, his voice now weak.

'And under these circumstances did you forget to do things you were supposed to do? Like being careful to avoid mishandling the sample?'

319

It was obvious to the lawyer that he wanted to answer. But he clearly didn't know what to say. Alex sensed that he had his man cornered: the witness could hold out no longer. He couldn't read Johnson's mind but he knew enough to see through him. His eyes met the boy's as if to say: *You can't hide your mistake.*

'I didn't make a mistake,' he said desperately. 'I followed procedure.'

This was the standard 'cover your ass' line at the lab. In training, they had been told that as long as you follow procedure, no one can blame you when something goes wrong.

Alex looked down at the worksheets before him. 'Before you amplified the evidence sample what did you do?'

'I . . . don't remember. I mean I'd have to check my worksheet.'

'I actually have a copy of your worksheet here.'

Alex handed two copies to the clerk who handed one to the judge and one to Johnson. The prosecution didn't need a copy as it was they who had given a copy to the defense. Johnson took it, his hands shaking.

'Now could you look at the lines above the line in which you amplified the evidence sample from the Bethel Newton case?'

'Yes.'

'What did you do?'

'I returned back-up copies of the Bethel Newton and Elias Claymore reference samples to cold storage.'

'And could you look at the line immediately before that.'

'Yes.' The voice was weak to the point of bordering on non-existence.

'Could you tell us what you did then?'

'I signed *out* the reference samples of Bethel Newton and Elias Claymore.'

On his chair, next to Andi, Claymore leaned forward, sensing a glimmer of hope in his fragile defense. 'And what was the time gap between these two actions?'

Steven Johnson looked down at the worksheets, but Alex sensed that he knew the answer to this question already.

'Four minutes?'

'And what was the purpose of taking out the back-up reference samples and putting them back four minutes later?'

Johnson started crying. 'I contaminated the evidence sample.'

Wednesday, 26 August 2009 – 14.50

Bridget Riley and Detective Nadis had finished at the Alta Bates hospital and written up their reports at the police station. Riley was being driven over to San Francisco International airport by Detective Nadis when a call came through on Nadis's cell phone. He listened mostly, prompting occasionally with a grunt or an 'uh huh.' When he had finished, it was hard to disguise the miserable look on his face.

'You look like you've just been tagged by the Grim Reaper,' she said, trying to put a humorous spin on it.

'That's what I feel like,' Nadis replied.

'Why, what is it?'

'We've just had the DNA report on the comparison between Louis Manning's reference sample and the Bethel Newton evidence sample.'

'And?'

'It's a match.'

Bridget felt a stab of shock. 'But it also matched Claymore.'

Nadis's face screwed up. 'It's Y-chromosome DNA. That's not as accurate as nuclear. They said on the TV that 1 in 500 African-Americans is likely to have this same DNA. And the defense pointed out that there are something like 37,000 or more blacks with that profile.'

'So Claymore can say it was Manning,' Bridget said. 'And

Manning will say it was Claymore. And they'll end up *both* getting off.'

'Unless we get some other evidence.'

Bridget raised her eyebrow. 'We've *got* other evidence. And it points to Claymore.'

'But that smart-ass defense lawyer is poking holes in the evidence.'

'And now we've got to disclose this to him.'

She looked glum. 'Well you know what they say: "Shit happens!"'

Wednesday, 26 August 2009 – 14.55

As Alex took in what Johnson had just said, the boy himself just stood there sobbing, covering his face with his hands.

'Would you like a few minutes to compose yourself?' asked Justice Wagner.

Johnson shook his head and struggled to continue.

'Why did you contaminate it?' asked Alex.

'What?'

It was almost like he didn't remember where he was.

'The sample – the nail clipping sample?'

'I didn't do it deliberately.'

'But when I asked you about taking out the reference samples, you said that you did it to contaminate the evidence sample.'

'No, it wasn't like that! I didn't take out the reference samples to contaminate the evidence sample. I'd *already* contaminated it.'

'How?'

'I sneezed.'

There was laughter in the courtroom. Justice Wagner silenced it with a steely-eyed stare.

'You sneezed,' Alex echoed. He wasn't trying to sound incredulous, especially as he didn't want to disrupt the flow that he had got Johnson talking. He just didn't quite manage to keep the surprise out of his voice.

'I felt it happening, but I just couldn't stop myself.'

'But weren't you supposed to be wearing a mask, in order to prevent just that sort of thing?'

Johnson looked helpless, even though he had already exposed himself and could hardly say anything to make it worse. 'I was supposed to . . . and I was going to. I'd just thrown away the old one and was about to put on a new one. But . . . like you said, we're working under so much pressure . . . I just forgot.'

Alex knew that this wasn't everything however. This was going to be painful but he had to press on. 'So what happened when you sneezed? Did it blow the sample off the table?'

Alex knew that he was being rather cruel here.

'No, but I knew it had been contaminated.'

'So what did you do?'

Johnson looked terrified. 'What do you mean?'

'You said that you checked out the back-up reference samples *after* you contaminated the evidence sample. *Why?*'

'Because I wanted to create a new one.'

A gasp went through the courtroom.

'A new sample?' asked Alex.

'Yes.'

'And *did* you create one?'

'Yes,' Johnson answered, his timid voice barely audible.

'*How?*'

'Using the reference samples of the victim and the suspect. I took a small quantity of each and combined them into a new sample and put it into the Thermal Cycler for PCR.'

'But didn't anyone see you?'

'No one was watching me. Everyone was doing their own thing. Like I said, we were all working under pressure.'

'But afterwards? Didn't they see that it wasn't a nail clipping with congealed blood?'

'It was a destructive test. Afterwards there'd've been nothing left.'

'And it was this *fake* evidence sample that was then separated and detected and matched to the defendant?'

'Objection, Your Honor,' said Sarah Jensen, rising swiftly to her feet. 'The question is compound and calls for a conclusion of the witness. This witness didn't do any of those other tasks, and unless he actually *saw* them being done, he isn't qualified to say that they were. And given that he has already stated that the lab was busy, I think we can safely rule out that possibility.'

Alex knew that he had them on the ropes now. That was why Sarah was objecting on such petty, technical grounds – because he had them beaten.

'Would you like to rephrase that question, Mr Sedaka?'

'Yes, certainly. Mr Johnson, was it this *fake* sample that you signed off on?'

'Yes,' he choked, the tears flowing profusely now.

'No further questions.'

He sat down looking solemn. Andi was smiling, but trying not to. Of all the reactions, Claymore's was the strangest. He was looking at Andi with a blank, neutral look on his face.

'Any redirect?'

'No, Your Honor,' said Sarah Jensen, uncomfortably.

Ellen Wagner looked at Steven Johnson as he sobbed uncontrollably into his hands. 'The witness is excused. I will not at this time direct that the witness be arrested. However, I am sure that the D.A. will look into this matter and take the necessary action in due course.'

Steven Johnson left the stand, his body shaking as he sobbed. Alex rose, keeping his face neutral.

'Sidebar, Your Honor,' said Alex.

'You may approach.'

Alex, Andi and Sarah Jensen approached the bench.

'Your Honor,' said Alex, 'in view of the fact this evidence isn't merely tainted but downright fake, I think that an uncontested motion for dismissal with prejudice would be in order.'

The judge turned to the Prosecutor, expectantly. 'Any objection?'

'Your Honor, this evidence may be tainted,' she replied half-heartedly, 'but we have a reliable back-up system in place.'

Wednesday, 26 August 2009 – 15.00

Gene Vance was watching the trial at the rape crisis center. She had returned to LA, explaining to Andi that she was needed there and couldn't take any more time off. But her mind wasn't really on the job.

A strange sensation of confusion wafted over her as she tried to take in what she had just seen. One moment the case against Elias Claymore looked rock solid. The next moment it was on the verge of collapse. Gene didn't know much about law in general but she knew about rape law and there was no way the prosecution case could survive the shocking revelation that had just emerged in court.

No matter the strength of the victim testimony, it was the DNA that incontrovertibly linked the rape to Claymore. Without that, Bethel's contradictory accounts of the assailant's age would make it impossible to convict him. Gene could only guess at what they were talking about at the sidebar. The microphones were switched off for that. But she assumed that there was some technical quibbling about whether the charges could be dropped without prejudice so that they could conduct a retrial without the tainted evidence. Not that they would. But it would be a face-saving formula for the prosecutor. The D.A. would announce later that they were dropping the charges. If the judge required that the charges be dismissed *with* prejudice now, then it would be a crushing humiliation for Sarah Jensen and she would take the rap, because the D.A.'s office needed a scapegoat.

Gene felt sorry for her. But she also felt sorry for Bethel. Bethel wanted some semblance of justice. Now she was getting nothing. She would be leaving the court empty-handed.

That wasn't right.

She picked up the phone and called a number.

Wednesday, 26 August 2009 – 15.05

'What do you mean?' asked Justice Wagner, leaning forward.

'We had three nail clipping samples, two from the index and middle finger of Miss Newton's left hand and one from the thumb of her right. These samples were all stored separately, so as to ensure that if they had to be tested destructively, some portion of the sample would be preserved. Therefore, although the lab assistant lost one sample, there are two other samples available for testing purposes and these two samples are still in storage at the Ventura lab. I suggest that the court grant a continuance so that we can process and test one of these samples.'

Alex was getting increasingly irritated, as he sensed victory slipping away. 'Your Honor, if this is so then why did this witness create a fake sample? Why did he simply not check out one of the spare samples?'

'I think the answer is obvious,' said Justice Wagner. 'He didn't want to admit his own mistake. Also he may not have known about the other samples. He only knew what he was told. Maybe he was just given the one evidence sample and was told to test it with no other instructions. At any rate, the other samples exist, so they *can* be tested.'

'Your Honor, even if this is so, in view of the behavior of this employee of the lab and the failure of the lab to stop him or even detect his misconduct, my client has legitimate grounds for concern over the reliability of any future testing procedures done by this lab until the matter can be thoroughly investigated. Moreover because of the evidence on record already, I would submit that this jury is tainted by that false evidence.'

'You could always move a mistrial *with* prejudice, Mr Sedaka. That way we could start again with a new jury.'

Alex hesitated. He knew that this would enable prosecution witnesses to avoid the pitfalls that they had fallen into the first time around. But then he realized that it might have the opposite effect. Alvarez could only answer according to the science and whatever the new tests showed, he would have to testify accordingly. But Albert Carter and Bethel Newton might be reluctant to testify at all – after the humiliation they been put through on cross-examination.

'I'm ready to accept that, Your Honor.'

But now Sarah Jensen was panicking. 'Your Honor, that would be extremely disruptive and would cause considerable distress to several prosecution witnesses who are clearly emotionally fragile and who have been testifying in good faith.'

Ellen Wagner thought for a moment. 'At this stage we don't know what the results of the tests will be. There seems to be no point in anticipating the results. If the new tests exclude the defendant then the matter will be decided for us. If not, then I'll hear legal arguments as to how to proceed at that stage. In the meantime, how long will the tests take?'

Justice Wagner had turned to Sarah Jensen when she asked this.

'We'll be using Y-STR again so four or five days should be enough.'

The judge turned to Alex. 'In the event that the new tests

fail to exclude the defendant will the defense be ready with legal arguments by Monday morning?'

'Yes, Your Honor.'

'Ms Jensen?'

'Yes, Your Honor.'

'All right, this case is adjourned until Monday morning.'

Wednesday, 26 August, 2009 – 18.00

Andi hadn't told Gene about the adjournment. Instead she decided to do what Gene had done at the weekend and surprise her lover with an unexpected midweek visit. Of course Gene might catch a TV news report in which they'd mention that the court wasn't due to reconvene until Monday. But she was unlikely to make anything of it.

It would be nice to surprise her.

She decided, when she arrived at the airport in the early afternoon, to go home while Gene was at work and have a hot dinner waiting for her in the oven, to be served on their best china on a lace tablecloth, complete with candlelight and wine. It was a long time since they had done anything romantic.

The house had been empty when she arrived and she took this as a sign that Gene was working late as usual. Now, as she prepared boeuf bourguignon in an empty house, she felt guilty about leaving Gene alone while she had been up in Oakland, fighting for that lowlife who was – as Gene had said – so unworthy of her efforts.

But at least, she told herself, it enabled her to surprise Gene with a beautifully laid table, when she finally came home. But as eight o'clock went by and blended into nine o'clock, there was still no sign of Gene. At first Andi tried to keep the food warm for Gene's arrival, but had finally given up and turned it off altogether, rather than let it get overdone and dried out.

But now with nothing more to do but wait, a desolate loneliness swept over her. Being here alone, made her feel uncomfortable and she realized now how difficult it must have been for Gene all these days in her absence.

Seized by guilt she went out to her car and drove off to the rape crisis center.

Wednesday, 26 August 2009 – 20.30

'Hi, Bethel. How are you holding up?'

'Okay,' Bethel replied weakly.

'Did you see what happened in court?'

'Yes . . . on the TV . . .'

'Me too.'

Bethel had been staying at a witness hostel up in Oakland because she had to continue attending the trial until she was discharged, in case either party needed to recall her as a witness. But after the adjournment she had got a message on her cell phone that had brought her back down to LA.

'I was afraid they were going to throw the case out.'

'But they didn't,' said Bethel.

'I know. I guess now we know why the DNA implicated Claymore.'

'Yes, but now that they've found out . . .'

Bethel trailed off, unable to get the words out.

'I know, I know. But that was always the risk. You know what the Italians say: *Que sera, sera.*'

'What?'

'What will be, will be.'

Bethel started to cry.

'Hey, listen. I don't want to hear any of that. At least you gave the bastard a good scare.'

337

'Yes, but that's not what I'm worried about.'

'There's *nothing* to worry about. Even if Claymore is cleared, that doesn't make you a liar. And they can't touch you. All it means is that it was a case of mistaken identity.'

'No, you don't understand! I scratched you *too*!'

'What are you talking about?'

'When I dug my fingers into your arm. Don't you remember?'

There was a moment's hesitation. 'That was your *right* hand. I'm sure of it.'

'Yes . . .'

'Well, which of your hands did they take the nail clippings from, left or right?'

'The left, I think. No, wait a minute. I think they took from both. Two from the left and one from the right.'

'Okay, well never mind. That's nothing to worry about. They're using Y chromosome DNA, and only men have that. Anyway, there's nothing to compare it to – nothing from me I mean.'

'All right.'

'Okay, well get a good night's sleep . . . and stop worrying.'

'There's something else . . . something weird happened on Saturday.'

'What?'

'I had a call from a woman. I don't know how she got my number. But she said that she was going to make sure that Claymore got what he deserved.'

'And it wasn't anyone you know?'

'It sounded familiar, but it was a bit distorted.'

'Did she say how she got your number?'

'No.'

'Did you ask her?'

'I didn't think about it at the time. She caught me off guard.'

'And did she say who she was? Or *what* she was? I mean, what she did?'

'No . . . but she told me a name. It was kind of a weird name.'

'Well, what was it?'

'I think it was something like . . . Lannosea. At least that's what it sounded like.'

'Lannosea?'

'Yes. Does it mean anything?'

'No. But I think I'd better Google it and see what comes up.'

Wednesday, 26 August 2009 – 21.05

As she drove to the rape crisis center, Andi thought about what she was actually doing: helping a rapist who had allegedly reformed but who had grown rich on the strength of his notoriety. And yet in terms of professional ethics, she was doing nothing wrong. It was these negative thoughts that went against the canons of her profession. People in her line of work were not supposed to get emotionally involved in their cases. Fight like hell for your client no matter what you personally believe. But if they go down for the crime, you'll know at least that they were given a fair trial and the system worked.

And what if, on the other hand, you manage to save them when they may in fact be guilty? How do you live with that?

She knew the answer. The system has its own kind of natural selection in the long run. A criminal who gets off may go one of two ways. They might learn from the experience of almost going down for the crime and be so frightened that they go straight. Or they might get cocky and think that they can carry on breaking the law with impunity. And the more they break the law, the greater their chances of getting caught in the future.

That's the way the system worked. It didn't catch all the bad guys and it didn't always spare the innocent. But in a rough and ready sort of way it balanced itself out and maintained some semblance of equilibrium.

And yet it made her feel uncomfortable. Even *one* injustice was one too many, especially when it was a crime like rape. But Andi knew that she couldn't allow herself to get personally involved – neither with the client nor the alleged victim. If she did, she wouldn't be able to sleep at night. But not everyone can switch off their emotions like that.

In truth, she wasn't sure if Claymore was guilty or not. He talked like an innocent man, even in the privacy of a conference with his own lawyers. And yet Bethel Newton insisted that he was guilty. The scientific evidence also suggested guilt, albeit inconclusively.

As she withdrew from these painful ruminations, she became aware of her new surroundings. Somehow she had arrived at the rape crisis center without noticing the journey. As she pulled up in the parking lot at the back of the building, she dreaded to think how she must have been driving on the way there.

She got out of the car and swept into the building, still rigid with the tension that she couldn't shake off. An armed female guard recognized her through the video-intercom and pressed the button to open the first of the reinforced glass doors. Andi entered the 'airlock' as she thought of it and the guard opened the inner doors to let her into the building. They exchanged a smile as Andi went upstairs to the first floor.

A few steps took her to Gene's office halfway down the wide corridor. But when she looked through the small porthole-shaped window in the door to see if Gene was alone, she got a surprise. For there was her lover engaged in earnest conversation with Bethel Newton.

Wednesday, 26 August 2009 – 21.30

Louis Manning was in a private room at the Alta Bates Medical Center, handcuffed to the bedrail, with a uniformed police officer sitting by the bed at all times. He had now been charged with the attempted rape of Martine Yin, but the arraignment had been postponed as he was in no position to be moved. His broken leg was still in traction. But at least it was a private room.

He smiled at the irony that he was getting better medical treatment as a criminal than he ever had as an ordinary citizen. However, he knew that his leg had healed enough to permit escape as soon as the opportunity arose. The trouble was the opportunity had yet to arise. He felt confident that he could walk – or at least limp – but he certainly couldn't run.

And the fact that he was handcuffed to the bed when not eating, meant that he could not run away when the officer left his bedside, as occasionally happened.

He had considered other options such as stabbing the officer in the eye with a syringe and then grabbing the keys for the handcuffs. There were sometimes syringes within reach, especially when they injected painkillers into the bag of his saline drip. But he dismissed the idea on two grounds. Firstly, the syringe was seldom inserted into the saline bag and then left there; when the saline bag was injected there was usually a nurse or a doctor nearby. Secondly, even if there were no other persons nearby, sticking a syringe into the cop's eye would cause the officer to scream with pain, thus attracting the attention of others, thereby making escape more difficult. He had to contend with the reality that he might not be able to walk but only hobble and for that reason he needed to escape without attracting the attention of anyone.

But he was working on another plan. Because a hospital is a busy place, even at night, the patients were offered night sedation to help them sleep. The sedation came in the form of a tablet to be orally imbibed. But over the past few days Manning had not been swallowing the tablet. Instead, he had been holding it under his tongue and swallowing the water that was offered with it.

It was a tricky operation: under the tongue, swallow, hand back the plastic cup, wait twenty seconds or so while the nurse went away, reach for a tissue and spit it out into the tissue under the guise of coughing or sneezing. When the cop went to relieve himself he would add the pill to the collection that he had accumulated, wrapped in a single tissue in the bedside cabinet. He was building up a nice little consolidated supply of sleeping pills and when he was ready, he would make his move.

Wednesday, 26 August 2009 – 21.35

Andi stood there for a few seconds, thoroughly confused.

Gene wasn't supposed to have any contact with Bethel Newton. She was under a legal injunction.

So what was Gene doing talking to Bethel now? And did this mean that she had been in contact with her the whole time leading up to the trial? How long had this been going on?

She needed to know. But would Gene tell her? If Gene was doing things behind her back would she open up now? Should she confront Gene and demand to know what was going on?

The trouble was that Bethel Newton was in there too. If she went in now and confronted her lover then what sort of effect would it have on Bethel? It would be frightening, traumatic. And Bethel had been through enough trauma to last a lifetime. What right did she have to add to her suffering by storming in there now to demand answers?

Her beef was with Gene.

And in any case, if she went in now, she had a duty as an officer of the court to notify the judge. That would lead to a mistrial and the whole process would start again, with Claymore still in custody. She had a duty to him too. He was in prison, in solitary confinement, living every day in fear that another inmate would kill him. If she caused a mistrial now, the next free slot for the trial might not be for months. They couldn't even argue that this would be a violation of his right to a speedy trial – because the defense would have *caused* it. She couldn't condemn Claymore to several more months in jail awaiting trial. She had to find a way to deal with this sensibly.

An idea struck her. It might *still* lead to a mistrial, but it was worth a shot.

She turned sharply and walked out.

Wednesday, 26 August 2009 – 21.40

'So it looks like both the Claymore and Manning tests are invalid,' said Sarah Jensen.

She had tried to call Detective Riley earlier in the day, after the courtroom debacle with Steven Johnson. But she was told that Bridget was in transit, and she couldn't reach her on her cell phone. Bridget was now back at home in Ventura and Sarah Jensen was filling her in on what had happened in court yesterday, with particular emphasis on the afternoon's proceedings.

'Still, it's funny that both results were positive.'

'Yeah, weird that,' said Sarah. 'But the evidence sample they compared it to was falsified, so the old result doesn't mean jack shit.'

'Yes, but that's what worries me. What if it happens again with the back-up sample? What if we get two matches?'

'It *could* happen. Sedaka's already established that there are 37,000 African-Americans with that same haplotype.'

'I have a bad feeling about this. I think Sedaka's going to try and throw up a smokescreen.'

'He's done that already. We're just going to have to point out that the DNA isn't the only evidence against Claymore. It's just one piece of the puzzle.'

Wednesday, 26 August 2009 – 22.30

It was later that evening when Andi came home. Gene was curled up on the couch in the den. She had seen the TV, but she leapt to her feet when Andi entered.

'Where were you? I was worried about you!'

'What do you mean?' asked Andi coldly.

'I found the dinner you cooked. Where d'you go? Andi?'

Gene had finally noticed the anger on Andi's face. The next thing she knew, Andi's hand was lashing out towards her. Instinctively she covered herself against it and blinked. But what she felt against her forearm was not a blow, but the light slap of a piece of paper. When she opened her eyes a split second later, she saw that the paper was an envelope. Andi made no effort to hold on to it and let it slip with her fingers. Acting more on instinct than reason, Gene caught the envelope before it could fall.

'You've been served,' said Andi coldly.

It took Gene a second to understand what was happening as she looked into Andi's piercing eyes and saw the intractable look. She tore open the envelope and read the page to see a subpoena ordering her to be available as a witness on Monday the thirty-first of August until discharged by the court in the case of the *State of California* v *Elias Claymore*.

'What is this?'

'I'm calling you as a witness.'

Gene looked at Andi helplessly, while Andi looked back, if not with confidence, then at least with anger. In this moment, their roles were reversed.

'Why are you doing this?' asked Gene.

'I have a duty to my client.'

Then, without another word she turned abruptly and stormed out.

But Gene realized that Andi could not remain strong for long. And only now, in Andi's absence, with the spell of anger broken, did Gene succumb to concern for Andi rather than fear for herself.

She leapt to her feet and ran out after her lover, flinging the front door open just in time to hear Andi's car roar to life and watch it speed away. She looked on helplessly. Then, unsure of what she was going to do next, she walked slowly back into the house.

Saturday, 29 August 2009 – 01.20

Paul Greenberg sat at the console of the computer, with a Styrofoam cup of coffee in one hand and a science fiction book in the other. It was a strange way to be celebrating his twenty-fourth birthday. But when you *look* like a nerd and *think* like one, you may as well act like one. In any case, the county of Ventura paid good money for systems administrators to watch over the network at the Ventura County Government Center, the building that housed the pre-trial detention facility, the court, the forensic lab, and the Local DNA Database Index.

And on the graveyard shift, it wasn't even hard work. At just after one o'clock in the morning there was virtually nothing for him to do. But there had to be a systems administrator there at all times in case anything went wrong with the network. The network and its peripherals had to be able to operate twenty-four hours a day. He was, in effect, the night watchman.

When the phone by the computer console broke the silence with its inordinately loud ring, it was so unexpected that he practically jumped out of his seat. The switchboard operated 24/7, but the loud ring only occurred when people called the number for the direct line.

'IT department.'

'Hallo, could I speak to Linda, please?' said a woman's voice. There was something warm and strangely seductive about the voice. But then again, most women's voices were seductive to an anorak like Greenberg.

'Linda?' echoed Greenberg.

'Linda Black,' said the woman.

'There's no Linda Black *here*. Are you sure she works nights?'

'Of course I'm sure.'

The woman sounded irritated. It put Greenberg on the defensive. 'I can't say I've ever heard of her. Are you sure you've got the right department?'

'What do you mean *department*?' Now the woman sounded bewildered. 'Who *are* you?'

'Paul Greenberg. I'm the systems administrator.'

'Systems what?'

'Administrator.'

It gave him a good feeling to say that. All of a sudden he felt as if he were the chief of operations in some major control room. The woman sounded like she was getting flustered but now she had given him a chance to flash his credentials at her. He hoped she was suitably impressed.

'Wait a minute, that isn't Ritchie's Pizza?'

'No it isn't.' By now Greenberg was thoroughly amused. 'This is the California Government Center.'

'Oh, God, this is so embarrassing,' replied the woman, gushing awkwardly. 'Gee, you must think I'm a right kook.'

'It's all right. We all make mistakes.'

'Look, I'm sorry I disturbed you. You must be terribly busy.'

There was an awkward silence, as if she was waiting for him to say something.

'No, not really. It gets kind of boring on the graveyard

shift. I mean the system has to be manned twenty-four hours a day just in case the network goes down, but it's basically only used during the day.'

'What, you mean like a computer network?'

'That's right,' said Greenberg, enjoying the warm enthusiasm in her voice.

'I don't really know much about computers. My ex-boyfriend tried to explain it to me once, but it was all too technical for me.'

She *did* sound impressed . . . and she said *ex*-boyfriend.

'Well it's a field that's got too much jargon. But it's really all very logical.'

'Oh, I'm sorry, I guess I should . . . My name is Barbie. Barbie Jackson.'

'Paul Greenberg. You can call me Paul.'

'Thanks. And you can call me Barbie. So what exactly do *you* do, Paul? I mean what's a . . . what did you call it? Administrator?'

'Systems administrator.'

'Is that like higher than a programmer?'

Greenberg smiled at the prospect of enlightening this neophyte. She sounded like she was in awe of his knowledge already. Maybe he'd get lucky with her. 'Not exactly. I mean I *am* a programmer. But that's not my job *here*. I'm in charge of the system as a whole. I make sure that it's working okay, that all the computers on the network are okay, that everything gets properly backed up and all the passwords stored safely.'

'You mean you know everyone's password? I guess they must really trust you.'

'No, but if they lose it I can access their files and give them a new password. I mean, they do trust me, I guess. I'm what's called a superuser.'

'*Super*user?' she repeated, rolling the words on her tongue. 'That sounds kind of sexy. What does it mean?'

He smiled, his ego well and truly buttered.

'It means I'm a highly privileged user.'

'You make it sound so *exciting*.'

Looking around at the dimly lit room and through the windows at the panoramic view of the lights around the bay, he realized that he had built it up out of all proportion with a few simple words. It was time to let her down gently. 'Believe me, it's not. It's actually rather boring.'

'Oh!' She sounded disappointed. 'I always thought that sort of work was terribly exciting. I mean, how do you do all these things? Do you have your own special privileged user password?'

'That's exactly it. I have a password which the computer recognizes as a superuser password and it gives me access to all sorts of things that other users don't have access to.'

'My ex-boyfriend used to have a password for his computer. But I knew what it was.'

She sounded like an airhead. But so what? She was fun, and she seemed to like him . . . at least over the phone.

'What was it?'

'It was a four-letter word,' she said, giggling.

He was now sure of his airhead theory. But then again, she had a kind of naïve charm. It wasn't her head that he was interested in. He imagined her with platinum blonde hair, silicone-enhanced breasts and wide childbearing hips. That was the marvelous thing about the phone – and the Internet – you could imagine the other person as whatever you liked.

'A lot of users are like that. They pick a four-letter word or a derogatory comment about their boss.'

'I bet you don't. You sound too intellectual for that.'

354

He was surprised that she even *knew* the word intellectual. It didn't seem to go with her overall vocabulary, at least not with the vocabulary that she had displayed so far. But then again, who could say for sure? She was just a voice on the other end of the phone.

'I'll plead guilty to that,' he said. 'Although usually they don't call us intellectuals. They call us nerds.'

'I can just imagine you picking some longwinded off-the-wall password like "Rumplestiltskin."'

Well, at least she reads children's stories, he thought. 'No, I use a short password. They're easier to remember and harder to mistype.'

'I can understand the bit about typing, but I'd've thought it doesn't matter how long the password is, as long as it's something you're likely to remember.'

'Well, I always use my mother's maiden name.'

'Isn't that two words?' she asked with another girlish giggle.

'Just the surname,' he said.

'Okay, well I won't ask you what it is. Listen, I've got to go now 'cause I promised Linda I'd call her. Look, maybe I could call you again tomorrow?'

'Sure. I'd like that. I'm on night duty all week.'

'Okay. I'll talk to you tomorrow. Can I call you during the day?'

'No, I'm only on nights: ten at night till six in the morning.'

'Okay, I'll call same time tomorrow.'

After she hung up, Paul Greenberg tried to get back into his book. But he couldn't concentrate on it anymore.

Sunday, 30 August 2009 – 9.50

But she did not call him back the same time the following day. The next time she called was Sunday morning.

'Ventura County,' said the switchboard operator, answering the call. It was a woman's voice, one of those artificially cheerful telephone voices that dripped saccharine from every word.

'Could you put me through to the IT systems administrator?' said the woman on the other end of the line. Her voice was deeper than the last time she called. Now she was trying to sound more like a serious, educated professional than an airhead. She didn't want her call to be diverted to some lackey away from the computer console.

'Who's calling?'

'Oh, er Barbara,' the woman replied. 'Barbara Jackson.' She sounded flustered, almost as if she had forgotten her name.

'Just one minute.'

'Systems administration,' said a man's voice.

'Hallo, can I speak to Paul Greenberg, please.'

Now she sounded like the airhead again. The voice was higher, almost squeaky.

'I'm afraid he's not here at the moment. He's on nights this week.'

'Oh, God, I'm sorry,' said the woman, sounding deeply embarrassed. 'I guess I'm making a bit of a fool of myself.'

'I don't understand.'

The systems administrator sounded confused, but there was a kind of enthusiasm in his voice.

'Well I spoke to him last night. I got a wrong number and we started talking. He sounded kind of cute.'

'Oh yeah, he—'

The systems administrator broke off. The woman well knew why. He had been about to say 'He told me all about you,' but realized it would have been tactless. It would have made Paul seem like a gossip.

'Yes?'

The systems administrator fumbled for something else to say instead. 'He's working nights all this week.'

The systems administrator realized that he had said this a moment ago.

'I don't suppose you could tell me if he . . . no I shouldn't ask.'

'What?' asked the man, smiling. He was enjoying listening to her. She had this kind of girlish way of babbling about her, just like Paul had said.

'Well, I was just wondering if he had a girlfriend.'

The systems administrator was grinning broadly at this. No wonder Paul couldn't stop talking about her.

'Not as far as I know.'

He will pretty soon though, thought the systems administrator. *It sounds like his luck is changing.*

'He hasn't?'

Greenberg's colleague realized that he had made a faux pas. 'I mean he just broke up with his girlfriend. He's kind of . . . um . . . upset about it. But he tries not to show it.'

'Oh . . . well . . . I was wondering if you could tell me a couple of things? I know I shouldn't ask, but it's just that I'm kind of curious.'

'Like what?'

If she hadn't sounded like such an airhead, his suspicions would have been aroused by this question. But she sounded too dumb to be a threat to security.

'Well like, he said he was five foot ten.'

There was muffled laughter at the other end of the line.

'Was he *lying*?' she asked, almost overdoing the girlish indignation.

'Well, I mean, not exactly lying . . . maybe just exaggerating.'

'And what about his eyes? What color are they?'

'What did he tell you?'

'Ah, no,' she said with another little nervous giggle, 'if I tell you that, then you'll just say the same thing.'

'Well, I've never really looked at his eyes.'

Typical of a man! 'Could they be blue?'

'I . . . I think so.'

The systems administrator breathed a sigh of relief. If she was some sort of a criminal, with infiltration in mind, she certainly couldn't slip in a ringer based on a mere description of Greenberg's eyes and height.

'Okay, now this time, you have to give me a straight answer without any help from me. How *old* is he?'

'Twenty-four.'

'Do you . . .' she broke off for a couple of seconds. 'Oh, God this is gonna sound *really* silly.'

'No, go on.'

'Do you . . . by any chance . . . know what his star sign is?'

'I'm not sure. Oh, wait a minute! Yesterday was his birthday.'

'So he's a Virgo!' she blurted out enthusiastically. 'And I'm a Taurus! That makes us compatible.'

She asked a few more questions. But that was really all she wanted.

Sunday, 30 August 2009 – 11.25

Lannosea's fingers were flying across the keyboard. She hadn't even needed to go to the public records office. All the records of births, marriage, divorce and death had now been put online. It always amazed her that so many people relied on their mother's maiden name for security purposes, when it's a detail so easy to obtain. She knew his name and she knew his age. She could have searched through the records based on his name and the quarter of the year in which he was born. But having his exact date of birth made the process even quicker.

So, after getting the information from the daytime systems administrator, she had logged on to the public records and looked for the record of Paul Greenberg's birth based on his age and birthday. This record included his mother's maiden name: Ruth Berman. And he had already told her that he used his mother's maiden name as his password.

But yesterday they might not yet have scanned the electropherogram from the new DNA profile into the computer. It normally takes four days from start to finish, and the judge had ordered it on Wednesday. They probably wouldn't even run the actual comparison until Sunday morning. That meant that she had her window of opportunity now.

Using the information she had, she set about gaining

access to the Ventura Local Database Index System. At the simplest level, with his password in her possession, she could try using a remote access program to gain direct access to the server.

But there were several problems with that. First of all she didn't know the IP address for that particular server. She had used various publicly available look-up tables to establish which *range* of IP addresses were used by the Ventura Government Center, but she didn't know which one was reserved for the LDIS in particular. She could try them all one by one, but that was risky. If she keyed in one stroke wrong, it might set off an alarm. Even if she did everything right, it might still alert someone. Some of the computers on the network might be set up to deny external access and warn the systems administrator as soon as a log-on attempt was made.

So instead she started off by logging on to the server used by the Ventura Sheriff's Department website. They couldn't have any alarms on this server, because it was intended to be publicly accessed. The most they could have was password control to anyone seeking to gain administrator or root level access. But that was a chance she had to take. At the root prompt she typed in 'pgreenberg' as the username and 'Berman' as the password. Her reasoning was that Greenberg was evidently a lazy person for using such a short and obvious password to begin with, so it was probable that he used some form of his name as his username.

In a matter of seconds, she had root control over the website server.

So far, so good. But now she had to find not only which other computers were on the network, but also the relationship between them. She did this by running a series of Remote Procedure Calls or RPCs. These were simply mini programs in which one computer contacted another computer and asked it to do certain things.

This process told her the IP address of the computer that housed the LDIS. But it also enabled her to build up a 'trust model' of the entire local network. That is, which of the computers in the network trusted which others. There was one computer in the middle of the hub – the network server, appropriately enough – that was apparently trusted by all the others. It was not online directly, but she could go from the website server to the network server and from there to the LDIS server. And once there – assuming the lazy Paul Greenberg used the same username and password – she could pretty much do what she liked.

Next she downloaded the evidence sample file. She was going to use it to create a new version of Elias Claymore's reference sample to match the minor contributor in the crime scene sample. But then she realized that this was a foolish idea. They could always get a new reference sample from Claymore if there was even the *slightest* doubt about its authenticity, whether now or at any time in the future.

But on the other hand, the evidence sample would have to be *destructively* tested. They *couldn't* create another. So she decided to change the evidence sample itself, to bring it into line with the Elias Claymore reference sample. To do this, she deleted the evidence sample file and then down-loaded Claymore's reference sample file. She then replaced the data on the evidence sample file, with data copied from Claymore's reference sample file, thus making it look like Claymore matched the source of the evidence sample. Then she uploaded this new evidence sample file and the job was done.

In theory, the time of this modification would be noted by the system. But the chances were that the original evidence sample file had only been uploaded from the lab that morning. Of course they could trace the IP address where it came from. But only if they were looking. And they would assume that their security was so good that there was no reason to suspect tampering in the first place.

She would have liked to go up one level to the California State Database Index System and poke around there, but that would have been a bit *too* risky.

Sunday, 30 August 2009 – 14.50

'You're spoiling me,' said Alex as Martine served him a plate that was full to toppling point.

Alex had invited Martine again for Friday evening dinner, which they had prepared together this time. Again it had been a traditional Jewish 'Sabbath' meal – even though he wasn't orthodox – egg and onions, followed by chicken soup with matzoballs, roast chicken with roast potatoes and a freshly made fruit salad at the end.

Like last week, Martine had stayed the night, as he had predicted she would from the overnight bag in her hand when he answered the door. But this time, she had stayed over till Sunday and was now reciprocating his culinary hospitality by treating him to a traditional English Sunday roast, complete with roast beef (he drew the line at pork), roast potatoes and parsnips, sage and onion stuffing, Yorkshire pudding, Brussels sprouts, carrots and peas.

'So they said they'll courier the DNA results over?' asked Martine.

'As soon as they get them.'

'Any bets on what they'll show?'

'Not with me. All bets are off.'

She was looking at him across the table. 'You look uncomfortable.'

'It's the waiting, it's the hardest part,' he said.

'Do you mean for us or for Claymore?'

Alex shrugged sheepishly. 'You're right. Here we are feeling sorry for ourselves when it's Elias whose fate is hanging in the balance.'

It was later, when they were clearing away the plates and loading up the dishwasher, that the doorbell rang. Alex went to answer it, looking through the spy hole first. It was a man in a brown uniform, a courier. Alex had been expecting this. He opened the door and signed for the envelope. In his excitement, he was already ripping it open as he walked back to the dining room.

'The DNA results?' asked Martine, meeting him in the corridor.

'Yes.'

Alex flipped past the first page to look at the crucial second page with its results. And what it showed was not good news.

Much to Alex's disappointment, it showed that the Y-STR profile of the sample marked as 'Ref, Elias Claymore' did match the sample, with no exclusions. Not that this made him guilty. They had already established that the chance of a random match between the evidence sample and an African-American was 1 in 500 and that was confirmed on this report too. But after the way Alex had exposed Steven Johnson's tampering, it was bitterly disappointing.

The question was, could he block this evidence? Technically, the prosecution had rested their case. Even if the case wasn't dismissed, Alex could argue that the prosecution could not introduce this report, as they could not now introduce any new material, except to rebut new evidence. And the defense had offered nothing to rebut. They hadn't offered any evidence that purported to show that the DNA was *not*

	DYS 19	DYS 385a	DYS 385b	DYS 389 I	DYS 389 II	DYS 390	DYS 391	DYS 392	DYS 393	DYS 438	DYS 439	DYS 437	DYS 448	DYS 456	DYS 458	DYS 635	Y-GATA -H4
Newton Finger nail (mid-finger)	4	5	2	4	5	3	2	5	2	2	2	5	5	4	3	5	2
Ref, Elias Claymore	4	5	2	4	5	3	2	5	2	2	2	5	5	4	3	5	2
Ref, Louis Manning	4	5	2	4	5	3	2	5	2	2	2	5	5	4	3	5	2

from Elias Claymore. They had merely discredited the evidence purporting to show that it *was*.

On Monday morning he would move that this new evidence be excluded. If the judge granted the motion, the prosecution would then move to dismiss the case without prejudice, intending to go for a retrial. He would then argue that there were no grounds for dismissal, as there had been no procedural errors. The prosecution had merely introduced flawed evidence that had now been discredited. If the prosecution were sloppy with the evidence they introduced then they must live with the consequences.

But then he noticed another line on the report that stated: 'Neither Elias Claymore nor Louis Manning can be eliminated as suspects on a basis of this comparison.' He flipped over to the grid with the comparison. He had been so focused on comparing Elias Claymore's line to that of the evidence sample, that he had missed the other line. Beneath 'Ref, Elias Claymore' was a line that stated 'Ref, Louis Manning.' And the numbers of repetitions in that line also matched the evidence sample.

Then, in the Frequency of Occurrence Estimates, it gave the figure for Caucasians as 1 in 4000, for blacks as 1 in 500 and for Hispanics as 1 in 6500.

So they had a second suspect, for what that was worth. But who was this Louis Manning? And why was his name so familiar? Whoever he was, this report referred to him as a suspect. But he hadn't been mentioned in the first report. Maybe he was someone who had come to the attention of the police since then. But why had Alex not been notified?

'What is it?' asked Martine, seeing the look on his face.

'There's another suspect. And he also matches the DNA sample.'

'Let me see,' she said, snatching the report from Alex's hand. 'Oh my God!' she blurted out.

'What?'

'It's Louis Manning.'

'That name sounds familiar?'

'Good God! For a lawyer, you sure could use a bit more attention to detail. That's the name of the man who tried to rape me!'

Sunday, 30 September 2009 – 22.15

Paul Greenberg was sitting at the console of the network server looking at an information log on the screen. It was one of the routine checks that he did at the start of his shift. He took his role as systems administrator very seriously, so the first thing he did whenever he started his shift was run a series of checks to find out in what state the system had been left by whoever was last on duty as systems administrator.

It was while he was making these routine checks that he noticed something unexpected. He leaned forward and peered intently at the screen. What he saw shocked him. It showed him logged on earlier during the day. That didn't make any sense. He was on nights.

He typed in an instruction and called up another screen of information. Not only did the user log show him as logged on to the system, but the activity log even showed him uploading and downloading files – something that he hadn't done all week. The only time he would download or upload files was if he was requested to help staff members of law enforcement agencies who were having trouble using the system.

A few more information requests gave him a clearer idea of what had happened. Someone had accessed the system from outside, via the web server and not only gained root control over it, but from there had gone on to gain access to the DNA database server via the network server. That could mean trouble.

He transferred his attention to the DNA database server and checked the activity log there. And what he saw filled him with horror.

Someone had remotely deleted a file and replaced it with another.

That wasn't right! The DNA server wasn't supposed to be accessed remotely. It was a Local DNA Database Index, with the emphasis on the word 'Local.' It was only supposed to be used by the local DNA lab in the government center itself. Indeed one of the conditions for the LDIS being allowed to upload to the California SDIS and the NDIS in Washington DC was that they disallow remote access to the LDIS server. But some hacker had evidently bypassed this by logging on to the web server and maneuvering their way through the internal trusted connections. And what was worse – Greenberg realized – they had done so by impersonating *him*.

He had to tell someone. But at this time there was no one to tell. He had to find out more.

Monday, 31 August 2009 – 10.15

It was Monday morning and once again the lawyers were in Justice Ellen Wagner's chambers to deal with the issues arising out of the results of the DNA tests.

As they were all familiar with the results already, Justice Wagner was taking the initiative.

'We have now established that neither Elias Claymore nor Louis Manning can be eliminated as suspects based on the DNA alone. As matters stand, the jury is aware of the falsification of the original DNA evidence by Steven Johnson. As they have been made aware of this, it cannot be held that this will have a prejudicial effect against the defendant. However, the new evidence cannot now be introduced by the prosecution because the prosecution has rested its case.'

Sarah Jensen leaned forward. 'Your Honor, we would seek to introduce this as rebuttal evidence.'

Justice Wagner looked at Sarah Jensen with condescension bordering on contempt. 'You've got to be kidding, Ms Jensen. There's no way this could be considered rebuttal.'

'Steven Johnson was a defense witness, Your Honor. It's in response to his testimony. Therefore technically . . .' She trailed off, realizing just how weak her argument was.

Justice Wagner spoke. 'This isn't rebuttal of Steven Johnson's evidence. This is *new* evidence. You're not challenging the fact that the State's own DNA testing was flawed by Steven Johnson's carelessness and subsequent chicanery. You're asking for a second shot to make up for the fact that your original DNA evidence was discredited.'

Sarah Jensen remained silent.

'I can understand your concern. You fear that if I declare a mistrial, even without prejudice, you won't be able to persuade Bethel Newton to testify at the retrial after what she's been through already. Mr Sedaka, you're also caught on the horns of a dilemma and you don't know whether to push for a mistrial or not. I've made it clear that I won't grant a mistrial with prejudice, but will simply order a retrial. You fear that if the case goes to retrial, Bethel Newton might yet be persuaded to testify and will be better prepared this time around. You also fear that a retrial will deny you the benefit of having discredited the prosecution's DNA evidence and even open the door to the people introducing the new DNA tests, although you will, for your part, be allowed to introduce the fact that that the genetic profile also matches Louis Manning.'

'I can do that now, without a retrial, Your Honor,' said Alex.

'Except that if you do, then I would have to rule that you have opened the door to the prosecution introducing *all* the results of the new tests including the fact that they match the defendant.'

'That's not fair, Your Hon—' Andi blurted out. She was silenced by a slight motion of Alex's index finger.

The judge continued. 'It's perfectly fair, Ms Phoenix. In order to introduce the facts pertaining to Louis Manning, the defense will have to introduce the results of the new test itself. Once the defense does that, the prosecution will be able to introduce whatever else is in those same tests. There is no way that the results can be separated or isolated.

'So the question that you *both* have to ask yourselves is would you rather continue or go to a new trial. As I have stated, I won't grant a mistrial with prejudice. But I will consider either a mistrial *without* prejudice followed by a retrial or proceed with the present trial. In the event that you agree to proceed, I will leave it in the hands of the defense whether it wishes to introduce the new test results or not.'

'I don't understand, Your Honor,' said Sarah. 'Why should the defense have the prerogative of deciding about admitting the tests results if we agree to proceed?'

'Because as a matter of law, the prosecution has rested and cannot now introduce new evidence. This is a court of law, Ms Jensen, not a court of whims.'

Now it was Alex's turn to sound confused. 'In that case, Your Honor, why is the court not making its own decision as to whether to carry on or go to a retrial?'

'Because, Mr Sedaka, this issue has become very complicated. Although I ultimately have the authority to decide, I can see that this is a dilemma for both parties. Whatever ruling I make, someone is liable to be dissatisfied, possibly both of you. So I'm leaving the matter in your hands – yours and the prosecutor. I'm going to adjourn this hearing and give both sides an hour to try to come to some agreement. Then if you agree, we'll do whatever you both agree upon.'

This was a very clever way to forestall subsequent objections – especially from the defense. There were pros and cons to both courses of action, and if the judge ruled unilaterally, they could lodge an exception for the record and then if the verdict went against them, they could appeal on the grounds that they had opposed the judge's ruling. This way Justice Wagner was effectively giving the parties themselves the right to decide – albeit camouflaged under the guise of seeking *agreement* between the parties.

Of course, they still might not agree. But the defense would have to make its position known. That meant they would have to make up their own minds where they stood in the face of this dilemma.

'What if we *can't* come to an agreement?' asked Alex.

'Then I'll have to make a decision. But I will ask both parties to state their positions for the record – including their fallback position.'

This confirmed Alex's suspicion. His primary position was that the judge should grant a mistrial *with* prejudice and effectively bar the case from being retried. But now he would have to state his fallback position. If the judge decided in favor of that position, then he couldn't use that as grounds for an appeal.

But how could he decide when he didn't have all the facts at his disposal – like *why* they had decided to test the DNA of the man who tried to rape Martine? Was this just random or had they tested others? Or was it because the woman he had tried to rape was a reporter covering the Elias Claymore trial?

Alex knew that he had to play for time. And he had to get some answers before he committed himself to a position that could land his client in prison for the rest of his life.

'Your Honor, these test results were the first time we were apprised of even the *existence* of Louis Manning, let alone his potential involvement in the case. As Your Honor may or may not know, Louis Manning – assuming that it is the same Louis Manning – was arrested for attempting to rape my . . . for attempting to rape a reporter who was covering this trial. Now he appears – somehow – to have become a credible suspect in this case. So much so that the police or the D.A. decided to compare his DNA to the evidence sample. Before we are able to make a rational decision as to whether we would prefer to continue or start afresh, we would like to file a discovery motion for everything the prosecution has on Louis Manning as it pertains to criminal convictions and the reasons why his DNA was tested in this case.'

Sarah Jensen looked panic-stricken. 'Your Honor, that's a pretty tall order with regard to the amount of information that the defense is seeking.'

To her credit, she didn't try to argue that the material was extraneous to the legitimate needs of the defense.

'We've wasted enough time on this. I see no reason why you can't provide the arrest report and his record by, say, 5 p.m. tomorrow. And to give the defense the opportunity to study the material we will reconvene at ten o'clock on Wednesday morning.'

Monday, 31 August 2009 – 10.40

Victor Alvarez was in his office at the forensic science lab when a tired and haggard looking young man walked into his office.

'Dr Alvarez, my name is Paul Greenberg. I'm the night systems administrator. I'm here about the LDIS server.'

'What is it?' asked Alvarez tensely. When the systems administrator on the graveyard shift walks into the office of a technical leader at the forensic lab, it's obvious that there's a problem.

'It looks like somebody's hacked in to database.'

Alvarez heard the tension in Greenberg's voice. 'Did they do any damage or just snoop around?'

'They deleted a file and replaced it with another.'

'Which file was it?'

'The new evidence sample from the Elias Claymore case.'

'Mother of God! How did they do it?'

There was a long pause before Greenberg spoke again. 'It looks like they used my ID.'

'*Your* ID?'

'Yes.'

'But how did they get it?'

'I'm still working on that. What I can tell you is that

according to the user log, they also downloaded Elias Claymore's reference sample.'

'But to log on with your ID wouldn't they have needed your password?'

Again the embarrassed pause. 'Yes, they did. But like I said, I don't know how they got it.'

'Can't you undelete the overwritten file?' asked Alvarez.

'It's not as simple as that. The original file hasn't just had its title deleted: it's been double deleted – physically overwritten.'

'Is that normal?'

'No, it isn't normal. But it's been done. It looks like someone deliberately changed a file and then set out to destroy any trace of the original.'

'And when was this done? Before or after the last comparison between the suspect samples and the back-up crime scene sample?'

Greenberg looked at the activity log. 'Before.'

'So you mean the last comparison was done with this *tampered* sample file?' There was alarm in Alvarez's voice.

'I'm afraid so.'

'*Damn!*' The frustration was mounting. 'Okay, you say it was overwritten. Does that mean it can't be recovered?'

Greenberg thought for a minute. 'Well, we do a back-up tape every day at 6 p.m. but it looks like this tampering was done after the new profile was uploaded and before the back-up was done.'

'So we've lost it for good! And the test was destructive so we haven't got the sample anymore. *Shit!*'

'There is something else we can try. If I can take a look at the computer that was used for the scan, I can check the outgoing packet log for the upload to the LDIS server.'

'Does it keep that data?'

'Only as a temporary file. But when the system deletes it,

it doesn't do a double delete like the hacker did on the database. It just frees up the area of the disk for reuse. If there hasn't been much more activity on that computer, I could recover the temporary packet log file with a standard utility and recover the raw data.'

'Okay, can you do that ASAP?'

'We have to. Let's take that computer out of use right away.'

'Okay, and then when you've done that, run another comparison between the restored crime scene sample and all three reference samples: that's Bethel Newton, Elias Claymore *and* Louis Manning.'

'All right, but I'll have to download the Louis Manning sample from the California SDIS. I think it was uploaded from the Oakland P.D. Forensic Lab.'

'Okay. Let me know when that's done.'

'Will do.'

Greenberg was about to say more when he suddenly remembered the airhead who had phoned up a few days ago. He hadn't told her the password. All he had told her was that it was his mother's maiden name. But he hadn't told her what that was. He had been hoping that she would call him back after she phoned during the day and asked one of his colleagues all those questions about him. They had teased him mercilessly about that afterwards.

She had asked about his age and his eyes and his zodiac sign.

He realized what had happened. She had social engineered him – *and* one of his colleagues. Once she had his birth details it would have been no problem to find out his mother's maiden name. But she had sounded so dumb on the phone.

An act. Of course!

How could I have been so stupid?

He tried to put it out of his mind as he looked at the file allocation table. Then he remembered something else.

'Dr Alvarez, I noticed that there are also extra reference sample files for Elias Claymore, Bethel Newton and Louis Manning. According to the properties, these are mitochondrial DNA profiles.'

'Yes, that's right. We do mitochondrial DNA profiles on reference samples as a matter of course. But we decided to use Y-STR on the evidence samples.'

'And you haven't got any more evidence samples?'

Alvarez thought for a moment. 'Let me just check.'

He typed in something on his own computer and smiled. 'Oh yes. There's another nail sample – from the victim's other hand.'

Greenberg smiled. 'Well maybe it would be a good idea to do a *mitochondrial* DNA profile on that last piece of evidence? Even if we can recover the overwritten reference sample file from the packet log, the defense might attack the results. But if we can also get a mitochondrial DNA comparison that matches Claymore but not Manning, then we've got him.'

Alvarez smiled. 'That's a good idea. I'll get right on it.'

Tuesday, 1 September 2009 – 6.30

Andi had had a sleepless night after yesterday's events in court. She had been expecting to call Gene as a hostile witness, but that had been postponed till Wednesday. So all Andi could do was worry. She had finally managed to fall asleep in the wee hours of the morning. But the silent peace of her early morning slumber was not to last long. It was shattered by a heavy pounding on the door. Squinting against the dawn light, she staggered downstairs to answer and looked through the spy hole to see several police officers.

What on earth was going on?

'Yes?' she shouted through the door.

'FBI, ma'am! Would you mind opening the door?'

She opened the door in haste.

'Special Agent Caine, ma'am,' he said, flashing a badge in her face. 'Are you Andromeda Phoenix?'

'Yes,' she replied hesitantly.

'I have a warrant for your arrest,' he said, holding out the warrant, 'and another to search these premises.'

'Arrest? What's the charge?'

'Illegally accessing a government computer without authorization.'

Tuesday, 1 September 2009 – 10.35

'Your Honor,' said the diminutive but feisty lawyer, 'my client is a man of limited means but has strong roots in this community where he has lived for twenty-seven years.'

Andi was sitting with a group of other unrelated defendants in a crowded district court, along with dozens of other defendants. She felt uncomfortable with Alex sitting next to her, yet comforted that he was there. It was embarrassing to feel that she needed his assistance, yet reassuring that he had dropped everything else at a moment's notice to come to her aid.

There were also quite a few journalists milling around. Usually an arraignment court isn't a particularly newsworthy venue. But someone had tipped off the press about the celebrity defendant and so the reporters were packed in along with the usual suspects and the low-life shysters looking for an easy fee – 'courthouse leeches,' Alex called them.

'Bail is set at $1,500,' said the arraignment judge. 'Next!'

Andi and Alex were signaled to step forward by a bailiff. When Andi took her place before the judge, Alex went with her.

'Case 08-29-09-2346, *United States* v *Andromeda Phoenix*,' said the clerk, rattling if off like a machine-gun. 'US Code, Title 18, Part I, Chapter 47, Section 1030, Paragraph 2, Clause

C, Unauthorized access to a computer used in interstate communication, one count. No priors.'

'Is the defendant represented by counsel?'

'Yes, Your Honor,' said Alex. 'Alex Sedaka. I appear on behalf of Ms Phoenix and my client pleads not guilty.'

'Does the prosecution oppose bail?'

'No, Your Honor. The accused has no previous convictions and strong domestic and professional roots in the community. Therefore the prosecution does not see her as a flight risk.'

The duty prosecutor knew that she would make bail regardless. Although Andi had been living in the community for less than three months, it was now her home and she had an unblemished record.

The US Attorney in charge of the case would probably offer her a plea bargain on the lines of probation and maybe community service – teaching computer skills to disadvantaged kids. Andi wasn't really a threat to anyone. As far as the duty prosecutor could tell she had just got overzealous trying to get information to help her client.

'Your Honor,' said Alex, 'in view of the prosecution's favorable statement, I would ask for R-O-R.'

'Does the government object to releasing the accused on her recognizance?'

'No, Your Honor.'

'In that case the defendant is released on her own recognizance. I'll set the pre-trial thirty days from now. Hopefully the three of you should be able to work something out by then.'

This was a coded suggestion from the judge that they should agree on a plea bargain.

Andi and Alex were led away by a bailiff to a clerk to get the paperwork sorted out. Later, a horde of news-hungry reporters swarmed around them as they left the Ronald V. Dellums Federal Building.

Alex put a protective arm around Andi as he shepherded her through the gauntlet of reporters.

'Ms Phoenix,' asked a man, thrusting a microphone into her face, 'does this case have anything to do with your defense of Elias Claymore?'

Alex turned her away without a word, shielding her from the reporter's inquisitive eyes with his arm. A female reporter was poised on the other side, waiting to pounce.

'Ms Phoenix, is it true that you logged on to the CODIS database in a desperate search for evidence to exonerate your client?'

'No comment!' snapped Alex angrily.

The female reporter pushed closer and held out her microphone close to Andi's mouth. 'Ms Phoenix?' she persisted.

Alex pushed the microphone away. 'Ms Phoenix has no comment,' he said again, firmly.

As the barrage of questions continued, Alex forced a path through the crowd of reporters and guided Andi to Juanita's waiting car. They got in the back and Juanita floored the pedal before Alex even had the chance to say, 'Drive.'

'I'm glad to see you've finally learned the art of keeping your mouth shut,' said Alex as the car roared away from the prying eyes of the reporters.

'She's going to pay – the fucking bitch!' said Andi.

'It's no use getting angry now. We've just got to figure out who's behind this and nail 'em.'

'Oh, I know who's behind it all right! It's that bitch Lannosea!'

'The person who's been sending you the e-mails?'

'Of course it is! Who else could it be?'

'But do you know who that is?'

387

'Not yet. But I intend to find out.'

'How?'

'I think it's one of Claymore's victims from the past.'

'What makes you think that?' asked Alex.

'The things she said . . . the anger . . . the bitterness.'

'Well, if you're right then she shouldn't be too difficult to find. That reminds me – call David.'

'Why?'

'When I told him about your call from the courthouse he told me that he had some results on some probes. He said you'd understand.'

Without another word, Andi pulled out her cell phone and pressed two keys.

'Hi Andi. Glad you made R-O-R.'

'How d'you know?'

'I heard it on the radio. Where are you now?'

'I'm in Juanita's car, with your dad. We're on our way back to the office.'

'I see that Lannosea has upped the ante,' he said wryly.

'It looks like it.'

'Anyway, listen, you remember those probes I set up on your account? Well, they've created a trace-route log of what happened these past few days.'

'What did you find?' she asked eagerly.

'That unauthorized access to the DNA database was done via your office wide area network but it ultimately traced back to the hotel where you were staying.'

Andi froze.

'They're doing it from the hotel?'

'It's worse than that. I was able to get the MAC number of the computer they were doing it from.'

The MAC was an identification number that identified an individual computer.

'And?'

'It came from your laptop, Andi.'

'*My* laptop!'

This sent a jolt through her. *When* could it have happened? She'd had her laptop with her at all times as far as she could remember. The only time when she had left it was when it was in the car when she went into the rape crisis center. Could someone have got into her car, used her laptop – via the WAN of Levine and Webster – and then switched it off and left the car looking untouched all in the space of a few minutes?

'Is it possible for someone to spoof a MAC number?'

'Yes. Anyone who can do an Internet search can download an off-the-shelf MAC spoofing program. You can get an evaluation version free or the standard version for thirty dollars.'

'But how would they have got my MAC address to spoof it? Only the IP address is transmitted with the message header. The MAC address is only transmitted to the initial service provider.'

'Maybe that's where they got it; from the company WAN.'

'You think someone at Levine and Webster . . .?'

'If the hacker could access the network there then they might be able to get the MAC address from there, if you use the laptop at work. Does anyone have access to your computer at all?'

Andi hesitated. She knew the answer to this. But didn't want to think about it.

'Gene wouldn't have the knowledge to do this sort of thing.'

'Gene?' he sounded surprised. She forgot that he didn't know what she had found out last Wednesday. As far as the rest of the world knew, Gene might have the opportunity, but she wouldn't have had the motive.

389

'She has access to my laptop . . . some of the time. But not recently.'

'And as you say, she wouldn't have had the knowledge of how to spoof a MAC address . . . let alone a motive.'

'So what do we do next?' asked Andi.

'Well, there's something you should be thinking about. Let's take an off-the-wall scenario and consider what if someone did somehow manage to gain temporary access to your laptop. We *know* that the person downloaded a file from the Bethel Newton rape case.'

'So?'

'That means then they might have left some telltale sign on your computer.'

'Holy shit! Of course!'

'Well, what I suggest is that you check it out when you get back to the office. Let me know what you find.'

'OK. Thanks, David. Bye.'

She put the phone away and became aware of Alex's eyes upon her.

'Good news?'

'It could be, Alex . . . it *could* be.'

Tuesday, 1 September 2009 – 11.05

Twenty minutes later they were back in the office. Alex had decided not to quiz Andi about this latest development immediately but to let her calm down first. Her animated conversation with David had perked her up somewhat but when he asked her about the good news, she had refused to elaborate. He sensed that she didn't want to jinx it by talking prematurely. She would tell him in her own good time.

So now Andi sat alone in her office, searching through her laptop's hard disk for any trace of what was downloaded from the DNA database. She was checking deleted files too. If Lannosea had really managed to gain access to the computer to log on to the Ventura LDIS and downloaded anything, then even if she subsequently deleted it, the ghost of the file would probably still be there on the system. Even if she overwrote it completely, there should be a record in the activity log.

She had to find it.

File by file, deleted file by deleted file, she searched the disk. Finally she saw something that made her eyes pop open. There was a file called EliasClaymore.dna and then another called nailmidfngr.dna. As she looked further, she discovered something very interesting. The nailmidfngr.dna file had been created locally on this computer, whereas the EliasClaymore.dna file had simply been downloaded.

But then as she continued to look through the deleted files, she found the shadow of another downloaded file, also called nailmidfngr.dna. This had been downloaded at about the same time as EliasClaymore.dna and then deleted. It was clear that the hacker had downloaded the EliasClaymore.dna file and then used it to create a false evidence sample file. But why also download the real evidence sample file if they were planning to overwrite it on the DNA server with a fake one?

Maybe it was because they needed to refer to the metadata in the file header, to get it right on the forged version. Or maybe Lannosea had originally planned to create a fake Elias Claymore sample – using the real evidence sample – and then changed her mind and decided to do it the other way round.

Andi decided to compare the forged evidence sample file with the retrieved file that she presumed was the real one.

But what she saw this time made no sense. Because the original evidence sample file that had been downloaded and deleted was the same as the new one that the hacker had created.

Why overwrite a file with another identical copy?

Wednesday, 2 September 2009 – 9.20

'But that doesn't make sense,' said Bridget.

She was talking on her cell phone to Victor Alvarez, from her car at San Francisco International airport, having flown in to be available to help Sarah Jensen on this, the most crucial day in the trial of Elias Claymore. It was going to be an uphill struggle winning the case if it continued. And if it didn't, they'd have a hell of a job persuading Bethel Newton to testify at the retrial.

'That's exactly what Paul Greenberg said. But he checked and double-checked. The fact is, whoever did it, all they did was delete the genuine evidence file that had been uploaded from a computer at the crime lab and then uploaded an *identical* copy from the remote computer where they were hacking in from.'

'But why would anyone do that?'

'Maybe the person who did it *didn't know* that it was the same profile.'

Bridget was trying to concentrate on what Dr Alvarez was telling her while at the same time navigating her way out of the airport parking lot. She didn't relish the prospect of the morning drive across the Bay Bridge in commuter time.

'Do we know who did it?'

'Greenberg said he'd passed on some information to the

FBI. I heard on the radio that Andi Phoenix was arrested. But she was released R-O-R and we'll have to wait for the evidence hearing.'

'In any case, that still doesn't help us resolve the question of who is actually guilty.'

'Not in itself,' said Alvarez. 'The way things stand now, we've got two suspects, neither of whom can be eliminated by the DNA, and in both cases the chances of a random match are 500 to 1.'

'It's worse than that, Victor. We've got one suspect who was identified by the victim and another who matches the age of the perp. We've got one who matches the description of the perp and the other who *used* to match that description when he was younger. We've got one suspect who owns a car that matches the one described by the victim and another who was caught *driving* that car with false number plates. We've got one suspect who was a rapist in his youth and another who has no *priors* for rape but was arrested *when he tried to rape a reporter who's covering the case.*'

'The thing is,' said Alvarez, 'I haven't been able to get through to Nick Sinclair or Sarah Jensen on their cell phones. And I don't want to leave a message with the Alameda D.A. 'cause that might dump 'em in the shithouse.'

'They're probably crossing the Bay Bridge. I know Nick Sinclair lives in San Francisco and I think Sarah Jensen may be staying there. She's been driving in with him.'

'Well, if I don't manage to get through to them, you'd better tell them.'

'But surely it doesn't make any difference if the results are the same.'

'Well, that's just it. You see there are some *additional* results.'

'What do you mean "additional"?' Bridget replied.

'We had one more nail sample – from the other hand.'

'But how does that help? You said the computer guy managed to recover the original evidence sample file from the second test.'

'Yes, but this time we swabbed the blood from the finger-nail clipping and did a *mitochondrial* DNA test.'

'And you've got the result?'

She could hardly contain her excitement.

'That's what I've been trying to tell you. It excludes Claymore but nearly matches Louis Manning.'

'*Nearly* matches?'

'Yes. Look, it's a bit complicated. Mitochondrial DNA testing looks at two blocks of nucleotides on the mitochondrial DNA ring called Hypervariable Regions, each block being 350 nucleotides long. The test doesn't look at repeated sequences or anything like that. It looks at individual nucleotides in the overall sequence. Siblings and people related by the maternal line have identical mitochondrial DNA sequences in these regions, whereas two maternally unrelated people have about ten nucleotide differences on average.'

'And if it nearly matches what does it mean?'

'Well, the general rule is that if the sequences are identical we call that a "failure to exclude." If the samples differ by two or more nucleotides in the sequences we treat it as an exclusion. And if there's a nucleotide difference at a single location, we call it inconclusive.'

'And is that what we've got in this case?'

'No. What we've got in this case is *two* differences.'

'And that counts as an exclusion?'

'Well it would, but there are a couple of other things we have to take into account. First, there's also something called Heteroplasmy.'

'Surprise me,' said Bridget, realizing that Alvarez was enjoying this game of I-know-something-you-don't-know.

'Heteroplasmy is the presence of more than one mito-chondrial DNA type in a single individual.'

'And what's the second?'

'The second is mutation. Mitochondrial DNA mutates as the cells grow and divide.'

'And what effect does this have on your findings?'

'Well, in the evidence sample we were able to identify Bethel Newton as the major contributor because of her matching reference sample. But then we looked at the sequence from the minor contributor – which we presumed to be the perpe-trator – and we found that it nearly matched Manning, but there were two heteroplasmic sites that did *not* match anything in Manning's reference sample.'

'And what does that imply?' asked Bridget.

'Well now this is the thing: normally a reference sample is more likely to be a complete sample than a crime scene or evidence sample, because of the clean laboratory methods we use to take and preserve reference samples. It doesn't matter whether it's from the suspect or the victim, if it's a *reference* sample, it should be complete. Right?'

'I guess so.'

'So if there was any mutation, we'd expect to find it in the reference sample – which is always a good sample – or in *both* the reference sample *and* the evidence sample.'

'Right,' said Bridget.

'But in this case we *only* found it in the minor contri-butor to the *evidence* sample, *not* in Manning's reference sample.'

'Is it possible that *the evidence sample itself mutated* after it was taken?'

'No. Mutations can only occur in living cells that are dividing and reproducing. Again, you'd be more likely to get it in the *reference* sample, because that's taken from the victim or suspect *after* the crime. That means the mutation could take place in the meantime, after the crime but before the sample was taken if you see what I mean.'

'So you think the evidence sample must have come from some one other than Manning?'

'I wouldn't go as far as to say that. But as far as generally accepted standards are concerned, we'd have to call it an exclusion, or at best an inconclusive result. Having said that, the fact that the samples are *almost* the same is quite surprising. Mutations generally occur in older people. This is the sort of result I'd expect if the source of the minor contributor sample was an older maternal relative of Manning.'

Now it was Bridget's turn to chuckle. 'Well, I think we can safely assume that Bethel Newton isn't Louis Manning's mother.'

Wednesday, 2 September
2009 – 10.05

'I want to know why you subpoenaed her.'

Alex and Andi were on their way into the judge's chambers, hanging back and keeping their distance from Sarah Jensen and Nick Sinclair.

'Not this time, Alex. You twisted my arm enough before, now you're going to have to defer to my judgment and trust me.'

'At least tell me what she's going to say.'

'I don't know yet.'

'Well, tell me what you're *calling her* to say . . . what you're *hoping* she'll say.'

'That's another way of asking the same question.'

'I could decide not to let you call her. I'm still lead counsel in this case.'

'Then you'll be blowing our best chance to clear our client.' She stopped, forcing him to do likewise and looked him in the eyes. 'Your call, Alex.'

Alex Sedaka looked at Andi Phoenix and saw a different woman to the one he had been working with these past few weeks. Here was a woman who was poised and self-assured. There was no trace of fear in her eyes this time, nor even a trace of doubt. This was a woman who knew that she was standing on rock-solid ground.

But it was the word *our* that tipped the scales. She had said 'our best chance' and 'our client.' That meant she was fully committed to the case.

Alex shrugged his shoulders and smiled, a tacit sign of consent to her request.

The judge was already waiting for them in her chambers.

'This in camera hearing is now in session,' said Justice Wagner. 'All right, I assume, Mr Sedaka, that you have now had time to read the arrest report and record of Louis Manning.'

'Yes, Your Honor.'

He had in fact read it through from start to finish, amazed at what it revealed. Not only did Louis Manning look like Bethel's original description and the FaceID image of the rapist, but he was also caught driving Claymore's stolen car – thus proving what Claymore had said all along about his car being stolen. But the question Alex asked himself was how could he introduce it, without also introducing the results of the new tests that tended to incriminate his client?

'And have you decided whether you wish to go for a mistrial without prejudice or to proceed with the case?'

'We'd like to proceed, Your Honor.'

Ellen Wagner turned to Sarah Jensen and Nick Sinclair. 'And the people?'

Nick shrugged his shoulders. Sarah spoke. 'We're only prepared to proceed if we can make the results of the new tests available.'

The judge turned to Alex. 'Any decision on that, Mr Sedaka?'

'Not yet, Your Honor.' The judge looked surprised. 'We don't yet know if we need to. Until we know we can hardly be expected to decide.'

'But the prosecution has to decide whether they want a mistrial or to go on. How can *they* decide on their position if they don't know your decision on this point?'

'I can understand their dilemma,' said Alex, 'but as a matter of law we have the right to decide whether or not to use a particular piece of admissible evidence at any time during our presentation of our case. Disclosure applies to what *might* be submitted in evidence, not what *will* be. Even the prosecution's disclosure doesn't oblige them to call a witness or present any particular evidence. The prosecution knows that this evidence exists and is admissible. That means it *might* be presented by the defense. We're not obliged to notify them ahead of time what we intend to do, only what we *may* do. They'll have to make their decision on that basis.'

'And when will you know if you're going to introduce the test results?'

Alex looked at Andi, inquiringly. She spoke. 'After we've called our next witness: Eugenia Vance.'

'Your Honor, that's another matter that I wanted to talk about,' said Sarah. 'We were given no prior notice of this witness until after she was issued with an emergency subpoena.'

The judge looked hard at Andi. 'Yes, she has a point there doesn't she, Ms Phoenix? You obtained this emergency subpoena via the Ventura County Superior Court, bypassing normal procedure and protocol.'

'Your Honor, I know that it's customary to obtain a subpoena from the trial court, but in this case, time was of the essence. I knew that the witness might be reluctant to come so that meant we'd have to give at least the statutory five days' notice or she'd file for a postponement. And we didn't want any more delays in the proceedings. The case was due to resume on Monday and it was late at night last Wednesday when we realized that this witness had relevant testimony. I was in Ventura County at the time, as was the witness. Therefore I resorted to the expedient of obtaining the emergency subpoena from the Ventura Court for Your Honor's subsequent approval.'

'And what exactly is this relevant testimony that this witness is expected to give?' asked the judge.

'Well, we don't actually know that she *will* give it, Your Honor. We were also planning on asking the court for permission to treat Ms Vance as hostile.'

'It gets better and better,' Sarah muttered under her breath, almost breaking into laughter.

'Okay, well let's *assume* for a moment,' said the judge, 'that she *does* give the evidence that you're hoping for. What evidence is that?'

'We believe that Ms Vance has been in contact with Bethel Newton, in violation of her promise not to do so. We think that she may have been influencing Miss Newton's testimony.'

'Great!' said Sarah, slapping her thigh. 'If that's the case then Ms Phoenix should step aside on grounds of a conflict of interest. In fact, as far as I'm concerned, she should also have to step aside over these pending charges of hacking into the DNA database.'

Andi looked round at Sarah and spoke quietly, whilst technically still addressing the judge. 'I may yet have to. But I think it's in everyone's interests that this case be expedited. It's already dragged on longer than expected and we're running up to the end of the slot in the docket that this case was assigned to.'

The judge spoke, to regain Andi's undivided attention. 'Ms Phoenix, is there any particular reason *why* you believe that Miss Vance has been influencing Miss Newton?'

'Yes, Your Honor, but I'd rather not state it just yet. Let's just say that Ms Vance was . . . observed talking with Miss Newton by . . . another person . . .'

'If so, she would be in contempt of court.'

'I know, Your Honor.'

'And you want to ask her this in direct examination?'

'Yes, Your Honor.'

'And to do so effectively you need to be able to treat the witness as hostile?'

'Yes, Your Honor.'

'And you believe that if the court gives you permission to do this, you can expedite the outcome of this case one way or the other.'

'Yes, Your Honor.'

Ellen Wagner looked at Sarah, expecting further objections. But this time Sarah remained silent and offered a slight shrug.

'I'm going to allow this witness to be called and allow the defense to treat the witness as hostile.'

Wednesday, 2 September
2009 – 10.35

They ought to have been enemies, but a bond of sorts was developing between Louis Manning and one of the cops who was guarding him. Maybe it was because this particular cop was going through a rough divorce and hadn't quite managed to rein in his subconscious misogyny. Maybe it was just because they were thrown together and sharing a set of common experiences born of mere proximity.

But, whatever the reason, the bond was there. That was why the cop had been only too happy to bring Manning a cup of coffee from the vending machine in the corridor, when he had asked for one, and also to bring one for himself. However Manning remained in handcuffs in accordance with police department rules. Fortunately this didn't prevent Manning from drinking coffee with his free hand. So he and the cop sat in front of the TV, their coffee cups in hand.

'Can you turn it up louder?' said Manning.

They were watching Court TV and were avidly following the Elias Claymore trial. For the last half hour, they had been treated to a long session of analysis by various lawyers and other experts, including a former prosecutor, a current defense lawyer and a jury psychologist. Now there was a flurry of activity and signs that the court was about to reconvene.

Suddenly Louis Manning clutched his chest and started coughing.

'What's the matter?' asked the cop.

'Ha . . . ha . . . heart.'

The cop understood immediately and, putting his coffee cup down on the bedside cabinet, went running from the room to summon a nurse or a doctor. As soon as he was out of the room Manning went to work, getting the sleeping pills out of the bedside cabinet and dropping them into the cop's coffee cup. He saw no need to stir it, as the heat of the coffee would surely dissolve them well enough. Then he went back to feigning the coughing.

The cop came back into the room with a nurse. Manning increased the time spacing between coughs, giving the impression of bringing it under control and then spoke to the nurse.

'Sorry, the coffee went down the wrong way.'

The nurse looked at the cop irritably. He shrugged sheepishly.

'I thought you said it was your heart?' said the cop.

'Sorry. I thought it was. I'm sorry. I didn't mean to start a panic.'

The nurse gave him a quick check and then left. The cop settled back into his chair with his coffee, keeping his eyes on the TV. But his mood had turned decidedly colder.

Wednesday, 2 September
2009 – 10.45

When the court reconvened and the judge was seated, Andi rose confidently.

'Your Honor, the defense calls Eugenia Vance.'

The bailiff opened the door to the witness room. 'Call Eugenia Vance!'

There was a tense moment as Andi held her breath, wondering if Gene was going to appear. Andi had not had any contact with her for a week and wasn't sure if she would even turn up. She had hoped that Gene would call her and start the first move towards making peace. But she realized that Gene was probably thinking the same thing. Besides, how could they reconcile themselves when this was still hanging over them? And how could Andi let it go when she still had a client whom she was sworn to serve according to her highest professional standards?

After what seemed like about half a minute, Gene emerged from the witness room into the courtroom. A few steps into the room she stopped and looked nervously at Andi. There was no anger now, nor even a trace of resentment, just a look of self-pity, and a residual trace of confusion. The bailiff took a step towards her and guided her to the witness stand.

The clerk established with a quick question that she was an atheist and gave her the card to affirm.

'I do solemnly affirm that the evidence I give the court shall be the truth, the whole truth and nothing but the truth.'

The clerk sat down, leaving Gene to face the penetrating stare of the woman who had once been her lover.

'You are Eugenia Vance?' asked Andi.

'Yes.'

She asked Gene to state her address for the record. It sounded silly, asking her to state the address, which they still technically shared. But it was part of the formality of trial proceedings and she had to do it.

'Miss Vance, I won't waste any time here. I'll come right to the point. You work at the Say No to Violence rape crisis center in Los Angeles, is that correct?'

'Yes.'

'And in that capacity did you have occasion to meet a young lady by the name of Bethel Newton?'

'Yes.'

'And were you on June twelfth served with an injunction to refrain from any contact with Bethel Newton?'

Sarah Jensen was poised to stand up and object if Andi crossed the line. But she sensed that something was going down and she wanted to hear the rest. Gene said nothing. Andi continued.

'We have already heard from Bethel Newton how she initially thought the rapist was a young man in his twenties and then changed her mind and said it was a man in his fifties. Did you have anything to do with this?'

'What do you mean?'

Gene was clearly nervous. She knew what was happening; they both did.

'Did you put her up to it?'

Justice Wagner stepped in. 'Miss Vance, you do not have

to answer that question, as it may incriminate you on charges of contempt of court and obstructing justice.'

'But you can answer if you want,' added Andi, giving her lover a hard stare.

'Why would I do that?'

Her voice was trembling now. The roles had now reversed completely. She was the weak one and Andi had finally done what Gene always feared she might do: seize control.

'Is it not a fact that twenty-seven years ago, Elias Claymore raped you, when you were twenty-one?'

The courtroom was filled by a huge collective gasp.

'Elias Claymore raped *white* women.'

'But before that, he raped three black women to "practice" his technique – as he described it in his autobiography. And you were one of them, weren't you, Gene? You were the first. But unlike the other victims, you never reported it.'

Sitting between Andi and Alex, Claymore looked nervous – indeed terrified.

'He never paid the price for what he did.'

Several jurors leaned forward in their seats. Andi waited for a moment, unsure of how far to go. This was the woman she loved, and she was destroying her . . . in public.

'What gave you the idea of framing Elias Claymore, after all these years?'

Gene choked as she tried to speak, and tears began to roll down her face as she struggled to regain her composure.

'After Bethel looked at the mug shots in the first photo line-up and didn't see the man who raped her, she came back to the rape crisis center to see me. She was crying. I knew what she felt like, because I'd been through it myself. I knew that feeling so well that I couldn't bear to see it again. So I just rushed up to her and met her halfway across the room. I put a comforting arm around her . . .

just like I did with another frightened little girl many years ago.'

Again she paused to dam up the flood of tears. Then she took a deep breath and continued.

'I offered her a set of darts to throw at our "poke his eyes out" dartboard. That's a corkboard with pictures of known rapists on it. The caption under the board says, "Rapist scum-bags of history." It's basically just a therapeutic tool we use to help rape vict—rape survivors work off their pain.

'Bethel started throwing the darts at the board. When she'd thrown a set of three darts at the board, she went over to pull them out and start again. But when she got there and saw the pictures up close, she stopped. You see she thought she recognized a face on the board. It was a picture of a young man and she thought it was the man who raped her. She started talking to me excitedly telling me that it was the man.'

'But it wasn't,' said Andi. It was a statement, not a question. She had more or less figured it out.

'No. It couldn't have been the man who raped her because it was an old picture of Elias Claymore. I knew he was in his fifties now and she'd said the man was in his twenties. So I realized that the real rapist had to be another man who just happened to look like Claymore. And I had to break this news to her after she was sure that she'd identified the right man. I had to let her know – just as she'd got her hopes up and was sure that the rapist was about to be caught – that he wouldn't be, because it was the wrong man. I had to look at the crestfallen look on her face when I told her that it was just a man who – when he was younger – looked a bit like the man who raped her. I had to watch her face contort in anguish and disintegrate into a torrent of tears when she took it all in. I had to see her beautiful young face ripped apart as she realized that the rapist wasn't going to be caught and punished after all.

'And I remembered how the man who raped me wasn't punished for that crime either . . . because, unlike most of his other victims, I never had the courage to come forward in time.'

'And that's when you got the idea? When you broke the news to Bethel that it couldn't be the man whose picture she had seen on the dartboard?'

'When I saw her reaction.'

'Okay, when you saw her reaction, you decided to get her to accuse Claymore.'

'Yes. I saw the chance to make him pay for what he did to me.'

'You *used* Bethel. You manipulated her.'

'I didn't manipulate her. I gave her the choice. I told her what happened to me and suggested the idea that she could help to punish the man who raped me and then later, if he was ever caught, someone else could help punish the man who raped her. But I didn't force her. She *wanted* to do it. And I thought it would be therapeutic for her.'

'For her? Or for you?'

'Do you really have the right to ask me that question? Do you know what it's like to bottle up the pain all these years, knowing that the man who inflicted the pain hasn't been properly punished, and watch him transformed by a public relations machine from a villain into a national hero? Do you know what it's like to—'

She broke down, unable to hold back the tears any longer.

Andi looked on helplessly, realizing that she had gone further than she intended. She looked sideways at Claymore and wondered if it had been worth it. Did he really deserve her help? Did Gene really deserve to be destroyed like this to get Claymore off the hook?

Claymore, for his part, was shrinking into his seat, as if trying to disappear from view, as if he at least had a sense of shame. But did that really matter? Surely it reaches a stage when it's too late for regrets? When one cannot be forgiven no matter how much remorse one feels or shows?

But then again, Andi realized, perhaps that was true of her too.

The judge's voice came out of nowhere to fill the silence with a gentleness that seemed appropriate for the situation.

'Does the defense have any more questions?'

'No, Your Honor.'

'Ms Jensen?'

'No, Your Honor.'

'Under normal circumstances I would order the witness to be taken into immediate custody. However in view of the circumstances I think the D.A. might want to deal leniently with her. Is that the case?'

'Yes, Your Honor,' said Nick Sinclair, rising slowly from her seat.

'In that case, the witness is excused.'

Gene was led shakily from the witness stand by a bailiff, sobbing as she walked away. As her cries faded into the distance, Sarah Jensen requested a sidebar.

'Approach the bench,' said the judge.

They approached the bench for a sidebar, Sarah, Nick, Andi and Alex. Sarah Jensen spoke.

'Your Honor, I'd rather not put the Newton girl back on the stand. If it was hard for that last witness, then we can all imagine what it would be like for her.'

Ellen Wagner nodded. 'If you meet with Miss Newton in private,' said the judge, 'would that be sufficient to give you what you need for a motion to dismiss?'

'There is still one outstanding question, Your Honor,'

Sarah Jensen replied. 'The DNA. I know that there's only a 1 in 500 possibility of a random match, but there are some issues we'd like clarified.'

'Your Honor,' said Andi, 'I think I may be of some assistance here. As you know, yesterday I was arrested by the FBI on Federal charges of illegally accessing a government computer – specifically the server for the local DNA database of the Ventura Sheriff's Department crime lab.'

'Go on,' said the judge.

'Well, it appears that someone else accessed it and tried to frame me. They logged on using my IP address and a spoofed version of the MAC number of my computer and basically deleted a file and then uploaded an identical copy of the same file.'

'And what is the relevance of this?'

'Well, it appears that someone has compromised the Ventura LDIS. This means that until further checks have been made, we cannot trust in the integrity of the local database – at least as it relates to this case.'

'But you said that they uploaded an identical file, Ms Phoenix,' said the judge. 'That means that they may have tried to frame you, but they didn't actually change any of the evidence.'

They were distracted by a sound at the back of the courtroom. Bridget Riley had just entered and was trying to get Sarah Jensen's attention.

Wednesday, 2 September
2009 – 11.20

'Can you believe that?' asked Manning, grinning from ear to ear.

They had just watched Andi's questioning of Gene Vance and the amazing courtroom scenes as they unfolded. The cop was barely taking it in, but Louis Manning was on the verge of laughter.

'Man, those bitches must really be suffering now.'

And this time he did laugh. The cop looked at him with disgust and tried to mouth the words, 'You bastard.' But it wasn't the courtroom scene that he was talking about. It was what was happening to himself. Because he now felt himself overtaken by a sudden wave of drowsiness and he realized that it was the coffee.

Manning had spiked his cup while he was out of the room. It had to be.

Why else would he suddenly feel so tired?

He realized that he had to do something. Drawing on his last reserves of strength, he staggered to his feet and lurched towards the door. Manning was constrained by his leg in traction, but somehow managed to maneuver his body to stick out his free leg, using his foot to trip the cop as he closed the gap between his desperately weary body and the door.

Although it was only the briefest and mildest of contacts between his shin and Manning's foot, the sudden, unexpected interruption of his motion, coupled with his precarious state of balance to begin with, sent the lethargic cop sprawling to the floor. He landed with a heavier thud than Manning had intended.

Still conscious, albeit barely, he looked round to see Manning struggling to extricate his leg from traction.

Wednesday, 2 September
2009 – 11.35

Fifteen minutes later, they were reassembled in the court-room after a short recess granted by the judge to clear matters up. Bridget Riley had briefed Sarah Jensen and they now all realized that it was Louis Manning and not Elias Claymore who had raped Bethel Newton. They had to avoid saying so explicitly, in order not to prejudice the case against Manning. But at the same time, the defense wanted some kind of acknowledgment that Claymore was innocent.

'Your Honor,' said Sarah Jensen, 'in view of certain new evidence that has come to the attention of the people, we move that the court declare a mistrial with prejudice and that the charges against Elias Claymore be dismissed.'

'Mr Sedaka?' said the judge.

'The defense has no objection.'

'So ordered. The charges against Elias Claymore are hereby dismissed with prejudice. The defendant is free to go. Court is adjourned.'

Andi felt a wave of relief. But it was tinged with dis-appointment. There was still some unfinished business. She and David Sedaka had discovered proof that the jury selec-tion software had been tampered with. Yet although the judge had passed the buck – understandably so – it was still some-thing that had to be dealt with.

Then there was also the matter of the illegal accessing of the DNA database and the attempt to frame her. And of course there were the malicious e-mail messages that she had been receiving. She assumed that it was all the work of the same person: Lannosea.

But the question remained: who *was* Lannosea?

'All rise!' intoned the bailiff.

Everyone in the courtroom stood. Only when the judge had left did the court erupt into pandemonium. Several bailiffs held back spectators as Andi, Alex and Claymore walked out the courtroom quickly.

Outside, Alex spoke to Claymore. 'We can go to the main lobby if you want to talk to the press.'

'No thanks. I just want to get my tail out of here. You can talk to the press if you like.'

'Okay, leave it to me,' said Alex.

He walked off down another corridor while Andi and Claymore continued walking to the side exit that took them to the museum parking lot. When they got there, it was deserted.

'Just tell me one thing,' said Claymore. 'How could you help defend me after . . .'

He was too embarrassed to finish the sentence.

'After I knew that you had raped the woman I love?'

'Yes.'

'I'll let you into a little secret. I was also raped once.'

Claymore looked frightened at these words.

'After *Gene* was raped she started working at a rape crisis center in New York. And then when I was raped, I was referred to that same center. That's how we met.'

'That's it?' he asked, hesitantly.

'Yes.'

'Then how could you help me?'

418

'Because I was raped again – this time by a colleague. Not *literally* raped, but figuratively speaking. My hands were tied and I was forced to conform to his will. Only this is the last time it's going to happen. I'm never going to have to look at him again. It's just a case of taking the plunge and moving on.'

She walked off angrily, got into her red Ford Mustang and drove off.

Wednesday, 2 September
2009 – 11.45

Louis Manning was struggling to pull the cop towards him. The floor was smooth but it was hard to get the necessary leverage. With his right leg in traction and his right wrist handcuffed to the bedrail, it was very hard getting into position. Sticking his free leg out had been easy enough. But reaching the cop's ankle with his hand was somewhat harder. So it used up precious time getting the necessary grip and dragging him back so that he could fumble for the key to the handcuffs and free his hand.

The cops had become blasé. There was supposed to be one in the room and one outside. But they had scaled it down to just one who was free to leave the room as long as Manning was handcuffed to the bed – as he was most of the time, except when eating. The only time there were two of them together was when a change of shift was due. The next change of shift was some hours away. And the doctors only came round at set intervals, in the morning and afternoon. But at any time a nurse might enter the room so he had to be quick.

After unlocking the handcuffs, it was a further problem getting his leg out of traction. He wasn't even sure how well he could walk with it still in the cast, but was surprised to find that it was relatively easy. But he couldn't run with it obviously. It was even hard for him to bend down, but he had to move the unconscious cop to the other side of the bed, so that he would not be so readily visible to anyone who might take a casual look into the room.

However, the hardest part was putting the pants on. The cast was too thick for the leg. Of course, he could cut them. But that would attract attention. And that would defeat the purpose. He wanted to escape undetected. Walking away in a police uniform with a leg slit up to the thigh would hardly be traveling incognito. So he struggled to pull the pants up without tearing them.

He was just doing up the belt when a nurse came into the room. She had walked in several steps before she noticed that the bed was empty and recognized Manning as the patient. She turned and was about to scream when Manning reached into the belt, pulled out the taser and zapped the nurse, bringing her quietly to the ground.

'I've got an old score to settle,' he said, stepping over her semiconscious form as he walked to the door and left the room.

Wednesday, 2 September
2009 – 13.05

Elias Claymore was watching the forty-two inch plasma TV in his balcony suite at the Hyatt Regency, San Francisco. He had decided not to travel back home right after the trial – he would be hounded by reporters. So he had phoned Alex and caught up with him when Alex had finished with the reporters. Alex had invited him back to the office, but Claymore had been reluctant to go there, anxious to avoid Andi's disapproving stare. So, at Alex's suggestion, he had booked this 585-square-foot luxury suite at the Hyatt Regency in Building Five of the Embarcadero Center, with a private 30-foot balcony and a magnificent view of the Bay Bridge through dramatic floor-to-ceiling windows.

He was sitting in the lounge, drinking a cup of coffee as he watched the TV report on the evening news about the outcome of his case. Alex had told him about Martine having to step aside from reporting the case for ethical reasons and he had been curious as to how her replacement was covering it. But what he really wanted to know was how he was being portrayed: as the aggrieved party or the lucky villain?

The reality was that the reporting was quite neutral and objective. The reports made it clear that he was innocent, but there was no hint of any emotion in the coverage, let alone sympathy. And as it was rolling news, it was becoming somewhat repetitious.

But something else was troubling him.

He went to the phone and called Alex. Juanita answered. 'Alex Sedaka's office.'

'Oh, hi, Juanita. Listen, I was wondering if I could have a word with Andi.'

'She's not here.'

'Has she been there today?'

'No, she hasn't. Weren't you with her when your case was dismissed?'

There was only the mildest note of suspicion in her tone.

'Yes, but I haven't seen her since then. Do you know if Alex has seen her? Or spoken to her?'

'Just a minute. I'll ask.'

She put him on hold and he heard music.

'Hallo, Elias.'

It was Alex.

'Yes, hi, Alex. I was wondering if you'd seen Andi. We split up after the hearing and . . .' he trailed off.

'No, I haven't seen her,' said Alex. 'Is it anything I could help with?'

'Well no, not really. Have you . . . have you spoken to her . . . since the hearing?'

There was a pause. 'Look, Elias, is there something wrong?'

Claymore sighed and tried to focus on how to explain it. 'Well it's just that we . . . that is, she . . . she seemed a little bit upset when we parted.'

Again the silence from Alex's end of the line. 'Did anything happen?'

'It depends what you mean by "happen."'

'I mean, did you have an argument?'

Alex sounded irritated when he said this, as if he resented

424

that Claymore was being so coy. Or maybe she *had* said something to Alex.

'No, not really. I mean, not exactly an argument. But she said something that—'

'What?'

'No, I mean it's not like it was one thing in particular. It was like . . . it was like she blamed me for what she had to put Gene through.'

Another pause.

'Yes, I can see why that might have upset her. I guess it's possible that she's gone back to LA to be with Gene.'

Claymore didn't buy this. 'I think after what happened in court . . .' There was no need to finish.

'No, you're right,' said Alex. 'But I don't know where she is. Maybe she's gone somewhere to work off her anger.'

'Do you know how she'd go about working off—'

'Now how the hell would I know that? Look, she may be jogging, she may be drinking, she may even be sitting in her hotel room sulking.'

'Do you have the number of her hotel? Or her cell phone?'

'Yes I do. Actually she's *also* staying at the Hyatt Regency. But if you exchanged rough words, it might not be too good an idea for you to call her. I'll call her now and if I get through I'll let you know.'

It was the best Claymore could hope for. 'Okay, thank you.'

Wednesday, 2 September
2009 – 13.20

Eleven stories down from Claymore, Andi was in her room swigging vodka and popping pills. She was supposed to check out today and return to LA. But there was no way she could go back to that house – not now. She wasn't afraid of Gene. It's just that the atmosphere would be too cold.

So instead she took comfort in the bottle, and when that wasn't enough she resorted to tranquilizers. The last time she had been on such a self-destructive spiral was right after she had been raped.

Then it was Gene who had got her through the crisis. But this time she couldn't call on Gene for support. Gene *was* the crisis.

Is it what Gene did to me or what I did to her?

It was all too fuzzy and unclear. Gene hadn't set out to do anything to her. Gene had merely set out for revenge against Claymore, having finally spotted the chance years later. But it was a reckless kind of revenge that hurt the innocent as well as the guilty. Bethel Newton was now robbed of her chance to see the real rapist brought to justice. Despite the mitochondrial DNA, they'd have a hell of a job proving Louis Manning guilty after Bethel had clearly identified Claymore in court. The DNA might prove sexual activity, but the defense could still attack Bethel personally, claiming that it was consensual and that she couldn't tell fantasy from reality.

They might have done this even without Gene's interference, citing the previous incident with Luke Orlando – as Andi herself had done, to her eternal shame. But the false accusations against Claymore and the ridiculous change in the rapist's age from twenties to fifties and then back again, would undermine her case completely.

But there was something even more troubling to Andi. She realized that even now she wasn't thinking about Bethel or even Gene as much as herself. She had been with Gene for so many years and now the fortress that they had built together – them against the world – had been destroyed.

But the hardest part to bear was that it was not Gene who had destroyed it. Gene could have had no way of knowing, when she embarked upon this crazy venture, that Andi would end up defending Claymore. That was why Gene had been so upset when Andi took on the case. Not because of what Claymore had done per se, but because it clashed with her plan for revenge. But by then it was too late to back out of it. By that stage there was no way she could stop it. She could hardly tell Bethel to withdraw the accusation against Claymore – not after she herself had urged Bethel to make that accusation in the first place.

But Andi had taken a conscious decision to go after Gene and force her to confess in public to suborning a witness. Yes, everyone would tell her that she had done her duty, that she had been right to put her emotions aside and act in strict accordance with the law and professional ethics.

Yet it felt so wrong.

She had done the 'right' thing and in the process destroyed the woman she loved and their relationship.

The phone rang. She couldn't bear to communicate with another human being, but instinctively she reached for the handset.

'Yes.'

'Andi . . . it's Gene.'

'What do you want?' Her voice was hardened by bitterness and guilt.

'Are you . . . are you coming home?'

Was it a cry for help or an offer of forgiveness?

She wasn't ready for either.

'I don't have a home,' she said, her eyes flooding with tears of regret, the moment the words were out of her mouth.

'Andi . . . baby . . . don't let that bastard Claymore destroy everything we had.'

'You don't get it, do you? The future belongs to the Claymores of this world. Everyone loves a repentant sinner. That's why he lives in a beachfront property in Santa Barbara. That's why he's in a fancy suite in this hotel while I'm in a basic business plan.'

For a second Andi almost mellowed. But then she realized that Gene had said 'had' rather than 'have.' They were too far gone for things to be as they were. Gene knew it too. You can't bring a relationship back from the dead.

Andi put the phone down and took another swig of the vodka . . . and popped another pill.

Wednesday, 2 September 2009 – 13.40

'Hallo. Could I speak to Martine Yin, please.'

Louis Manning was in a payphone. He didn't like the feeling of not being mobile. He had lost his car – or rather Claymore's car – and he didn't have as much money on him as he would have liked. There was a bit of money in the cop's wallet, which he had augmented by a couple of quick muggings across town.

But now he felt exposed. The cops would surely be looking for him and he had to lie low. He'd been living out of Claymore's car when he first drove up to Oakland. But back in LA he had his own pad, albeit rented. His common sense told him that he should get on a bus and hightail it back to LA, where he could lie low for a while. But the BART station would be crawling with cops and they'd certainly be on the lookout for him. He had just about enough in his pocket for a set of wheels and some gas. But like he had told the nurse, he had some unfinished business to attend to.

'She's not yet back in LA. As far as we know she's still in Oakland. May I ask who's calling?'

'But I thought she stopped covering the Claymore case and was replaced by someone else? Besides, the Claymore case is over.'

'Yes, but she stayed on in Oakland. That's all the information we have at the moment. Could you tell me what this is about? There may be someone else here who could help you.'

'No, I can't do that. I only deal with Martine.'

He put the phone down, confident that he had not set off any alarms. They would assume that he was one of her sources and that he didn't trust anyone else. He wasn't surprised by what they had told him. Martine Yin had a thing going with Alex Sedaka and so it made sense that she'd stick around.

The question was, had she gone back to San Francisco with Sedaka or was she still in Oakland? On the phone they'd said the latter. But then again they probably didn't know about Sedaka – or at least not the whole story. If she was staying with Sedaka, then she might be hard to get at. But he had to try.

The first stage was finding out for certain. That meant he had a few phone calls to make.

Wednesday, 2 September
2009 – 14.25

'You want the light on, Your Honor?'

Justice Ellen Wagner had been sitting alone in the dark in her chambers when her clerk entered. It was light outside, but the judge had closed the curtains against the early afternoon sun to sit there quietly, contemplating in peace.

'No, that's all right. I prefer the dark right now.'

The clerk was a girl of twenty-three, full of the enthusiasm of youth and the excitement that a young person feels at the beginning of an adventure. In this case, the adventure was the start of her career. Ellen Wagner saw so much of herself in this girl. That bright-eyed look of wonderment at all that was possible, with all the hopes and dreams for the future spread out before her. And this girl would grow up in a world made all the better by what Ellen Wagner's own generation had done – by the battles they had fought and won.

But how much had they won? And how much had the world changed? Was it a case of *Plus ça change, plus c'est la même chose*? Was it true that what goes around, comes around? Had they replaced one stereotype with another? Had they traded in rights for some rights for others, yet still not achieved that elusive nirvana of rights for all?

Claymore had walked out of court a free man, legally innocent. But one of his victims was now facing the prospect of many years' imprisonment for obstructing justice. Was that right?

Claymore might even be able to resume his life as a celebrity. It would be hard, but everyone loves a repentant sinner, especially in America. He had proved that before and he'd probably prove it again.

'Do you want to talk?' asked the clerk.

'No . . . no, that's all right. You can go home for the day.'

Wednesday, 2 September
2009 – 15.10

Smoke hung in the air and the sound of gangsta rap filled the room, punctuated occasionally by the staccato sound of the cue ball ricocheting off its target.

Gene ignored the wolf-whistles and vulgar jibes as she stood a few feet into the bar looking around. It had taken her a few phone calls and a few face to face encounters in some seedy back alleys and side streets, but she knew how to talk 'street' and it was only a matter of time before she finally found out where she needed to go. And here she was.

She took a deep breath as she thought about what she was planning to do.

Yes, she told herself. *It is right. It is fair, it is just.*

The only thing she couldn't tell herself was that it would do any good in the broader scheme of things.

Steeling herself to face up to it, and trying very hard to stay focused, she walked up to the barman. Before he could ask her what she wanted to drink, she whispered a few words into his ear and pressed a ten-dollar bill into his hand.

He whispered a word back in hers and nodded in the direction of a corner table. She turned casually and walked towards it. At the table sat a solitary young man, smoking what may have been a joint and trying to look like he didn't have a care in the world.

435

'Are you Joe?'

He looked up at her without smiling.

'Who wants to know?'

'Jane.'

'Cute name,' he said, this time giving in to the urge to smile, imperceptibly. 'I know a lot of Janes. Most of 'em work the streets.'

'I don't work the streets.'

'No, I didn't think so. Are you the Jane that's looking to buy a piece?'

Wednesday, 2 September
2009 – 16.30

'Hallo, can I speak to Martine Yin please? I'm not sure what room she's in.'

At the other end of the phone, someone was looking up the name in a perfunctory fashion, with no recognition of the name.

'What was that name again, sir?'

'Yin, Martine Yin.'

'I'm afraid we have no guest of that name at the hotel, sir.'

'Oh, sorry. I guess she must have checked out. Well, thank you anyway.'

'You're welcome, sir. Have a nice day.'

He broke the connection and crossed the name of the hotel off his list.

Wednesday, 2 September
2009 – 16.55

Elias Claymore was debating whether to call Alex again. He assumed that if Alex hadn't called him then it meant he hadn't been able to contact Andi. He had debated going to reception or the concierge and asking what room she was in. But they wouldn't tell him any more than they would reveal which room he was in. The most they would do is let him call her on the courtesy phone.

Actually that was all he needed. He would call using a one-digit prefix and the room number. But what was the point? If she was in her room, then Alex would have been able to reach her. The fact that he couldn't meant that she wasn't in her room and her cell phone was switched off.

There was a knock on the door.

'Who is it?' he called out.

'Maintenance,' said a female voice.

This caught him by surprise. He associated maintenance with men.

He opened the door to find himself confronted by Gene. This in itself would have been frightening enough, but she was holding a pistol in her hand and it was aimed at his chest.

As he backed into the room, she followed him, closing the door behind her.

'Don't look so surprised,' she said quietly. 'Justice has finally caught up with you after all.'

He looked at her with pity rather than fear or anger. 'Justice . . . or revenge?'

'Do you think you even have the right to *ask* that question?'

'It seems like a long time to wait for revenge. You must have known who I was a long time ago. Why wait till now?'

'Until recently I was on the other side of the country.'

'That's not the reason. Not if you were really determined.'

'Apart from that, I never had the opportunity.'

Claymore shook his head. 'Not to do it the way you did with that Bethel Newton girl, maybe. But to do what you're doing now . . . you could have done that *any* time. Why now?'

'You think I didn't do it a hundred times in my mind?'

'But you didn't have the courage?'

'I didn't have the anger.'

'No . . . you *had* the anger. But you didn't have the courage. It took what happened in court today to *give* you the courage.'

'What happened to me in court today is nothing.'

'No, but what happened to Bethel Newton in court today is everything. Because she reminds you of another young girl who went through something similar . . . and there was only a limited amount you could do for her too.'

The implacable expression on Gene's face didn't change. 'You know, pain is a funny thing,' said Gene. 'Wounds heal. But scars never do – and every now and again they start to itch.'

'And did your scars start itching?'

'Let's talk about you, Claymore. You say you've changed. That you could never hurt a woman like you did before. But I'd like to try to understand you. Do you know how much pain it cost Andi to defend you?'

440

'I know. That was the strange thing . . . she didn't say anything about—'

'I *know* she didn't say anything,' Gene interrupted angrily. 'That's Andi. She keeps things bottled up. But that isn't really the point. There's a limit to the amount of suffering anyone should have to bear.'

'I tried to object to Andi taking second seat. But Alex insisted.'

'Yes, Alex is a bastard. Figuratively speaking, he's a bit of a rapist himself. At least he knows how to use coercion of one kind or another to force other people to conform to his will. *What?*'

She was looking at him bewildered. He realized the expression on his face betrayed his thoughts.

'That's exactly what Andi said.'

Wednesday, 2 September
2009 – 17.20

> You may have thwarted my plan, but there is a price to be paid for doing so. I am now going to kill Andi. Her blood is on your hands.
>
> Lannosea

She had finished keying in the text message to her cell phone and was now keying in the number to the intended recipient: Alex Sedaka. But then she had second thoughts. Why Alex? Was it really Alex that she wanted to hurt?

Alex Sedaka was insignificant. He meant nothing to anyone. There was someone else who deserved to be hurt much more. And he had a weak spot: his conscience.

She had read somewhere that it was wrong to punish a person using their own conscience, because conscience was a virtue. To punish a person through his own conscience was to punish him for his virtues and not for his vices.

And yet it made perfect sense. You punish a wrongdoer by attacking his weaknesses. If his weakness is his conscience, then so be it. If he *has* no conscience then maybe you have to use other means. But why use more force than necessary?

And if Claymore *did* have a conscience, then how did it make him a better person if he protected that conscience through denial? That conscience was only worth something to his victims if it was pricked by self-awareness. Absent that awareness, his conscience was a disembodied attachment – a conscience without a consciousness.

So she deleted Alex Sedaka's cell phone number and replaced it with that of Elias Claymore.

But as she was about to press SEND, she hesitated again.

Wednesday, 2 September
2009 – 17.30

'Do you know how painful it is to bottle it all up inside like that?' asked Gene, still holding the gun close to her side, aimed squarely at Claymore's torso. She had ordered him to sit down on the couch, from which position it would have been hard for him to take any hostile action. That meant that he was facing the TV on the wall, with his side to her, forcing him to turn his head to give her his full attention.

'That's what I don't understand. Why didn't the anger come out *sooner*? Why only now?'

'I guess it's because we have a duty to ourselves to go on living. That's how I got through the pregnancy.'

He was confused.

'What pregnancy?'

'You don't know, do you?' She looked at him for a few seconds, alternately angry and then contemptuous at the blank look on his face. 'When you raped me you got me pregnant.'

For a few seconds he was dumbstruck. But he had to know. 'And did you . . .?'

'Have an abortion? I couldn't.'

'Why not? It was after *Roe* v *Wade*.'

'That's not what I mean.'

'No one could have blamed you.'

'Not even born-again fundamentalists like you?'

'The Bible says "Judge not, that ye be not judged."' he said, lowering his eyes in shame. 'And I'd be the *last* person to sit in judgment . . . Why didn't you? Couldn't you afford the costs?'

'Oh, I could afford it. There are always organizations ready to come forward and help in those circumstances. I could barely afford *not to* considering my lack of job skills at the time and the fact that I couldn't provide for the baby. It's just that I couldn't bring myself to do it.'

'Even though it was mine?'

'You mean even though it was the fruit of an act of violation?'

'Yes,' he gulped, barely able to speak.

'But, don't you see, that didn't matter. Because it was mine too. And when I felt it inside me I didn't think of you. I saw it as . . .' Tears welled up in her eyes. 'I don't know. I just couldn't bring myself to kill it. It was life and if I was going to go on living, as I resolved to do, I guess I had to let the baby live too. I didn't know how I'd feel when it was born, but I couldn't destroy it when it was inside me. And when I held him my arms, he was so weak and vulnerable and I knew that I was there to protect him.'

'Where is he now?'

'I got rid of him.'

'But you said . . .'

'I said I couldn't bring myself to have an abortion. And I tried to bring him up on my own. But it was hard. Everyone told me I should try and find a man. They said forget the looks. Just find yourself an ugly, lonely guy with a pocket full of money and a heart full of empty. At least he'll provide for you both and he won't leave you. That's what my friends said. And maybe my friends were right. But I wasn't ready to deliver myself into the hands of another man. I was

446

looking for someone gentle to share my life with, even before that.'

'You mean because of your sexual preference?'

'If that's what you care to call it.'

'But what about . . . getting rid of him?'

'You think I . . .? Oh no, not even *you* could be sick enough to think that.'

'I didn't mean . . .'

'Oh, I know what you *didn't* mean. But what you *did* mean is that you weren't sure. You actually needed some reassurance that I didn't . . . Oh God, *that is sick*.'

'I never said . . . Look, after what I put you through I don't know what effect it might have had.'

'Okay, well let me put your mind at rest. I gave him up for adoption.'

'But not because of you and Andi? And not because of me. I mean you *said* you wanted to keep him. Couldn't you have found a way – I mean if that was what you really wanted?'

'You don't understand. Of course I wanted to keep him. I wanted to love him. He was my child. And when he was a baby, weak and helpless, I could do that. I didn't think of him as part of you, I thought of him as part of *me*. But when he got towards two, things started to change. His facial features started to develop and he began reminding me of you. Also he was stubborn. He was developing a mind of his own. Instead of being the baby who responded with a smile when I scooped him up in my arms, he became this strong-willed brat who wanted his own way every time. And then it all started coming back. All the memories of another over-grown little boy who wanted things all his own way and didn't care who he hurt to get it.'

There were tears in both their eyes. If Claymore's pain

failed to equal that of Gene, it was offset by the knife of guilt that twisted in his gut.

'So you gave him up after you'd already bonded with him?' asked Claymore tensely.

'*Yes!*' said Andi, choked up with tears.

'But you still loved him?'

'Of course I still loved him!' By now she was crying more hysterically than she had been in court. But she still held on to the gun aimed squarely at Claymore.

'And that's what you've had to live with all these years?'

'Yes.'

He leaned forward. 'I can help you, if you'll let me.'

He started to get up, but stopped in his tracks when she raised the gun and aimed it at his face.

'I don't need your help! I can handle my own pain.'

'Look . . . I know it's an impertinence for me to offer *my* help. But like you said, you've been bottling it up all these years. You're entitled to some relief, some rest, some inner peace.'

'I wasn't talking about *me!*' she screamed. 'When I said how hard it was to keep it all bottled up, I didn't mean *me!*'

'Then who?' he stuttered, helplessly.

'I was talking about your other victim who didn't come forward at the time you raped her! *I was talking about Andi!*'

Wednesday, 2 September 2009 – 17.45 PDT (20.45 EDT)

Bethel Newton was going home.

She had boarded the flight at noon and touched down at Miami International Airport five hours and twenty-five minutes later. She had taken only hand luggage, having ditched practically everything that reminded her of her all too brief stay in California.

Her folks were expecting her. But she remained uncertain of what to expect. She had told them of her plans by text message while the taxi snaked its way to the airport in Los Angeles. She had used up practically the last of her precious cash to make the journey. But she didn't have the courage to speak to them by phone and they hadn't replied to her message.

She wondered how they would take it. She had rejected their overtures of support during her ordeal in California. Would they want to have anything to do with her now?

These thoughts were playing on her mind as she raced from the arrivals lounge past baggage collection and into the arrivals hall.

'Bethel, honey?' a woman's voice shouted. 'Over here!'

She looked round to see a somewhat plump thirty-nine-year-old woman waving to her. It was her mother. And she wasn't alone. Her stepfather Jack, twelve-year-old sister Judy and two-year-old brother Benny were also there.

Bethel Newton's eyes flooded with tears as she raced towards her waiting family.

Wednesday, 2 September
2009 – 18.00

Claymore had been silenced by Gene's words and was still struggling to take it all in. He had long suspected it – since the day he had first walked into the meeting room with her and Alex. But he hadn't been sure. And she had said nothing.

After a long silence, Claymore finally spoke. 'I *thought* it was her.'

'What do you mean, you *thought*?'

'It was so long ago. She was . . . I don't know how old.'

'Fourteen.'

'Fourteen,' he repeated quietly, as if the magnitude of his crime from twenty-five years ago was only now sinking in. 'I still remember her face. It's haunted me ever since. That was why I stopped, you know. It wasn't getting caught. It was her eyes . . . those wounded eyes.'

'*Shut up!*' Gene yelled.

'I'm sorry. I wasn't trying to torment you. And I wasn't making a play for sympathy. I just want you to know the truth. When she first came into that room and Alex introduced her . . . the face had changed of course. But I still remembered. When he said the name, it didn't confirm it because I never knew the names.'

'Of course you didn't! What did the names matter? We weren't people to you.'

'That's what I was like *then*! It's not the man I am *now*! The men you should really hate are the men who are *still like that* – like that scumbag Louis Manning.'

'Who?' She seemed stunned by this.

'Louis Manning. He's the guy who really raped Bethel Newton.'

'How do you know?' asked Gene, confused.

'They were talking about it after Andi finished questioning you. That policewoman, Detective Riley, came up and told them about the new DNA tests. The DNA came from some guy called Louis Manning. We both matched the DNA in the first tests – but that didn't mean anything because they said that something like 1 black man in 500 has that same DNA. It was from the Y chromosome or something like that. So then they did another test and that cleared me and implicated him.'

'What sort of a test?' asked Gene.

'It's kind of like the opposite of the first test. The first test looked at DNA from the father. But the second test – the one that cleared me – looked at DNA that comes from the mother.'

'Mitochondrial DNA?'

'Yes, that's it.'

'And you say this test cleared you?'

'Yes – and it implicated the other guy.'

'But how did they get him in the first place . . . this Louis . . .?'

'Manning. Well what happened was he tried to rape one of the reporters covering the case . . . Martine Yin.'

'Holy shit!'

'Holy shit's the word. And then they checked out the car he was driving. You see it was a Merc and he crashed it into a police car – or rather the cops crashed into him. And it was *my* car.'

'*Your* car.'

'Yes, my car. The one that was stolen two days before Bethel Newton was raped. And that's when they started figuring things out. One of the cops noticed that he looked a bit like the suspect description in the Bethel Newton case. So they decided to test his DNA too. And at first there were some shenanigans at the DNA lab – and with the computer too. But then they did those new tests and they got him.'

'So is he in custody now?'

'As far as I know. I think he's in the hospital or something, 'cause he broke his leg when then the cops sideswiped his auto. But I think they've got him under arrest.'

Gene took a deep breath.

'And you think that because this Louis Manning is the man who raped Bethel I should just blame him and forget about what you put Andi through in that courtroom – forcing her to relive the experience?'

'But I wasn't sure it was her. And what was I supposed to do? I didn't want her defending me. I tried to say so. But I couldn't say why without making it worse – for *both* of us. But how come she never said anything? I mean she must have known it was me?'

'Because she bottled it all up inside her. *That's* what I meant about keeping it all locked up. It wasn't *me* I was talking about. It was *her*. She sat next to you the whole trial and she didn't even remember that twenty-five years ago you were the one who raped her!'

Claymore's head dropped. Only now the full measure of his shame and guilt weighed down upon him.

'Turn that up!' snapped Gene.

He looked up to see a mug shot of Louis Manning on the TV. Picking up the remote hesitantly, he complied with Gene's command.

'Manning was only being guarded by a single police officer at the time and it appears that he took advantage of a moment of distraction to drug the officer's coffee with sleeping pills that he had been stockpiling while at the hospital. Police are refusing to say anything about the state of the injured nurse, but according to unofficial sources he said something to her just before he left, about having an old score to settle. Neither the police, nor the hospital, will confirm or deny these reports.'

'Oh my God!' said Gene as the report continued. She turned sharply on her heel and raced out.

Claymore could breathe again, but not easily. That maniac Louis Manning was on the loose with a grudge. Who would he go after? Sarah Jensen? Bridget Riley? Bethel Newton?

As if reading his mind, his cell phone beeped and flashed, alerting him to the fact that he had a message. He picked up the phone and pressed the button to retrieve the text.

You may have thwarted my plan, but there is a price to be paid for doing so. I am now going to kill Andi. Her blood is on your hands.

Lannosea

454

Wednesday, 2 September
2009 – 18.20

'Hallo, can I speak to Martine Yin please . . . I'm not sure what room she's in.'

Louis Manning was still checking hotels in Oakland. He was getting to the bottom of his list and wondering if perhaps Martine was staying in San Francisco. Certainly they had better hotels on the other side of the Bay Bridge. But she had been sent here to cover a trial in Oakland and it was unlikely that she'd want to face that commuter crush on the bridge every day.

Then again, she had come off the case – probably because of her relationship with the lawyer. So maybe she was staying with him. Or maybe at a hotel nearer to where he lived or worked.

He realized that he'd probably have to check out the hotels in San Francisco too.

'Putting you through now, sir.'

His heart leapt. *He had found her!*

A few seconds later, he heard the ringing tone. He should ring off now, so as not to alert her. But he had to make sure. Maybe they had misheard the name.

'Hallo.'

He recognized the voice – the voice that he had heard on the TV. The voice of the woman he had tried to rape.

The woman who had squirted pepper spray in his face and escaped his clutches. The woman who was responsible for the fact that he had broken his leg and been arrested . . . and now been ID-ed as the man who had raped Bethel Newton.

He put the phone down, slamming it harder than he intended.

The bitch was going to pay.

Wednesday, 2 September
2009 – 18.30

Martine Yin was undressing in her room at the Waterfront Hotel on the East Bay, curious about the phone call that hadn't got through. It was probably from Alex, she thought. But then he'd have tried her cell phone.

Whatever, she told herself. *If it was important, they'd call back.*

She had used the excuse of the trauma of the attempted rape to get herself relieved of reporting on the Claymore case. This avoided having to tell them anything about her relationship with Alex. But she had also used the trauma as a pretext to ask for a leave of absence until the following Monday, the seventh. That left her free to spend more time with Alex, including – she hoped – another weekend.

It was a little too early to think about moving in together. For a start, it wouldn't be easy to coordinate, workwise. She was based in Southern California and he was firmly rooted in San Francisco. Secondly, he wasn't yet ready to tell David and Debbie. And it wasn't yet clear whether or not they approved of her. She didn't want this to turn into one of those ongoing feuds between the daughter and the 'step-mother' who is only a few years her senior.

Still, Martine was already hoping . . . and planning.

Alex had invited her out for dinner tonight at Sens, an

457

exotic southern Mediterranean restaurant in the Embarcadero Center. She had spent the morning on retail therapy, but still hadn't decided what to wear. It would definitely have to be white. The question was, should it be the dress with the single shoulder strap and long slit up the leg or the medium length number with the tantalizing keyhole? She had laid them both out on the bed, but couldn't make up her mind.

But there was still time. Meanwhile, she headed for the shower.

Wednesday, 2 September
2009 – 18.35

Alex was in his office cleaning up the paperwork from the Claymore case, when another call came. Juanita had gone home, so Alex took it himself.

'Alex Sedaka.'

'Hallo, Mr Sedaka.'

It was a woman's voice. He hadn't expected that. He thought it would be Claymore calling about Andi. He was all set to tell him that he had no news and that he should stop worrying. Women weren't as emotionally fragile as men seemed to believe. Martine had proved that when she had brushed off his excess of sympathy and concern after the rape attempt. But this woman *did* sound emotionally fragile, even from the few words she had uttered.

'Yes. Who is this?'

'It's Gene – Gene Vance.'

'Oh, hallo, Gene. What can I do for you?'

'I'm worried about Martine.'

'*Martine?*' He had thought she was going to say she was worried about Andi. Alex hadn't seen Andi since he went off to make a statement to the press about how his client was relieved that it was all over. But Claymore had said that Andi was in a state of distress when they parted. When Gene came on the line, he thought it was going to be more of the same. But Gene had said *Martine* . . .

'Why? What's the problem?'

'I think she may be in danger.'

'*Danger?* What sort of danger?'

'Didn't you hear?'

'Hear what?'

'Louis Manning escaped from the hospital—'

'How?'

'He drugged the cop who was keeping an eye on him and got the key to the handcuffs. Then he stole the cop's uniform and escaped.'

Alex was in shock at this revelation. But he stayed calm until his sense of logic kicked in. 'But I don't see that he'd be stupid enough to stick around. I mean, he knows they're looking for him. And if they know he's wearing a cop's uniform then they'll be looking for that too. And that means he'll be looking for a change of clothes. He's more likely to attack a man to get some new threads than go after Martine.'

'No, you don't understand. It was on the news.'

'*What* was on the news?'

'He tasered a nurse who saw him making his getaway. And it was reported that he said something about having an old score to settle before he hightailed it.'

'But that could mean anything.' He was rationalizing now – and he knew it.

'No, think about it for a minute. Who else would he go after? He could hardly go after the cops who busted him: he wouldn't dare. He has no reason to go after Bethel Newton, 'cause she never accused him. It was others who ID-ed him. He wouldn't go after Detective Reilly or Sarah Jensen 'cause they're probably too well protected. So who else does that leave?'

Alex could think of several answers. There was Andi,

who had discovered the tampering at the DNA lab that had got the police and D.A. to look again at the DNA evidence.

No, he told himself. That doesn't make sense! What *Gene* had said made sense. If Manning *was* stupid enough to stick around in an attempt to exact revenge, then Martine was the logical target. Who successfully fought him off when he tried to rape her? Who maced him in the face and left him defeated and humiliated? Who sounded the alarm that got the cops racing to the scene, so that when he tried to hotfoot it out of there he got sideswiped by a squad car and ended up with a broken leg?

'Look, I was supposed to be meeting her tonight. I know where she's staying so I'll call her right away and warn her to be careful.'

'Okay, but keep me posted. I don't want anyone else to get hurt because of . . .'

He understood why she had tailed off. She felt guilty, as if she had caused all this – which in a way she had.

'Okay. I'll call you right back as soon as I've spoken to her. Are you on this number?'

'Yes. I'll be waiting.'

Wednesday, 2 September
2009 – 18.40

Andi was driving north along Drumm Street in the direction of Sacramento Street. On the dashboard in front of her was a note in an unfamiliar handwriting that said: 'Golden Gate Bridge, sunset. The truth shall set you free.'

At Washington Street she turned right, glancing at the green wall of the outdoor tennis courts to her left. The street was divided by a stretch of grass with three or four trees. Behind her the sun was setting, but she still had about an hour before it dropped below the horizon and maybe an hour of twilight after that.

There was no particular urgency to the way she was driving, but a barrage of thoughts was racing through her mind. Anger, guilt, vengeance. On the front passenger seat was the vodka bottle. But she wasn't driving erratically. Still . . . maybe she'd get pulled over by the cops. Maybe she wouldn't. To tell the truth, she didn't care.

She was headed east on Washington towards the Embarcadero intersection. The southbound traffic seemed heavy. She remembered that today was a baseball day, the Giants were at home to the Dodgers.

Old rivalries. They could bring out people's anger more than politics, more than religion. Funny, people's values. When they couldn't find something to fight over, they invented something.

As if there wasn't enough pain and suffering in the world. Maybe that was precisely *because* most people had it too easy. They could afford to fight over the most trivial things in life.

The one thing that *ought* to bring people out onto the streets and get them to storm the barricades was injustice. But that rarely happened these days. America's anger with itself had burnt itself out in Andi's infancy. It wasn't that America was now at peace with itself. It had merely succumbed to complacency. And there was no room in all this for someone who had a passion for justice.

She had reached the intersection just as the light turned from green to yellow. As she pulled out on the yellow, the light turned to red. But a gray pickup truck behind her tried to beat the lights and shot out into the intersection close on her tail. Maybe if Andi had been quicker across the intersection, things would have been different. But the alcohol and pills had clouded her judgment and she was driving not with speed and aggression but slowly and passively – oblivious to the danger.

Meanwhile, the traffic headed south on Embarcadero towards the ballpark was taking no prisoners. And when their light turned green they *went* for it. So it was no surprise that a bus that was headed straight across the intersection slammed into the pickup truck. Meanwhile another car on Washington took a risky right turn on red. But when the bus plowed into the pickup truck, the pickup truck was sent careening sideways till it skidded to a halt, thus making it too a perfect target for the stream of southbound traffic on Embarcadero.

For a second the air hung still. Then Andi – who had caught only some of this with a quick sideways glance – heard an almighty crash. As she completed her left turn into Embarcadero, she heard the sound of cars crashing and turned again to see an almighty multiple pile-up across the entire intersection.

Wednesday, 2 September
2009 – 18.45

Martine was sitting on the bed in her bathrobe, drying her hair, and she barely heard the knock on the door.

'Who is it?' she shouted, moving the dryer away from her hair but not switching it off.

A muffled voice came at her and all she heard was 'iss.' She switched off the hair dryer.

'Pardon?'

'Room Service!'

'I didn't order anything.'

'I'll leave the tray out here.'

She heard the faint sound of receding footsteps.

'No, you didn't hear me! I said I didn't order anything!'

She waited for a response. But heard nothing.

What kind of a moron was that?

She walked over to the door and peered out through the spy hole. There was no one there. But to the side of the door, she could clearly see a tray on the floor with a covered plate together with a coffee pot and a cup. Angrily, she opened the door to take a proper look. Realizing that the food tray was probably intended for someone else, she looked left and right, but saw no sign of the waiter. There was another corridor, branching off, and for a split second, she thought she sensed a human presence there, the movement of a shadow or maybe the sound of breathing.

But before she had time to think about it, her cell phone rang. The erroneous delivery would have to wait. She turned and went back into the room, but before the door closed behind her there was a flurry of movement from the branching corridor and Martine found herself hurled into the room and thrown onto the bed.

When she spun round, in preparation to spring back to her feet and fight, she saw the door shutting behind Louis Manning who stood there with a menacing smile on his face.

Wednesday, 2 September
2009 – 18.50

Claymore was stuck in the logjam on Washington Street. Something had happened just ahead at the intersection with Embarcadero, but he didn't know what. He wished he had gone the other way, via Broadway. But it was too late now. He would have liked to turn back and go that way even now. But with the traffic clogged up all the way up his tail, there was no possibility of that. He was stuck here until something gave – and he didn't know how long *that* would be.

In his mind he kept thinking about Andi. He couldn't get the thought of her out of his mind. He wasn't worried about Gene. She was too strong to worry about. Whatever weakness she had shown in court had been short-lived. She had the kind of inner strength that enabled her to come bouncing back.

But not Andi. Andi was fragile. He had seen that over the two and half weeks of the trial. And after Gene had told him, he knew how thoroughly he was responsible for that fragility.

Nietzsche had said: 'That which does not kill me makes me stronger.' But this wasn't true of everyone. It's like paternal bullying in childhood: it toughens up the first son, but turns his younger brother into a wimp. And Andi may have put on a dazzling display in the courtroom, but every time she did that, it was followed by an internal collapse. He had seen that after the voir dire, when she came back looking crushed after Alex had spoken to her. He had seen how she cried after she'd taken Bethel Newton apart on the witness stand. He had even caught a glimpse of it after she had finished cross-examining Albert Carter. And he had no doubt that she was feeling guilty beyond belief at what she had done to her lover on the witness stand.

But it was actually Gene's words that were haunting him right now.

'She sat next to you the whole trial and she didn't even remember that twenty-five years ago you were the one who raped her,' Gene had said.

She had been bottling it all up, just as Gene had. But Gene had now opened the bottle. Had she opened it for both of them?

He had to know, because *he* was responsible. But right now he was powerless as he sat here, snarled in traffic that wasn't going anywhere.

He whipped out his cell phone and tried to call the number that had sent him the text message in the hope of reasoning with the person at the other end.

But there was no answer.

Wednesday, 2 September
2009 – 18.55

Alex was calling Gene. She answered almost immediately.

'Hi Gene, it's Alex. Listen. I've tried calling Martine several times but she's not answering.'

'You think we should call the cops?'

'And tell them what? That we *think* Louis Manning *might* try and attack her but we're not sure and we're not even sure where she is.'

'We can tell 'em that we can't contact her and that we're worried about her.'

'And you think they'll do anything?'

'So what are *we* gonna do?'

There was no question in Gene's mind that Alex would want to do something.

'Well, I'll keep trying to call her, but I'll have to go there myself.'

'Where are you?'

'I'm in my office in San Francisco, the Embarcadero Center.'

'And is she in San Francisco?'

'No, she's in Oakland. She's staying at the Waterfront Hotel.'

'That means you're gonna have to drive across the Bay Bridge like, *now.*'

It was commuter time: the worst time to be traveling and the worst time to be crossing the Bay Bridge. The fact that the Giants were playing the Dodgers made it even worse.

'I've got no alternative.'

'I'm also in San Fran. But I'm right by the bridge. And I can ride a motorbike. That makes me a bit more mobile than you.'

'Have you *got* a motorbike?'

'Not yet. But I can get one.'

'You can't buy one at such short notice.'

'Who said anything about buying?'

'No, wait, listen! Don't do anything illeg—'

The line went dead. He knew that he was going to have to go there himself – even though there was no doubt in his mind that Gene would get there first.

Wednesday, 2 September
2009 – 19.00

The fear Martine had felt when Manning tried to rape her in the multistory parking structure was nothing compared to the terror she felt now, secured to the bed with duct tape. For this was the terror of uncertainty. Then, she was in a public place and his options were limited. Here they were away from public view and he had much more scope and much more available time.

The phone had rung a couple of times since Manning had forced his way into the room and Martine suspected that it might be Alex. But she wasn't sure. And anyway, he had no way of knowing that anything was wrong. She might be out, or in the shower. In fact, when she was in the shower, she had thought at one point that the phone was ringing.

For a brief moment she had considered putting up some resistance. It had been her courage in the parking structure that had saved her from being raped and helped the police to catch Manning. But this time it was a whole different ball game. For a start, she no longer had the element of surprise. He was alert to any sudden show of resistance. Secondly, even if she managed to make a break, she would still have had to open the door and get out of the room. That would have cost her precious extra seconds. But the third and most important factor was that this time Manning had a gun.

That last one was the clincher. She knew that this time she didn't dare resist. And he knew it too. But just to make sure, after ordering her to remove the bathrobe, he was quick to handcuff her wrists together in front, before he forced her to lay down on the bed.

Words could hardly describe how vulnerable she felt. And yet in some way, once she accepted the reality, it was strangely liberating. She knew that her only chance – if indeed it was a chance – was to reason with him, to open up the lines of communication.

'There's something I don't understand.'

'Did I tell you to talk, bitch?'

For a second she was filled with an even deeper terror and thought that perhaps she had misjudged the situation and misread Manning. But then she realized that he was not completely free of fear and even though he had the upper hand, much of what he was doing was still an act and not an expression of any real belief in his own invincibility. She decided to put her strategy back on track and tried to sound nonchalant, without being contemptuous.

'Oh, come on, you don't have to impress me with that macho performance. You've got me right where you want me. There's no reason why we shouldn't talk.'

He was so taken aback by her response that he actually smiled for a second. 'You're right there.'

She breathed a sigh of relief. The tacit acknowledgement of his power had assuaged his anger. But she waited for him to speak again, not wanting to sound too eager.

'So what is it you don't understand?'

'Well . . . you raped Bethel Newton . . . then you tried to rape me. I was just wondering if that was a coincidence?'

'Not really. Raping Bethel Newton was something I did on the spur of the moment. God knows why, she'd probably have slept with me anyway. Or maybe that's why. I'm into power. Life is just one big power game, from the submissive oriental wife who walks four paces behind her husband to the man with his finger on the nuclear trigger.'

'Yeah, okay. But what about . . .?'

'What about you? That's easy. I knew all about you and Sedaka.'

'How?'

'I was paying close attention to the Bethel Newton rape case, for obvious reasons. After Claymore was arrested the first time, I saw a story on the news about it. They said Sedaka was his lawyer as well as his friend and that he was supposed to be a good lawyer. Anyway, I was a bit curious, so one time when he left the jail, I followed him around and I saw him pick you up and take you to a restaurant.'

'You were playing a dangerous game. It's like going back to the scene of the crime.'

'Maybe. I find it hard to let go. It's like I have this urge to go back to where things started. You know, retracing my roots, like that fish that swims upstream to where it was born.'

She looked surprised. 'Salmon?'

'Yeah.'

She was looking at him, unsure of what to say.

'And you thought I was just an ignorant nigger.'

'I never said that.'

'Oh I *know* you never *said* that. That's 'cause you're a cultured, educated Chinese-American. Now if you were an Alabama redneck, you *would* have said it. But then again, if you were an Alabama redneck you wouldn't know about the mating habits of fish.'

A gleaming smile came to his face and he put on a high-pitched Southern accent to taunt her.

473

'But I *saw* that flicker of surprise in your eyes when I said that about swimmin' upstream. And I gahts to tell you, ma'am, thaz the fahst time in mah life ahhhz ever bin compared to a salmon!'

He held the smile a while longer, before his face hardened.

'I think I'd better gag you too,' he continued, his voice deepening. It's not like you're gonna say anything that I can't already figure out. The parody accent came back. 'Nothin' personal, ma'am, but you *is* kind of *pre*-dictable.'

Wednesday, 2 September 2009 – 19.05

Claymore was sitting at the end of Washington Street in his rented car, desperately trying to figure a way out of this logjam. But at the back of his mind he was remembering Gene's words.

'Alex is a bastard. Figuratively speaking, he's a bit of rapist himself. At least, he knows how to use coercion of one kind or another to force other people to conform to his will.'

This was remarkably similar to what Andi had said after the trial: 'I was raped again – this time by a colleague. Not *literally* raped, but figuratively speaking. My hands were tied and I was forced to conform to his will. Only this is the last time it's going to happen.'

There were signs of things moving ahead and Claymore breathed again. Then he remembered the text message that he had received. He had tried the number but got no answer. So he called the one person who might be able to help him.

'Hallo.'

'Hi, Alex. It's Elias.'

'Elias. Hi, listen, don't take this personally, but I'm kind of busy right now. Something's come up.'

'Something to do with Andi by any chance?'

'No. With Mart— Look, you're not still worried about her are you? I'm sure she's all right.'

'Okay, but just tell me one thing, does the name Lannosea mean anything to you?'

There were a few seconds of silence on the other end of the line.

'Why do you ask?'

'I had a text message from a number I didn't recognize, from someone who called themselves Lannosea. I presume you *do* recognize the name?'

'Okay, look, *save that message*. It might help us later.'

'Help you how?'

'Lannosea is the name of the person who's been sending threatening messages to Andi. We think that it was the same person who tampered with the jury selection software and who tried to frame Andi for hacking into the database. We think it may be another woman that you . . .'

Neither of them spoke for a few seconds. In the end it was up to Claymore to break the silence. 'But you don't know who it is.' It had the finality of a statement.

'No. Although my son and Andi were going to pool their expertise to try and find out. Why, do *you* have any idea?'

Now it was Claymore's turn to hesitate. Alex had said that something had come up. And he sounded like he was driving. He wasn't in any position to handle more pressure.

'No . . . not really,' said Claymore, as the traffic ahead of him finally started to move.

Wednesday, 2 September
2009 – 19.10

Gene hadn't lied about getting to the Waterfront Hotel quickly – and she hadn't been joking about getting a motorbike either. Starting the bike had been easier than finding it. The irony that Oakland was the birthplace of the Hell's Angels was not lost on her as she stole the bike and raced across the Bay Bridge.

By the time she rode into the hotel parking lot, her heart rate was as fast as the rev counter on the engine. She got quite a few stares as she dismounted the bike. But she was too preoccupied to notice. Instead, she raced into the hotel lobby and up to the front desk. There were several people ahead of her, but she used her intimidating height and build to face them down as she pushed her way up to the desk.

'I need to speak to Martine Yin *now!*'

She reached into her inner pocket as if she were reaching for a police badge – or a gun. It did the trick – that and the continuous eye contact. The frightened girl at the reception desk keyed in the name on the computer and stuttered: 'You can use the white courtesy phone. Number 9214. You're the second person who—'

Gene had already shot off towards the staircase. She knew exactly what that four-digit number meant. The first digit – nine – meant that you were calling a room in the hotel, rather than any of its services. The other three digits were the room number. The second digit was the floor and the last two digits designated the room itself. Martine was in room 214 on the second floor.

But the thing that had spurred Gene into action with such haste was the additional wording that the receptionist had tacked on to her answer: 'You're the second person who—'

At the second floor, Gene looked at the arrows indicating which way the room numbers went; 214 was to her left. She turned and strode briskly in that direction, looking at the door numbers as she went past them to make sure that she didn't overshoot the mark.

Then, as she got to the room, she stopped abruptly and pounded on the door.

She was greeted by silence. But she thought that in that split second before she knocked, she had heard the sound of a voice . . . a male voice.

She pounded again. 'Louis! I know you're in there!'

She heard a sound inside the room and then the sound of a door handle turning. The door opened slowly to reveal a young black man in his late twenties standing there with a beaming smile on his face and his leg in some sort of a synthetic cast. As the man stepped aside, still holding the door, she noticed two other things. One was the supine, terrified figure of Martine on the bed, gagged and handcuffed. The other was the gun in Manning's hand, held loosely at his side with an almost insultingly casual indifference.

With an arrogant flick of his head he motioned for Gene to enter the room. She complied, the look on her face quite neutral.

'Hallo, son,' she said, as he closed the door behind her.

'Hallo, Mom,' he replied.

Wednesday, 2 September
2009 – 19.15

Andi had turned off the road just before the Golden Gate Bridge and was driving to the Golden Gate parking lot. But she had no recollection of how she had got there. When she pulled up, she lowered the visor with the vanity mirror and started fixing her make-up. She couldn't remember what she was doing there or why she had decided to come there. She just had a vague awareness of her new surroundings. She wondered if perhaps she was just a puppet and that someone else was pulling the strings.

Then she remembered.

She got out of her car and smoothed down her rumpled dress with a few brisk movements of her hands.

'I'm never going to have to look at him again.'

Of course she wouldn't: the case was over. She started walking towards the nearby bridge. There was pedestrian access from this side.

She walked along the footpath from the parking lot that led to the bridge, bypassing the tool gate. It was a slow leisurely walk. There was no reason to run. She might as well take in the views and savor the atmosphere as she remembered her final words to Claymore in court.

'It's just a case of taking the plunge and moving on.'

Wednesday, 2 September 2009 – 19.20

'I bribed a girl at the records office to let me see the file,' said Louis Manning.

He was talking to Gene Vance like she was an old friend. But she sensed that he was taunting her. And she couldn't ignore the helpless figure of Martine on the bed, breathing heavily with a look of terror in her eyes.

'I didn't think it was that easy. I thought it was only on TV soaps and cop shows that public officials were all on the take.'

'Oh, I didn't bribe her with money.'

'Then what?'

'I got her hooked on crystal meth. That made it easier to control her.'

He seemed to be taking pleasure in the way he described it, like he was taunting her.

'How much did you find out?'

'Both my parents' names. I'd never heard of you until then, but I knew who *he* was. There it was staring me in the face – my father a convicted rapist and political activist. So I started reading about him and learned all about who he was and what he stood for, not to mention how he turned his back on it and joined the establishment. Then I checked up on you and found out where you worked. That's when I realized what had happened.'

'When was that?'

'A while back.'

'So at the time of . . . you knew.'

'Yes, but I didn't do it 'cause of that. And then when you got involved – and Andi – that was just like . . . kind of like the icing on the cake. How did *you* figure it out?'

'Elias Claymore told me—'

'How the fuck does *he* know?'

'Not about you. I mean not directly. He told me that the Y-chromosome DNA – when they finally got it right – matched both him and you. That didn't mean much because it also matched thousands of others. But then they did another test with the last remaining evidence sample, a mitochondrial DNA test—'

'What the fuck is that?'

'It's a test for DNA that's inherited from the mother. It can't identify an individual but it can identify sisters and brothers and any relatives from the same maternal line, like cousins and things like that. And it matched you.'

Manning looked puzzled.

'But if it goes back through loads of generations, then somewhere along the line it probably matches others too.'

'Yes, but how many of them have their father's DNA matching Elias Claymore?'

'So it was the combination of the two that gave it away.'

'Actually, no. You see what I know, and what nobody else knows, is that the DNA in that third sample didn't come from the rapist. It came from me. I was assigned to Bethel Newton before they took the evidence samples and when we met, she was so emotionally overwrought that she gripped my arm and dug her nails into me, or at least one nail. That was the third nail clipping sample.'

Manning was wide-eyed with incredulity.

'You mean they realized it was me, and all the time it was based on false evidence?'

Wednesday, 2 September
2009 – 19.25

Elias Claymore pulled up in the Golden Gate parking lot and leapt out of his car without even bothering to check if he had parked it straight. That was the least of his worries.

He looked around and wandered round too. Then he saw it: a red Ford Mustang. Was it Andi's? Or just another like it? It was the only one in the lot. He raced over to it and looked inside. There was no obvious sign that it was hers. But equally none that it wasn't.

It has to be, he told himself.

But where was she now? And how long ago had she got here? It was a long walk to the bridge. And when he last saw her, she wasn't exactly dressed for running.

Was there still a chance? Could he get to her?

Certainly there hadn't been any incidents on the bridge recently because otherwise this whole area would be buzzing with activity – not to mention gawking members of the public.

He looked round at the Bay. To his right the sun was low in the sky but still above the horizon.

Maybe she had got held up in the logjam on Embarcadero too. Maybe she had also been delayed. Maybe she had only just got here.

There was only one way to know for sure.

He sprinted towards the bridge, up the slope, chugging

away breathlessly. He hadn't put on rolls of fat like some men his age. Nevertheless he was no longer a young man, and although he could run, he felt it in his lungs, his heart and the sinews of his thighs.

He was panting and hunched with cramp in his ribcage when he got onto the pedestrian walkway of the bridge. But he didn't know whether to be relieved or worried when he saw Andi walking the same path, almost staggering, as she receded from him in the distance.

All he knew was that he wanted to sprint towards her, but his legs wouldn't let him.

Wednesday, 2 September
2009 – 19.30

'Looks like it,' said Gene, taunting him right back. 'Maybe you shouldn't have escaped. Maybe you should have brazened it out.'

'No, they still had me for the attempted rape on . . .' he half turned to indicate the terrified young woman on the bed. 'But if the last DNA sample was from you – and if you *knew* that – then how did *you* figure it out?'

'It was the coincidence that got me thinking. You see, the very fact that Bethel ID-ed the picture of the young Elias Claymore on the corkboard at the rape crisis center was itself interesting. I knew the rapist couldn't be Claymore, because of the age factor. But still, there had to be a reason. There had to be a cause. And the obvious cause was the son that I gave up – the son that Claymore never knew he had. That also made the match of the Y-chromosomal DNA somewhat less of a coincidence. It meant all of a sudden that there was a causal explanation.'

'So now we *both* know. What about my father? Does *he* know?'

'I didn't tell him.'

'Why not?'

'I had to see you first. I had to speak to you.'

He shrugged his shoulders. 'And am I what you expected?'

'When I gave you up, I didn't expect anything. I was only thinking of myself.'

'Well, at least you're not a hypocrite. But what about now?'

'I knew you raped Bethel . . . knew you tried to rape Martine—'

'Still intend to,' he cut back almost under his breath. The contempt was manifest in the quiet, off-the-cuff tone.

'Look, I admit that I wronged you. I could make excuses and say it's because of what your father did to me, but – yes – I still wronged you. But Martine didn't. All she did was defend herself when—'

'You don't get it, do you? What Claymore did was part of his nature. It's in a man's genes. It's part of their nature. Men try to reproduce their genes. And the stronger men succeed.'

'But not by rape.'

'They don't need to. In the animal kingdom the concept of rape is meaningless. The males fight amongst each other to establish superiority and then the females go naturally and willingly with the strongest males. The weaker males get the leftovers. It's only in the human species that women look for other things like sympathy and kindness and wealth. A female animal doesn't want a good provider, she gathers or hunts for the food herself. She just wants strong genes to bind with hers to make sure that her own genes survive in her offspring. Even in the human species most women know that the best provider isn't necessarily the best biological father for their children. That's why they marry rich men and then cheat on them with working class hunks. Adultery's as natural for a woman as it is for a man.'

'How do you know all this?'

'I've done a few spells behind bars. Books are one of the few things they give you. Some cons like to toke. Some like to work out. I liked to read books. I've messed with my head enough with all that shit and I'm fit enough already.'

'But not strong enough to get off drugs for good?' asked Gene, holding her breath against Manning's possible response.

Wednesday, 2 September
2009 – 19.35

Claymore was sprinting along the pedestrian walkway as fast as he could, trying his best to keep Andi in his line of sight. But his heart sank when she arrived at the southern suspension tower and moved off the walkway and round the tower, onto the observation platform behind it. That – and a similar platform at the northern suspension tower – were the points where suicides jumped off.

He arrived at the suspension column in time to see Andi clambering over, with what looked like a bottle of gin or vodka in her hand. He felt a knot in his stomach as terror swept over him. If he shouted out to her he would frighten her. If her decision was final, it would make her jump. If she was still undecided, it would take her by surprise and might very well startle her and cause her to lose her grip. If he rushed her, it would also frighten her.

He stood there frozen with indecision, his feet stuck to the ground beneath him. As she completed her climb to the other side, she held on with one hand as she took a swig from the bottle.

And then she saw him.

For a second his heart went into his mouth as he thought this was the end for her. But instead, she simply smiled.

'Oh, hi, Elias,' she said, in what sounded a bit like a little girl voice.

He looked at her, feeling helpless, and yet in some way liberated from fear by precisely that sense of desperation. Behind her the sun was setting and he couldn't make out the features on her face. Was she happy? Sad? Lost? Already too far gone?

He looked around. There were plenty of cars on the bridge. But here, behind the suspension column, they were virtually concealed from public view. And at this time on a baseball day, there weren't many pedestrians about. They were, effectively, alone.

He had to reach out to her in the only way he could. But that meant not with his body, but with his mind, with his words.

'Andi, don't do it.'

Even though she was in silhouette, he sensed that she was smiling, maybe from the girlish shake of her head, freeing her hair to the tender mercies of the breeze.

'What do you want?' she asked hesitantly, putting the bottle down on the ledge and holding on with both hands now.

'Don't do it. Don't jump.' At that height, hitting the water would be like hitting concrete.

She half turned her head and looked round at the water hundreds of feet below.

'Why not?'

He tried to take a step forward, but she released one of her hands, as if warning him of how easy it would be to jump.

'No! Wait!' he pleaded, stopping in his tracks and holding up his hands in a gesture of surrender. 'Andi, listen to me. You've blotted it out of your mind. The rape. The pain. It was *me*. I was the man who raped you all those years ago. You've closed off the past and shut it out of your mind. But it's been there all the time, in the background.'

'I don't understand,' she said weakly, her voice now distinctly like a little girl's as some distant memory pierced her consciousness.

'You've been doing these things to yourself,' he said. 'The messages, the threats, switching the DNA files and then leaving a trail for them to get back to you. It was *you* all along, Andi. You were doing it to *yourself*!'

'Why would I want to do those things to myself?' she asked.

He didn't know about the pills or how much she had drunk. But she was clearly out of it.

'It was your way of handling the pressure . . . the painful memories. You couldn't take it, so you blotted it out. And then you must have created another person to carry the anger for you, so that you could get on with your life.'

'What do you mean, "created another person"?' she asked, crying with the pain of recollection as memories of the rape came fleeting in and out of her mind.

'I don't know all the reasons. I only know that it's because of what I did. You wanted revenge. You wanted me to be punished – as I deserved to be. But you also wanted to forget your pain. And I guess you couldn't handle both. The one wasn't compatible with the other. So the part of you that wanted to forget blotted it out. And then the other part of you set about getting revenge. But then, just now at the trial, because you were *helping* me, the other part of you didn't just want revenge on *me*. It sought revenge *on you too*.'

'Revenge?' she echoed, confused, as her mind drifted into some far-off world.

'Yes. *You* were the one who modified the jury selection software.'

'No!' Andi whined, wiping back the tears with the backs of her free hand. 'It was Lannosea!'

'Don't you see Andi? You *are* Lannosea. She's part of you – the *strong* part. She's the part that wants revenge, the part that wants to punish the other part for helping me. Lannosea is just the angry side of *you*. She carries the anger, but you still carry the *pain*. That's why she hounded you with those e-mail messages and threats. That's why she broke into the DNA database and framed you. It was you doing it to yourself to punish yourself.'

'No, you're wrong! It can't be that! I wouldn't betray someone who trusted me.'

'Andi, I'm not blaming you. God knows, I've got no right to blame *anyone*! But you need help.'

'I don't need any help from *you*!'

It looked like she was about to jump. He had to stop her.

'Lannosea!' he shouted desperately. 'If you let her jump, you'll die too!'

Wednesday, 2 September
2009 – 19.38

Alex, meanwhile, was going nowhere. He was snarled up in traffic on the Bay Bridge.

He had tried calling Martine's hotel room several more times, but got no answer. He had considered asking the hotel to send a member of staff to check. But they would probably think he was crazy and even if they didn't, they were unlikely to treat it as a matter of any particular urgency.

But Gene must be there by now.

It was strange the way she was suddenly helping him after what she had been put through in court. And yet in a way it made perfect sense. She probably felt guilty about what she had done herself. And this was her way of trying to redeem herself.

But was she right to fear for Martine's safety?

Alex had no way of knowing that. But he knew that Manning had escaped. He had heard the news reports on the radio, so he knew that what Gene had said about Manning's veiled threat was true. And he knew that there was a certain underlying logic to her theory that Martine was the intended target.

There was nothing he could do about it until the traffic cleared ahead of him.

But what about Gene?

He phoned her and waited desperately for an answer.

'Hallo Ale—'

Gene's voice was cut short abruptly.

Something had happened. It sounded like some kind of a struggle, albeit a very brief one. The next thing he heard was a man's voice.

'I've got your bitch here.'

Wednesday, 2 September 2009 – 19.41

Holding on with only one hand, Andi swept her hair back with a self-assured, almost arrogant gesture. Then she gripped the rail with both hands. The tears seemed to dry up in an instant and her face grew in confidence. Even her posture and body language was different. This was no timid little girl anymore. This was a woman with attitude.

'You were pretty smart to figure it out, Claymore.' The voice was deeper now. 'How did you know?'

'Some of the things you said— *she* said.'

'Well that's pretty smart, for a nigger. You're right too. I *was* the one who hacked the jury selection software. I mean I literally hacked it to pieces with two snips of my intellectual scissors. Two lines of code swapped round, two memory heaps expanded and that was it. I did it five years back in the Big Apple. Actually, it was very easy.'

While she was talking, Claymore was surreptitiously taking off his jacket.

'The source code was on public record and all I had to do was get my hands on it, switch the object calls in the main object and recompile it. The hard part was slipping it into the system afterward. Most of the States have firewalls in place on the jury selection systems. But I beat them. I beat the bleeding-heart, liberal motherfuckers! I'm good at what I do, Claymore, just as you were good in *your* chosen vocation.'

'Then I guess I deserve to die too.'

'Probably,' she said, with an indifferent shrug of her shoulders.

'Then maybe *I'm* the one who should jump.'

'It's up to you.'

Seizing his opportunity, Claymore edged nearer and began climbing over the rail, making sure that none of his movements seemed too threatening.

Now, with the menacing waters far below them, they were facing each other on equal terms for the first time in their lives. But he still had to get through to her.

'Why did you frame Andi for the break-in at the DNA database? I mean I can understand why you did the break-in. That was to frame me. But why frame Andi?'

'I should think that's obvious. Andi was making trouble for me. I had to stop her.'

'But in the end that was what gave her the ammunition to save me.'

'Yes, she's a smart girl, that Andi. But then again that's not surprising. She's got part of me in her. But none of that really matters because it's the end of the line for both of us.'

'Us?' he echoed nervously.

'Me and her.'

Claymore was desperately trying to think of something to say – something that would persuade the strong-willed Lannosea to reconsider.

'But *she* doesn't deserve to suffer – and neither do *you*. I'm the one who hurt both of you. And *I'm* the one who should pay for it.'

'What are you saying, Claymore? That you care about Andi? That you care about a weak, white bitch whom you raped?'

'Yes,' he said, weakly. She still had the upper hand, and they both knew it.

'It looks like you're pretty weak too.'

Claymore shrugged his shoulders helplessly. 'It's true. I *am* weak.'

'And you used to be so strong.'

'I guess I was strong then because I was driven by anger. Now I'm weak because I'm restrained by guilt.'

'But if you're weak, you're also vulnerable.'

'That's true. But *I'm* the one who deserves to be punished, not Andi.'

'But it's the *form* of your weakness that interests me. Your weakness is that you *care* for her.'

'Yes.'

'And so, ironically, now that you've learned to care about your victims, you're more vulnerable to punishment than when they meant nothing to you.'

She was holding on with only one hand again, and starting to turn, as if ready to jump.

'Yes, but why should *she* suffer for what *I* did?'

'Because she's weak too,' said Andi with a malicious gleam in her eyes. 'And because she sold out.'

'Andi!' he shrieked. 'It wasn't meant to be like this!'

She stopped turning and gripped the rail with both hands again.

'What do you *mean*?'

She was whining again. *Andi was back*, possibly.

'I thought all the suffering was over – for my victims as well as for me! When I came back to America to serve out my sentence, I was a different man. I thought when I turned my life around I'd lost the capacity to inflict suffering on anyone. I thought from then on the pain would only diminish. I thought that in time all the pain and suffering

I'd caused would fade away, maybe not completely, but at least enough to be bearable.'

Her eyes were welling up with tears again. 'You think the pain of your victims ebbs into oblivion just because *you* turned *your* life around? You think it's that *easy*? Don't you know that for the victims the pain *never* goes away! And sometimes it just keeps getting worse. That's why it's better to end it.'

She let go with both hands and turned.

'No!' screamed Claymore.

He grabbed her torso with his legs, clinging on desperately with his hands. He didn't think he would have the strength to hold onto her if she struggled. But there was no struggling – and no cooperation either. As he looked down at her, he noticed that she had lost consciousness.

It must have been the drink, he thought.

Here he was holding onto an unconscious woman with a leg scissor lock, while supporting the weight of both of them by clinging on to the Golden Gate Bridge for his life with his hands.

Wednesday, 2 September
2009 – 19.44

'I can understand why you blame me,' said Gene, fighting back the tears. 'But I don't understand why you blame women in general so much, and your father so little.'

'I told you. In the animal kingdom there *is* no such thing as rape.'

'But we're not animals. We don't live by the law of the jungle. We live by the laws of civilization. And your father broke those laws.'

'Not the law of nature. Everything he did was strictly in accordance with the laws of nature. But you rebelled against a woman's nature. A woman's nature – a mother's nature – is to nurture and protect her child, not give it away to strangers. You should have been proud to carry a child with strong genes like mine – even if my daddy did have to force you.'

'You don't think that maybe the circumstances in which you were conceived made that unbearably painful for me?'

'Sex is always painful. All the physiological responses that go with sex are part of the pain mechanism. That's true of men as much as women.'

'But rape isn't about sex. It's about power.'

'Oh yes, that old feminist cliché. But it's meaningless, because *sex itself* is always about power, whether it's the men

501

fighting to get the pick of the females or the power involved in the transaction itself. Why do you think in sex there's nearly always someone on top? Why do you think there are so many S & M sites on the web?'

'Okay,' she said, struggling to keep pace with his self-serving rationalization, 'and what about all those men who go online in search of some leather-clad dominatrix to whop their butt?'

'But don't you get it, that just proves my point? It's the same process with the polarity reversed. Sex is about an exchange of power. It doesn't matter whether it's the exercise of power over the other person or giving in to their power. It doesn't even matter whether it's real power or just make believe. Either way, it's not about equality. Never was!'

Gene thought about this for a moment and realized that it was true, even in her own relationship with Andi. All those role-playing games they played. What were they if not ritualized exercises in power and control?

'Okay, look . . . maybe you're right. Maybe sex is just one big game about power. But it's a game with *rules*. Society has *rules*. We call it the *social contract*. And people have *rights*. And we all have a duty to obey those rules and respect the rights of our fellow human beings.'

'Uh uh! I never signed up for no social contract.'

She noticed that as anger got the better of him, his grammar was slipping, like a façade that couldn't stand up to the inclement weather.

'The social contract never did a thing for me. I got jack shit out of other people's social contract! So why should I abide by it? This animal lives by the law of the jungle. And I'm proud of it.'

'Then go back to the jungle! Don't bring your jungle into our cities.'

He looked at her with a wide-eyed smile. 'I prefer to do it this way, to take my jungle with me wherever I go. And that's not a race thing either. Most kluckers would agree with me on this one. At least they would if they had the brains.'

He turned to the terrified Martine on the bed and smiled not with delight, but with the bitter anger that he had carried around with him.

Wednesday, 2 September
2009 – 19.47

Claymore was desperately looking around as the sun set over the Bay. But there was no one there to help. On other days, there might have been, even at this time. But not today. Right now those people who weren't on the road were sitting in front of their TVs glued to the final day of the baseball game.

With an almighty effort of his stomach muscles, he heaved Andi's lifeless body up to the level of the rail and then rested his elbows on the rail, still clinging on with his hands. It gave him a breather, although her body was still held there only by the pressure of his torso. But now he was able to plant his feet again on the girders of the bridge and free one hand.

He leaned back, encircled Andi's waist with his left arm and heaved her with all his might, so that he could deposit her onto the railing. From there he turned her over onto her stomach, flopped across the railing and maneuvered her down back onto the observation platform.

Climbing back himself was easy after that. But then he realized that his problems were just beginning. For as he surveyed her crumpled, motionless body he saw that there was no sign of breathing or movement of any kind. And she had almost turned blue.

505

He realized in that moment that she wasn't merely unconscious. She had gone into cardiac arrest.

He scrambled frantically to his jacket, whipped out his cell phone and punched in 911.

'I'm on the Golden Gate Bridge with a woman who—'

'Have you got a potential jumper?'

'No, I've pulled her back in. But she's gone into cardiac arrest. She's been drinking heavily – and maybe popping pills too. I need an ambulance right away.'

'Is she still breathing?'

'No, and there's no pulse either.'

'Okay, I'll send an ambulance right away. Do you know how to do CPR?'

'I've seen it on TV, but I'm not really sure. I mean I never learned how to do it properly.'

'Okay, I'm sending an ambulance now. In the meantime I'll explain to you what to do. Lie her down on a flat, hard surface.'

'I did that already.'

'Okay, now tilt her head slightly back to clear an air passage.'

'Okay,' he said, noting the instruction, but not yet acting on it.

'Now with a pumping wrist action on both hands, do fifteen sharp compressions on the left side of her chest.'

'Fifteen?'

'Yes.'

'And then what?'

'Then you do two ventilations. That means you pinch her nose shut and breathe into her twice, gently. Don't breathe too hard or it can burst her lungs.'

'Okay, I'll try that.'

He put the phone down and crouched down next to Andi, engulfed in sorrow. He knew that he had lost – that he had killed her twenty-five years ago. What he had before him now was merely the culmination of his wickedness. But he had to try to save her. He owed her that at least. He had hurt her in every way possible, including driving her to this. But he couldn't fail her now.

He looked around in blind panic as if hoping to see someone who could help him. But there was no one.

And as misery and fear engulfed him, it finally dawned on him that he was well and truly alone.

It hadn't merely been idle talk at the trial when he said: 'Since I came back to America to serve out my sentence I haven't been able to touch a woman.' It had been the truth.

But he remembered what Andi had told him at their conference before he testified.

'Sometimes the greatest test of courage is standing up to the enemy within.'

In his case the *immediate* enemy within was the fear of touching a woman, knowing what he had done to women in the past. But the *latent* enemy was the knowledge of how little his own life was worth.

Only *now* it was different. Now he *could* do something. If he could bring himself to overcome his own self-loathing.

But if he couldn't overcome this terror in this moment, then he would do more harm by his *inaction* now than he had ever done by his actions in the past. It would be the ultimate guilt: the guilt of indifference.

One of his fellow revolutionaries had once said: '*If you're not part of the solution, you're part of the problem.*' If this applied to problems that affected him, then it must surely also apply to the problems that afflicted others.

So now, he knew, it was time for the hands that had once violated to become the hands that heal, in a final act of redemption.

Wednesday, 2 September 2009 – 19.50

Alex had phoned the cops and tried to explain the situation, to no avail. The more he explained, the more convoluted it sounded. Up till the point when he got through to Gene and Manning had addressed him directly, he couldn't really cite any reason why they should even bother to pay a visit to Martine's room because all he had was conjecture piled on top of paranoia.

When he finally told them about the phone call to Gene and Manning's response, they sounded interested. But when he admitted that he couldn't be sure that it *was* Manning – and also that he reached Gene on her cell phone rather than the landline in Martine's room – they seemed to lose interest. The dispatcher even pointed out that Gene could have been anywhere and that 'Manning' could have been anyone.

So all Alex could do was make his own way to Martine's room and hope that he had the wherewithal to deal with the situation.

When he arrived at the parking lot of the Waterfront Hotel, he leapt out of his car, tossed the keys to the valet and ran inside. He knew which room she was in, so it was just a case of racing up the stairs and getting there. He thought about the possibility of calling 911 again, so that they would hear what was going on when he got there. He knew that there was no way that he could take on Manning – especially as he almost certainly had the cop's gun.

But Martine was in danger and he had to save her. He hadn't been there for Melody when she was in danger. But he was here for Martine now. He had to justify his existence, even if it meant risking it.

When he got to the door, his courage almost deserted him, but in his mind, the faces of Martine and Melody merged into one and he knew what he had to do.

He banged on the door even more aggressively than Gene had done fifty minutes earlier.

'Martine! Martine!'

There was movement inside, followed by the sound of the door handle opening. Slowly the door opened a crack . . . then a little more. Finally it opened enough for Martine's frightened, huddled figure to become visible. But what surprised Alex was what happened next.

The door was flung open and Martine staggered out in her bathrobe. She collapsed into his arms.

Wednesday, 2 September 2009 – 19.53

Slowly, Claymore's hands reached down and took their place over Andi's heart – the same hands that had once fondled her breasts while she lay there on the grass, sobbing profusely and begging for him not to hurt her, in that secluded area of woodland where he had raped her. As the woman on the phone had instructed, he began the manual compressions, pumping her heart with a double-handed action, counting as he did do.

'One, two, three, four, five, six, seven, eight, nine, ten, eleven, twelve, thirteen, fourteen, fifteen.'

He leaned over and opened his mouth. For a moment he hesitated, remembering how he had pinioned her to the ground, holding her thin, frail wrists together with one of his giant hands while he leaned over her and thrust his mouth onto hers, kissing her in a way that was so possessive that it made him feel as if he owned her for life, regardless of her wishes.

I have to do it, he told himself.

He placed his mouth gingerly over hers and did the first ventilation, breathing into her and silently praying that it would be the breath of life. He paused and did it a second time. Then he straightened up into a kneeling position and did the next fifteen compressions.

'One, two, three, four, five, six, seven, eight, nine, ten, eleven, twelve, thirteen, fourteen, fifteen.'

He did two ventilations and then went back to the compressions again, repeating the entire process three more times. He felt exhausted, and defeated. There was still no sign of life. He straightened up, remembering how he had grabbed the throat of fourteen-year-old Andi when she tried to scream. But this time, when he reached for her throat it was to check if there was a pulse. As he touched her, he saw a slight movement of Andi's chest and felt the pulse that he had been praying for. The heart was beating and she had resumed breathing. Through his tears, Claymore smiled a bitter smile and sighed heavily with relief.

Then he staggered to his feet, turned away and wept into his open hands.

Wednesday, 2 September
2009 – 19.55

Martine stood there clinging onto him as he encircled her waist with his arms. But strangely there were no tears, just a kind of heavy gasping as if she were trying to recover her strength.

'Where's Manning?' he asked, urgently. 'And Gene?'

'Inside,' said Martine, her voice rasping from shortage of breath.

He looked over at the door nervously and tried to edge Martine away from it, to get her out of harm's way. But she resisted his efforts.

'We have to help her,' she said, releasing her grip and half turning towards the door.

He nodded, unsure of what she meant, or what danger lay behind that door. She turned her back on him, opened the door and walked into the room. He followed and saw Gene in a kneeling position, cradling Louis Manning's bleeding head in her arms, rocking backward and forward gently as if rocking a baby to sleep.

There was no movement from Manning. His eyes were open but unblinking. And the only sound in the room was a faint murmur from Gene's throat as she sang the lullaby from Robert Munch's *Love You Forever*.

Martine turned to Alex, and this time a couple of tears were forming in her eyes. 'He was the salmon,' she said softly.

'The salmon?'

'Swimming upstream, to the waters where he was born. Only he never made it.'

Wednesday, 2 September
2009 – 22.00

It was later that night when Claymore stood dry eyed on the Golden Gate Bridge looking out at the waters below. He had gone with Andi in the ambulance and was still with her at the hospital when Gene had arrived with Alex and Martine. Andi had been slipping in and out of consciousness, but she seemed to respond to Gene, at one point even squeezing her hand. Alex and Martine had left shortly after that, and Claymore realized that he too was in danger of outstaying his welcome.

So now, with no one else about, he stood here looking east towards the city where he had been judged not guilty by the system. But it was not so easy to escape the judgment of his own conscience.

It would be so much simpler to end it here. He had given Andi back her life, but he could not restore her youthful joy of living that he had robbed her of forever. Neither could he banish her pain. Like all human beings he could do limited good but unlimited evil.

His moral account was overdrawn.

And yet . . .

That didn't make him morally bankrupt. The words 'temporarily insolvent' came into his head, bringing a wry smile to his lips. He still had a few good years left, and if he chose to use them wisely he could repay at least part of his debt. But he could never give back to Andi what he had taken away from her.

To do away with himself now – as a means of paying for his sins – was as tempting as any temptation life had thrown at him. But it was tempting for all the wrong reasons. It would be like the trick that those smarmy, crooked business corporations sometimes play: filing for Chapter 11 protection to duck their obligations toward workers, creditors and shareholders.

He knew that he had a duty to pay back what he had taken out of society. If he couldn't pay it back to Andi, he could pay it back to others – helping some future potential victim before it was too late. He had thought, for many years, that he had repaid the debt already by standing up for 'American values.' But paying tribute to American values – whatever that meant – didn't expiate his sins or purge him of the guilt that he still carried. Whatever those ill-defined values were, they weren't a model of perfection any more than those other political and religious systems that he had experimented with and that had left him so thoroughly disillusioned.

'American values' was just a convenient package deal that he had accepted wholesale to get back into the fold of public popularity.

All we can do, is go on striving for perfection, even if we can never reach it, some poet had said before. And another had said that you can't even dream if you're dead.

But it was Gene who had really hit the nail on the head. 'We have a duty to ourselves go on living.'

To *ourselves* if we're the *victims*.

And to *others* if we're the *victimizers*.

He was both.

He turned away from the water and began walking slowly toward the flickering lights in the distance.

Read on for an exclusive extract from the next book by David Kessler. *Marked for Death* features Alex Sedaka and will be published in 2011.

It wasn't exactly a gay bar. San Francisco was progressive enough that gays and straights could mingle in the same bars. So it wasn't clear to the bar tender whether the two men who staggered in were gay or not.

Certainly they were in each other's arms. But it looked to the barman as if one of them was supporting the other – as if one was a little more sober than the other, or at least a little less inebriated. It also wasn't clear if they were down-and-outs. On the one hand they looked somewhat unkempt. But on the other hand they looked rather well-fed – not fat, just well-fed. Down-and-outs tended to look under-nourished, whether it is thin from too little food or fat from eating the wrong kinds of food.

Of course they might not have got to that stage yet. They could be only recently homeless. In any case, the barman had learned not to judge people. In his line of work one would see a lot of people, and it was all too easy to play guessing games about them. But however much you thought you knew about human nature, you could never be sure.

The man at the corner table looked up for a second, as if taking in the change to his environment. Now *he* was homeless. You could see it not just in his clothes and unsuccessful attempts at personal hygiene, but even in his demeanour.

He was a man who had no home to go to, with no light of hope in his eyes.

'What'll it be?' asked the barman as the less inebriate men propped up the other on a bar stool.

'A Jack Daniel's on the rocks for me and an Irn Bru for my friend.'

The barman poured the whisky and slammed a can of Irn Bru down on the bar for the semi-conscious man. The man who spoke paid up and the barman went back to cleaning the glasses in the almost empty bar.

The half-sober man tore the ring off the Irn Bru can and practically poured it down the other man's throat. Only when he had finished, did he down his Jack Daniel's in a single swig. Then he stood up and looked at his drunken friend.

'Sorry Corny, gotta go.'

And with that he abruptly stood up and left.

The drunk, looked after his friend nervously and then looked around disoriented, as if trying to get his bearings.

'Where am I?' asked the drunk.

'*The Call of the Wild.*' The drunk looked at him blankly. 'A bar . . . just off Folsom Street . . . San Francisco?' The barman waved his hand in front of the drunk hoping to verify that the man was this side of reality.

'I have to go,' said the drunk, sliding off the stool and unexpectedly managing to stay on his feet.

'Are you sure you're okay?' asked the barman.

'I'm fine,' said the drunk, apparently sobering up, possibly from the caffeine rush. 'How much do I owe you?'

The drunk took out a sizeable wad of cash, bringing a gleam to the barman's eyes. But the barman sensed a setup or sting operation and kept the lid on his greed.

'That's okay,' he said, shaking his head. 'Your friend already paid.'

This seemed to confuse the drunk even more, but his hand went back into his shirt pocket and when it came out again, the money was nowhere to be seen but the pocket was bulging. He turned and staggered out.

It was no more than a few second later that the down-and-out in the corner got up and left, walking with a surprising sense of purpose and pace for a man without a home to go to. He stepped out into the dark night, his eyes focussed on the drunk staggering away a few yards ahead of him. Even though the nocturnal atmosphere of this near deserted street was menacing, he was unafraid. This was his turf and he knew what dangers lurked in its dark corners.

When the drunk was almost level with a nearby back alley he pounced, closing the gap with a couple of brisk, hobbling strides. Sensing motion, the drunk reared up and turned, just in time to see the down-and-out's advance. But his soporific reactions were not quick enough to respond to the knife as it plunged first into his liver and then his gut.

He tried to let out a cry, but a hand clamped over his mouth stifled it. He bit down hard, and it was the homeless man who let out the cry that attracted the attention of others. Panicked by his own action, the down-and-out pushed the drunk hard into the alley, out of sight of any other people who might be walking down the street. The drunk slumped into a seated posture, clutching his wounds and then lay back, almost as if accepting his fate. With a stab wound to the liver he had about twenty minutes to live, unless help arrived. And he wasn't expecting any help.

The man who had stabbed him made no further effort to approach him. Instead he turned and started hobbling away. He heard a police siren in the distance, but was unsure of the direction from which it was coming. By the time he realized that it was approaching him from in front, it was too late. He turned sharply and tried to retreat in the other direction. But his abrupt turn merely served to capture the attention of the cops in the squad car. When they ordered him to stop, through the car's public address system, he kept hobbling. When they leapt out with guns drawn and again ordered him to stop, he ignored them, praying that they wouldn't shoot.

They didn't. Instead the younger cop brought him down with a flying tackle so hard that the down-and-out's prosthetic leg came off.